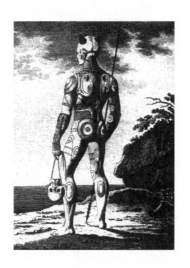

RONALD WRIGHT

A NOVEL

Henderson's

Spear

ALFRED A. KNOPF CANADA

PUBLISHED BY ALFRED A. KNOPF CANADA

Copyright © 2001 by Ronald Wright

All rights reserved under International and Pan-American Copyright Conventions. Published in 2001 by Alfred A. Knopf Canada, a division of Random House of Canada Limited, Toronto. Distributed by Random House of Canada Limited, Toronto.

Knopf Canada and colophon are trademarks.

Half-title illustration: *From Voyages and Trends 1803–07*, Georg Heinrich von Langsdorf. London: Henry Colburn, 1813. Permission of Pitt Rivers Museum, Oxford

NATIONAL LIBRARY OF CANADA CATALOGUING IN PUBLICATION DATA

Wright, Ronald
 Henderson's spear

ISBN 0-676-97389-2

I. Title.

PS8595.R62H46 2001   C813'.54   C2001-930056-5
PR9199.3.W74H46 2001

First Edition

www.randomhouse.ca

Text design: CS Richardson

Printed and bound in the United States of America

10 9 8 7 6 5 4 3 2 1

To the memory of my father
A.E.A. Wright
1914–1995

Keeper of the family stories
and the spear.

No one lives under palm trees unpunished.

—Goethe, *Die Wahlverwandtschaften*, 1809

One

<§>° °<§>

TAHITI

Women's Prison, Arue. April, 1990

A NOTE IS ALL I HAVE FROM YOU. I think of it as yours despite the
formal stationery and wary tone: *We have recently been contacted by
a young lady whose particulars appear to match your own.* It found me
here just before Christmas—a few weeks after my arrest.

I'd left my name with the contact agency several years ago,
long enough to grow discouraged and then push discouragement
to the back of my mind. So your note was a shock, though I'd
invited it—a shock followed by relief and joy. You were alive! You
wanted us to find each other. You weren't hiding, weren't exacting
a sullen revenge that might last until I died.

Particulars. They mean dates, ages, numbers on certificates.
These aren't always reliable in our family, as I shall tell. But there
can be no mistake; only your particulars could possibly "appear"
to match my own. This young lady is you. And this older one is
me, who gave you life at sixteen, and gave you away.

1

• • •

Who are you now? And how and what and where? I'm brimming with questions. I'm ready for the best, the worst, the in-between. Like most of us you're probably in between. And twenty-two is so damn young, but for the first time in your life you're feeling old. You're thinking of endings and beginnings, which is why you've begun to look for me. But maybe you haven't yet made up your mind you'll even see me. So I'll go first: Olivia Wyvern, Cell 15. Your mother.

There's this tiresome obstacle to our reunion: I'm imprisoned on the far side of the world (assuming you're still in Britain). It's not a bad jail. How many have palm trees in the yard, French bread, an ocean view? And a good friend is moving heaven and earth to get me out of it. My government—I'm a Canadian now—is sympathetic. The consul here is on my side. Ottawa is asking questions about the charge, the so-called evidence. People are beginning to see that I've been framed.

It can't be easy finding your mother after all these years, only to learn she stands accused of murder—well, for *complice*, which means "accessory." But truly there was no murder. Or if there was it had nothing to do with me. I was simply in the wrong place at the wrong time.

She would say that, wouldn't she? Will you allow me the presumption of innocence, which is more than I've had from the Napoleonic Code? (Tahiti's a French colony.) I am not guilty. But I do plead guilty to a charge concerning you: I threw away the life we might have lived together. No law sets penalties for that; it was a crime of the will and the heart. Both you the innocent and I the guilty have served over twenty years for it.

• • •

The people in London who matched our particulars have also offered advice on how to proceed. Phone calls out of the blue are not recommended. Start with a letter, they say—enclose photos, snippets of hair, take your time. Phone calls and meetings will come later. Phoning is difficult here, anyway, and a meeting out of the question. But I have plenty of time. So this is a long letter to prepare you for the next step, if and when.

Already I've a lot to thank you for. Without your note I might still be stewing in the bath of outrage, fear, and hate in which I fell at my arrest. You've kept me busy writing this since January. They let me spend four hours a day in the library. The light's good in the morning, a breeze comes through the bars, mynah birds squabble in the palms, and it's the only room without a reek of sewer. This place is so French: good food, bad drains. The washbasin in my cell is a mixed blessing—no plug or trap to keep down smells and cockroaches. Until Pua showed me the remedy (chewing gum and a coin), I thought I might be gassed in my sleep or nibbled raw. Tahitian roaches are as big as mice and they go for the dead skin on your feet.

I don't mean to make too much of these discomforts. My hotel in Papeete was much the same, at ninety dollars a night. In French Polynesia they know how to let off nuclear weapons but they've never grasped the rudiments of plumbing.

I know I should start with *I love you.* But how can I say that without it ringing false, the sudden intimacy of salesmen and seducers? We're strangers, you and I, despite our blood. I don't even know your name. And I may as well tell you straight that I've never been very good at love, though I am working on it. Often I think love stalled in me the day you went away.

So this won't be that kind of letter. What I can give you, for now, is my story. And in return I hope someday you'll give me yours. I'll try to stick to the point, though it doesn't come easily—my mind's a sackful of cats and they're all clawing their way out at once. Be patient while I let them go in an order that makes sense, at least to me. Mine isn't the usual tale of a girlish mistake with a pimply boy in the bicycle shed. This stretches across a hundred years and half the world. I'll start with me, but you must hear from Frank Henderson too. I'm enclosing copies of his papers. More than a century ago, when he was about your age, he sailed to the South Seas aboard a warship. It's ultimately because of him that I'm here now.

We seem to be a family of writers—diarists, memoirists—the kind with secrets to dribble onto paper and hoard away. For whom, I wonder. For posterity? Or as a form of exorcism? Of course you may decide, after reading what I have to say, that you want nothing to do with me. How far can we go with genes; do they call to one another like the deeps? *Damn the genes, let me choose my friends, and to hell with blood relations.* I can hear myself saying something like that in your position. That's your right, and if it's your choice I'll respect it. But if ever you change your mind, know that I'll never hide from you again.

I was kept in the dark all my life, until after my mother died. You musn't wait that long. I thought I knew my past but didn't, and this ignorance is half to blame for many things. Hear me out and at least you'll be able to make an informed decision after learning what I've learnt, much of it just recently, about who we are. Knowing is in our power. And knowing may kindle love, which is not.

⇜ ⇝

In the beginning we were four: my parents, my sister Lottie, and me. Soon we became three, when Jon, my father, failed to come home from the Korean War. He was a pilot in the RAF, until then a brave and lucky one who'd flown against Hitler long before Lottie and I were born. We've always called him Jon, perhaps because Mother did, or because *Daddy* wouldn't do for a father who was . . . missing. We were a family of three women for so many years that it seemed to us (though never to our mother) the natural order of things, an order without men.

I didn't leave home until my twenties, but once I did I kept going—from England to Canada, a land where pasts are easily forgotten. I've settled in the west, on the coast of British Columbia, where I make a living making films. Nothing grand. You won't see my name in lights, though you might spot me now and then if you look at documentary credits. This too, for all its precariousness, had become an order of its own.

Then Mother died.

One day she'd been perfectly well, a sprightly sixty-seven who walked an hour in the park every day, rain or shine; the next she was dead. *Cardiac arrest, possibly induced by chronic stress.* Lottie's voice in tears from London, in the middle of a wet Vancouver night two years ago. I was in England the next day, the phone ringing with distant relations. And the worst of it was that we could hardly bring ourselves to tell anyone—except her closest friends, who knew how she lived—exactly what had killed her. How can you tell people that your mother died over a parrot?

Soon after I was born our father had brought home an African grey, rescued impulsively from a pet shop window, a "good talker" who uttered nothing but parrotish clicks, warbles, and rending shrieks. He named this bird Lord Jim, and told Mother it'd be no bother at all—it would learn to speak at the same time I did, and would keep her company whenever he was away.

Jim was a quick study. Soon he could chime like the door-bell and sing snatches of aria complete with the record's hiss. He did a faultless imitation of Mother's telephone hello, terrified the red setter next door by barking back verbatim, mastered the clank and whoosh of the downstairs loo. His command of the noises made by babies and toddlers in distress drove Mother up the wall. Many was the time she woke in panic, ran to Lottie or me, to find us blissfully sleeping and not a peep from the wily bird under his velvet cloth. Many was the time, she told us, that she sent Jon off to his squadron with *Don't expect to find that bloody parrot here when you get back.*

But Jim also learnt a great many things from our father, besides the usual jokes: Jon's catch of breath as he dozed off after lunch, his RAF expressions, the *Lord! Who's that?* he'd exclaim when someone knocked at the front door, and a squeak the stairs made under his weight only.

For all this Mother grew to love Lord Jim.

The bird was accustomed to our father's comings and goings, his long absences and sudden returns, but he knew something dreadful had happened when that telegram came in 1953. July 20th. One week before the Korean armistice.

Ministry of Defence <STOP> To Mrs. J. B. Wyvern, 84 Tilehouse Street, Hitchin, Herts. Regret to inform you <STOP> Group Captain Jonathan Barkley Wyvern reported missing over Yalu <STOP> Plane and parachute not located <STOP> Details to follow soonest.

No details ever did.

The parrot went silent, refused food, began to moult. He plucked out his remaining feathers until he was bald everywhere except the back of his head—a revolting sight, raw and primaeval like an embryo dinosaur.

When we'd got over our own grief enough to deal with Jim's we tried tempting him with favourite morsels—pistachio nuts, dried apricots, brandy-soaked croutons (Jon used to get him sloshed). The parrot wouldn't even leave his cage, and when Lottie put her hand in he bit her finger so hard that she had to have stitches and a tiny cast. Had Mother been herself, Lord Jim might have met his end that day, but she said she couldn't face another loss. The bird was given one more chance, and seemed to understand he'd done something unforgivable but had been spared. Slowly he began to eat. A downy coat of grey sprouted on his nakedness. And a few weeks later she heard him say, *Lord! Who's that?*

Jim learnt nothing new after 1953. Television, when it came, made no impression. Other parrots picked up the *I Love Lucy* theme, or the William Tell overture (which only a true high-brow can hear without thinking of the Lone Ranger). But not Jim. In the sixties he ignored the Kinks, Janis Joplin, the Singing Nun—all the records Lottie and I played to destruction. But neither did he lose the things he had, especially our father's voice and personal sounds. More than thirty years after he'd last heard it, Lord Jim could reproduce Jon's sudden snore so faithfully that Mother, absorbed in knitting or a crossword, would start from her chair with a terrible little cry.

To Lottie and me the parrot was a veteran of the heroic age of our father's photos, his uniforms, his old motorbike outside. To Mother he was an archive of her husband, a medium who could raise his presence at the fireside, his tread on the stairs.

One May morning two years ago, Mother found Lord Jim dead among the nut shells on the floor of his cage. We'd known the day would come (the bird must have been at least forty, perhaps much more) but neither Lottie nor I had foreseen what his death might do to her. After we'd left home—Lottie at seventeen, to model and act in London; I for Canada—he was the only living creature who could bridge the years between Jon's life and Mother's. All the frail hopes that Jim's cracked incantatory voice had nourished for thirty-five years died with him. A tide of silence, swollen by the greater silence she'd denied, welled up in the house, drowning the past.

Our response as daughters was inadequate, and arguably fatal. I, finishing production of a CBC special, sent flowers.

Lottie came down and stayed for a few nights, but had to go back to her Rosalind (a critical success) at the Haymarket.

Mother died ten days after Lord Jim.

The importance that had kept us away dissolved immediately in grief. I was on the next plane to London, walking in the front door, into Lottie's arms, to an island in time I had thought would last forever. Through all the years I'd lived in Canada, Mother had been kept from time and change, no matter what I saw on visits home. Whenever I came over for Christmas or a summer break I re-entered a childhood landscape, seeing her and her house not as they really were but as they'd always been.

Now that she was dead I felt her not as an external presence watching me or flitting from the corner of my eye—nor as an absence, like Jon—but within me, looking through my eyes, guiding my hands and footsteps, her words and intonation falling from my lips. I'd walk into the garden, feel sunlight on my face, and know that the dead don't go away, they live inside us. The dead make us alive. I rejoiced in being possessed by her, resolving not to let the texture of the world wear smooth again, or Mother's spirit separate from mine.

⊰⊱ ⊰⊱

Tilehouse Street was the home of the Wyverns, and before them the Hendersons, for nearly two hundred years. For us it was a women's house full of men's things—things from a lost world of empire and unreconstructed manhood. A dinner-gong hung from a tusk mounted on the back of a wooden elephant with a missing ear. A forbidden cupboard under the stairs held shotguns, fishing rods, an array of lures and flies with faintly risqué names: Pink

Ladies, Royal Coachmen, Woolly Buggers, a Nympho. Dragons guarded our underwear in Burmese lacquer chests. And in the drawing-room, ranged above the mantel mirror, was a great spear more than twice the length of a man.

"Oh that," Mother would say crisply to visitors. "That's an assegai, you know."

Sometimes she'd add that it had been there a century, ever since Henderson came back from Africa where he'd lost an eye in some native war and won a medal from Queen Victoria which was somewhere in a box. As a child I never wondered how she knew the thing was specifically an *assegai*, beyond asking what an "assy guy" might be. "That's what they call a spear in Africa, darling."

"Can we take it down so I can hold it?"

"No, Livvy. It's not a toy. Spears are dangerous. Anyway, it's much too heavy."

"Have you held it, Mum?"

"No, dear, I haven't. And I don't intend to."

"So how do you know it's too heavy?"

"Olivia!"

The spear was never taken down, not even when painters came to exorcise the ghosts imprinted by smoke and time on the plaster round the fireplace. They wrapped it in paper and dabbed their brushes expertly behind. I remember climbing their freckled ladder for a look (I must have been eleven or twelve), noticing for the first time that the blade, shaft, and a small pommel at the base were made from a single piece of wood. The spear seemed to belong to a place or time where metals were unknown. Yet there was nothing primitive about the thing; it was as finely worked and polished as a piece of furniture, the mere look of it conveying poise, authority.

The ghosts hid for a summer beneath pale green, resuming their haunts when winter rain trickled down the flue. My sister and I were glad to see them back. They had names: the Dark Lady, a triangular silhouette we knew to be a woman in a cloak; above her the Man in the Moon, a round stain the size of a dinner plate which, in the last of day, before curtains were drawn and lights switched on, was a mottled face. Lower down were two sinuous forms we named the Lizard Twins. Lottie, who is two years older, used to say the Lizard Twins were trying to scamper up the Lady's skirt. When she turned thirteen she got a knowing look and pointed at some small spots (hitherto identified as lizard turds) and said she thought they must be the Dark Lady's Curse. This was overheard by Mother, who called her out of the room. A day later, by the iron warmth of the kitchen stove with its smell of old roasts and fuel-oil, my mother appalled me with the facts of life.

The most recent male things, our father's, were mainly photographs he'd taken in two wars: young men on windscoured airfields, brave grins behind goggles and leather, white scarves flowing like contrails from their necks; the ruins of Berlin and Hamburg, smoking silhouettes at dawn; Oriental temples in strange gardens of raked gravel and big stones. He was good, very good—I can see that now—though as a child I merely gazed at these images for hours in fascination, absorbing something of him there. His ruins have a jagged grandeur, his airfields (always a difficult subject) are balanced foreground and horizon, detail and distance—a radial engine like a metal sunflower, a dark propeller against a mare's-tail sky, fatigue and fear behind brave smiles.

And Jon himself: as a boy at the seaside, in his RAF uniform, astride his motorbike, outside a country pub with his wife (impossible to think of her as Mother). Now that I'm in my thirties, he looks so young and handsome, a stranger who is and is not my father. How old do you have to be before you can see your parents as young people, glowing with reckless love?

Downstairs were his books. A lot about planes and engineering, also Greene, Conrad, T.E. Lawrence, Greek plays, Romantic poets. His Leica in a brown leather case. A shelf of 78s. A wireless-set with faraway cities etched on phosphorescent glass: *Hilversum, Lisbon, Oslo, Prague*. And in the greenhouse, under an old carpet, the motorcycle he'd bought new in the spring of '53 and ridden only a few times before he went away. "A motorbike, Vivien," he'd told Mother when he brought it home, "is the closest you can come on earth to flying."

She couldn't bring herself to part with anything of his. At first because she expected news of Jon's return daily, running at each ring of the phone or doorbell. Then, as years went by, because there *was* still hope. And when hope had shrunk to a small irrational lump like the residue of a religion in which one no longer believes, still she kept all his things because getting rid of them was tantamount to sacrilege.

Korea and career. My three-year-old mind construed them as the same: fathers are detained by careers and Koreas, especially military careers.

The Korean War never ended; it was merely put on hold. History sees it as a postscript to the second war. At the time it must have seemed like the beginning of the third. But who remembers now? How many people even know that British forces took part? Korea has been shouldered out by its noisy neighbours in time: World War Two on one side, Vietnam on the other.

There were "reports"—of prisoners held in North Korea, or China, or the Soviet Union—which degenerated into rumour. Defectors from the East would revive old stories of men heard speaking English in Siberian camps or tropical prison farms. Enough to quicken hope, to make us wonder, to let ourselves pick at old scars on our hearts. Could he still be alive? Had he for all these years had a life somewhere, planting rice inside a barbed wire perimeter under a molten sun? Could he *be* there on the dark side of the earth—be looking up at the moon, seeing the full moon I could see when I ran outside on a summer evening? Sometimes I felt sure that the moon was a mirror in which, with a big enough telescope, I'd be able to see his face.

In those hollow days after the funeral Lottie sat beside the fireplace in Mother's leather wingback; my sister's theatrical way of saying she was head of the household now.

I remember her frowning and staring at the hearthrug, her face pulled out of symmetry by an active bulge in a cheek where her tongue explored a tooth. After some minutes she said: "A friend of mine's sniffing round the two-wheeler. Says it's a Royal Enfield, a 'Super Constellation' or something. Sounds more like a

13

plane, doesn't it—I wonder if that's why Jon chose it? Anyway, he reckons the old heap's restorable. And desirable. Worth a lot more now than when it was new. We could be quids in."

She had on a bulky fisherman's sweater and black leggings, shoes kicked off and feet tucked under her bottom. A mermaid pose. Her lips were dark red, her sapphire eyes skilfully framed with liner. We'd been out to see our solicitor that morning, and Lottie never could greet the world without her "face," though she was just as lovely without it. (I wasn't bothering at all; I'd just round up my springy hair in a clasp and pull on a sweater and jeans.) The will, read to us a few days before, had not been helpful: *I hereby give devise and bequeath all my real and personal estate to my dear Husband Jonathan Barkley Wyvern absolutely, in Witness whereof I have subscribed my name this seventh day of July, One thousand nine hundred and forty-nine.*

The day after their second wedding anniversary. Lottie was one; I did not exist. The solicitor said there had to be a later will somewhere. Our mother would have made a new one—handwritten, at least—after her husband disappeared. We searched her desk but we knew better. Her wishes changed no more than her belief in Jon's return.

Lottie poured herself a whisky, lifted an eyebrow. "Go on, Liv. Get a glass. I know it's only eleven, but who's here to tell us off? Time we acted like grown-ups, you and me."

"I suppose this 'friend' of yours is some biker shag-bandit?"

"I wish. Sugar daddies are more my line these days. The offers I get! Sixty-year-olds! No, Piers is just a sweet young guy I tell all my dankest secrets. Runs a junk shop in World's End. 'The

Den of Antiquity.' Name's better than the stuff inside. But he knows the price of absolutely anything. Anything old. . . ."

"And the value of nothing? You, for instance."

"Not my sort, Liv. Too serious. You'd like him."

She topped up her glass, set the bottle down on the floor beside her chair. "Poor Mum. What are we going to do with this place? Can you see yourself living here? I can't. I'm a London girl, and the trains are no good. And what are we going to do with that sodding one-eared elephant? Someone told me it's illegal to sell ivory now, even antique. All the books! They must weigh *tons*. And what about this spear?" She rolled her lovely eyes at the weapon above her. "How *do* you flog a spear? I'm going to re-open the grate this minute and break it up for firewood." Lottie leaped to her feet, kicked at the asbestos board that sealed the chimney, tugged at a sprung corner, gave up. She sank back into the chair, chewing her bottom lip. Then: "Have you found his eye yet?"

"Eye?"

"Henderson's. The only thing I know about Henderson is that he wore a glass eye. A lion's eye he got from a taxidermist."

"A tiger. Mum said it was a tiger."

She peered at a photograph across the room, at an upright chap of thirty or so in the dress of a late Victorian naval officer, firm gaze to the lens, sharp chin, nose, and shelving brow carved in shadow by a studio skylight, gloved hand on the hilt of a sword. Many Hendersons had lived at Tilehouse Street, but this was the one we called simply "Henderson," known to have been in Africa, owner of the spear.

15

"Never noticed before, but he was rather tasty, wasn't he? Wouldn't kick him out of bed for farting if I was a nice Victorian girl. Not while he still had both his own eyes anyway. Have to admit that's quite good, though—a tiger's eye. Almost worth losing one to do something like that."

When Lottie acts tough it means the opposite. I could see by the way she'd curled herself. And she was shivering, though the house wasn't cold. I'd flung aside the heavy brocade curtains of indeterminate colour (they looked like they'd hung in the room as long as the spear) to let the spring sun pour its honey on the floor. Mother kept the front drapes drawn for privacy, but you never shut out the sun if you live in British Columbia.

"Liquidating heirlooms isn't going to make us feel any better, Lot. Let's not do things we might regret. We can always rent this place out for a while. Don't make any big decisions for six months—that's what everyone says. I'll take the spear. Mother always said she wanted me to have it."

"You're right. I'm babbling. God!" she added. "What are we worrying about the junk for? What about poor Mother's stuff? I can't go near it. Her clothes, Olivia. Mummy's clothes!" She burst into tears, whisky spraying from her mouth, her eyes red and piggy. People always say that Lottie has the world by the tail; I'd never seen my sister so diminished.

⋘ ⋙

It was August 1988 when we finished emptying two hundred years of life from Tilehouse Street. Perhaps one day you'll see the place, if Lottie and I keep it. Or you could have a snoop if you live nearby—Hitchin's about thirty miles north of London. (Where *do* you live, I wonder. Not knowing where you are makes you almost as unimaginable as not knowing your name.)

We started with the attic and worked down, putting things in storage, taking a few for ourselves, leaving furniture that might do for tenants, pieces without much market or nostalgic value. I stayed in the bedroom Lottie and I shared when small—still the same teddy-bear wallpaper—and did the bulk of the work. She appeared and helped (talked, mainly) whenever she could get away from London.

The house had begun as the home and office of the Hendersons—Scots originally—Quakers entrusted with money and legal matters by less godly folk. It's red brick, tall and narrow, a short walk from the River Hiz, whose name I've always adored. The faintly classical façade, suggesting exactly the sort of place a banker or lawyer should live, is right on the street. "This house has never been the same since the motorcar," Mother used to say, quoting one of Jon's old aunts. True enough: I remember the mirrors trembling at each bus and lorry, the lurching shadow-play thrown by headlamps on our bedroom curtains. But the back was quiet and private, a long, slim, high-walled garden, with a copper beech, a catalpa, and a gentle upward slope to a ruined greenhouse crammed with gardening tools and Jon's old bike.

In Victorian times the Hendersons went into the Navy and the Church, forsaking Quakerism for the Queen's shilling. Among the tintypes in the study were a whiskery admiral and a deacon. Money had come and gone with empire. Mother raised us on Jon's pension and little else. Financial crises—her teeth,

Lottie's drama school, dry rot—were met with the arrival of a van. One by one a piano, a portrait, a Tang bronze, a Tompion clock departed over the years, until little remained of the family hoard except the bric-a-brac.

I filled five boxes with Jon's photos and negatives, and shipped them to Vancouver. Lottie wanted only a few snaps, a concise history of our parents' courtship and her origin: in front of the King's Oak with cocktails in their hands; at a churchyard lych-gate on their wedding day, beaming at the future through the door by which a body leaves the world.

Five boxes of Jon's past, yet nothing of Mother's. Not even one shot of her girlhood or her single years. Only those taken by Jon before he went away. One side of the family had too much history, the other much too little.

She wouldn't talk, and we learnt not to ask. All she told us was that she was an orphan, a Barnardo's girl, and the nice people there had been very kind to her. Once, when I was still quite small, I found her on the landing, stricken, clutching a piece of paper in a sodden hanky. She'd drawn me to her and hugged me half to death. "Oh, Livvy! My darling." Her voice faint and scratchy, far-off yet shrill like an old record. "If *only* you knew! If only . . ." I stamped my foot and begged to be told. And she said—so softly I doubted later what I'd heard—that she'd been "disowned."

Lottie and I discussed this at night in whispers. We concluded that disowning someone had to be a secret but common practice among grown-ups, like what they really knew about God and did in bed together. Mother never spoke of it again. Many years later—just before I went to Canada—Lottie asked her point blank about that long-ago meeting on the stairs. Mother laughed and said she couldn't remember it at all.

"Perhaps you did hear wrong," Lottie said at Heathrow. "Or she was off her head for a while. Over Jon. But I doubt it, Liv. The laugh was wrong. I'm *sure* that laugh was wrong. In my line of work you get an ear."

Mother's words came to mind as I went through her desk. I hoped to find that piece of paper, whatever it was, and other letters, especially from Jon during the Korean war, though she wasn't a keeper when it came to correspondence. Every year, on Twelfth Night, she threw out the year's letters with the Christmas cards. I found four—just four!—all from their early days before I was born, before Korea. The most recent was dated May '49, and sent from a base in Scotland. I felt shabby, snooping at my parents' intimacies, and very sad, yet the hope of finding a clue she'd missed or forgotten or hidden was irresistible. All I discovered were some names to put to faces in the photographs, and crazy post-war dreams I'd never heard her speak of: to start a flying school at a Battle of Britain airfield, or buy a small hotel in Cornwall, or leave England altogether and grow peanuts in the sun.

The attic had yielded more than four letters from Henderson alone, but they mainly concerned wills (his brothers and sisters had all died childless before him). There was also a rather pathetic correspondence about fruit trees. After retiring at the end of the Great War, he and his wife had tried to establish an orchard on their property in Suffolk, hoping the venture would keep them in old age. It hadn't done well. The letters spoke of declining years spent fending off blight and creditors. A sad end to a life I'd always pictured as romantic and adventurous.

Often during that summer my thoughts turned to Henderson. He was a welcome distraction from my grief, a detour into a past inviting because it seemed irrelevant. Francis Barkley Henderson, known as Frank, was the last of his line. Mother sometimes called him "one of your ancestors" but that wasn't strictly true because he died, as lawyers say, without issue.

"Well," Mother had added with a don't-confuse-me sigh. "If he wasn't an ancestor he was some kind of cousin. Second or third or twice removed. How does that go? There was also a link by marriage. A Wyvern and a Henderson married Barkley sisters. They had a double wedding. Those two families *must* have been close. Instead of going away on holiday they'd swap houses every year for a fortnight. To save money, I suppose. Though if they'd been really hard up they couldn't have afforded houses like this in the first place, could they? It was the Scottish blood! Your father has it. He never threw away a thing."

Henderson had died in the 1920s, leaving Tilehouse Street to my grandfather. "The Wyverns must have been his next of kin," said Mother. "Or the only ones he wanted to remember in his will. Your father's relations were all rather peculiar."

This last was a remark she often made. She said it almost admiringly, the English love of eccentrics. But there was also regret and resignation, as if she suspected that Jon—and we—carried a hereditary flaw, like a rare medical condition passed down by inbred royalty. Almost as if eccentricity might explain his absence. The Eastern bloc was starting to crack. That nice man

Gorbachev was setting prisoners free. Why was there still no word? Could it be—she hinted—that Jon had "gone native" somewhere, was alive and well but no longer wanted to come home?

"Of course it may have been the times. I mean, why Henderson left everything to your grandfather. A lot of families died out in the First War. The boys were killed. There weren't enough left for the girls to marry. Some of them did marry but couldn't have children. Shell-shock. Gangrene. Bits shot away. . . . Ghastly!" She grimaced. "You don't know how lucky you've been. Your generation is the first in a century without a bloodbath. And yes—all right—" Her palms went up. "I know you've had to live with the Bomb."

She'd paused and shrunk slightly in her chair, for despite her handsome airman in a silver frame on the mantel and her two girls either side of him, and various suitors (always unsuitable), I think she saw herself as an old maid. Certainly her life was blighted by war. She never found it in her to remarry, which was odd because it's mainly from her that Lottie gets her looks. She never said much to us about marriage, either. That seemed odd too.

"I wish I knew more. I think your father said Henderson's papers were burnt. For security reasons. Towards the end of his career he was involved in intelligence. In MI5—if that makes any sense. Was there such a thing as MI5 back then, in the First War? These things only seem important when it's too late. No one left to ask. I only wish I knew more, so I could tell you."

But I knew my mother well enough to hear a sprung note. She *didn't* wish to tell us. There was something about Henderson,

21

something shocking or shameful, that she didn't want to send on down the generations.

Not until I was going through Mother's desk for a second time did anything from Henderson's early days turn up. Fallen or hidden behind a drawer was a small cardboard box. Inside was a weighty spherical object in a chamois purse. The famous eye. I was right: a tiger.

With this were two cuttings, short obituaries. He'd made a good start in the Navy, winning a gunnery prize (absurdly named the Goodenough), but had retired for health reasons while still a junior officer. A decade later he went out to West Africa and took part in the Ashanti wars. There was also a medal in the box, a Distinguished Service Order awarded in 1898 for bravery in action the previous year. One of the cuttings, entitled "Henderson, the Man Who Fell Asleep and Doubled His Life," launched into a colourful tale, but half was missing. All I could glean was that an African chief had threatened him with death, and he managed to escape somehow by dozing off. Mother had told us this too, adding that Henderson returned with the spear.

As if to underline this last point, she'd enclosed a snapshot of the weapon, perhaps the only photo in the house taken by her. (It seemed too inept to be one of Jon's, foggy with movement and overexposure.) The intriguing thing about the picture was a human figure: a man I didn't know—certainly not my father—the cut of his jacket suggesting a demob suit of the late 1940s. He was tall and broad-shouldered, yet stooped, his back to the camera, his head just turning towards the lens, a hand stretching for the spear. The figure seemed furtive, yet familiar, like a glimpse of the auteur in one of Hitchcock's films.

Lottie came to help less often towards the end. By then I was down to the cellar, to jelly moulds, canning jars, and baffling Victorian gadgets.

The last thing I dealt with was a plywood cubicle in the corner furthest from the window. My father's darkroom.

We burned with curiosity about this place when we were young. It was always kept locked. Mother said it was full of poisonous chemicals, and anyway she'd no idea where Jon had kept the key. This may have been true; I couldn't find one. But the little room had to be cleaned out now. I forced the hasp with a screwdriver, a deed that seemed a greater violation of the past than anything else I did that summer at Tilehouse Street.

Dust lay in a fine snowfall over a sink, draining-board, an enlarger, and shelves of squat brown bottles. I lifted a glass stopper and got a brassy whiff of hypo. The last person to breathe that was my father; for a moment he was a presence, not an idea.

Beneath the enlarger was a metal box, heavy and padlocked. So I did another break and enter. It was full of photographic paper, yellowed and useless. But underneath were several notebooks. Jon's! I thought. But they were dated 1899 and filled with a scrawl I'd seen before, though here it was shakier and more crabbed than in the letters about fruit trees.

Henderson's papers. Some of them, at least. But why would my father have locked them away down here?

23

The handwriting was a challenge. I didn't have time to read the notebooks properly until I got them home. The first two or three were about Africa, the rest about a long voyage, many years earlier, to the South Pacific. Apart from dog-ears and some wine or tea stains, they seemed to be just as Henderson had left them. There were no notes from Jon, no torn-out pages, no indication why he'd hidden them away. The memoirs seemed nothing more than a curiosity, a relic like so many others from our family's past.

Months later, in Vancouver, I began to see their true significance. I brought photocopies on my own trip to the South Seas; now I've read them through so many times I know whole passages by heart. And I believe I've retraced a wheel of cause and effect, set in motion by Frank Henderson, which has rolled down upon our lives through a century: on Jon's, Mother's, mine, and therefore yours. I hope my conclusions are the right ones. To me they seem inescapable. I long to know how all this looks to you.

Over to Frank.

Two

⋖≋⋗ ⋖≋⋗

ENGLAND

Frank Henderson's first notebook:
Tilehouse Street, Hitchin. April, 1899

NEARLY TWO YEARS SINCE I LEFT AFRICA, and they've passed like
a rail journey one hardly notices because one's been absorbed in a
good meal, a conversation, a card game, a burgeoning romance,
whilst hundreds of miles rush by beyond the carriage window.

I've neglected these "Occasional Papers" of mine. When one
is busy living life one can't find the time to record it. I'm not
among those diligent souls who produce a journal entry every day,
if only to note the weather and that nothing happened to them.
When on duty, of course, one has to keep a field diary, but despite
many resolutions to continue such a regimen on leave, I seldom
stick to it. The best I usually manage is a few scribbles on the
backs of envelopes, scraps of cartridge paper, brown bags, and
the like. I simmer upon a subject that interests or troubles me;
then, when a head of steam is raised, I ransack these fragments,

gather my recollections with a good cigar, and set down an account in the belief that it may be of interest to myself in later years when memory shall have dimmed, and perhaps to members of the family. A curious habit—to write to one's future self, of whose existence one can have no certainty, but enough of us do so that we human beings must be a hopeful lot. Or is it simply that we're vain?

Much has happened, of the best and worst, and before returning to duty I feel compelled to set down certain things.

Whilst up in London in the autumn of '97 to deliver my report to the Colonial Office, I was asked to lunch at York House by an old shipmate, Prince George. He was most eager to hear about my African experiences, especially the time I'd spent as a captive of Samory, self-styled "King" of the Sofas. I felt well enough to accept this kind invitation, and we had an animated evening.

Just as I was leaving (after brandy, of which we had both partaken rather freely), the Prince gripped my arm.

"They've broken her up, Jackdaw—had you heard?—and not before time." For a moment he'd lost me; nobody had called me that in years. It was the nickname he and his late brother, Prince Eddy, had bestowed on me when we were all in the Navy together. He was referring to our old corvette *Bacchante*, whose decks we'd trodden from '79 to '82.

"Don't you ever wonder whether that voyage of ours lay under a curse, Jackdaw? Dear Eddy dead within ten years! The admiral nearly dead. You half dead at twenty-five. And that poor devil who saw the Flying Dutchman and fell from aloft. Not to

26

mention the time she nearly sank. I say *Bacchante* was a dashed unlucky ship!" He downed his glass and gave a searching look. "No sailor should say this of any vessel, especially one he's served in. But I'll say it now—I'm glad she's gone!" His look changed to one of shock at what he had just uttered.

It didn't surprise me to learn that *Bacchante* had gone to the scrapyard. She sailed like a bathtub, and though she handled well enough under power, her bearings sometimes heated up at speed, a habit the engineers were never able to cure. But I was indeed surprised to hear him speak about those years at all, given other things that happened on that voyage, and the low, sensational attacks on Prince Edward's memory more recently. *Bacchante* and Eddy were subjects I preferred to avoid.

Before I could think how to respond, the strange look was gone from the Prince's face, and he was speaking with his normal geniality:

"And now! What if you don't go and get yourself captured by fanatical savages! My God, Henderson, you've a gift for being in the wrong place at the wrong time. Maxwell cabled. It's good to see you alive. We feared the worst. Rotten luck about the eye, but at least it's not your shooting eye. Come to Sandringham when you feel up to it, and I'll wager we'll see you get as good a bag as ever. Now off you go, Jackdaw, old man." He gave my shoulder a farewell pat, then spoke again as I reached the door.

"Wait. Do you remember what I asked you last time we met, before you went out to Ashanti?"

I said I wasn't sure. We'd had a long conversation.

"I asked whether you thought it a good idea for me to become engaged to my late brother's fiancée."

"I hope I said yes, P.G."

"You did. Nearly everyone thought it was a capital scheme. Including May herself, thank goodness. There *were* one or two wet blankets—churchmen for the most part—who thought it a trifle soon. But dash it all, we waited over a year. Anyway, my point is this: Don't *you* wait too long. What are you now? Wrong side of forty?"

"Thirty-eight last month. But I dare say I look twice that."

"I must say, Jackdaw, that you haven't looked so seedy since they took you off the active list. For heaven's sake go down to the country, get some rest, and find a good woman to look after you. Do as I say. A good woman. Not the other sort. Goodbye, old man."

We Hendersons are not the marrying kind. My father was the only one of five to succumb to domesticity, though he and my mother made up for the others by producing nine children, of whom seven live. Of these, I'm the first to wed and, I fear, may be the last, all of us now getting on in years.

Since the recent events in the Gold Coast I'd become resigned to the prospect of a bachelor life. What woman would want a man with a lonely eye and his constitution racked by equatorial fevers? But, as it happened, Prince George's advice did not fall on stony ground.

Last summer, whilst visiting my mother in Suffolk, I was invited to a garden party at Bifford Hall near Sudbury, and there ran into someone I'd not seen in almost twenty years. Ivry Fonnereau and I had been close as children. Our parents were fast friends, and we'd struck a youthful echo of that friendship, climbing trees and poaching birds' eggs at nine or ten, teaching one another waltzes at twelve or thirteen, and going on sketching picnics. Ivry was the first person who said I could draw (the first whom I believed, at any rate). For my fourteenth birthday she gave me a box of watercolours, and in an amateurish way I've painted ever since. At about this time we declared ourselves madly in love, but that bud was nipped when I had to sign aboard the *Swiftsure* as a cadet. We wrote back and forth, but saw little of each other over the next few years, and in the awkwardness of late adolescence nothing more was said of love.

In 1879, when we were both just twenty, I sailed on *Bacchante* for the three-year voyage around the world with Prince Eddy and Prince George. (The young Princes were then midshipmen; I, their senior by a few years, was a sub-lieutenant.) On my return to England in 1882, I learnt that Ivry had married. She was widowed most sadly a few years later when her husband lost his life during the attempted relief of General Gordon. They'd had no children.

It was a glorious afternoon at Bifford Hall in the rolling west Suffolk countryside, the gardens a sparkle of colour around emerald lawns, the whole in a golden setting of ripe wheat. The air was rich with floral scents, both from the blooms and the assembled ladies, and beneath the murmur of human voices lay a drowsy hum of bees. I recognized Ivry immediately—she'd hardly changed, except in the acquisition of a fetching maturity and grace. This thought prompted some childishness in me, and I thought I'd have a spot of fun.

A circular thatched summerhouse romantically sited beneath a tall wellingtonia gave me the idea, for it reminded me of the West African fetish-hut that claimed my eye. I slipped inside. "Frank," she called. "Come out of there. I saw you go in. It *is* you, isn't it? They said you'd be here. Why are you hiding from me?" While she approached, I popped out the artificial eye made for me in London—a good replica of my lost organ—and slipped in a tiger's eye I'd chanced to buy that week at an Ipswich taxidermist's. It had been lying in my pocket for days, irresistible as a firecracker; this seemed the ideal chance to let it off. Attempting a tigerish stance and growl, I emerged from the summerhouse blind side to Ivry.

The wheeze was a great success. For all her misfortunes and her grace, she was still the spunky girl I remembered. Her champagne flew one way, her hat into a hydrangea, and the two of us seized one another by the elbows and laughed our heads off. She was looking splendid in a slim lavender skirt that flared just above her neat ankles, her blouse was the last word in fashion, with those puffed sleeves that show off a slender woman's frame so well.

I confessed to her that my prank was not original, relating how some years ago in the South China Sea I'd met Sir Charles Brooke, the famous White Rajah of Sarawak. He'd lost an eye during a battle with headhunters in his jungle kingdom, and the only replacement he could obtain locally was one intended for a hunting trophy. "It keeps the wizards away and draws the girls," the Rajah had confided with a feline wink. "Don't know why, but it does. Best damned thing I've bought in all me life."

"Frank, really!" Ivry exclaimed—she kept glancing up at my face and biting her lower lip to stifle her amusement. "You always were a naughty boy. Your stories are improper as ever. Obviously you've been a bachelor much too long."

Ivry and her unmarried sisters were living only three miles from Riverhill, my mother's house in the country near Ispwich, where I spent as much of my convalescence as possible.

After the wild savannah, the many months under canvas and stars, and the roomy life of the colonies, I find I cannot long remain content here at Hitchin with sundry brothers and sisters, older than myself and still disposed to treat me as a boy—at thirty-eight! The hemmed streets and suburban atmosphere of the town become irksome. Our narrow house, so capacious in my child's eye, appears to me as a birdcage. I prefer Suffolk, England's sunniest county, projecting like a squire's belly into the sea. The tropics it will never be, but it strikes me as the most agreeable spot within an hour or two of London for someone who has shaken out his tent in empty places. Such splendid open vistas and weather-beaten coasts.

Riverhill commands a fine view of water-meadows falling down to the River Gipping and Bramford church. The locals say a hunting lodge once stood on its lofty site. The present house is about thirty years old and vaguely Elizabethan, its promiscuous architect allowing himself a crenellated tower. The owner, having built so solidly and fashionably, expected to enjoy the bucolic pleasures of the place for many years. But scarcely had the mortar set between the bricks when evil befell him in the shape of the Great Eastern Railway. Surveyors determined that the Norwich line had to run between river and hill, cleaving his property—its very name—with steel.

Having exhausted himself in futile litigation, the poor fellow watched while an army of navvies advanced with picks and shovels, with moleskin trousers and steaming mugs of tea, to carve a muddy wound across the land he loved, not a hundred yards from his French windows. This done, the iron Behemoth rattled the panes, snorting past at fifty miles per hour, leaving a sooty dragon in the sky that sank upon his garden with the breath of hell.

Riverhill's owner fell into melancholic decline, becoming so withdrawn that his own servants scarcely saw him. Old friends were sent packing. Health and hygiene were neglected. One day a maid found him hanging from an attic beam, martyred to the modern age by his own hand.

Soon the unfortunate's ghost was seen, rushing from the house to shake its airy fist at passing trains. The property was put up for sale by the man's estate. Needless to say, prospective buyers were not abundant. The servant who would work there after dark could not be found. So it was that this roomy house and still delightful garden (winds obliging) fell within the slim resources of my widowed mother and my brother Henry, twelve years my senior and a confirmed bachelor. My devout mother has no dread of ghosts, and Henry has been enthralled by trains since he was a boy. For staff they manage with two or three worthies of the Nonconformist chapel, who venture from the village in daylight hours. In short, they are happy at Riverhill, and I am always glad to impose upon their hospitality, staying with them for as long as they will have me, between obligatory Hitchin visits.

Ivry and I were therefore able to see rather a lot of one another, and I grew stronger daily in her company. We took long carriage rides and country rambles, went painting as we'd done so many years ago, sailed at Woodbridge, golfed at the Aldeburgh links. At Ivry's side I felt fourteen again, and my old affections were rekindled. I hardly dared hope that these feelings might be reciprocated, but to my great surprise and joy they were. On a glorious Sunday afternoon last November, a thirsty walk made us stop for drinks at the Wild Man. She joked about my being a wild man, and I asked if she would marry such a creature. Ivry agreed there and then to become my wife! Our wedding is to be in June.

❧ ❧

Riverhill, Bramford. September, 1899.

IN THE MONTHS SINCE MY LAST ENTRY I have decided, after much reflection, that I must go into matters I should give a great deal to leave untouched. What follows is strictly confidential, to be seen by no one, not even my dear wife, until after I am dead. It is mainly for her sake that I write, for should my end come sooner than expected, or in a way that seems sudden or strange, these scribbles may afford her something of an explanation. And I have always believed that explanations, however distressing, are more consoling than mysteries.

Before I am again posted overseas these papers will be left with Mr. Gerald Samuels, a London solicitor unconnected to the family whom I have known most of my life—we were at school together. He is a man in whom my eventual reader may place the utmost trust.

It was my intention, until now, to write nothing of my capture and confinement by the Sofas—especially the personal aftermath of that experience—beyond the official report I filed two years ago with the Colonial Office. During those early months back in England a certain euphoria came over me, despite my physical weakness, followed by a disinclination to say another word on my African troubles. I think this began soon after the visit to Prince George, when my tongue had wagged rather freely under the influence of the royal decanter.

I should perhaps abide by the secretive instinct and cast aside this pen. But now that I'm a married man, I can no longer think only of myself. A conviction has come over me—or comes over me at times—that a sinister pattern may lie behind widely separated events: namely, that my West African difficulties may not be altogether unrelated to certain things I witnessed many years before, as a young man in the South Seas. Should anything happen to me I could not bear for my beloved wife to blame herself, to think there was something she might have done or might not have done that could have made a difference. I am also sensible that my "explanation" may be nothing more than the ravings of an Englishman who has spent too long in the tropics, far from home, hearth, and the clime for which Nature intended him.

That will be for my widow to judge, and perhaps also for the police.

I am not at all sure how to broach this narrative. The very act of trying to write makes it seem beyond expression. It cannot be done briefly, for to compress events would be to drain them of their ambiguity and impose an order not apparent at the time. Yet these matters were already raised by Dr. Part, and now they have been raised again by my dear wife. What wouldn't I give to have spared her any glimpse of them!

Ivry said nothing of this on our honeymoon, and no shadow passed across her lovely face—a wise face, I might add, for it is subtly etched with its own share of cares—until after we honeymooners were returned and comfortably installed at Bramford. My mother and Henry offered us a wing of Riverhill for which they have little use, pending my return to Africa. Here we enjoy the best of both worlds: the society of family and, when we wish it, we are self-contained.

"Frank," said Ivry in a fraught voice one morning after breakfast. "I should like you to write to Dr. Part. I remember you saying he saved your life when you escaped from the Sofas."

"Part? Is he in England? Of course, we'll have him down."

"Not as far as I know. If only he were."

"Escape is rather overdoing it, dear girl. Samory let me go."

"Frank, please listen." She was pouring us both more tea. "You mentioned once that he spoke to you about talking in your sleep."

"That's all over and done with, Ivry. Please don't bring it up again. Let the dead bury the dead."

"Frank, I do not believe it *is* over and done with. You know how tired you feel every morning, how many cups of tea you need before you go to your study—tea you could stand a spoon in. The truth is you're not sleeping well, and I keep hearing things. Names of people I don't know—or perhaps some of them are places—and they all seem to be doing their level best to kill you, whoever they are. And the odd thing is it doesn't seem to come just from your time with Samory, because I distinctly hear you speak of 'poison.' From what you've told me of the Sofas, Frank, they don't sound like the sort who go in for poison." She took my hands in hers across the table, and looked into my eyes. She was doing her best to make light of it, but I could tell how worried she was.

"And these places, Frank. A lot of it's a jumble, but I'm sure it harks back to your time at sea. You're talking about ships. Voyages. The South Seas. You were in Sydney and Fiji and Tahiti, weren't you, my dear—all those years ago, when we lost touch and I married Reginald? I envy you, you know. Isn't it an earthly paradise down there? Of course, I can imagine you may have reasons for not telling *me*. . . ." She laughed coquettishly. "But you should know me well enough by now to see I don't care a fig about things like that. In your past, I mean. I'm hardly an ingenue, Frank dearest. I know what sailors get up to."

"Ivry, please," I said, making the painful decision to be less than candid with her. "Sydney, yes. And Fiji—*Bacchante* called there. But not Tahiti. The French have it. A British warship wouldn't go there. Not without a very good reason. Anyway, if you want to know what we did on *Bacchante*, you have only to look it up in Reverend Dalton. Though be warned, he makes a devilish dull read of an extraordinary voyage."

I gestured towards my study where, in a glass-fronted bookcase, repose the obese tomes of the royal tutor's exhaustive, and exhausting, narrative—the routes and ports, each breath of wind, each foot of sail, every pound of coal that propelled the royal

corvette. To say nothing of the learned man's potted history of each colony and nation visited, descriptions of their flora and fauna, analyses of produce and industry, and prospects for British settlement, right down to the cost of a third-class ticket from Liverpool.

"He says he merely compiled the account from the Princes' journals, Ivry. But of course he wrote the thing himself. One can't imagine those two youngsters sitting down night after night and penning anything like that. It was hard enough getting them to write to their grandmother. Imagine that when your granny's Queen Victoria!"

"Don't try to divert me, Frank. I'm worried."

"Well, whatever this is you keep hearing, let me assure you it has nothing to do with sailors' doings. I'm sorry if I'm still raving occasionally, but that's all it is. Raving. Old Part did say it takes some people years. Perhaps we should sleep in separate rooms, just for the time being."

Ivry replied, with characteristic verve, that she had not remarried in order to sleep alone so soon. I guessed more or less what she must have been hearing, though in my waking life I fought it down, hoped it would unravel each morning the way dreams do, even the worst of nightmares. But the truth is that the dreams have not been fading. Quite the reverse. My time with the Sofas has unearthed a Pandora's box from dark recesses of my mind.

⊰⊱ ⊰⊱

Things could hardly have looked better for me in the mid-nineties, my first years on the Gold Coast. The illness that had

forced my retirement from the Navy was by then a memory, and I rediscovered youthful springs of energy and spirit that I had feared might never flow again. I became Secretary and Aide-de-Camp to the Governor, Sir William Maxwell, accompanying him on the Ashanti Expedition of 1895–96, in which all involved could take pride, for it was both bloodless and decisive.

With the might of Ashanti broken, the way seemed clear to consolidate our own influence in the North. To this end Sir William made me Travelling Commissioner in the Gold Coast Hinterland, empowered to visit distant kings and chiefs with whom we had treaties, to show them that though they were out of sight they were nonetheless dear to the heart of the Colonial Office.

I set out late in 1896, accompanied by the Colony's Surveyor, Mr. George Ekem Ferguson, one of the most remarkable men and staunchest friends it has ever been my privilege to know. Ferguson was a man in a million, one who moved with ease and brilliance between the African world of his birth and the English world he served. A member of the Fanti tribe (with perhaps a Scot somewhere up the family tree), he spoke eloquent Ashanti, half a dozen other local languages, better French than I do, and each evening on our travels he was reading Caesar and Tacitus in the Latin. His knowledge of local geography, flora and fauna was unsurpassed. Had our Hinterland duties not intervened, Ferguson would have gone to London that November to address the Royal Geographical Society and receive its medal, the first African to be so honoured. Instead, he met an untimely death in a remote and lawless corner of the globe, an end witnessed only by his killers.

Since we expected no trouble, our column was small: one hundred Hausa rifles under Captain Irvine and Native Officer Gimalah, a flinty old warrior from Timbuctoo, plus a medical contingent in the capable hands of Dr. Part, Colonial Surgeon.

About ten days out from Accra, after marching inland through the grand and gloomy jungles that surround the Kingdom of Ashanti, we entered Kumasi. The Ashanti capital was much changed in the months since I'd last seen it, having a forlorn and desolate look, a far cry from its glory days when the native rank and beauty flocked there for the glister of gold and the gore of human sacrifice. The Ashantis had promised to give up that cherished custom, but found they could not deny themselves after their victory over Nkoranza, when King Prempeh, like some modern Montezuma, consigned captives in their hundreds to the sacrificial blade.

Royal Engineers were at work on the British fort, using hewn granite brought in originally by King Kofi for his palace. The Residency was complete enough that Ferguson, Irvine, and myself could lodge within its walls. Ferguson remarked how these very stones, in their former life, must have heard many a toast quaffed from the royal goblet made of Sir Charles MacCarthy's skull.

We pressed on north into the Hinterland, the great woods slowly fraying into scattered bush and undulating plains where elephant grass grew high and thick. I soon began to hear reports of a new scourge in the region: encroachment by invading Sofas, the followers of Samory and his warlike sons. Until then, these marauders had seldom been met with east of the Black Volta. Now they were crossing the river in strength, seizing our traders' goods and carrying them back to their headquarters behind the French Ivory Coast. There the plunder—mainly slaves and tribute extorted with unspeakable cruelty from any native kingdom unable to resist—was exchanged for the latest weaponry, to be employed in further outrages.

Although addressed as King, and assuming the pomp and state of royalty, Samory himself was only the son of a petty Mandingo trader. Also styled by his people the *Almamy*, or High Priest, he sanctified his ambitions by invoking the name of the Prophet. His so-called empire was, however, nothing more than a sticky web of terror stretching across the Hinterland beyond the reach of the Great Powers. His followers were a mongrel lot of no particular tribe or nationality, the word Sofa, or "Horseman," being applied to any brigands claiming to have horses, sometimes with as little reason as the term Cavalier during our own Civil War.

We travelled many weeks, reaching a country whose isolation and wildness surpassed anything I had seen. The eye fed upon waving plains turning sere, with acacias, baobabs, and other trees dotted about sparingly. The people, who wore little but leaves and not many of them, were known as a turbulent race who might welcome the stranger with a poisoned arrow between his ribs.

At a fortified village where we camped, we saw a pond full of tame crocodiles, reared and held sacred like those of ancient Egypt. On learning that they often took a stroll about town after dark, I was careful to fasten my tent securely against these festive Saurians.

I was stricken, however, by dysentery, an old foe from my Navy years. Our stores had nearly run out, and milk—the diet prescribed by medicos—was almost unobtainable. Ferguson's knowledge of the climate and diseases made him especially anxious that I should not quench my thirst with water, a beverage harmful under any circumstances. He scoured the country to get milk for me from nearly anything he could find that was female and walked on four legs.

At length we reached Wa, in the northwest, where we set up a temporary headquarters. My people settled down comfortably, the Hausas making their usual huts of poles and grass. The town looked prosperous and substantial, well built of rammed earth finished with swish (mud plaster) and the dwellings arranged in compounds.

Complaints about the Sofas soon came in from all around, especially from the people of Bona who had recently fled to Wa when the raiders occupied their capital. In some places hardly a hut was unburnt, hardly a field free from charred and mangled corpses. This was the work of Samory's eldest son, whom the Sofas knew simply as Famadeh, or "the Prince."

Affairs came to a head when the king of Wa, emboldened by our presence, refused to fulfil a Sofa demand for five thousand slaves. I decided to go with a portion of our force and occupy Dawkita, a town on Wa's frontier with Bona, in the hope that my presence would deter the Sofas from invading a land where the Union Jack was flying.

❦ ❦

It was the second of March when I set out on this ill-fated mission, accompanied by Mr. Ferguson, Native Officer Gimalah, and forty Hausas, leaving Captain Irvine in command of Wa. At noon the following day we reached the steep wooded banks of the Black Volta, a fine stream broader than the Thames at Windsor. The water was low, and we got across easily. On the west bank we met more refugees, who told me that Sofas were on the march.

Upon reaching Dawkita I told the chiefs I had come to protect them, and did not expect the Sofas would attack me. I then sent a message to the Prince, explaining which kingdoms were under British protection and must therefore be left unmolested. He sent a threatening reply, telling me that all the Hinterland belonged to Samory, and that if I wished to die, Dawkita would be a perfect spot for it.

We prepared by occupying three large compounds, each with thick mud walls about ten feet high and a single narrow entrance. The rooms inside had flat roofs about seven feet high, thus leaving a parapet to protect defenders on the roof. All was quiet for some time, the weather very hot, and we watched in dismay as the small Dawkita River became dryer each day, until there remained only a waterhole in its bed.

One morning before dawn, Ferguson shook me awake with news that the whole Sofa army was approaching. Shortly past noon they came in sight, advancing over the hill in a huge square, numbering about seven thousand. These were flanked by four hundred horsemen, who veered off along the riverbank and took our waterhole. Late in the afternoon the Sofa bugles sounded, and their riflemen opened fire from the edge of the bush. We had no more than 120 rounds per man. I gave orders that only picked shots were to fire, but when a rush was threatened a volley should be given. The

Hausas showed admirable steadiness throughout our four days and nights under siege, and I cannot speak too highly of their courage.

On the last day of March, there came a sudden pause in the firing, and a messenger approached with a letter in a cleft stick. In this the Prince said that we had better go away across the Volta. My reply was that the Sofas had attacked me, and had better retire themselves, for I should not do so.

This decision seems to me now to have been foolhardy, and I have repented of it bitterly through many a wakeful night. But only hindsight can trace the line between arrogance and fortitude, and there is no telling what treachery we might have met with had we left our compounds.

There was enough water for only one more day, and our ammunition was nearly at an end. Next morning the Sofas renewed their attack with undiminished ferocity, and by mid-afternoon compounds 2 and 3 were in flames. The defenders retreated to mine, losing on the way one killed and six wounded, one mortally. Mr. Ferguson took a bullet through his leg. The enemy then occupied the buildings we'd abandoned, put out the flames, and resumed firing from there.

At dusk we decided that our position was untenable. Our only chance—and, though no one said so, we all knew it to be slim—was to fight our way out, withdraw across the Volta under cover of darkness, and fall back on Wa.

It then occurred to me that I might see the Prince and induce him to cease hostilities. I knew him to be untrustworthy and cruel, but thought the risk worth taking in view of the great loss of life, to say nothing of guns and equipment, which would probably result on our retreat. The other officers strongly objected, saying I should be uselessly courting death—very possibly in some unpleasant form.

In the end they agreed. We decided that if negotiations failed, or if I were detained, the rest should make their escape that night. I must add that poor Ferguson, though he spoke most gloomily of the fate that would befall me, was restrained only with difficulty from coming along, wounded though he was.

At first light I started for the enemy camp, carried in state by my hammock-men in their uniform of dark blue pants and frocks trimmed in red, with sashes and caps to match; myself with white flag in hand.

I was met by a Sofa priest, a refined man of Arab type named Abu Bukari, who asked me to wait for a short time. I was then taken to the place of palaver.

The Prince was tall and good-looking, but there was weakness in his countenance—perhaps, thought I, the weakness of a cruel man. Surrounding him were chiefs and courtiers, many of them very young. Some carried umbrellas, at one time reserved for royalty in Africa, but nowadays borne by pushing and pretentious individuals with no better claim than those who call themselves "Esquire" in England. Behind them stood a semi-arch of a thousand riflemen.

The Prince said that my people should surrender and come into his camp with all our stores and weapons. I told him this was out of the question. I was then placed under guard in a compound, Abu Bukari letting me know that he and several older chiefs had begged the Prince to spare my life. Late that night I heard firing in the direction of Wa, and could only guess at its meaning. Was Irvine breaking through at last? Or was this the end for the others? My hammock-men, who had bravely chosen to remain with me, now said that our heads would soon be off, and we should therefore finish the whisky.

On the next day I was brought again before the Prince and his chiefs. He said they had "examined my head" (figuratively thus far) and found I was a good man. He would do me no harm and send me back to the coast, but I must first go before his father, Samory, at Haramonkoro, some fortnight's journey to the west.

The Prince added that as I had not been afraid to come to him, my men would not be killed. I demanded to know what had happened to Ferguson and the others, and the meaning of the shooting last night towards Wa. But he would say no more, and I received no further news of my friend until his death was communicated to me many days later in a most grisly manner.

The Sofas brought in stores of ours that they had seized, and I had to explain their use. The surveying equipment baffled them; the gold (about £100 brought for friendly kings) aroused glee; and certain medical appliances, namely syringes and enema bulbs, afforded them infinite amusement.

The next day we started for Bona, which lay *en route* to Samory's headquarters. A lame Rosinante was my mount, all knobs and saddle-sores. As the day wore on, my skin wore off, until parts of me resembled the condition of my steed. The country we traversed was mostly dry upland, lion-coloured and dotted with thorny acacias and other hardy trees. The baobabs had lost their leaves, as they always do in this season, but great cylindrical seed pods still hung from them like salami in an Italian butcher's shop. Whenever we stopped beneath one of these trees I begged my Sofa jailer, a surly old ruffian named Siraku, to split open a pod and let me have the pith, which serves as a tart and refreshing sherbet.

Bona was a good-sized town, on a rise, with a small mud-brick mosque. Here and there, less prominently sited, were the mysterious abodes of local fetishes, the palings around them decorated with animal skulls. There seemed an uneasy truce in the war of the One God of the desert against the many spirits of the bush—not to mention my bottled spirits from the misty glens of Scotland, for the Sofas were rigid teetotallers.

The Prince and his chiefs put on a triumphal reception, arraying themselves and their horses in all their finery. The men played music and fired off guns, while about twenty of the Prince's wives began to sing and dance before us, lightly clad. Notwithstanding their Mohammedan faith, the Sofa women go unveiled, and in their ways rather resemble the native African; some indeed, in their free conduct, might pass for local examples of the "new woman," if one may picture such ladies largely bare except for an exiguous breechclout or a skirt of leather thongs resembling nothing so much as the fringe of a lampshade.

The Prince seemed astonished that I had no wife, and offered me one on terms much easier than those of the marriage service. Had I accepted, however, it would have been difficult to enjoy the honeymoon, for a constant flow of visitors came to my quarters to stare at me, saying they had never seen a white man.

On the next day I was sent under guard to Haramonkoro, the Sofa capital. For a week we rode through an unhealthy land, stony and barren, its streams dry. Here and there were great piles of rock, the leopard-haunted homes of the baboon. These primates often sallied out and perched on boulders, shaking their fists at us and making other manlike gestures.

Monkeys have become rare around our colonies. The great trade in skins has rendered the country all but silent wherever commerce penetrates. A trumpeting elephant is now almost as rare a sound on the "Tooth Coast," named for his white gold, as it is on the coast of England.

The gold of most interest to the Sofas was the black kind, still much in demand across the Soudan and Arabia, though it no longer commanded the prices known in the heyday of the Atlantic trade. All work in the Sofas' domain was done by slaves, and I witnessed a great deal of disgusting cruelty. At Bona I saw a sick slave, whose recovery was hopeless, dragged out of the town to die. On the march, if a woman who was carrying a child as well as a load began to flag, her burden was lightened by throwing the child in a thornbush.

After a week we reached the Komoe River, where the land improves. Three days later I entered Samory's seat of government. Haramonkoro resembled Bona in size and architecture, though without obvious fetish houses. Around the outskirts of the town were lyre-horned cattle, all showing their ribs and bawling pitifully as if trying to call down the rain.

I was brought before Samory without time for a wash, let alone a rest. Weeks had passed since the loss of Dawkita, but I'd had little opportunity to recover from the extreme fatigue we all experienced there. I do not believe I'd slept a night through since hostilities began, for I was woken often by dysentery and even more by the sad procession of events which passed before my mind's unquiet eye like scenes from a baleful lantern show. My thoughts could not abandon the débâcle at Dawkita, playing day and night over each moment when I might have made a better decision, or given better orders.

Samory's army was drawn up around him in an oval formation of about four thousand, with the townsfolk beyond. The spoils were carried round this *circus maximus* in a kind of Roman triumph, saving the best for last: myself paraded in my hammock. After this I was called before the King.

He was about fifty years old, a tall man with a rather pleasant face which lacked the weakness of his son's. He was wholly bald, only the muscles of his scalp betraying ripples of emotion and cunning, which he was expert at stifling in his sloe eyes. He had the slender build of the Mandingo, with long fingers in which he clasped a rhinoceros-tail flywhisk. His clothes were of Arab type—white cotton robes over trousers, with a purple silk sash. He had a loose turban embellished with leopardskin, and was augustly seated on an old iron bedstead.

Signs were made to me to kneel before him. These I disregarded, shaking him by the hand instead. I then sat down on a chair beside him and watched the rest of the review. It was a performance much like the one at Bona, but grander, with the troops attired in booty from a dozen campaigns. Samory had his Household Brigade of five hundred riflemen march past in full uniform, though "uniform" is hardly the word. One was arrayed in a frock coat, a pair of pyjamas, and a fireman's helmet of French make; the next in top boots, a tail coat, and a tall hat; still another in a soldier's tunic and a bowler, but with bare legs; and one with a morning coat and tam-o'-shanter.

Within the oval, four regimental bands were stationed, one having wooden dulcimers, another horns made from elephant tusks, the third a kind of four-stringed harp or lyre, while the fourth consisted of the King's wives, uttering that eerie African cry called ululation—a trilling of the tongue at the back of the throat, accompanied by bells and cymbals.

The sun set smartly, as it always does in the tropics, swallowed by the rippling darkness of the hills. The Sofas adjourned their revels to wash and prostrate themselves at prayer, rank after rank of warlike figures meek beneath a violet sky, the Holy City in their wild minds. Then night was upon the town, and straw bonfires were lit beside the bands. Young men, oiled and nearly naked, came forth from the Sofa army to engage in wrestling matches, glistening in the firelight. Each champion's name was announced and celebrated by drummers who circled him, beating out his accomplishments with flying hands upon the "speaking" drums. It was like something from the ancient stadium of Olympia, a weird, romantic scene—now dim as the fire died, now bright as grass was cast upon the blaze. I steeled myself to remain alert, keeping in mind that any sign of weakness might prove fatal.

The climax of the evening could not have been more shocking, or more unexpected after the generally civil treatment Samory had shown towards me until then. I heard a scuffle at the edge of the firelight. Prominent Sofas I'd not seen before came brusquely to their monarch, bearing a bundle in a cloth. They glared and pointed angrily at me, as if demanding to know why I was still alive. When Samory seemed unswayed, one of them unwrapped the cloth, revealing a man's head. It was flourished before the King, held aloft in hideous triumph for the throng, then shaken before my eyes and cast at my feet. They brought a firebrand to illuminate the object, and in this savage manner conveyed to me beyond all hope the fate of poor George Ferguson.

I will forbear describing the condition of the remains, except to say that his hour of death was clearly many days in the past. I could scarcely recognize his face, but the patterns of hair and beard allowed no doubt that the head was his. I cannot adequately describe my feelings at this abrupt news of the barbaric death of such a brave and loyal friend. Horror, pity, fury—above all, guilt and remorse—surged within me, as they have done ever since when I ponder these events.

I might easily have said or done something then to bring a similar end upon myself. But exhaustion held my tongue, whilst darkness hid the trembling I experienced throughout my frame. Samory, his face dull red in the light from the embers, regarded me silently for what seemed a long time. Then he began to speak through an interpreter, saying he was sorry for what had happened, claiming his son's men had exceeded their orders. When I recovered enough composure to reply, I attempted to find out the details of Ferguson's last moments. I also demanded to know what had happened to Gimalah and my other men, and to the rest of our forces at Wa. But he would tell me nothing.

Next I heard the word *brune*, "white man," repeated vehemently by several of Samory's councillors. They were discussing whether to kill me on the spot. Or perhaps when to kill me. Or how. I have only a smattering of Mandingo and was too tired to parse the grammar, but their gesturing spoke volumes.

I told the interpreter to convey to them that I knew very well what they were talking about, that I was too worn out to care, and they should wake me when they'd come to a decision.

I then lay down on the ground and fell asleep.

Three

⋖⋗ ⋖⋗

TAHITI

Arue Women's Prison. April, 1990

HENDERSON'S FIRST NOTEBOOK ENDS THERE at the warlord's
feet, as if he meant to leave his reader panting. An odd thing to
do for one who hopes he'll never be read; he wasn't quite out of
pages.

As I go through these photocopies, typing them up for
you, I remember the originals back in Vancouver with my
stolen life—their look and feel, their covers of black or green or
pinkish marbling, their cellar mustiness and tang of horsehoof
glue. New decipherments still leap out, the mind pulling a
squiggle into focus, a stranger recognized, so obvious that I
smack myself.

Reading Frank in this way makes me feel that I know him
(insofar as you can know anyone by what they write!). Is it fever,
or pain, or an articulate madness in his giddy loops and lines? I
like him. I like his affection for his wife and friends, his open-

mindedness, his freethinking sense of the absurd, his painting—
especially that he never claims to be much good at it—and his
love of the tropics.

Years later, when he retired after the Great War, he built a
steam-heated conservatory against the Suffolk house, filling it
with orchids and hibiscus, bromeliads, strangler figs. As blight
and winter claimed the orchard outside, he'd retreat to this tiny
jungle, sink in a rattan armchair and talk old times to a scarlet
macaw who flew down to eat grapes from his hand.

Whenever I feel too sorry for myself, I reread his captivity
in Africa. I am merely inconvenienced, I have friends nearby,
assurances that this will end, and I've my health. Henderson had
none of these, yet he went on, a man from a hardier time.

Like you, he's a comfort to me now.

I'm locked up in a historic building, a tropical Bastille built by the
last king of Tahiti. Picture a stone fortress scrambling up a hill,
spacious and old-fashioned, no razor wire or swivelling cameras.
Over the main gate, where you half expect to see *Abandon hope*,
are the words POMARE V REX 1879. It used to be the men's
jail, the only jail, until things started going wrong in these islands
and the French had to build a new one. That's overflowing, but
we female crooks are rare.

My cell has aquamarine walls and red tile floor. No rug—
they worry about people unravelling rugs and hanging themselves with the twine—but they provide a pink curtain in my
tiny window, a poster of Bora Bora on the wall, and they allow
a few personal things, some photos, a calendar. I even have a

small TV, high in a steel cage bolted to the ceiling. This is an extra I pay for. Not much worth watching except the news, but it helps me pick up Tahitian, and my French has improved no end. Above all, they've let me keep my papers and my clothes (I had horrid visions of striped pyjama suits).

My fellow inmates are what you might guess: pickpockets, druggies, hookers, wives who topped their husbands with a breadfruit pounder. Only three or four whites. The rest are Tahitian, Chinese, various mixtures, and homesick girls from outer islands—from Rangiroa, the Australs, the Marquesas. A sad rather than a vicious lot, yet I often hear them laugh.

No one laughs more than Pua, who knifed a sailor in Quinn's Bar. She admits it cheerfully (he deserved it). She's nineteen, slight and graceful, wavy hair to her waist, the very image of a *vahine*. I never believed her capable of violence until one day I glimpsed a mongoose quickness in her wrist and eye.

Twice a week she teaches us Tahitian dance, a flowing semaphore of hips and arms: *marama* the moon, *anuanua* the rainbow, *mata'i*, the wind. We do this at the top of the yard, where we can look out over the parapet and rusty roofs and flame-trees to the sea and mountains, our only sight of the world. Down there is Matavai Bay, where the *Bounty* anchored; Point Venus, where Cook tried to measure the distance of the sun; and a strange tower beside the water containing the pickled bones of the last Pomare, builder of this place, who gave his kingdom to the French and slowly killed himself with Benedictine.

On Sundays, if the wind's onshore, the hymns of Cowper and Wesley waft up above the traffic, faint tunes I half remember sung in old Tahitian at a frumpy royal chapel built by Methodists from Wapping.

But you don't want to hear my prison memoirs. When I was free, I hardly had a moment. Now I'm getting long-winded. This will land on your doormat with a thud.

⤝⫘⤞ ⤝⫘⤞

Your father. I must be careful what I say, and *how*. I've promised you the truth and you shall have it, but there's no need to make it any bitterer than it is. For me, Victor Lumley is a sour memory in a shallow grave; for you . . . well, he's your flesh and blood.

Until lately, until your note, your father was seldom on my mind. Usually he's underground, a sort of troll or goblin, which is as close as I come to banishing him altogether. But he gets out and about when my guard is down, as it was on the flight here, a long haul through the night from Los Angeles. In those shiny cocoons of rancid air and rushing noise, where life hangs on a single flaw or stroke of malice, I often think over the inches burned from my candle of unknown length. On the ground, dazzled by the steady flame consuming time, we live as if our light will burn forever. But eight miles high above the world, where humans have no right to be, the flame sinks and I see it as it is, faltering in the gale of chance.

So Lumley came to visit me in that close darkness, the other passengers asleep (all but a scatter of insomniacs in yellow pools). He appeared, smiled, lowered himself onto me. An incubus.

•　•　•

In the spring of 1966 this letter arrived at Tilehouse Street on Ministry of Defence writing paper:

> Dear Mrs. Wyvern,
>
> Certain evidence has recently come to our attention which we would be pleased to be able to discuss with you. While we do not wish to raise hopes more than is warranted, it would greatly assist our continuing investigation into the disappearance of your husband and other persons missing in action during the Korean Emergency if you would kindly consent to a visit from the undersigned at your convenience.
>
> Yours sincerely, V.C. Lumley, Wing Cmdr. (ret.)

Such an innocuous name, Lumley, Wing Commander, retired. We imagined a moon-faced jovial fellow, maybe not the sharpest knife in the drawer, but the owner of a splendid handlebar moustache. And those gallant initials, V.C.—how easily we fell for false suggestions—a brave man, a hero, coming to see us.

"Oh, Liv! We mustn't let ourselves. . . . Of course it'll be nothing. Just some War Office mistake—the Ministry—whatever they call themselves now. How I wish your sister were here. That silly girl isn't even on the phone."

Lottie *was* on the phone. Of course she was. You don't get modelling jobs without one. But I was sworn to secrecy—she'd never forgive me if Mother rang up and heard the row she lived in. I'd already visited my sister at her "flat," only twice the size of her bed (a mattress on the floor), the smallest inhabited room I'd ever seen. It was in a Clapham terrace with a greasy kitchen and a bathroom shared by eight. Her walls were draped with melting psychedelic posters: Jefferson Airplane, *OZ*, sundry gigs and clubs. She was barefoot, in a long Indian-cotton skirt and sheer blouse revealing pink rosettes. I didn't dare—still owned a bra, always wore pullover and jeans. Bursts of music and laughter came from upstairs doors. Hollow-chested men strolled about as if I wasn't there. There was a smell of joss-sticks and fish on the landing, and another smell I didn't know until that night, when I smoked a joint for the first time. (Coughed like hell and didn't get high.)

At dawn came a clopping of hooves outside, and I thought I must be stoned after all, but it was a real rag-and-bone man with a horse and cart, sleepwalking between the Minis and Vespas parked along the street. London! Half Dickens, half Swinging, and my sister here living it all, and I so impressed, so envious, and I'd have given myself away to any of those young hairies if they'd asked. But none did, and the only one who even gave me an up-and-down look was Lottie's boyfriend, Art, who shook his locks at me and said, "Lottie's little sister! You two are so different. Far out." And Lottie said, "Mitts off, Art. She's not even legal. You can sod off and doss somewhere else tonight. See you."

All this I'd kept from Mother, who thought I'd gone up with the school English class for *Romeo and Juliet*.

So it was just my mother and myself there to greet V.C. Lumley, Wing Commander (retired), when he turned up on a wet afternoon in the spring of 1966.

I remember opening the door, dizzy with longing and apprehension, to a tall man, a friendly face, square bone structure like a Scandinavian's. He stood there in a damp tweed jacket with leather elbow patches, an open-necked white shirt and spotted burgundy cravat, a gust of March at his back. No moustache. A grey drift at the temples. Dark hair and clear grey eyes that seemed to look into my heart, twinkling, roguish, pleading.

"Come in."

I got the tea things and a plate of biscuits, catching: "—bored stiff since I retired, so I run errands for the Ministry. Enjoy it immensely. Gets me out and about, and I meet charming people like yourself."

"A biscuit with your tea, Wing Commander?"

"Just plain Lumley now, I'm afraid. Victor Lumley. Silly to use one's rank so long after. Korea did it for me, too, Mrs. Wyvern. Though my troubles are trifles compared to . . . to yours. Health bother. Something in my tum. Still there. Doctors haven't a clue. Ever had Korean food? Don't—that's my advice." He accepted a jammy dodger. "I regret to say I never met your husband. We were there at slightly different times."

"I'm sorry . . . ," Mother said.

I was watching him. He looked fit enough to me. A vigorous man in his forties, as Jon would be. What really had forced him to retire? Were some bits and pieces shot away? He was fascinating, though I wasn't sure I liked him.

Mother noticed me for the first time. "This is my daughter, Olivia." We shook hands, his large and muscular, the hand of someone who makes things or plays an instrument.

"What really happened to you? In Korea?"

"Liv! That's very rude. Sorry, Mr. Lumley. She's only a child. She looks older. People don't realize."

"You don't want to hear about *me*. You ladies'll be wanting to know why I'm here."

I liked being a "lady." He'd brought a tan dispatch case with RAF wings stamped on the pigskin. From this he took a folded cloth. Inside it were a few small objects wrapped in tissue paper. Moving his teacup to the carpet, he laid out cloth and contents on the table.

"Bloody bought it, poor chap! Bloody bought it, poor chap!" called a maniacal voice from the pantry.

"Heavens! Who's that? Sorry. Not my business."

Mother laughed nervously. "No need to apologize. It's only Lord Jim. The parrot. Something in your voice must. . . ." She fell silent, fingering her necklace.

"A parrot! My auntie had a parrot—her late husband's. Navy man. Torpedoed in the Med. That bird said frightful things whenever the vicar came to tea." Lumley laughed easily, then composed himself. He had a generous mouth, good teeth, the lips full, a perfect Cupid's bow.

"Let me say at the outset that there's nothing conclusive, one way or another. We still can't say whether your husband survived the downing of his plane in '53. There's still no wreckage. We haven't a shred of evidence to support—or dismiss—the speculation that he or others might have been taken alive. What I've brought are these. I can't tell you exactly how they came into Ministry hands. Don't know the answer myself—those Whitehall types have lockjaw. But they have asked me to ask you to take a look. Can you bear to?"

Lumley unwrapped the things and passed them to Mother. They were small. Corroded and pitted. Like ancient coins.

"Condition's poor, I'm afraid. More or less what you'd expect for the soil conditions over there." He lowered his voice. "They grow everything with nightsoil, you see."

Mother clenched her fist around them suddenly. She was crying.

"Take your time."

She sat up on the edge of her chair, dabbing at her eyes with a lace hankie she always kept in her cuff. "I remember buttons like these on my husband's uniform. There's a uniform upstairs. We could check if they're the same. But surely these could have come from any RAF officer of the time?"

"I'm afraid that's so."

"Then why come all this way to show them to me? I'm sorry if I sound ungrateful. I just can't see the point."

"I . . . we have no wish to distress you, Mrs. Wyvern. But we feel it important to include you in any findings. Some people in your position have told us that we go about things too . . . quietly."

"Can I see, Mummy?" She poured the things unsteadily from her palm to mine.

Two brass buttons and a cap badge. Heavily verdigrised, as if they'd been in the ground for centuries, like Roman coins.

"There's one thing more. The most important, actually. It *is* rather fragile. I must ask you not to take it out of the wrapper."

From the dispatch case he withdrew a small document sheathed in cellophane. Mother examined it, looked up at me with watery eyes. She passed it over, turning quickly away.

It was a fragment of my father's handwriting. I recognized it from old birthday and Christmas cards I kept with my jewellery. I didn't understand what it might mean. It was just a scrap—not much bigger than a cigarette paper—crumpled and stained. I could read five words: . . . *recce SW quadrant and report* . . .

"Where did you get this?" Mother asked. "And when? Surely you must have some idea."

"Then it's authentic?"

"Yes. Unless. . . ."

"You have any doubts?"

"There've been false trails before, haven't there? Cruel hoaxes. . . ." She began to cry again.

"I know. . . . I can't imagine how one copes. If I may say so, you strike me as a very brave woman, Mrs. Wyvern. And so do you, Miss Wyvern. Other people I've seen recently have responded—how shall I put it?—irrationally. People need to believe." He sat quietly for a moment. "I can tell you only what I know. These things have come from overseas sources we believe to be reliable. As to what their appearance, or release at this time may mean, I'm as much in the dark as you are. I'm awfully sorry if my coming here's upset you. As I said, there's been a change in policy at the Ministry under the Labour government. They feel that next of kin should be kept abreast of developments. That hasn't always been the case."

"You mean there's other information—kept from us?"

"I honestly don't know. Probably nothing of substance. As you perceive, even physical evidence like this is open to a number of interpretations.

"I'd better be getting along. Here's where you can reach me. Though don't be surprised if you have trouble getting through. The right hand never knows what the left hand's doing up there. They won't even tell you if it's raining outside in case it's a state secret. Speaking of which, I must ask you both to sign this. Silly. Just routine."

Lumley produced a form entitled *Official Secrets Act*. We read and duly signed. Though it seemed so pointless. Thirteen years ago was an age to me. Most of my life. The images of Jon in my mind—real ones, not photographs—were fleeting, indistinct. He'd died. . . . He'd "gone missing," as Mother insisted, when I was three, an age when you can't distinguish between the height of your father and the height of a tree—I remember thinking that the crown of his head and the treetops were equally far out of reach. I'm left with bits of him. Big hands clasping my waist as I learnt to ride a trike. A stern face and a spanking when I chased a neighbour's chickens. The sandpaper of his cheek at bedtime. His smell of wet tweed, jet fuel, pipe tobacco. Now, of course, I can see how recent it still was in 1966, how to Mother it must have seemed that Korea had ended only yesterday, that the trail was warm, that her husband could still come back.

"Good Lord, that's rather fine. Looks terribly old. What exactly is it? Suppose I ought to know. Never much good at history." Lumley laughed. Mother made her usual little speech: "I believe it's called an assegai. An ancestor of my husband's brought it back from Africa."

"May I?" He stood up and approached the spear, ran a caressing hand along the polished wood. "People used to make things so beautifully, didn't they? Reminds me of a wooden propeller we had in the mess. Same craftsmanship. Fascinating."

He opened his case, gathered the things he'd shown us. "If it was up to me I'd leave these with you, but I'm afraid the Ministry won't allow it. Force of habit. They've a grip like Scots on a ten-pound note. On anything at all. What I *can* give you is a photo of the small finds—here—and a copy of the paper fragment. I'll be in touch the minute I hear more."

That evening we had a cold supper of bread and cheese. Mother drank several whiskies, something she rarely did. She even gave me a small glass.

"You know what's odd about those things, Liv? I wish I'd thought to ask that man before he left. Those buttons and the badge, they're from Jon's—from someone's—dress uniform. Why would he have been wearing, or carrying, a dress uniform on a mission? It doesn't add up."

It wasn't long before she had a chance to put that question. About three weeks later Lumley rang, said he was nearby, thought he'd pop in. I was at school. He told her nothing new. Had no idea why dress buttons had been recovered from a combat zone. But she was tipsy when I got home. Mother and Lumley had had a rather cosy afternoon. He'd revealed why he had to leave the service: malaria and deafness as well as an "uppity amoeba." And as for her, it was just so marvellous to talk about things with someone who'd been there, who understood, who remembered. Who hadn't forgotten what we'd fought for, and who wasn't out in Trafalgar Square chanting from Mao's wretched little book.

Mother loathed the sixties. "Everything I've believed in," she used to say. "Everything I've paid dearly for is now held cheap and ridiculed." I tried to persuade her that it wasn't like that. That she and Jon, and their parents before them, had fought those terrible wars to end all war, and my generation was agreeing with them, saying *hell no, we won't go; make love not war*. But our style put her off—the music, the hair, the clothes—too big a step from ration cards and Vera Lynn. I always won the argument, but she never changed her view. She'd throw up her hands and say, "Olivia, darling, you could talk the hind leg off a donkey."

Throughout that summer Lumley came to see us every few weeks. He said he lived nearby, in Royston, which is why he'd been given our "case." He took us there once to see the Royston Cave, a vault hollowed down into the chalk beneath the town centuries ago. The bottle-shaped cavity was dank and smelt vaguely of pee. By the light of a dangling bulb I saw writhing figures and cabbalistic symbols, scratched crudely on the pale stone. A creepy place, more dungeon than cave, where witches and heretics were said to have hidden in the Middle Ages, or been imprisoned, or tortured.

Afterwards Lumley drove us past a house he said was his—quite grand with a circular drive, barely visible from the road behind curtains of rain—but he couldn't ask us in because of his old mother. "I feel I know you ladies well enough by now to be perfectly frank. You see, the dear old thing's off her rocker. Senile dementia."

Embarrassed by this disclosure, neither of us thought to question it, slumped as we were in the warmth and soft leather of his Alvis after the crypt-like chill of the cave.

Were Lumley and my mother lovers? I doubt it, but I think she was tempted. Mother was a heavy smoker in those days, though she gave it up later on. It used to be "Run down to the corner and get me twenty Seniors, will you, dear? There's a good girl." Now she was smoking a Turkish job with a gold ring round the filter, and there were no more errands to the corner shop, which didn't stock exotic brands. They were his. I would come home to find a dozen in the ashtray, six on one side, six on the other with scarlet daubs.

Later I wondered if he came to me because she turned him down. I'll say one thing for the cad: he didn't kiss and tell. Discretion was his stock in trade. He was as secretive by nature as that Ministry of his.

He was, I suppose, what is nowadays called a sexual predator, with a taste for widows and daughters. Though predator's a bit strong. In my book seduction's an art, not a crime. As far as I know he never used force, only deceit. He knew exactly what he was doing: not a finger did he lay on me until I turned sixteen. Perhaps confidence man is the term. Lovable rogue? You decide. (I'm cutting him all the slack I can for you.) He even gave a sort of warning that wasn't a warning, like a cobra that mesmerizes before it strikes. He said, as if advising in a fatherly way on boyfriends, "All's fair, little Liv, in love and war. Remember that."

A stroke of genius, *little Liv*. From a shorter man I'd have suspected sarcasm, but I believed him because he was tall. It was the afternoon of the World Cup final, the one when England beat Germany and the Germans said we cheated. Perhaps we did. Perhaps dishonesty was in the air that day.

I'd gone to the Saracen's Head with three or four friends. Kenny Watt for one, showing off his red motorbike, taking those who dared for a quick burn-up round the block until he got too pissed for anyone to risk it. Sarah and Jane turned up in a back-seatless Beetle with two boys I didn't know.

It was a bright long late summer day, and people had spilt out around the country pub like drunken bees. Indoors, on a shelf, a TV was blaring live from Wembley Stadium to a rolling surf of cheers and jeers. You couldn't move or speak. The mood was tribal, one big boisterous family: England. England was going to beat Germany. Again. Just to remind them who won the war. And to hell with all their money and Mercedes-Benzes and that Common Market rot.

Songs arose, peaked, died away. "Rule Britannia," "Yellow Submarine," "Deutschland über Alles." Not that there were any Germans present. The Nazi hymn, with its sublime music and mad words, was belted out mockingly, out of time and tune. Two gins down my throat and I was singing it too.

Commotion somewhere over my shoulder, Lancashire vowels. "I didn't lose five of me best mates to a U-bowt to coom in 'ere and hear poncey long-haired pups like you singin' for fookin' Hitler!"

"Sorry, mate. Don't mean nuffink. Just sarcastic, like."

GOAL! Germany scores! A simian howl. *Yellow submarine, yellow submarine . . .* And so it went on until the referee's call. Pandemonium, the floor awash. Rattles ratcheting. Whirling dervishes in England scarves. I was dressed up for once, Kenny's arm around me, hoping he wouldn't throw up on my Mary Quant. Everyone's arm around me, all of us singing, singing. *Land of Hope and Glory.*

"My God! It's little Liv! Does your mother know you're out?"

"What are you doing here?"

"You *do* sound pleased to see me. Actually, I was looking for your mum."

"She'd never come down here. If she did I wouldn't. She's at home, glued to the telly like the rest of the country."

"I can't bear that song, can you?"

"'Yellow Submarine'?"

"The one I really hate's the 'Deutschland.' Lost a brother to Adolf."

"Was that you? Were you one of them making all the fuss over there?"

"No. But I'm with 'em. You young have no idea. . . . Buy you a drink?"

"So here we are, all on our high horse about the war, trying to corrupt a minor?"

"I mean a Babycham. How old are you, Liv? Fifteen?"

"Sixteen last month. Old enough."

"Not for drinking."

"I bloody work here two afternoons a week! Pulling pints. One of my regular's a copper. Nobody checks. They think I'm twenty. And don't you dare blow my cover! I'll have a gin and lime, thanks."

Outside, dusk now, the crowd thinned.

Cars driving by blowing horns, bursts of song:
I've seen it, I've felt it,
It's just like a bit of velvet. . . .
Summer sounds calling back from shadows, crickets in the grass, rooks squabbling in the churchyard's blighted elms. (All gone now. I can hardly remember what an elm tree looks like, and I bet you've never seen one in your life.) Kenny wobbles over, asks if he can give me a lift to Sarah's place, "Party's moving over there. Her old man's away." He winks. Lumley and I (I *will* not call him Victor) look at each other and smirk.

"If I were you, young man, I'd toddle off and come back for that bike of yours in the morning. I'll bring Liv along presently." Kenny leaves, suggestible.

"Your boyfriend?"

"Just a friend."

"That's the idea. Keep 'em guessing."

Mist rising off the river.

"I'm getting cold."

Lumley's smoky tweed around my shoulders. "Have you eaten?"

"Not hungry. Full of bloody gin."

"You swear too much for a nice young lady."

"Who says I'm nice?"

"I think you're sweet. I'm sure it isn't easy, being you."

"You should meet my sister. She's the pretty one."

"I don't believe that for a second. I've seen your mother's photos. I think you are." Flirting with me! Should I have been flattered or outraged? Of course, being me, tall me—twenty at sixteen, far too old for twerps like Kenny—I *was* flattered.

Did I find him attractive, this man old enough to be my father? Maybe. But it wasn't really about being attracted. I can see that now. He never claimed to have known Jon (he knew better than to play that card, too easily called) but he'd known the ground, that faraway land that had swallowed my father. Victor Lumley's grey eyes had seen what Jon had seen. His nearness to that mystery drew me to him, gave him power. And his coming back alive made it seem less impossible that Jon might do so, made Lumley an envoy from the past, my father's proxy. And even though he'd returned with only minor scars, he had my admiration and my pity. A woman's pity sinks her every time.

He was going to buy me dinner. Somewhere in town. My choice. No man had ever asked me to dinner before, not like that—long-stemmed glasses, candlelight, glances across a red carnation. I saw myself very elegant, hair up, in my Mary Quant. (It had black and yellow bands, like a wasp.)

Out along the lane in his sleek car with its walnut trim, green leather, and smell of an old glove. Leather and strong out-landish tobacco—the exotic smell of Man.

"Christ! A copper. Why isn't the bugger home watching the match?" Lights off. Lumley did something clever with the hand-brake that turned the car half-circle. Tyres sowing gravel, snarls from the big engine.

"Don't you need lights to drive?"

"Didn't need 'em to fly. Eyes like a cat, I have. I'll shake him behind the turnips. He should be going after the likes of your friend Kenny."

"Poor Kenny."

"All's fair, little Liv, in love and war. Remember that." The car rushing on in the night, Lumley driving by the sky's glow, braking and turning, hedgerows hurtling past like unlit trains. He was good.

"Slow down. Please."

"Soon."

"Please. I'm frightened." I may have put a hand on his knee. Bumping down a track. Slower.

"Stop here! I think I'm going to be sick."

It was a good place for it. A gravel pit in a wood. I got out and retched. I thought, That does it. That'll cool him off, a puking girl. At least that's what I think I thought. I hadn't been so woozy since the night at Lottie's. But did I want to put him off? Why not get it over and done with, become a woman and make an old man happy? Now that I'm telling you this it makes no sense at all, but it made sense that night. It made sense to the person I was at sixteen.

"Hold me up, or I'll fall over."

Lumley's arms around me. "You'd better lie down."

"I know your sort. My mother's warned me about men like you." The sandpaper of his chin. He was kissing me, and I was thinking, How can he bear to do that?

"Because I love you."

"You can't. I'm a mess. I'm at my worst."

"I'll always love you, Livvy, at your very, very worst."

And so it happened, on the back seat of an Alvis. And that was only the first time. Being desired seemed to feed desire. I loved him, thought of him all the time, thought of ways to see him, to please him. We'd meet twice a week, around three, when I finished serving at the pub. We usually went to the gravel pit. When school resumed it wasn't so easy to get together, but my uniform drove him crazy when we did.

He bought me "the Pill," as we called it then, a ring of twenty-one days. "More infallible than the Pope, Liv," and I found that very funny. The pills made me keener—though whether it was the hormones or the freedom, I don't know. Perhaps it was simply that *he* had got them for me, a secret calendar of love.

Once a week, once a fortnight, once a month. As the weather cooled, so did Victor Lumley. His work, he said, hardly a moment to himself. Each wait seemed an age; I became sad, suspicious, angry. My schoolwork suffered. And I got careless with the plastic wheel of fortune. I was on Sunday when it was Wednesday, didn't know if I'd taken too many or too few. I "missed."

One day Mother said, "Pop round to the corner for twenty Seniors, would you, Liv? Be a dear." He was slipping away from us both.

By the middle of November I knew about you. I was sure. I told him. And of course that was the end. He took it calmly, like a thief who's always known he'll be caught. We wriggled into our clothes on the back seat of his leathery car. He drove me home. Said nothing. Nothing until he pecked me on the cheek. *Goodbye, little Liv.*

You were born in a discreet nursing home in Harrow. All winter and spring I tried to believe a message would come, or the bell would ring and there'd be Lumley on the doorstep: Get your hat and coat, little Liv, I'm taking you away from all this. Or at least a solicitor's letter in Dickens mode, saying an anonymous bene-factor had made provisions for your upkeep. (The things one imagines at sixteen!) But by June, as I waited to burst like an over-watered melon, I'd faced the obvious: your father had van-ished from the Earth.

There'd been no sign of him whatsoever since the November day I told him my news. I kept it from Mother for another six weeks—until she made a remark about my figure: "I think you've had too much Christmas, dear. You're looking rather plump." I burst into tears. It was Twelfth Night. We were going round the house gathering up cards and decorations. Lottie had just gone back to London. Mother used to say the Christmas magic turns bad if you leave decorations up after Twelfth Night.

She guessed immediately who it was. "Oh, Livvy," she said, "you're not! How *could* you? Oh Livvy, if only you knew! If only. . . ." (At the time I thought she meant nothing more than if only I knew the consequences.) There were scenes, tears, late-night conversations. And anger. How I'd let her down. Let down my father. "What will I tell him if he walks in that door tomorrow? What will *you* tell him? Go on, Olivia. Answer me that!" I felt kicked. And I fancied that you spun inside me, a dolphin somersault of fear, though surely it was much too soon. Then Mother turned her anger on herself. "Where have I gone wrong? I ask myself that every night, wide awake at three in the morning. I should have foreseen this with fatherless girls. I should have been stricter. I should have sold this house and raised the money and sent you to boarding school." And she'd looked at me with swimming eyes, "Oh, Liv. Not you! Not you. With Lottie I . . . I shouldn't say this, but your sister's. . . . She's flighty. But not you. Not my solid, sensible Olivia!"

"You mean your big frumpy Olivia. Who'd want her? Isn't that the real reason you're so surprised? Go on, say it! Anyway, I seem to remember I wasn't the only person in this house rather charmed by the cad in question. . . ." I was full of tearful apology as soon as I'd let that out.

Lottie should have been the one in trouble. And part of me was glad I'd beaten my sister to something, even heartbreak and disgrace. Mother had never said so, but we knew that in her eyes Lottie had the looks and I was the brain.

I remember reaching the age when one first becomes aware of looks, of lonely selfhood staring from its cave of flesh and bone. Lottie had taken off her dressing-gown at bedtime and was studying herself naked in the bathroom mirror: a northern blonde with narrow hips and our father's level sapphire gaze. I joined her: a tall Mediterranean brunette, darker and more strongly built, with a nose like the sharp edge of the number four. Straight and classical, Mother said, but I knew it was too big. Lottie said I must have been switched by Gypsies, or adopted. (That will strike you as ironic.) She meant, of course, *I am lovelier.*

I found consolation in the puddly old looking-glass beneath the spear. Unlike the bathroom mirror, this was a lens of magic possibilities. If I stared hard enough I could see an African girl gazing back at me: her dark eyes, full lips, pantherine body, the ripple and spring of her hair. I would never grow up to be one of these English with their cracked-meringue complexions. I was the fruit of Henderson's love for a native queen, descended from people who fought lions and tigers, tamed elephants, tossed assegais. Mine was the dark beauty of the spear.

Years later I learnt there were no tigers in Africa, and no blood line between Henderson and us. Now, when I look at photographs of Lottie and me in our teens, it seems silly to have been so insecure. If my sister's looks hadn't been so exceptional, I wouldn't have felt outshone. I was leggy and coltish, not plain. I drew my share of stares from men who should have known better. Men like Mr. Lumley.

We got beyond recrimination and began to talk over what to do. Mother pestered the Ministry until there was no room for doubt: the RAF had never had a Victor Charles Lumley, wing commander or otherwise. Who he was, how he'd found us, and how he forged Jon's handwriting, we never found out. I suppose he went through public records. In those days handwriting was in wider use; it can't have been hard to dig up a licence application, a building permit.

The buttons were explained by a dealer in militaria who'd moved to Hitchin from the Portobello Road. "I've 'eard it said, miss—you didn't get this from me—that if you want to age a bit of metal you bury it in a chicken run. Don't know what it is those birds eat, but a couple of months in there is good for two 'undred years." The Royston house with the grand drive turned out to belong to a stockbroker who spent half his time in Spain. And I'd never thought to note down the number of the Alvis that smelt like a glove.

Mother was too embarrassed to approach the police until some time after our own investigation stalled. An inspector listened sympathetically. "If your daughter had been under sixteen at the time, madam, we could do him for offences against a minor. You might consider a civil suit, breach of promise for example. But unless you've got physical evidence—a letter making explicit undertakings, a ring, preferably inscribed—breach of promise is a hard one. Paternity suit might be an option, once the child's born and you know its blood type. Also difficult to win.

"Fraud, however, is a criminal matter. So's impersonating an officer of the Crown. I'll check and see if that applies to retired officers. It may not. Our friend seems to know what he's doing. And we still have to catch him first." Then he brightened. "But there's a good chance this gentleman may be 'known to police,' as we say. You'll be hearing from me in due course."

He did ring two or three times to say he was still on the case. I think he felt sorry for us. But it was the sixties—drugs, sit-ins, Vietnam demonstrations, the crime wave. How much police time would have gone to tracking down a confidence man whose only loot was a woman's self-respect?

"Whatever decision you take, Livvy, I'll support you in it." Mother was hard to read. Was this support, or fence-sitting? It was already a bit late in the day for the first option. You may not believe me when I say this, but I never considered it. I can't say why. It wasn't religious scruples. Or even ethical ones. I just knew it wasn't something I could do. Perhaps you owe your existence to nothing loftier than my dread of hospitals.

So, keep you, or give you up? Picturing life after you, with or without you, took a stretch of imagination I couldn't manage. In the small hours, those four o'clock oh-my-God awakenings, I'd be ruled by the heart: how could I even think of giving up my flesh and blood? But in the day, struggling with school, I'd harden. You were still a hypothetical being. (Until you got too big to ignore, till the heartburn, the itching, the sweats.) My life as a mother was as hard to conjure from the future as my life on the old-age pension.

There was also Lottie. I hesitate to say this because I don't want you to blame her. If you blame anyone it must be me. Perhaps you've had a happy life so far, a better upbringing than I could have given you. Perhaps the decision I took was for the best. (How often I've told myself this!) But I feel I owe you a full account. Lottie did not sit on the fence. "Liv, understand. You've got to ask yourself what kind of life you and the child will have. If you keep it you can forget about university, film, career. You can say goodbye to marriage, or any kind of live-in man. Men don't take on other people's brats. The few that do are nutters and diddlers, most likely. Come to London right away, there's someone you ought to meet."

This person was Annette, a former housemate of Lottie's who'd made the same "mistake" as I and taken the high road. She was living on National Assistance in a tower block. There I saw a future all too clearly. No sleep, no job, no friends for more than half an hour, an endless round of noise and nappies. And other women in the building—five, ten years further down the same road, their children like vicious monkeys, and tales of pederastic babysitters, loopy social workers, court orders, foster homes.

Mother offered help, of course, and if we'd been closer she might have swayed me. But the thought of being cooped up in Hitchin for the next twenty years, dependent and beholden, frightened me as much as Annette's tower block. I decided there was no life for you and me together. My course no longer seemed selfish, merely the best thing.

The nursing home people knew exactly what to say. An older, financially secure, childless couple "from a good background." Able to offer you the best in life. A fresh start on both sides. Complete anonymity and confidentiality. Your existence legally erased from my life; mine erased from yours. Once you left my body we would never meet again. And no, Mrs. Wyvern—we call everyone here "Mrs." by the way—no, we always find it's best for all concerned if you *don't* hold the baby. Not even for a moment.

Four

⊰⊱ ⊰⊱

ENGLAND

Frank Henderson's second notebook:
Riverhill, Bramford. September, 1899. No. 2

I AWOKE AFTER ONLY AN HOUR OR SO. The bonfires had been revived, and by their light I saw Samory and his chiefs watching me. Their expressions seemed to have changed for the better. They told me they had once again "examined my head" and found I was a "good man," adding it was a lucky thing for me I had not been afraid to visit the King, and had not spurned his splendid hospitality.

From what Abu Bukari and Siraku later told me, it is clear that I owe my very life to dozing off. There were two factions among Samory's thanes: one wishing to cultivate good relations with us; the other favouring my execution, for reasons of revenge and as a warning to the Great Powers that they should stay out of the Hinterland. Until my nap, these foes of mine had been on the point of carrying the debate, for the column that had brought in

Ferguson's head included many Sofas who had lost sons and brothers to our marksmanship at Dawkita.

Siraku—reluctant jailer!—told me later that it was past his understanding why all our heads hadn't been cut off at once.

Despite his men's thirst for revenge, my falling asleep in Samory's presence had precisely the opposite effect such behaviour might produce before Her Majesty the Queen Empress. To nod off was to pay him the ultimate compliment on his hospitality and rectitude. My snores fell on their ears as the very balm of diplomacy. To do mischief to such a trusting soul was, for them, unthinkable.

I have spent enough time in Africa and other parts of the world to comprehend their logic, and I wish I could claim that I had had the foresight, sang-froid, and Thespian gifts to counterfeit such an efficacious snooze. But I confess I was simply worn out. I would have slept on a railway track or a Hindoo fakir's bed of nails. It was pure luck.

Samory began our new *entente* by allowing a semblance of a Christian burial for poor Ferguson's remains. He appealed to my brotherly feelings as a co-religionist, alluding through his interpreter to those parts of the Bible shared by Christian, Mohammedan, and Jew. "English, Sofa, both are people of the Book!" He smiled broadly, uttering the names of Abraham, Ishmael, Moses, the Angel Gabriel, and other patriarchs and celestial characters familiar to us all. Samory then offered a burial site not far from the Prophet's hallowed ground.

This I couldn't accept, having heard Ferguson's opinion of

the Prophet on many occasions. I believe I fulfilled what would have been my dear friend's wishes, choosing a pretty spot under a venerable baobab beside a striking outcrop. Here the fields ended and the bush began. Ferguson's sagacious spirit, thought I, would be happy roaming the wild Africa he loved, and to which he was born, for all his cultured ways. I fashioned a little cross of acacia wood, and uttered what I could muster of the burial service, which, as a boy, I'd heard my father perform so many times with far greater eloquence.

Samory gave me rather comfortable quarters—a compound of three huts on a small courtyard, the fourth side being a wall with a door to the "street," a malodorous alley in which both cattle and citizens routinely ease their bodies, as they do in all these towns. He told me I should have the same rights "as a son," and would be secure against intrusion, for these included the right to flog anyone who was tiresome. The people were intensely curious, many never having seen a white man. The length and straightness of my nose (often compared by my friends to a jib-boom) excited interest; they stared at my proboscis and then patted their fingers in a straight line against their own squat snubs, uttering *brune, brune* with much laughter.

Samory laid great stress on his friendship for the English, disclaiming the need for any border treaty. As for the "incident" at Dawkita, he accounted for it in an original manner, saying that it was not his son's fault, nor my fault, "it was God." Be that as it may, he was not disposed to leave further campaigning in the hands of the Deity alone. Rifles and ammunition were the object

80

of his desires, and he asked me whether I would have these sent to him when I returned to the coast, along with friction tubes for the guns, percussion caps, and brass for cartridges. Such matters, I told him, rested with the Governor and not with me. Clearly he had decided to let me go, probably to have me gone before I died, causing him further political embarrassment.

The dysentery was upon me again, and I kept indoors for some days, feeling very much the want of meat, which I had eaten only three or four times in the past month. The stores given back to me by the Prince were biscuits, tinned jam, and whisky. Once, I found old Siraku helping himself to my biscuits while he thought I was comatose, and I spoke pretty sharply to him. He said he would tell his master that I was treating him badly and not giving him food. I said, "Go! And I shall tell your master that whenever my men have biscuits, you have biscuits; and when they have whisky, you have whisky." His jaw fell some inches at this, and he implored me not to do so, for whisky-drinking would mean death.

One afternoon, as I was resting, I heard a feminine giggle at my door, and sent Siraku to investigate. The rascal returned with a young girl who, he said, had been sent by Samory to be my "wife." She entered casually, wearing nothing more than a scanty loincloth and some strings of shell beads. She was disgracefully young, her half-grown bosom firm and high, almost at her armpits. I could not avoid a close inspection of her person for she herself invited it, drawing my attention to a sunburst tattooed around each nipple. More exactly, it was scarification, inscribed for life on her dark skin by means of small

81

raised cicatrices neatly laid out in lines and spirals like the tooling on a Spanish saddle.

I declined this signal act of hospitality—gracefully, I hoped—by pleading illness. Siraku shook his head and muttered, saying the mother of the girl would not be pleased.

I left Haramonkoro in the first week of May, near as I can reckon, having with me sixteen of my own people and an escort of nine Sofas, bearing a letter and a gift of two heavy gold anklets for the Governor, Sir William. The rains had still not broken, though their threat could be read in the sky: great purple cauliflowers rearing in the west. Samory himself saw us off, accompanying us a mile or so on a sorrel pony. He took these moments to reveal more of poor Ferguson's death.

It seems that after I went out to palaver with the Prince that day at Dawkita, and it became clear no truce would be arranged, Gimalah and Ferguson fell back on Wa after dark as we had planned. They formed the men into a hollow square, with Ferguson and the other wounded in the middle. It was pitch black, and they were under fire from Sofas hidden in the woods, shouting, "The English run! The English run!"

The square could not be maintained; the only thing was for the Hausas to make their way to the Volta as best they could, and regroup there at first light. In the course of this rout, Ferguson fell from his stretcher. He lay on the ground all night, unable to move or even crawl for cover because of the state of his leg. Two Sofas came upon him in the morning. He held them at bay with a revolver, which afterwards proved to be empty. When he refused to give up this weapon, they shot him and cut off his head.

Samory did not exactly keep his bargain with me to release all my surviving men and stores, saying that he would give the rest to the next Englishman commissioned to visit him.

I tried to recover some of my own necessaries from the hand of the plunderer. At length my toothbrush was graciously restored, also a shaving-glass, one side of which was a magnifier, deemed by the marabouts to be uncanny. My hairbrushes I demanded in vain; Samory refused to hand them over. Since he is bald as a coot, it's a mystery to me what on Earth he did with them.

He did however release the promised bullocks for food along the way, but my men and I saw precious little of the meat, our Sofa guards regaling themselves upon the glutton's share. I resolved that once I reached civilization I should not again eat biscuits and jam for a long time. And I haven't.

At night the distant cloud formations flickered and flashed as if lit up by a titanic artillery battle below the horizon, and far-off detonations of the Thunder Fetish rolled towards us through the stifling air. It is hard to say which was worse, the airlessness of the hours without wind, or the scorching harmattan, which blew steadily each day, drying up the waterholes, cracking lips, filling the ears and eyes with a fine dust, corrosive as Portland cement. After three days I was too ill to ride. The bloody flux had returned and with the chafing of the saddle I became mindful of Dr. Part's dire warnings of rectal gangrene. How I longed to see

that good medico with his pince-nez and black bag of tricks—
notably his opium digestive powders!

The carriers put me in a hammock and I passed the hours
on my side. The sweat streamed down their backs, whilst their
feet, calloused and spreading like the feet of camels, sank rhyth-
mically into sand and alkali. For long hours I kept my eyes closed
against the sun. The only sensation of travel was the cradle-like
rocking of my hammock and a procession of smells that for me
will always be Africa: dust, cow dung, wild bees, acacia resin, and
dead things here and there in the dry grass.

The drought was now severe. Anything that could move
had gathered at the waterholes, where crocodiles lurked in the
mud, and vultures jostled like mad priests on every leafless
branch. Thirst had banished natural fears: the gazelle and baboon
came down to drink beside the leopard, running off no more than
a few yards when one of their kind was suddenly seized and torn
to bits. For the first time ever I saw baboons with blood on their
hands. Desperation had made them carnivores, and they too were
taking a share of the weak.

There is something unmistakably kindred about baboons.
Their lively golden eye is the most intelligent of any animal I
know, and their mischievous, snatching, sometimes vicious nature
so much like that of small boys—or grown men.

During the twelve days it took to reach Bontuku—the last town of
any size in Samory's domain, and the midway point to Kumasi—we
passed through a number of villages, all drought-stricken. My men
found little enough to eat. One night, while dining, I became

strongly aware of a disgusting stench emanating from my attendants. They were consuming what is commonly called "stink meat"—the decomposing carcass of some animal, in this case a lion. Next morning a local fellow came to me with the lion's skin to sell. I did not want a skin, but he looked so dejected that I offered him half a sovereign for it. This he wouldn't accept, saying that the lion was worth at least a whole sovereign, because it had eaten his wife!

At another village we had a lamentable encounter with a bull elephant, heard trumpeting and rollicking about all night. The great beast came early in the morning, attracted by the smell of water which women were drawing in leather buckets from a well. I was leaning against the hut in which I'd slept. Several villagers ran up with nothing in their hands, as if to welcome him. Then one of the Sofas fired a flintlock and hit him above his eye. The elephant came on at the same slow walk, seemingly calm and unprovoked, until he reached the riverbed. There we saw him standing in a garden, breaking down the palms.

About forty more shots were poured into him. Blood ran down his wrinkled hide from dozens of small holes, but he did not stir, except to flap his enormous ears. Then a village boy crept up behind with a knife and, taking hold of the tail, started to cut a piece off. With extraordinary speed, the elephant bundled the boy up in his trunk, threw him down and trod upon him. Some Sofas opened fire again, but the elephant walked softly to the riverbed until he came to some mud, where he lay and rolled to salve his wounds.

After a little while in the river, he approached a house and knocked down a wall. Now the shooting was resumed, until at last—it must have taken an hour from start to finish—the great beast went down slowly, in stages, like a sinking ship whose bulkheads rupture one by one.

Soon waking and sleeping ceased to be separate states for me. I became oblivious of the country travelled, and at night I felt as if I were still on the move. The creak of the hammock poles and the fetor of bush and carriers never ceased, except for episodes of blankness that I can't call rest.

The cowardly slaughter I'd just witnessed ran through my mind obsessively, mingling with the sight of poor Ferguson's ruined but still noble head.

At last we descried Bontuku's defensive walls quavering in the heat, rustic minarets rising gauntly above them like termite hills, and it seemed a fabled Eastern city. For the first time in weeks I felt that I might be within reach of deliverance, that I might yet return to the soggy island of my birth, hear church bells and steam engines, and see Jersey cattle eating fresh green grass.

We entered at sunset, the thin Arabian stream of a muezzin's cry cutting through the drumming of Africa and the braying of skeletal donkeys. My Hausas soon made contact with kinsmen of theirs, finding a clean room where I could rest before continuing. They also found a runner willing to take a dispatch to end-of-telegraph at Kumasi. I kept the message to essentials: for myself I asked that a doctor be sent to meet me at the frontier of Ashanti, as my strength was failing fast; to the Governor I said simply, "Ferguson is dead."

I well knew what effect those words would have when they reached Sir William, and, worse, when he carried out the sad duty of communicating them to George's widow, son, and two little girls. But knowing also the swift and crooked wings on which rumour flies through the bush, I thought it right that they should have reliable word from a friend at the first opportunity.

The sky was a vast bruise when we pressed on, the air so heavy and foul that the lungs derived little benefit from it. Breathing was like trying to slake one's thirst on thick, turned cream.

That night the weather broke with a deafening barrage.

The following day's march was a new trial for the men. Every gully was a torrent, every low-lying spot a khaki lake. Cakes of mud lifted with their feet, exposing the dust and hard-pan underneath.

On the third day my fortunes took a sudden turn for the worse. The rain had stopped about eleven, the sun showed itself, and steam rose from the earth like smoke after a grass fire. The men's spirits lifted, and they began to sing. We had a quick lunch at noon, and carried on while the going was good. At about three, dark tongues licked across the sky in minutes, and we were pounded by raindrops fat as musket balls, which danced on the ground.

We had been approaching a village. Not far off, outside the main fence beside an old baobab (known in West Africa as the "upside-down tree," because its branches, when leafless, look like upended roots), was a small round hut with a conical roof and an abandoned air. My hammock-men had been relieved by Sofa guards, as was often the case when we entered a town. These were Mohammedans from Mandingo country. Spying the shelter of the hut, they trotted there as quickly as they could, unaware of its peculiar nature. Blinded by rain, they failed to notice the skulls beside the door and the frieze painted in mimicry of a python's reticulations around the top of the wall. It was the lair of a fetish priest.

These practitioners may be of either sex, and range in their arts from healers and black magicians to high-class fortune tellers. Like the table-rappers of Mayfair, they question their familiar spirit upon all matters relating to a client's future, convey the answer of the oracle, and call the attentions of the dead to questions asked by their relations left behind on Earth.

My men, who understood very well the taboo nature of the place, ran up and began to shout, but I was halfway across the threshold by then. There now ensued a tug-of-war: those in the van trying to enter; those in the rear trying to pull hammock, white man, and bearers out. In the confusion I was shoved up near the overhanging thatch, where a long, stiff straw pierced my left eye.

At my shout the men dropped me and fled. I was alone in the intimate tholos of the Python Fetish.

I became aware of an old half-naked woman bending over me, her lined, toothless face; and the fanged face of a large snake, its tongue testing the air and its tail coiled around the withered breasts of its attendant. There was a stench of sour milk and rotten meat from offerings given to the sacred reptile. Then the pain was on me like fire, my sight failed altogether, and I blacked out.

I came awake in a stifling hut inside the village. A bandage was around my head. The men were murmuring with worried voices, and someone was making me drink from a gourd. They asked me what to do. I said we must press on, faster than before.

We travelled for another week. Gradually, the savannah became more overgrown as our bedraggled column was swallowed by outlying patches of woodland. These thickened by degrees into the primaeval forest of Ashanti. The pain in my eye came and went in waves, seeming to alternate with the pangs of dysentery. I could see only a little with my good eye but could smell familiar resins, leaves and blooms—a greenhouse scent I knew from the Ashanti campaign—welcome as the scent of home to a horse. It cheered me to picture the bosky tunnels down which we marched, the sunbeams and blue orchids, the towering bombax and mahogany rigged with monkey-ropes, the roof of glossy foliage on which the rain drummed now and then like hail.

I urged the men to be punctilious about changing the dressing on my eye, but this was difficult to do on the march. The wound leaked fluid constantly, attracting flies, which had hatched in large numbers with the wet. After some days it was maggoty, and I knew I should not have sight there again.

On the tenth day from Bontuku, at a small village within three days of Kumasi, I was greeted by my deliverer, Dr. Part. By great good luck he had been in the Ashanti capital when my message arrived. His was the first white face I had seen in months, and what a shock it was! I had forgotten how we Europeans look: eyes like water, skin like bloody milk. In native belief, ours are the hues of death; and in those first moments—I was delirious much of this time—Dr. Part appeared to me as a strange, colourless being, come from the spirit world to fetch me thither.

He cleaned the wound (relieving me of the eyeball, which could not be saved), gave me opium, fed me beef tea, and made me as comfortable as it is possible to be in the bush once the rains have begun. In short, he saved my life, for without his timely arrival I doubt I should have lasted to Kumasi.

In the long half-year since Ferguson and I had passed through that famous town at the start of our mission, the Royal Engineers had completed the new fort. Telegraph had been established to Cape Coast Castle, and from there to Accra. Kumasi no longer seemed abandoned. Trade, the all-important factor, was coming back; Ashanti was beginning to feel the benign embrace of the World Market.

After some time at Kumasi, Dr. Part pronounced me fit to be carried with him to the coast, where the Governor, Sir William, took one look at me and booked me aboard the next steamer to England. He insisted I postpone my official report until I felt well enough, and that I send it straight to the Colonial Office. I was at least able to pass on the details I'd gathered of Ferguson's death, and to impress on him the bravery of the Hausas at Dawkita. No troops could have behaved better under fire, and their discipline was all that could be wished. I ventured to suggest that the West African medal might fairly be awarded them.

⟨⟩ ⟨⟩

The passage home, via Freetown on the *Carthage*, was not the most pleasant. The steamer's black hull soaked up the midsummer sun, releasing heat all night into the cabins, to say nothing of more heat and mephitic vapours from the boiler-room. My stateroom (as it was grandly styled) was an oven. I awoke many times each night drenched in perspiration. Dr. Part, who had taken passage on the same vessel for some overdue leave, swore he could hear me "rambling" in my sleep through the bulkhead.

One day he came aft to stand beside me at the taffrail, where we could speak privately, and asked who exactly I thought was trying to kill me.

"Not you," I told him. "You're off duty, anyhow. Leave me to the ship's M.O."

"You're still my patient, man," he replied in his reassuring Glaswegian. "This has been going on since Kumasi. You keep crying out, 'My God, they mean to kill me!' Easy enough to account for, given what you've been through. But it seems—don't be alarmed—as if your recent experience has loosened other things more deeply buried in your mind. Who's 'Eddy'?"

"No idea. One of my best men was named Idi. Had to leave him behind with the Sofas, poor chap."

"I think you should be prepared," he answered gently, "for it being a good while before these troubles leave you. They'll keep returning from time to time. Mainly in dreams, but you may also experience dreamlike conditions when awake. You mustn't be alarmed or ashamed. I've known chaps—men with much less to get over than you have—who needed years."

I did not reveal to Part that these troubles had begun soon after I arrived at Haramonkoro, when Samory had offered me a "wife" on easy terms, and that they had plagued me, on and off, throughout my delirious journey to Kumasi.

After I'd refused the cicatriced girl, Siraku had entered my hut the following afternoon with a sleek boy, equally young. The creature had parallel scars on his cheeks (symbolic leopard scratches, I was told) that did nothing to dignify an insolent, debauched expression. He was carrying an ostrich feather cushion, which he placed on the foot of my cot, and sat down like a debutante before I could get over my astonishment.

"The Almamy savvy," Siraku said with a smirk, in his atrocious English. "Englishman, Arab man, same thing. Woman good! Boy better! His name Amadou." He let out his usual cackle, making with his hands a repulsive gesture, the meaning of which was ineluctable. Largesse of this kind is hardly rare in warm places where the chilling breath of Christendom has yet to blow, but it was the first time I'd been offered it. I didn't know what to do. Given the paramount importance, when dealing with a potentate such as Samory, of avoiding any offence against the local code of hospitality, there seemed only one solution.

"This Englishman," I said to Siraku in my best Ashanti, stabbing a finger at my chest, "does not like boys in the way you suggest. No doubt this boy you've brought me is a fine boy, an excellent boy. But in my country a boy is not a fitting wife. Please tell the Almamy that if his generous offer of yesterday still stands, it will not be refused." Siraku seemed crestfallen at this; doubtless he had hoped to retail some gossip at my expense around the town.

While I waited to see what would happen next, recollections of the late Prince Eddy swam into my mind. Eddy would not have been so fastidious. Indeed, there was no escaping the view that Samory's second offer might have been to Eddy's taste. I then felt horribly shabby—shabby as old Siraku himself—in entertaining such thoughts about someone far above my station who had treated me as a friend, and who was no longer alive. Only five years had passed since his untimely death at Sandringham in 1892, when pneumonia took him soon after his twenty-eighth birthday.

Of course, should the girl reappear, it would be a simple matter, so I thought, to avoid conjugal duties on grounds of ill health. She would merely stay in my hut as a companion. I need only say that in this resolve I was mistaken, for I had not reckoned with the girl's initiative and considerable erotic talents.

During the relatively tranquil interlude while Samory was trying to mend fences with me, and the girl Fatouma shared my hut, I began to sink (so I see now) into what Part would call a melancholic decline. My career—indeed my whole life—appeared to me as nothing but a catalogue of disaster. Far worse, my failings were not merely private (*that* I might have endured); they had led to death and untold suffering for people entrusted to my care.

No doubt the melancholy had been building for weeks, but it was precipitated, I think, the moment I ceased to resist Fatouma, allowed myself to be seduced by her (tho' it was only

twice), debauched a woman little more than a child, however
worldly she may have been, and in so doing debauched myself.

The thoughts of Prince Eddy brought to mind a strange meeting
I'd had in London about three years after his death—shortly
before my posting to the Gold Coast as Sir William's ADC.

One February morning in 1895 a letter on Home Office
stationery had arrived at Tilehouse Street. The sender was someone I knew from my midshipman days. He had always struck me
as just the type who might go into Government—a thin-lipped
fellow with a calculating, aspiring nature, and not a whit of fun or
genuine good humour. We had messed together for a year, yet I
couldn't recall him doing a single spontaneous thing. He'd been a
middle-aged man at sixteen.

This man (I think it better not to name him, though he
could be traced if need be) summoned me to London on "official
business." He met me at King's Cross, where we got into into a
yellow motorcar of French manufacture, the first I ever sat in. I
was startled by the noise it made and the way the coachwork rattled from the gas engine's vibration, even while the machine was
standing. When the driver made it move off there was none of
the breathy ease of steam; it leaped into the traffic like a snarling
greyhound, frightening horses right and left.

I *was* impressed that my erstwhile shipmate should have
such a vehicle at his disposal. Yet it all seemed rather pointless, as
a man with a red flag had to precede us on foot the whole way.

We lunched at his club, during which we drank rather a lot
of claret—at least, I did. He hadn't changed a bit. Still the same

crashing bore, with the preening self-importance of mediocrity.

He then took me to a large, modern office building off Whitehall, where we entered a panelled boardroom blue with cigar smoke. Three others—of much the same stamp as my escort, differing only in the style of whiskers, the degree of baldness, etc.—were seated at the table, where they had evidently taken lunch. The room overlooked a lane with a slim view of the Thames, the window admitting a grey pallor and a draft. My escort made no introductions.

"These gentleman are here to ask certain questions of a delicate nature," he said. "I need hardly add that what is discussed today must remain within these walls, and should you meet any of us by accident at some future date, we will not know each other."

"But I already know you!" I protested.

"You used to know me. If we meet again, you have not seen me since our *Swiftsure* days. You've brought the note I sent?" I had done as asked. He took the letter from me, and its smoke soon curled up from a brass ashtray, adding a pale spiral to the blue haze in the room. One of the men opened a briefcase, taking out a thin, cheap-looking broadsheet which he slid across the table.

"Have you ever seen this before, Lieutenant Henderson—or another number of the same pamphlet?" It was entitled *The Liberator*, and the leading article bore the headline: Future King of England Is a Bigamist! The printing and paper were very bad, but the content was clear enough. The article claimed that Prince George had married, quietly but lawfully, at Malta in 1890, and that he'd concealed this prior marriage in order to marry Princess

May, his late brother's fiancée, in 1893. (The royal wedding had taken place that summer, and I had been among the many guests invited to the garden party at Marlborough House.)

"Certainly not."

"Have you anything to say about these allegations?"

"Only that they're rubbish, as if you didn't know. Just two years ago Prince George was asking my advice about his marrying Princess May. He'd hardly do that if he was married already. He was asking lots of people. We would have known. It's unthinkable. Why ask me?"

"*We* are putting the questions, Lieutenant. You are here to answer them." Only one inquisitor did the talking, as if delegated by the rest; he continued, "*The Liberator* is published irregularly in Paris by republican extremists seeking to blacken the name of the monarchy and to bring Her Majesty's Government into ill repute. Their technique is to cast any filth that comes to hand in the hope that some of it will stick. We assume that French agents are involved, along with a small cabal of British exiles. Anarchists. Communists. Fugitives from justice." The man prodded the pamphlet in front of me with a nicotine-stained finger. "There are other examples, worse than this, often nothing more than a single sheet. Usually they affect a portentous title— *Liberator, Intelligencer, Free Briton,* and the like. Many of their calumnies concern the late Prince Albert Victor, Duke of Clarence, known as Prince Edward or Eddy. We believe you knew him as a young man?"

"That's a matter of public record. He and Prince George and I were on H.M.S. *Bacchante* together for three years—there's an exhaustive book about that cruise. You'll find it at any library or bookseller's. . . ."

"Please refer yourself to a part of that voyage, in the autumn of 1881, which is not on public record. We believe you were with Prince Edward on a . . . special excursion. To the Tahitian islands."

"I'm not prepared to discuss anything of a private nature, or anything I was asked to keep in confidence. That is simply a statement of principle, not an admission that there is anything at all to hide." I began to rise from my chair.

"Please keep your seat, sir. This is part of an official enquiry, at the highest level. I advise you to co-operate." My wits were not about me. The claret had turned acid in my innards. The fact that they seemed to know something confidential disarmed me. Had I been thinking clearly, I should have asked them for proof of who they were and what they were doing. As it was, I merely reacted to their questions like a simpleton, a habit ingrained by years of naval discipline.

"We want to find out where these republican elements are getting their ideas, Lieutenant. Of course it's fabrication and distortion. We are well aware of that. But lies, in order to be effective, require trappings of verisimilitude. These same treasonous elements are, in all probability, at the bottom of the rumours about the late Prince Edward and the Cleveland Street affair."

"Cleveland Street?"

"I forget—you Navy chaps are out of the country a lot. A libel concerning a bordello of a special . . . specially depraved kind. Telegraph boys were said to have been involved in unnatural practices with certain gentlemen. Titled gentlemen. Prince

Edward was never named—indeed he was in India by the time the matter came to trial—and the proprietor of the one newspaper to publish the allegations in this country is now behind bars. But rumours are not so easily locked up. From the Cleveland Street business they've taken ever more preposterous flights of fancy. Now it is the common gossip of the East End that the late Prince had something to do with the Whitechapel murders—in short, sir, that the former Heir Presumptive was the so-called 'Ripper'—though as far as we're aware none of that has yet shown its face in print.

"We know, as I'm sure you know, that *that* charge can't possibly be true. But there's the rub, Lieutenant. For the anonymous authors of this filth, and for their ignorant and impressionable readers, the mere suggestion of impropriety on the part of the late Prince is enough. That is why these will-o'-the-wisps, these mere whiffs and ornaments of scandal, are so damaging.

"This brings me to the reason we have asked you here. Namely, *we* want to know what *they* might know—or might have been able to find out—about a violent incident during your Pacific voyage. One that took place on the territory of a foreign Power."

Again I rose from my chair. "I've told you before, I can't possibly discuss anything of the sort. Good day to you!" A murmur passed around the table, and the speaker then asked me to wait outside for a minute. I did so, feeling like a schoolboy sent out of class. Through my mind ran a low satirical ditty then going the rounds, about Eddy's Indian tour:

And this is what impressed me most,
Whilst Hindustan I travelled o'er:
A laundry boy named Chundra Dass,
Who won my heart at Shuttadore!

Before I had time to collect my thoughts, I was summoned back inside and offered a cigar, which I accepted, then instantly regretted—I had no wish to be beholden to them for even the slightest hospitality.

"Lieutenant Henderson. I'm not going to beat about the bush any longer. It would help us—and therefore your country—enormously if we had a precise idea of what the late Prince did, or was believed to have done, that caused so much offence to the Tahitian natives. We are certain the information, however distorted, will get into republican hands sooner or later, if only because it could be used to add credence to the foulest lie of all."

"What might that be?" I asked. My interrogator glanced around at his colleagues, two of whom gave barely perceptible nods.

"It will be all over London soon enough." He paused to relight his Havana, then resumed, emitting puffs of information like a train. "Their latest"—*puff*—"and vilest"—*puff*—"calumny is that"—*puff*—"the Prince's death may not have been purely accidental. That it was . . . given his character . . . dynastically convenient." He paused again, scrutinizing me with wolfish eyes through the pall he had emitted. "Pamphlets to this effect have been intercepted at Dover. Doubtless others will get through."

This was no great revelation—I'd heard it at least once elsewhere, and almost said so. But that seemed unwise; the cigar had revived a few of my wits. "Good heavens!" I exclaimed.

"I'm afraid we are up against more than mere extremist rags, Lieutenant." He removed a clipping from a folder and slid it across the mahogany, scattering crumbs and ash. "This article appeared in *The New York Times* at the height of the Cleveland Street affair. A full two years before Prince Edward's death. Today there are those who take it as a sinister prophecy."

I can't remember the whole of it, but a certain paragraph to which my attention was drawn still stands out clearly:

From a London Correspondent: There has come to be a general conviction that this long-necked, narrow-headed young dullard was mixed up in the scandal, and out of this has sprung a half-whimsical, half-serious notion which one hears propounded now about clubland: that matters will be arranged so that he will never return from India. The most popular idea is that he will be killed in a tiger hunt, but runaway horses or a fractious elephant might serve as well. What this really mirrors is a public awakening to the fact that this stupid, perverse boy has become a man, has only two precious lives between himself and the English throne, and is an utter blackguard and ruffian. It is not too early to predict that such a fellow will never be allowed to ascend the British throne.

Poor, dear Eddy, I thought. To them I said, "The boy was no ruffian. Simple, perhaps. But not capable of violence. I've never known a boy of his age with so little drive, so little interest in the world around him. It was all we could do on *Bacchante* to roust him out of bed each morning. Is that the portrait of a blackguard, a ruffian? I think not."

They then asked me again the same question as before. Again I told them nothing.

"Look here, my dear fellow," my old shipmate spoke up. "Tell us what you know. It's vital to the national interest. If we know what these swine are working with, we can make preparations to counter it. Tell us, Frank. There's a good chap." It was the first time he had called me Frank. Surnames had been *de rigueur* in the *Swiftsure's* gunroom. His gauche familiarity set me on guard, the reverse of his intention.

"What do you suspect?" I asked. "If I had the faintest notion of what you're driving at, I might be able to help."

"Enough of this!" my inquisitor announced. "Within these walls we'll call a spade a spade. I refer, Lieutenant Henderson, to the sin of Sodom. I mean buggery, sir. Hardly unknown to a Navy man, surely? What is it you chaps say—'rum, bum, and baccy'— the three solaces of life on the ocean wave? Isn't that what it was, with a deadly degree of coercion? That and a political manoeuvre disastrously ill conceived by persons who had no business meddling in affairs of state."

"You needn't try to shock me into revelations," I replied. "Look here. At the time you mentioned—the autumn of '81, didn't you say?—Prince Eddy wasn't yet eighteen. Don't you think that's rather young for him to be involved in intrigues, political or otherwise? Throughout his entire, short life that poor, gentle boy was notoriously immature for his age."

"Don't pretend to be naive, sir. Information has come into our hands that you yourself were also morally compromised. Perhaps you will tell us about that."

I surveyed the figures in the darkening room. Rum, bum, and baccy! I'd be damned if I'd listen to anything more from these wattled and bewhiskered badgers.

"I decline to answer charges of buggery," said I sarcastically. "Even at the 'highest level.' Though I suggest this inquisition of yours is at the lowest."

I made for the door and left without hesitation, angry words following me down the passage.

Five

❧ ❦

TAHITI

Arue Prison

THE TAHITIAN SUN BURNS WHITE AND HAZY at this time of year, as if through hothouse glass. Thunderheads build high on Mount Orohena, congealing from the overcast. For a while they seem tethered to the peak. Then one by one they slip their moorings and sink low over the coast like great black airships, lashing the land with aerial waterfalls and threads of light.

Pua breaks off her dance lessons, but my hour outside is too precious. I stay at the top of the yard to watch the storm, feel the sting of raindrops in my mouth, the deluge in my hair and between my shoulderblades, and running away through the toes as if I were a tree or a young girl.

Being in jail is being a child again, all decisions made by others whose keys and purposed footsteps echo down long corridors. Freedom's always been the dearest thing in life to me. I made my choice: love or liberty; and you know which I chose.

103

Some think children are free, but I know better. I remember those years too well, each one slow as a decade. I couldn't wait to grow up. Be careful what you wish for.

I expect you're wondering what it is they think I've done. Not easy to explain just yet. Better to tell you how things happened in the order they happened. But you may as well know it was a death on the ocean, possibly but not necessarily suspicious, a body surrounded by water. All I did, all any of us did, was fish her from the sea about five hundred miles off Tahiti. International waters, technically, but the French don't see it that way.

We still don't know where she came from, how she died. We don't know her name or nationality. If only we did! It'd be so much easier to disprove any link with ourselves. We reported to the authorities thoroughly, if slowly. And that was our downfall. Our report became evidence against us, a gift to powers-that-be with motives of their own.

There are consolations in being not guilty: I am clean and good, whatever the law may say. But I often think I could put up with prison a lot better if I deserved it.

Captivity isn't just being in a room, a building. It's the loss of possibility. When I brood on how I can no longer command my own body to walk out of this door, let alone to the shops or the beach, I feel a landslide of despair. And rage, the opposite of a landslide, a hot mass gathering itself and rushing upwards.

Not only am I innocent but those who've put me here are guilty, at least of perjury. It's enough to make me want to do what

I'm accused of—on bad days I'd cheerfully murder those faceless Robespierres, whoever they are. And I must fight this down, for it means they're winning, making me become what they've said I am and I know I am not.

<✥> <✥>

I was a late starter, for obvious reasons, loitering at Tilehouse Street in indecision and disgrace. Twenty before going to university, twenty-three before leaving England for Canada. I told myself—told everyone—I'd be back in three years. I didn't foresee how experience transforms, how time would make me into someone who could never go back to Britain's fifty million people and five thousand years; and the smothered memory of you.

I began in Montreal, with the National Film Board's Studio D. It wasn't quite a *job*. I was a lowly researcher, no contract, paid by the day. And paid with compliments—she liked to hire Brits, my producer said, because we brought a level of literacy, by which she meant familiarity with the great books drummed into us at our Dickensian schools. Canadians, she said, knew *of* such things but didn't *know* them.

It is true that in those days Canadians were not great ciné dramatists (English Canadians; Quebec mined its own Gallic veins of mime and masquerade and *noir*). But they had a way with documentary, and that was what I'd come for. It was wonderful to break from Britain's wartime legacy of Pathé newsreels, with their scoutmaster voices and chirping pizzicato violins. Canada, where the war cast a shorter shadow, had moved on.

Then the world moved on, a sharp right turn. The public

arts became a shrinking waterhole surrounded by corpses of the
bold. So I migrated again, to the rim of the Western world, where
Canada rucks up into the Rockies and falls in tiers of stone to the
Pacific.

A few weeks after my thirtieth birthday, I stuffed my
Montreal life into a U-Haul trailer, hooked it to my car, and
drove west three thousand miles. There's an old joke: if your dog
runs away in Saskatchewan you can watch him leaving for a
week. But the prairie held surprises I'd never guessed from the air:
an oceanic swell, spare luxuries of light and contour, hills and
badlands tearing the net of ownership.

I've watched the mountains many times from a jet chasing
the sun. I never tire of that sudden barricade at the end of the
plains, as if God piled it there to stop us making the whole continent a chequerboard of wheatfields. Four squares to the mile,
every ten miles a village, every hundred a town, every thousand a
city.

Escape from predictability to mystery—*that's* what I wanted —from the flat-earth utopia of grain to the Rockies' muddle
of pyramids and tarns and icefields, and rivers of cloud flowing
down to the sea between walls of sunlit stone.

When I fly over those mountains I look down amazed, a
Martian viewing Earth for the first time.

There's Hollywood, which needs no introduction. There is
Bollywood, its Bombay avatar. And there is Brollywood—the
lovely, loopy, brash, soaking city of Vancouver, a place of umbrellas and webbed feet, a city where a rainforest should stand (and

did), a winter wetness in which even uprooted Brits can drown.

Visitors from Montreal or Toronto (or Hollywood, for that matter) don't understand if you break a date because the sun has shown itself for the first time in ninety-three days and you're going up on the roof to let it pour into your skull through crimson eyelids. The oyster sky shucks away and forests hang above the streets. Rotting Bic-lighter towers become Cambodian temples; grimy girders turn into gold; dazzled drivers crash their cars. Then just as suddenly the clouds descend, the woods withdraw and fade to bits of bristle clogged with mist, leaving only a smile, the mountain ice.

Brollywood thrives because it's a cheap, photogenic location for our American cousins. It might be Seattle or Portland, but our streets are safe, we have public health, our dollar's a bargain, our talent less litigious. If you watch trash on the box (it's all right, I do) you've seen Brollywood, though you may not know it. All those Siberian gulags in B-movies, those stump-ranches full of aliens on *The Outer Limits,* and the corpse-sown woods of serial thrillers—these are the picturesque glens of British Columbia. The secret files are in a derelict mine beside the Whistler highway, and the leafy neighbourhoods of arts-and-crafts bungalows with eyebrow porches, where boy meets girl and spy shoots spy and terrible mutilations take place, these are Kitsilano, Shaughnessy, West Vancouver.

My business card: *Olivia Wyvern, Producer-Director, Wyvern Films.* My name (it can be yours if you like) comes with a logo: a griffin with a devil's tail, copied from the few bits of family plate that haven't been pinched or pawned. The name's mine, and so are one or two little follies that get built, but for bread and butter I make other people's films, mostly for TV. Canada has been good to me; I'm a modest success in that wide cold country subtended from the Pole.

⋘ ⋙

A man and a small girl who hardly knew each other. The girl is holding pictures of smiling men beside old-fashioned aeroplanes, smoking ruins, odd rocks. These she spreads out on the floor in rows and ponders often. Sometimes she arranges them by subject: all the men, all the planes, the stones, the melted buildings, all the pictures of a young man and a young woman who is, yet cannot be, her mother. Sometimes she sets them out by what she thinks of as their "colour"—tone and contrast, the grain, the darkroom burns and fades.

I hadn't understood, not until I unpacked Jon's photos in Vancouver, spreading them out for the first time in a new land: my father made me a filmmaker. He'd sent this gift down the years. And I hadn't known what he'd done, any more than he had. I was ashamed. How could this be a surprise? How could I have failed to recognize his eye—for near and far, foreground and horizon, sharp outline and soft light—as mine?

Only then, far from the house where my small self lingers with the other ghosts, did I see how film has been my way of putting life into the still-lifes of the past.

All these words from Henderson, but no pictures. All these pictures from Jon, but hardly a word. Henderson's engaging voice—

all the more engaging because I'd unearthed it where he grew up, reading the first pages in the very window, perhaps, where he started writing—his voice was filling the silence where my father's should have been. And I saw then how words bring one nearer to the past than pictures ever can. Images emphasize the farness of that other country, make it seem more outlandish than it really was, a silent film where troops march jerkily to battle and die like puppets. But words show it to you through the eyes of its inhabitants, make you wait in a sodden dawn for the shout to go over the top.

Through many years when I might have searched for Jon, Mother had claimed the quest for herself, her right as next of kin and family head, in a way that brooked no help. And I'd acquiesced because there seemed plenty of time, expecting her to tell me one day, show me his letters, discuss lines of enquiry. But now she was gone and I couldn't even ask *why*. Why nothing from Korea? Was she unable to face opening her desk to a Korean stamp? How many letters had she thrown away? Or had Jon simply not written, inhibited by the thought of wartime censors grubbing through his words?

Once I began to question the past, the possibilities grew so outrageous that I felt ashamed for thinking them: could he have killed himself? Deserted? Even defected? Had Mother guessed, or known? Was that the hidden thing?

I'd moved to Canada, away from an addled life. But what had stopped me from writing to the Air Force, tracking down Jon's old comrades? It's easy to blame *your* father, to say a long paralysis afflicted me in this area since Victor Lumley. He'd poisoned the waters in which I might have searched, and the poison stayed fresh for twenty years. Memories do not decay at a uniform atomic rate. Happiness has the shortest half-life, a quick fade to oblivion or nostalgia. But shame, guilt, anger, remorse: these are heavier isotopes, remaining toxic for a lifetime, even generations.

Now I saw these "reasons" as nothing but excuses. That summer when we packed up Mother's house was also when the adoption law changed—not enough to let me find you, but enough to let myself be found. So I began two searches, to the right and left, after twenty years of staring straight ahead.

A man who'd flown with Jon in Korea had become a dealer in old books. He'd sent a sympathy note over Mother, enclosing his card. *Morley Cosworth. Rare and used books. Houses cleared.* I decided to go and see him with old books, and take a further step if possible.

I remembered him coming to Tilehouse Street when we were young, a diffident figure, not warm but kind, with a funny remark and a half-crown each for Lottie and me when he said goodbye. In those days he lived in London. Now he had a farm cottage in Cambridgeshire, only an hour away. I hadn't seen him in nearly thirty years. Mother had always called him by his Air Force nickname, Mole. "Dear Mole," she'd say. "Straight out of *Wind in the Willows.*"

Time had made the nickname even apter. He was stooped and blinking behind thick glasses at his dark front door, in an old black sweater like the fur of a mole, clasping my shoulders in large pink hands.

"Livvy! My dear! Come through. Business first, then tea.

We'll take the books out back." We carried my boxes through the house and down the garden to an ancient henhouse patched with plywood and tarred roofing. Smells of creosote and buckram, an undertow of rot and chickens. Books lined the walls and rose from the floor in wobbly towers, others were stacked in open cartons as if awaiting burial.

He put mine on a desk under a dusty window and began riffling through boisterously, plucking out titles and holding them to the light.

"Ah!" he exclaimed with mock excitement, "*The Royal Windermere Yacht Club 1910–1950*. Now there's a work of special interest."

"Signed by the author," I said. But he set it down without looking. The hands lifted up another. "*The Application of Modern Magnets*. Hmm. . . . Title says it all, really, doesn't it?" He went on like this for some minutes. "Will twenty be all right for the lot, Livvy? I know it's not much, but at least you'll be shut of them. Some dealers only take the good ones."

His vast stock looked undisturbed, roughly sorted into novels, travel, religion, art, historical and scientific subjects, separated by narrow tunnels just big enough for Mole. I wondered if he ever sold books at all, or merely hoarded them compulsively.

"I can tell by your silence, Livvy, that you're unimpressed. Try to see my difficulty. If I give you twenty quid today, I may sell them over the next six months for thirty. Thirty-five if I'm lucky. Good thing I've got my pension."

"I'd better stop looking around," I said, "or I might leave with more than I brought."

"Ah! Now I can tell which side you're on."

He pointed to heaps of books like mine, forlorn and sunbleached, from the century's middle years. "Interior decorators take 'em for filling shelves in boardrooms and hotels. You know, touch of class, aura of a gentleman's library. They pay by the foot."

"I've stayed in those hotels. I've run to those shelves, looked through top to bottom, and never found a single thing to read. Always wondered where they got them."

"Exactly. There's nothing there at all. If there was I wouldn't have done my job. You don't sell *reading* books by the foot.

"Tell you what," he added. "I'll throw in another fiver. How's that?"

It was a low moment, flogging stuff that wasn't really mine, that might have meant something to my parents. The deal done, I had a Parthian glance, noticing a tatty atlas. I remembered Mother saying it had been Jon's, when he was a schoolboy. Lottie must have tossed it in the box.

"Can I keep this, after all? You keep your fiver."

Mole took the atlas for a moment, fingering red expanses of lost empire. "Won't miss it, Livvy. Have it on me." He touched my arm. "Why don't we go in now for a cuppa?"

He served very weak tea with a very stale biscuit. His house smelt damp and forgotten, like the biscuit. No woman had lived there for years. The wallpaper—1920s floral in oxblood reds, hot pinks, ochre and baby blue—had once been ugly. Now it was faded enough to have a vague period charm, like a stage set. A grandfather clock ticked in the passage hesitantly, as if about to stall.

"Do you keep in touch with any of the people you knew in Korea?"

"Nobody's asked me about that in years." He thought for a moment. "Half of 'em have fallen off their perches. Dare say a few still go to reunions. Pilots mainly. Once my eyes started to go they only let me fly a desk. Couldn't recognize myself across a room now. Anyway, it's all so bloody long ago. When you get to my age, you see how long ago everything is." He halted, as if out of practice with conversation.

"And how recent, too. I know that sounds utter rubbish, but the other day it struck me I've lived through a tenth of the time since Magna Carta. Imagine that! Ten of me end to end and you're back in the thirteenth century." He paused again. Loneliness comes in two kinds: one chatters on oppressively, the other can't find words. Mole seemed to oscillate between the two.

"Being old's a bit like flying. When you're up there at forty thousand you see how big the world is, and at the same time how small. My early years seem prehistoric. I mean, look at things now. Korean cars!" He stared into the ticking darkness of the passage. "I think time must have gone by more slowly in the past, don't you? Before the steam engine. That's when people began to feel it. An avalanche. Change running away with their lives. All of Victorian literature's about change."

"Yes," I said. I was thinking how slowly childhood had passed, until sixteen: a long steep hill, a penance in advance for anything I might do later. Then a greasy slope on the far side.

The tea was cold. The evening had clouded over, drizzle flecking the window. The feeble light seemed to soak into the brick floor, which had sunk over the years below ground level. Mole took the tea things out, and came back with a dusty bottle.

"Must drink to your father's . . . er. . . . Whisky all right? Been saving this for a guest. Livvy, I'm so sorry about your mother. And your father, of course. But you knew that."

"Were you two close, or more just comrades-in-arms?"

"I like to think I was your father's friend." Silence. I'd hurt him.

"I remember you coming to visit us in the early years. It meant so much to Mother. To all of us."

We drank, he asked about my life and Lottie's. But my pulse was racing with the big question I had to ask: Did he believe the official version of my father's disappearance?

Mole thought a long time before answering. "As I was saying, I like to think I was your father's friend. . . . But I can't say he confided in me. I doubt anyone was close enough to Jon for that. In a war you live on the surface. Got to. Your friends go out and come back, and then one morning off you all go and two or three don't come back. So you keep a certain distance. But Jon seemed unusually . . . withdrawn towards the end. As if something had upset him. Some news perhaps. One worried a bit. One got a feeling."

His voice fell to little more than a whisper. "Nobody saw him go down. Never found a trace, did they?"

"How do you mean, a feeling?"

"Nothing really. Nothing at all. I've said enough."

"No you haven't. Look, never mind old loyalties. Do you think my father could have killed himself? Or even deserted? I want you to tell me if you do. I often feel he's still alive somewhere. That he's alive as you or me."

"If he's alive, Livvy, he'll be *more* alive than me." Mole gave a bleak chuckle. "He always was. You're doers, you Wyverns. Not bookworms. He'll be like you."

"If I was such a doer I would have come to see you years ago."

The remark seemed to reassure him.

"I *have* thought from time to time there's a chance he didn't go down in action. That he just. . . . He wouldn't have been the first. Once in a while a chap simply flew and flew until the juice was gone, and bailed out. Over Formosa. Or a small island. You could get about a thousand miles in a Meteor. Less in a Sabre. Cowardice, they called it then. I wouldn't have said so. Certainly not in Jon's case." He cleared his throat and took a sip, blinking. The clock gathered itself to strike six, each chime preceded by a struggle, old clockwork mustering a sneeze.

"Your father hated that war. The more he knew it the more he loathed it. A lot of us did. One day I expect it'll all come out."

"What will?"

"What we really did over there."

"Your squadron?"

"We the Free World, Livvy. We the People. Yanks ran the show. Rest of us had to take everything on trust." He clasped both hands around his glass, as if warming his fingers, his eyes fixed on the window. A farmer was passing on a tractor, followed by a pack of beagles.

"They said we mustn't let ourselves be fooled. We were

dealing with fanatics. Automata. An enemy who held life so cheap he was capable of anything. They said there were no such things as civilians." Mole took off his spectacles and wiped them carefully. "You'd see these bedraggled peasants, Livvy. Local people. In coolie hats. Hundreds of 'em straggling down muddy tracks in the hills, mile after mile. Carts and bundles and pigs and whatnot. Yanks said they weren't peasants at all. They were infiltrators. Chinese and North Korean regulars, cleverly disguised." He gulped his drink. "Perhaps some of them were. They showed us films. Old women unmasked as young soldiers, confessing on their knees. We believed it at first. But when they started ordering chaps who'd flown over Germany—chaps like Jon—to mow down peasants. . . ."

A pink hand reached for the whisky, refilled his glass, the neck of the bottle drumming on the rim. He was silent again. I waited.

"I remember something he said, Livvy. Not long before he disappeared. *If those are Chinese troops, Mole. . . . If those are Chinese troops, what are all those children doing down there?*"

⋘ ⋙

About a year before Mother's death, I bought a flat on the strength of the Nova deal (U.S. network, good money). It's the top of a fifties walk-up on English Bay, a pile of mildewed stucco in a jungle of morning glory and azaleas near the old Sylvia Hotel, where Errol Flynn is believed to have died of some sexual excess and raccoons climb up the ivy to steal chocolate from the rooms.

I painted everything white, for the light. For colour I had cyclamens and flowering cacti, Rivera prints, Mexican rugs. Sparrows nesting in a soffit showered guano down my kitchen window, but I loved the cheeps and little bald heads popping out to be fed when the parents came home.

I bought it (the bank did) for the view. I can walk along the bay on summer nights beside water like silk, lights staining down from the far shore, gulls palely sleeping at the edge of the dark. On the boulevard are small Asian palms and a smell of seaweed from the beach, and cedar bark, cherry blossom, mock orange.

The afternoon sun burns through a drift of woodsmoke from a lumber mill; out on the bay a seal rises in a tanker's wake; and islands stand on the water, some helmet-shaped, others like drowned bodies, all furred with trees, olive-black in winter and lettuce green in the glycerine light of spring.

So I see my home, a mind's-eye view. Strange to picture that cold arm of this ocean whose warm heart I hear beating on the reef. As I describe it for you I'm back there. Each hour in memory is an hour of parole.

Film's an ephemeral art. One idea in ten gets taken seriously, one tenth of those get developed, and a tenth of the survivors make the screen. Odds of a thousand to one. But I love the process, the research. Suddenly, overnight, I become expert in something I've never thought about: the French and Indian War, the Dead Kennedys (the band), life in deep-sea vents, the drinking feats of Malcolm Lowry, the diving feats of the sperm whale (it can go ten times deeper than a nuclear submarine). In the past few years

117

I've lost myself in all the above, ransacking libraries, interrogating illustrious professors. Things I've scarcely heard of become my life, keep me up late, invade my dreams. They become affairs. Which is why filmmakers, like actors and artists, are impossible to live with.

Several men have tried it over the years. The one who lasted longest was a seaplane pilot. Michael. He used to take me across to the Gulf Islands. *Fly the Saltspring Quickie: Easy, affordable, and over in 20 minutes.* He owned a piece of woodland with a cabin up the Sunshine Coast (one of Canada's great wishful thoughts, he said, like the Progressive Conservative Party). We'd go there weeks at a time, until the world beyond the huge trees would disappear and we were at the centre of everything, a feeling I'd never had in England. I know what Dr. Freud would say about my pilot, but what I really loved about him was his love of the outdoors. Michael gave me that, and I still have it, though we lost touch some years ago when he moved to Venezuela.

The illustrious professor I'm "seeing" is married, older, an authority on Pacific writers—by which he means any author he admires who's written about this ocean or lived beside it. I'll call him Bob. It is he who's come to rescue me, at great risk to marriage and career. Bob is my friend on the outside.

Our relationship was the stolen kind, little holidays from reality at my flat and out-of-town hotels. But when Bob heard I was in prison, he dropped everything and flew out to Tahiti. He says he's combining my rescue with research for a book on Pierre Loti's *Mariage*—his "first real book" in years—and I suppose that's what his wife thinks. I know he's here because he's a good man and he loves me. He must. All this way, all this risk and expense, to hold hands with an accused murderess through bars.

He made it clear from the outset that he would never leave his wife because of their children (two boys, the younger still at school), and this suited both of us just fine. I think he used to worry about my childlessness—that a woman at my time of life might be in the grip of womb-hunger, fishing for sperm with a Ph.D. behind it. I didn't tell him about you (I've told nobody in Canada). I merely said I'd had enough of children when I was one myself.

You may have guessed by now that although I've never married I like men. Perhaps my interest is anthropological, the lure of the Other. When you grow up without them in the house, men are a strange tribe at the fringe of civilized life. I've gone a bit native in my fieldwork among them. I look around me nowadays at the new man—the kind who changes the baby's diaper in the airport washroom—and think I may have become a throwback, a Neanderthal, loyal to an earlier incarnation of the race.

Our first meeting was professional. I'd begun work on *Great Lives*, a series on dead Canadians, in this case gin-soaked Malcolm Lowry, who wrote *Under the Volcano* in a squatter's shack outside Vancouver.

I'd been reading *Lowry's Labyrinth* for days before I realized that its author taught locally at UBC. It was a good book, lean and confident, a contagious smile in the prose. I rang the English department and arranged lunch with Professor Bob.

The manly figure on the back cover was now slumping, as if muscle had melted and slid down. He was wearing a brown belt with black shoes (or vice versa) and a comfy old blue sweatshirt inside out. (How can you not want to hug a man who wears his shirt inside out?) Months later, when we knew each other well enough to hand out free advice, I got Bob exercising and taught him some rudiments of style. He's still an inch shorter than me and balding in the same places as Prince Charles. His brain is the prime erotic organ.

He's also kind to animals, considerate with women (except possibly his wife, but I understand she was the first to stray), funny, and has a bottomless fund of stories and wry wisdom.

We arranged to meet with a cameraman at Burrard Inlet, the site of Lowry's hideaway. "Dress bright and casual," I said, "and you'll look great on air."

The beach was a rough one of shingle and oyster shells. The sun had come out after a wet morning, strands of mist were snagged in the trees. Even the flaming stacks of an oil refinery across the reach seemed calm below the wooded hills. That was there in Lowry's day, its sign short a letter: HELL would blaze all night outside his window, which the writer, depending on his state of mind, found either amusing or terrifying.

A man appeared in red-and-green check shirt, scarlet cardigan and grey slacks, picking his way between tidal pools in a pair of white golfing shoes. Professor Bob, attired for television.

He pointed to a black stump. "One of the old piles. Not Lowry's. His place was round the point. Of course there were three of them, three Lowry cabins. The first two burned down, along with drafts of his book. Careless drinking, so they say."

"I've read *Volcano* twice," I said, detecting booze upwind, though Bob wasn't visibly pissed. "The first time I never finished it. The second time I thought it was brilliant. But I was drinking. Now I've got to where the consul's low on funds and what he has left will buy him one bottle of Johnny Walker or nine bottles of mescal. Of course he goes for the nine."

Bob laughed, a laugh that fitted naturally into his face, its magnetic field of lines. There's nothing like laughter for seduction.

"Friends used to call him 'the Malcohol'," Bob said to camera. "Many an aspiring novelist has drunk himself to death at the Lowry school of writing. But no one's ever written another *Under the Volcano*. And that includes the man himself. It was his one great work."

I remember Bob finding a broken bottle in the water. "Looks almost old enough. . . ." In handing it to me he cut himself slightly. The fumble seemed characteristic, a man at odds with physical things. I hoped this didn't extend to things of the flesh.

After the shoot we had coffee at a nearby Starbuck's. Bob regarded with disdain the green tile and black metal chairs. *"By their cafés shall ye know them,* said Lowry, of Canadians."

"Starbuck's is American."

"I wonder," he asked the ceiling dourly, "if they named these places for the mate in *Moby Dick*?"

Months later, when I was back from that summer at Tilehouse Street, I rang Bob at the English department with a new project.

"It's Liv Wyvern. You were kind enough to let me interview you about Lowry last spring. . . ." Noises I was hoping for came down the line: snorts of warm and instant recognition.

"Is Herman Melville one of your Pacific writers?"

"Of course. The greatest novelist ever produced by our neighbouring republic. And one of the most uneven."

"Hang on! I'm not taking notes. Can you let me have it again, later? Can we meet? Lunch this week? I can offer somewhere nice. TV's paying."

The film was about whaling, beginning when the Nootka sallied out with stone-tipped lances in canoes carved from giant cedars, and ending in a less heroic age of factory ships and explosive harpoons. There was, in truth, little room for Melville in the film. It was political, a hard-hitting plea for conservation. The Whaling Commission was about to allow Norway and Japan to slaughter hundreds a year for "research." I'd borrowed a fine edition of *Moby Dick* for its old engravings of the hunt.

A day or two later my back went out. This trouble started at Hitchin, soon after you were born, when I tried to move Jon's bike and it fell on me. I can go years without any bother, then one day when I'm off guard, tense, I'll bend down to pluck lint from the floor and find I can't stand up. Codeine, heating pad, and days in bed are the cure. That and a good big book.

There could hardly have been a better way to read *Moby Dick*, sailing across high seas of pain, pierced by shafts of agony, Melville's prose breaking over me, the heating pad rendering my flesh.

I suppose every age gets the *Moby Dick* it deserves. The greatest tragedy, it seemed to me then, was not the death of the *Pequod*, or her crew, or even the agony of the white whale; but the passing of a world in which such things were possible. Only two human lifespans since Melville went to sea—and in the distance gone they might be a thousand years.

"You're right," Bob said. (He often says that as if he means it, and I love him for it.) "You're right, Liv. Melville saw what was coming. 'Humped herds of buffalo, not forty years ago, shook their iron manes where now the polite broker sells you land at a dollar an inch.' Buffalo, whales, Indians, everything—he foresaw that it won't stop, can't stop, until the ship goes down. That's what I think *Moby Dick*'s about. But that's a reading for our time. Like saying *Othello*'s about race relations."

We finished lunch—a rather liquid one—and he came back to my flat before an evening class. I kicked the door shut, reached both arms behind his neck, and kissed him fiercely.

I needn't have worried. He couldn't tie a shoelace but he didn't fumble love.

We agreed that I would never call him, even at work. I wondered what she was like, his wife, and whether I'd hear from Bob again. A fortnight later the phone rang: "Wanna come to Yoho, a bottle of rum and an old man's chest?"

"Where?"

"Yoho Lake, next week. High in the Rockies, remote, romantic. Sorry for the short notice. Wasn't sure I'd be alone until just now."

Bob slipped away from a literary conference in Banff.

We threw down our bags in the still cabin. He lifted the coat off my shoulders, brushed my hair aside and kissed the small of my neck.

"I don't know you," I whispered.

"That's the point, isn't it?"

Afterwards, I drifted on a silence rippled by his snores. He was like a dear old dog asleep by the fire. Probably what they call dead wood at university. Was it disloyal to think this? Did I owe him tender fibs?

He woke and regarded our bodies in the half-light, a light of contrast. "Look at us, Liv. I'm white as a cod's belly and you're golden. Either you go to a tanning parlour or you're not entirely Anglo-Saxon."

An innocent remark but it touched a childhood wound. On one of our brittle, three-bottle days after Mother's death, Lottie had picked at that particular scar for the first time in years. We were standing under the spear, staring at it vacantly, and our eyes strayed down into the glass.

"Didn't you ever wonder, Liv, about Mum?"

"How do you mean?"

"You know. The milkman, the dustman. Jon *was* away a lot. Even before."

"Lottie!"

She took a swig, unabashed. "Or maybe that pedlar chappie who used to come round door to door when we were little. Remember? Ribbons and buttons. From India, wasn't he? I mean, just look at us, Liv. Do we look like we share a lot of genes?"

"We all share ninety-nine per cent with chimpanzees. Even you, Charlotte. So I imagine you and I have some in common."

Bob tipped the maître d' for the best table in the old log building at the heart of the lodge. He took it upon himself to choose the wine, locking eyes with me over the list. There were no prices on my menu. He suggested raw Arctic char, followed by grilled caribou. "All the meat and fish are wild. It's the only truly Canadian restaurant I know." He was such a nationalist. The wind had to be let out of him, or this getaway would be disastrous.

"I've had Canadian food before," I said. "There's this great little place in Medicine Hat. Did a shoot there once. The PDQ Lounge, *Chinese and Canadian Cuisine.*"

"I bet they don't serve caribou."

"He. An old Cantonese in a sailor's hat folded from a sheet of newspaper. He does soggy chips, burgers mixed with breadcrumbs, and gravy like carpenter's glue. I'm not a kept woman, you know. You get the room. Dinners are on me."

Back at the cabin we sat on the balcony in our coats. I hadn't seen a night so clear since Mother took us to the Scottish highlands. I was eleven, and I thought then that no matter how sad life might be, I could always look into those endless deeps of light and see how small my worries were.

In the morning, wet snow was sticking to the windows, melting and sliding down. We spent the day in bed, except for a lunchtime foray to the lodge, where Bob procured two bottles of "the Widow," his favourite bubbly.

"I can see why you like Lowry," I said. "You drink about as much."

"I like Melville, but I don't hunt whales."

"I've been thinking about what you said. The only truly universal American writer. Isn't that a bit heretical? I've read that the whaling ship is meant to *be* America. All its nationalities forged into a common purpose."

"That's what American critics often say. Even if they're right, it's hardly good news. The *Pequod* sinks like a stone."

And so it went on: I objecting, he parrying hyperbolically.

"Henry James. Just as universal, just as great."

"If you think the parlour's as interesting as the world. Who remembers a title of his unless they've seen it televised?"

"How about . . . Twain?"

"Twain's funny, and funny goes a long way. But sentimental as a made-for-TV movie."

"I give you Faulkner. Local yet universal. Incontestably major."

"Faulkner did more harm than General Sherman. The South has never recovered from his prose."

"Bob."

"Huh?"

"You're pissed."

"You think I'm mad at you?"

"I don't think you're angry. I think you're drunk. And you've just given yourself away. In this country, if we mean angry, we say pissed *off.* Where are you from, really? Come on. A straight answer." He bowed his head and looked up sheepishly, as if peering over spectacles. Caught out. Also an obscure pride.

"A little place you wouldn't have heard of."

"Try me."

"Vandalia, Connecticut. It's not on any map. True places never are."

"Aha! A self-hating Yankee. Draft dodger, were we?"

"War resister, please. I was never actually drafted. Past the shelf date for prime grunt."

"So why leave?"

Bob's smile drained away, its lines of force like arid gullies. He went quiet, staring at the mountain that filled our window: a castle of layered rock, snow massing on the battlements.

"I *will* tell you, Liv. But not right now. People think it's easy, attractive even, leaving home and country. Maybe it was for you. Maybe you're the slash-and-burn type. It was the hardest thing I've ever done. Can you wait?"

"Of course." I was wondering where his wife was from.

"Will you ever go back?" I said. "Now things have changed?"

"Doubt it. Will you?"

"I've been thinking about it lately. Since my mother died. There's nothing stopping me. Except me. You need to be a very urban person, and I'm not. England feels so . . . spoken for. Nothing unclaimed. Nothing unsaid. The whole place seems to say: never mind what *you* think, *this* is what you need to know, and you'd better get it absolutely right. It's part of that British arrogance—the way they always think they know what matters. And that what they don't know is so far off the map it doesn't count."

"Americans do it too. It goes with being an empire."

"I remember thinking, If I stay in this country I'll be arguing with everyone for the rest of my life. But I miss it. God, I miss it! I watch *Masterpiece Theatre*—you know, 'The Morris Minor Murders'—and I think I could go back to those riverbanks and sunny afternoons at the drop of a hat. I have to remind myself of things. Crowds. Crowds of shoppers with push-chairs. The smell of the Underground. Country footpaths ankle-deep in lager tins and dogshit. Did you know most of the dust in the Tube is flakes of human skin?"

Bob got up, went to the bar fridge, came back with flutes of champagne.

"Maybe when I'm old," I added. "A Wisteria Cottage with my sister and some cats. But you get used to all this! Places like this change you forever. Unfold you so you can never get back inside the box you came in."

The glacial crest of the mountain was shedding tiny avalanches caught by the afternoon light, puffs of mauve confetti falling to the lake. He kissed me on my shoulder, on my ear. He touched a cold glass to my nipple.

"God!" he said. "You've no idea how good it is to talk. People talk best in bed, don't they? Even about books."

"Haven't you been talking books all week?"

"Don't imagine, Liv, that we do anything so passé at literary conferences as talk about *books*. Nobody's done that in twenty years. We talk about ways of talking about talking about books. . . . I need a smoke! Trossil was in Cuba. He has theories about Hemingway, but he knows tobacco. Do you mind?"

"I like it. It's part of your smell."

He knuckle-walked off the bed like a great ape and fossicked in his jacket. "What I mean about Melville is that he's a writer of and for the world. After *Moby Dick* we had the Civil War. Then the huddled masses. Americans became obsessed with what the heck an American is, and precious little else. Melville was writing about what it means to be a human being at large in this . . . this mystery. . . ." Bob summoned infinity with a circular wave of his Havana. "Melville wanted all of culture and nature. All the piled centuries."

He lit up, drew the smoke in a blue stream from mouth to nose; sent a dragon-breath forking from his nostrils. "If we don't look out the window, or up at the sky, or down at our monkey hands and ask ourselves unanswerable questions now and again, we're not half alive. What's an American is pretty small potatoes. But it's gotten worse. Now it's lifestyle stuff. The cultural Balkans. No great and enduring volume can ever be written on the flea! That's what I tell my creative writing class churning out watered-down Updike."

He halted to catch a breath and scratch his balls, which had rolled onto his thigh like a pair of onions in a string bag. "In my experience, Liv, people who think their 'gender identity' is the most important thing about them are usually right." He butted the Havana. "Sorry! This isn't what you came for. I guess I'm still not decompressed."

He stroked under my chin, as if caressing a cat. I bit him on the shoulder.

"The ear, Liv, please—the ear. For some reason you can bite the earlobe all you like and it never shows."

He bent and kissed the nipple stiffened by the icy glass. His lips lingered there just long enough, and wandered south. A finger brushed a haiku down my back. A hand found an ankle, clapped me in irons. I lit up like a switchboard.

Does this embarrass you? Well, you're a grown woman by now, and if you can't imagine your batty old ma as a sexual animal that's your problem. If I were not, you wouldn't be here with these pages in your hand. A word in your ear: There are things to be said for older blokes. They take their time. They know what they're about. And they're so grateful.

Six

⟨⟩° °⟨⟩

ENGLAND

Riverhill. September, 1899. Notebook No. 3

THE RECOLLECTION, DURING MY MISFORTUNES in West Africa, of that sordid fellow and his Whitehall confederates raised certain chimerical thoughts that ever since have caused me profound distress. Who were they really? Who the devil was he working for? Why such an air of menace and intrigue? The more I've thought over that afternoon, the likelier it has seemed that the motorcar, the interrogation, and so forth were mere props in a charade designed to further the very treachery they pretended to be uprooting.

It is not given to a member of Her Majesty's Services, except perhaps at the highest rank, to be privy to the source of orders and the policy behind them. To question an order is tantamount to mutiny, and I have never done so. But it appeared to me, as the men trundled me towards Ashanti, my mind racing hither and yon over our failed expedition, that to have gone where

I had gone, with a few dozen Hausas against well-armed forces in their thousands, was nothing short of suicidal.

Yet how can one apply the word *suicide* to events one hasn't invited and over which one has little control? It is true that the advance to Dawkita was entirely my decision, but I now believe that even had we stayed at Wa, we should still have been attacked and overwhelmed. If the Hinterland catastrophe stood alone in my life, I could not construe any link between it and earlier events. But my extreme condition after the loss of my eye brought vividly to mind that voyage with the Princes many years before, and the illness that threatened me soon afterwards—an illness never explained or identified but which ended my naval career and very nearly my life.

Although the more lurid rumours about Prince Eddy raised in that Whitehall room were, to my knowledge, without foundation, there was no denying they were nourished by certain flaws in his character. Flaws so worrying in an eventual heir to the throne that (once one allowed oneself to entertain speculations such as those purveyed by *The New York Times*) Eddy's sudden and fatal illness could indeed be seen as suspiciously convenient. From this it was only a short step, in my agitated state, to conclude that I myself—being one of a mere handful privy to a fiasco with the Prince in the South Seas—might be seen as a weak stitch in the cloak of secrecy that had descended over those events of 1881. In short, that certain people might view my own removal as convenient, even necessary.

I should elaborate here on Dr. Part's conversations with me during the voyage home two years ago.

"We don't get many originals like you out here on the Coast, Henderson," he said one day over backgammon in the *Carthage's* saloon. "Types, certainly, but not originals. You're a queer fish, if I may say so, and that's a compliment. An interesting fish. I wish we saw more like you." His brow creased with professional concern. "From the little I do know, and I refer to things your unconscious mind has disclosed while you were asleep. . . ." Seeing I was about to protest, he held up his hand like a constable stopping a carriage. "No, no. Be assured of my absolute discretion. How shall I put this? Medical science is getting rather good at healing the body, Henderson. But with the mind . . . well, until recently we'd not come very far since Galen and Imhotep." He then dilated on new research in Germany, drawing my attention to an article in *The Lancet* on the work of a Baron von Krafft-Ebing. Later, when I'd perused this (I found it far from a transparent read) he came at last to his point.

"Forgive me for what I'm about to say. We medicos usually keep our patients pretty much in the dark. The less the average chap knows, the less he worries. That's all right for average chaps and average complaints. But in the case of your . . . utterances—the talking in your sleep and so on, I think it advisable to let in a little light. From what I've overheard, you—or rather your unconscious mind—your mind, as I say, seems to picture itself at risk. A delusion involving a fear of death by foul play. And—here's the queerest thing—foul play due to some conspiracy aimed at silencing you. As Krafft-Ebing puts it, you seem to be experiencing delusions of persecution allied to an exaggerated sense of—forgive me—self-importance. These symptoms accord well with what students of that German's ideas term *paranoia*."

"You mean I'm mad? That's what you're telling me?"

"Not at all. The modern use of the word is quite specific. It refers to a single condition. As I said, delusions of persecution and importance."

"And what remedy does our Teutonic friend suggest? A long leave spent in a bath chair by the seaside, with a straitjacket and improving books?"

"We're only beginning to describe these things. We really don't know how to treat them. You're not far off the mark, though. Rest, good fellowship, diversion—the bosom of family and friends—all this seems to help. Make sure you don't rush things when you get to England. Take as long a rest from duty as possible. After what you've been through, I'm sure the brass-hats will understand."

"Brass, by its nature, is incapable of understanding."

"Quite so! You're obviously on the mend. I can see I needn't have spoken."

Nothing more on the subject was said by Part for about a week, not until we'd crossed the Bay of Biscay and were within two watches of Southampton.

"Look here, Henderson. We'll be going our separate ways soon. I hope you don't think . . . What I mean to say is, I've been reconsidering what I said the other day. It's too easy to fall head over heels in love with newfangled ideas. My wife always tells me I go soft in the head at the newest thing. Professionally, that is." He chuckled awkwardly. "I've underestimated you. I'm sorry. It's good of you to put up with me the way you have. I now believe I may be mistaken. I now think there *is* a pattern—a narrative consistency—in what I've been mistaking hitherto for mere ramblings." He sent the steward off to get us sandwiches and bottles of beer, then resumed.

"You seem to have made quite a career of singeing the Frenchman's beard. I confess I don't like 'em, though one can't help admiring them. Pasteur, Voltaire, Montaigne! Yet the hecatombs of Kumasi were as nothing to the Terror of Paris. It's my belief that the more civilized the nation, the greater its capacity for savagery. We Scots have some experience with the Sassenach in that regard. Give me an honest-to-God savage with a bone through his nose any day. I wouldn't want the French to pick *me* out as a marked man. No thank you. But they may well have picked out *you*. I wouldn't put it past them to have been egging on Samory's lot from the start. It's a wonder you're here at all. Even paranoiacs can have enemies, don't you know." A nervous laugh accompanied his *bon mot*.

"There's no need to humour me, Doctor. Samory and the French hate each other far more than either hates us. I'm damned if I can see this consistency of yours. I intend to take the relaxation you suggest. No doubt everything will appear in its normal light once I've been home a few weeks."

Thank God our passage together was nearly at an end! I was now worried that Part was going to deduce the very thing above all else that was tormenting me. To put it plainly, in my more "paranoiac" moments I wasn't at all certain from which I had more to fear: a foreign Power, or my own country? Samory might have been a possible instrument, but the design seemed to lie elsewhere. I considered changing berths, so the doctor couldn't eavesdrop on my unconscious indiscretions. But such a move would only have made him more tenacious.

I wish to make it clear that my suspicions have alighted only on faceless individuals such as those who badgered me in Whitehall, whether they be out-and-out traitors or merely pushing and unscrupulous underlings driven by their ambition to take dirty business into their own hands. History is full of such men, witness Becket. I had no opportunity to discuss any of this with my friend the Governor, Sir William Maxwell. Only weeks after handing in my report to the Colonial Office, I learnt that fever took him at Accra. God rest that good soul! Among Sir William's last deeds was to secure support for Ferguson's family, and to see that my Hausas were awarded the West African Medal with special clasp.

Samory, too, has passed on—to the voluptuous paradise of the Mohammedans, or perhaps, in Allah's wisdom, to their counterpart of the other place. (In a bid to convert me, Samory once revealed that the Prophet's heaven abounds in naked houris, with whom the moment of ecstasy lasts twenty-four hours. He was selling me short, I replied, for Gibbon assures us that the said moment endures one thousand years! Samory laughed uproariously at this, declaring he would never understand the English.) Not long after he let me go, a French column surprised and captured him. He died soon afterwards, conveniently enough for them.

What a difference in two years! The boundaries between the Great Powers' African possessions are now agreed by protocol, and civilization makes its inexorable march across the continent's interior. A railway cleaves the ancient forests of Ashanti, and the copper threads that bind the globe run all the way to end-of-telegraph at Wa! In sanguine moments I reflect that the ultimate sacrifice made by Ferguson and the other men I lost in that country, and now by Sir William, was not made for naught.

Even in my most feverish imaginings, I had and shall always have unshakeable faith in Sir William. Even had I not, no governor of the Gold Coast would have risked the life of Ferguson recklessly. But a foreign Power with designs on our Colony might have counted it a great bonus to dispose of him while getting rid of me. Alternatively, it also seemed just possible that an unscrupulous fanatic in Whitehall, of the stamp I met, with concerns far removed from those of West Africa, ignorant of Ferguson (or seeing him only as a native interpreter)—and thinking *me* a potential traitor—might have misjudged the costs and gains involved in my elimination.

So it seemed during my injury and convalescence. And so it still seems, from time to time, in recurring attacks of the same nervous condition. I do not know what to believe. I can only let the readers of these pages (if ever they are read) draw what conclusions they may.

Of Africa I have told all I can remember that seems germane, and doubtless much besides. Now I shall relate much earlier events. I must speak of that ill-starred voyage to the Pacific which began in the summer of 1879. Some of the salient occurrences are on public record. Others I have retrieved from notes and sketches made at the time (strange how the sight of a drawing or watercolour one did long ago can release a tide of memory, just as a tune one hasn't heard since childhood can bring back a conversation, a chess game, a summer afternoon). Yet others I can only set down as I recall them unaided, there being no memorial on paper and nobody with whom it is possible, or prudent, to consult.

⋘ ⋙

Had there been women on board *Bacchante*, even one sympathetic woman, things might have turned out quite differently. How plainly I see this now! Eddy and George had grown up in a world of women: their lovely mother, their sisters, governesses, ladies-in-waiting. Then they were wrenched from drawing-room cushions, French gowns and perfume, the trill of girlish laughter, and thrown into the tarry hold of the Royal Navy.

They had already undergone some cadet training on H.M.S. *Britannia*, but she was little more than a wooden school, a three-decker from Nelson's day, stuck in the Dartmouth silt. *Bacchante's* voyage was a very different proposition. Three years round the world is a long time for anyone, much more so for youngsters. They left England as boys and were expected to return as men. And no ordinary men, but imperial Princes: steeled by the Navy, schooled by their tutor, and awakened to the duties of empire by having circumnavigated the globe and strolled beneath palm and pine.

George was all right within wooden walls. A robust boy with boyish interests, notably gunnery and stamp collecting, he affected the rolling gait of a seadog, took each day as it came, seldom let anything bother him, got along well with shipmates, superiors, and subordinates. Hail-fellow-well-met was his way with every-one. But Eddy withered when torn from the maternal soil. His cheeks grew hollow and his eyes more glassy with each day. He shirked both duty and devotion, said nothing, did nothing, liked nothing better than to stay in his bunk staring at the port-hole. He was late for every lesson and drill, shivered at the sound of guns or the snap of a sail, shrank from the touch of hemp and canvas.

One might have thought him a bookworm, only he never touched a book if he could help it. Reverend Dalton tried every-thing—including things that were better left untried—to ignite the damp fires of his soul and intellect. In three years on board, that boy learnt next to nothing, except a self-preservational detachment and some verse by rote, which he recited abstract-edly like a man recalling a trek through endless wastes.

Even before we set sail, *Bacchante* herself had been the subject of heated debate. Some navy men doubted she was seaworthy enough to carry the Queen's grandsons. Disraeli thought it mad-ness to put both royal "eggs" in one basket, no matter how sound the vessel. Dalton, however, who knew the Princes better than anyone—not excepting their parents—overcame all opposition on that point, threatening resignation to get his way.

The Rev. John Neale Dalton had been the boys' tutor since they were small, when he used to run like a deer through the Sandringham woods while they took potshots at him with rubber-tipped arrows. He had the ear and absolute trust of the Queen, and was of the firm view that the best hope for Eddy's improve-ment was to keep him with his younger and abler brother

George. Perhaps he also wished to preserve his own monopoly of influence. Whatever his motives, I think he was right to keep them together. Certainly the results were catastrophic on the one occasion when he deviated from that policy.

The royal tutor, quite a fancier of ships, did not like the looks of *Bacchante* either, advocating the *Newcastle*. The First Sea Lord didn't agree, saying the *Newcastle* was an old tub full of bilgewater, while *Bacchante*, being new, would be free of rot and vermin. Dalton pointed out that because she was new, there was no telling what she might do in an emergency. He lost this argument, though his fears turned out to be well founded.

Bacchante was neither fish nor fowl, the offspring of a time when tradition and innovation were at war. She had an iron hull and wooden decks, and was built slim in a futile quest for speed. She measured, in round figures, 300 feet from stem to stern, 40 in beam, and weighed 4,000 tons with a complement of 400 men. Her single gun-deck classed her a corvette.

She carried a full square-rig on three masts, but old tars from the frigate days, seeing her silhouette against the sky, would have noted something odd in the spacing of her trees, for the mainmast was set aft to make room for two squat funnels. From these issued the breath of thirty furnaces, firing ten boilers, which fed two Rennies driving a single screw. In an ingenious but cumbersome compromise between the motive powers of man and God, the screw could be rove—hoisted into a well beneath the poop—to prevent drag when the wind promised a good run under canvas.

The weight of her machinery and coal made *Bacchante* a slow sailer, except in a stiff wind, and whenever the boilers were alight her rigging and brightwork soon became begrimed and tarnished. Keeping her spars and planking clear of soot was indeed the chief occupation of the bluejackets, who had little else to do when her five thousand steam horses were furrowing the waves.

Looking back on *Bacchante* now, after years of rapid advance in ship design, one can see what a far cry she was from the floating steel castles that the world's great navies have become. Her ordnance belonged to the days of powder and shot, and I doubt whether a full broadside could match the destructive force of a single high-explosive shell from a modern ten-inch gun.

Her Captain, Lord Charles Scott, was however a great believer in the march of science. Shortly before we sailed, he took delivery of an electric-lighting apparatus—a particular interest of his—worked by a hand-crank and pulley wheels. He had imagined that this would be a capital thing for excursions ashore, for lighting up caves and climbing mountains after dark. He was rather disappointed to find that, when unpacked and put together, it required a dozen men to lift it. The equipment proved good for little more than evening entertainments in the after-cabin where, with lamps doused, we saw glass tubes light up with ghostly sparks and twirls of pink and green.

It was August 6, 1879—my twentieth birthday, as it happened—when the Princes joined the ship. We were in Cowes Roads for the regatta. But it was neither my own anniversary nor the sight of so many fine yachts that made the day memorable. Nor, even, was it the private visit to *Bacchante* of the Prince and Princess of Wales.

I took it upon myself, as sub-lieutenant on duty that day, to make sure the royal midshipmen were settled in their cabin and to show them the gunroom, where they and their fellows would take meals and spend free hours. *Bacchante's* gunroom was a pleasant place, like a prefects' common-room, except for its ship-shape compactness. If memory serves it was about eight feet wide and twice as long, filled by a dining table surrounded on three sides by mahogany locker-seats with red leather cushions. On one bulkhead was a large mirror to add illusory space. Two large ports admitted light and air, though it was wise to keep them shut when under way, lest a sea came lopping in. A shelf above the seats held books, photograph albums, chess and backgammon sets, and battered telescopes.

The Princes' own cabin was similar, though much smaller, with George in the upper berth—a reversal in their status due to Eddy's dread of ladders. The other mids had no cabins, slinging their hammocks in the steerage, but the Queen's grandsons could hardly do that, though in most other respects they were treated like the rest. Prince George, just fourteen, was still very much a boy, slight, not yet five foot; Eddy, well on in his sixteenth year, was a good nine inches taller, and looked already a young man.

What I remember is Prince Eddy's languid countenance, a long face that seemed lost to the world, or utterly expressionless; if a person can be devoid of expression yet at the same time give an intimation of troubled depths beneath a glassy surface. And just when I had begun to think I was reading more of the mind's construction in that face than a stranger could possibly divine, there came a cheerful warbling of female voices, and three ladies appeared—two rather forgettable (I have forgotten them), the third like a radiant bloom between mere leaves.

Stunningly beautiful, gay and bright, well-spoken yet not a member of the aristocracy, this gorgeous creature seemed, in the way she commanded attention with her measured azure gaze, a woman of the stage. Indeed, I half thought I'd seen her in a play somewhere—though perhaps memory is playing tricks, for in those days her acting career had scarcely begun. She opened her arms to Eddy, drawing him against the well-filled sail of her blouse. (George was off somewhere among the guns.)

"I'm going to miss you two rascals most dreadfully, my dear. And I don't want you to forget me. Even though your Papa may well do so before you get back." At that moment I knew who she was: Lillie Langtry, rumoured to be their father's mistress. (Happy dog! thought I.) She was utterly unselfconscious; not because I was too lowly a species to be noticed in the background, but because it was her manner to give rapt attention to the person she addressed.

"Look, Eddy dear, I've brought you something. Keep it somewhere safe, and whenever you take it out you must think of me!" She put her hands on her shapely hips and sighed theatrically. "You *will* remember me just a little bit, won't you, dear boy?"

It was a small gold locket. (Not until Eddy showed it me some weeks later did I see the bewitching miniature within of its presenter.) For the merest instant, the young Prince's face came galvanically to life. He gave her a smack on the cheek, and said, very sweetly, "I'll put it here on my watch chain. Though I'll have to take off Grandmama's to make room for it."

143

I'll wager Mrs. Langtry wasn't acting her delight at the thought of displacing the Queen from Eddy's fob. She turned and gave me a complicitous wink. Then she and her friends were gone. For a long time, her rose perfume seemed to hang about the half-deck, vanquishing manly odours of new oak, tarred lines, and linseed oil.

With Mrs. Langtry's departure, Eddy's countenance relapsed into its prior state, which is best described as a look of pained torpor. At the time, I thought perhaps he favoured his father's mistress over his mother and sisters, and was desolate to see her go, but that was only because I didn't see his goodbyes to the others. Later I understood that he adored the feminine, that most of his childhood had been spent in the society of women (his father being absent much of the time for the same reason, but to a rather different end), and that the thought of three years aboard a man-of-war was more than he could bear.

The ship spent a month in the English Channel, undergoing trials. These showed her to be a good enough steamer but sluggish under sail, even for a warship. A forecastle gun was taken off to improve her trim. In the end she was pronounced generally satisfactory, like a dull student who graduates through sheer persistence.

But a new ship is never truly known until her mettle has been tested in a gale. Captain Scott did his best to push her into a thunderstorm or two, but we found nothing a sailor would call a hard blow. The weaknesses in *Bacchante*'s character were to remain hidden for two years—until unmasked by a tempest in the Indian Ocean.

Whilst the trials proceeded, the Princes spent a lot of time ashore. Their father was on the South Coast officiating in various capacities, chief of which was to lay the foundation stone for the new Eddystone Light.

It was late September when we lost sight of Land's End. It would be my last glimpse of England for three years.

The booming voice of Reverend Dalton, both royal tutor and Acting Chaplain, was soon heard everywhere on board. "Look, dear boys!" he cried, trying to stir some romance of the sea in their pedestrian hearts. "Look, a shoal of porpoises coming to welcome us!"

We ran south to Gibraltar, then set course for the Canary Islands. As the youngest of the sub-lieutenants and the one most often detailed to the Princes' routine supervision, I was responsible for delivering them to, and collecting them from, their forenoon lessons with the polymathic parson. This afforded me snatches of Dalton's erudition—tail-ends of historical lectures, fragments of verse and prose by modern and classical authors.

Dalton was often moved by nature's displays to literary allusion, a source of merriment among the ratings and the more philistine officers. On balmy shipboard evenings his voice could be heard like a distant gun, firing a volley of Milton or Keats, or the ornate sentiments of Charles Kingsley. George might say, "What a jolly pretty sunset!" And the tutor would declaim: "The evening skies are fit weeds for widowed Eos weeping over the dying sun." Eddy seldom said a word.

145

Dalton was a tall, vigorous man, about forty when we sailed. He had light hair, starting to bleach a little, and what he proudly referred to as "sea-blue" eyes, considering himself a born mariner on their account. These beamed owlishly through large round spectacles. Perhaps to make up for the receding foliage on his crown, he affected long sidewhiskers that ran from temple to collar—not exactly a full muttonchop; more a chop with the tenderloin devoured.

Like me, he was a country parson's son, which fostered a certain camaraderie between us. Beneath his severity and pedantry he was a sincere, kindly man. A confirmed bachelor, so it seemed, he surprised everyone by marrying a midshipman's sister not long after the voyage, a very Casaubon with a bride half his age. At about the same time the Palace rewarded him for his loyalty, his patience, and for the circumspect chronicle of the voyage he penned under the Princes' names, by making him Canon of Windsor.

Dalton had taken a First in Theology at Cambridge and another degree in Classics. He was an untiring teacher who went to extraordinary lengths to instil in his royal charges some of the boundless curiosity, energy, and natural sympathy he himself possessed. Prince George soaked up what took his fancy, leaving what didn't (languages, for one), but with Prince Eddy the tutor's Herculean efforts were not merely fruitless but overwhelming, a vast bolus of knowledge the boy could never hope to swallow, let alone digest. This contributed, I believe, to the disastrous turn of events I shall relate in due course.

Despite his learning, Dalton was hardly as conventional as many judged him. Once established on board, he began to voice libertarian opinions, for the most part harmless but often outspoken and eccentric. In later years he became a sympathizer with the "New Thought," a friend of Carpenter, Shaw, and other sandal-wearing, vegetarian exponents of Hindu mysticism, sexual reform, homespun clothing, and the utopia of William Morris. Such a fellow was *rara avis* on a warship. Certain senior members of the wardroom made it clear they found him a prig and crashing bore. They also resented his royal connections—feeling unable to speak freely when he was present—and it was even hinted he was the sort of man to listen at keyholes and pass intelligence to the Palace.

Dalton's chief tormentor at the wardroom dinner table was Smyth, Lieutenant of Marines, who had a quick but entirely practical mind and pale brown, almost yellow, eyes—eyes as hard and discomfiting to his subordinates as those of a wolf. Smyth soon discovered that a sure way to rag poor Dalton was to cap his deviations into humour.

"It is often remarked," Dalton essayed one night off Tenerife, "that people resemble their dogs. This is less remarkable than generally supposed, for what can it be but narcissism, the same unconscious self-regard that results in the resemblance one often sees between husband and wife? The long-chinned man chooses the long-chinned woman, and she him, without either being aware they are drawn by their own echo in another's person. More remarkable, I'd argue, is the likeness between a man's profession and his surname. From my personal acquaintance alone I can adduce a banker named Banks, a politician named Tory, a painter called Prime, a policeman named Grab, and two undertakers, one Body and the other Death!"

"Speak up, Padre!" Smyth struck in before a polite murmur could escape the diners. "Since childhood I've suffered from a disorder of the ears, requiring a regular sluicing out. The man who treats me is a Dr. Wax."

This was met with brays of laughter, while Dalton's observations had fallen on the same stony ground that greeted his weekly sermon.

⫷ ⫸

Sad news was awaiting me at the telegraph office in Tenerife. My dear father had died. Consumptive for many years, he had not looked well when I'd sailed four months before, but I need hardly say that this was a shock. How cruel of the fates that he should go while I was far away, his last moments unknown to me! My next thought was for my mother. There being no possibility of compassionate leave, all I could do was send condolences and flowers by wire, and write a long letter which went through many drafts before I could bring myself to post it.

Not far beyond Tenerife lay doldrum weather, holding us limp-sailed on a bald ocean beneath a brassy sky. A laziness fell upon ship and sea. Even the flying-fish seemed torpid, skimming just inches from the surface like little glass-winged birds. Prince George caught some and dried the wings for bookmarks.

Bacchante flumped about for several days, her head all round the compass, while I drifted through my duties grief-stricken, in doldrums of my own. Then Captain Scott ordered fires lit, and we steamed to the West Indies at half speed, the stiff new engines sending pulses of vibration through *Bacchante*'s frame. Every glass and metal object rattled, my outline in the shaving mirror was blurry as a ghost's, and there was a leaden smell of baking paint from funnels and steampipes.

This was my first crossing of an ocean, an immensity that cannot be grasped in abstract. In quiet moments I stood often at the taffrail and gazed, as into a cold fire, at the churned glass flowing from the stern day upon day for weeks, reflecting there upon the great size of the world and the smallness, brevity, and loneliness of our places in it.

Landfall at Barbados on Boxing Day could hardly have brought a greater contrast to these musings. Swarms of shore-boats, filled with laughing washerwomen, descended on us in a loud flotilla. On still nights, the rhythmic gruntle and squeak of frogs carried across the water. And when we went ashore even Eddy was intrigued by the hummingbirds—little flashes of crimson and emerald darting in the sun like fairy arrows.

When I was a youngster my uncle and namesake, the late Francis Morris, had tried to infect me with his mania for ornithology. Seeing these tiny and outlandish living things—more insects than birds, now hanging in mid-air like hoverflies, with a blur of wingbeats and a sound like a spinning top, now darting after one another in aerial combat—I fancied that I knew a little of the wonder Uncle Frank had known. It was a joyful counterpart to that melancholy awe I'd felt whilst gazing at our wake across the boundless sea in contemplation of my father's death. First, a gloomy intimation of the world's vast indifference, then a vision of its exquisite delicacy. At twenty, such moments mark one deeply; they are the moorings of our lives.

· · ·

"Look well, boys. You'll see the hummingbird *only* in the Americas—North, Central, and South." Dalton's stentorian tones carried down the wooded path behind the Governor's residence, where bearded figs and Spanish moss festooned majestic trees. "Observe how the males fight. They are quite capable of impaling each other on those needle beaks, though they rarely succeed, for they are masters of evasion. Note the fearless aggression, the quick resort to violence, and you understand why the tiny hummingbird was, for the mighty Aztecs, an emblem of the God of War, who quaffed human blood the way these little creatures sip nectar from the hearts of flowers."

"I say, sir! How did the God of War drink blood?" This had piqued the interest of Prince George. "I mean he wasn't real, was he?"

"Don't take everything I say so literally, P.G. Of course he wasn't real. Diaz describes a terrifying statue on top of a great pyramid in the Aztec city. Blood was offered to it, wrung from the palpitating hearts of human victims." Dalton opened and shut his palm in a squeezing motion to illustrate. "All this you would already know, boys, had you been reading your Prescott! Better get on with it—you have a test on Friday."

"I say!" replied George. Eddy, as usual, said nothing.

In Dalton's programme for the Princes' development, he emphasized study at sea, and strenuous physical culture when ashore. The New Year—1880—found us on St. Vincent, where we scrambled up the Soufrière volcano. A few days later we climbed Diablotin on Dominica, an ascent of five thousand feet.

Dalton did not, at this stage in the voyage, share confidences with me, but I couldn't help overhearing a remark he made to another officer. Eddy, he noted, had just turned sixteen, but it was George, younger by a year and a half, who was "Eddy's mainstay and chief incentive to exertion."

There were many Caribbean ports of call, excursions, dinners. Trinidad stands out in my mind for its primaeval woods, covering most of the island. As we steamed into the Gulf of Paria, the hills were so green that from a distance they seemed cloaked in moss from their summits to the water's edge, but as we drew nearer this resolved into a feathery mass of great trees.

We saw tropical hardwoods I knew only from planks in timber yards—mahogany, conocaste, silk-cotton, locust—and smaller trees whose costly fruits appear sometimes in London markets. A black man led the way through the forest gloom, swinging a cutlass through saplings and lianas as if they were so much asparagus. He showed us the trees that yield indiarubber, and bade us drink from the famous *bejuco de agua*, or water vine.

"Know your plants, boys," Dalton intoned, "when you help yourselves to a free drink in the woods. And abstain from the vice of alcohol, or you may end up like the indiarubber man!"

"The rubber man?" said George.

"Quite so. An inexperienced traveller hereabouts, having slaked his thirst from a water-holding vine of the forest, had a nip of rum when he got home to his plantation. Shortly afterwards he died in great agony. He had drunk, boys, from *Mimusops balata*, the juice of which coagulates and sets in alcohol. A postmortem revealed a solid rubbery cast of his intestines."

"I don't believe it!" said Eddy, his first utterance of the day. "It's all made up, like *Gulliver's Travels.*"

"And how are we finding our Swift, may one enquire?"

"I don't believe a word of it, sir."

"Ah, you're in good company there, Eddy. You and the Bishop of Connemara."

Summer found us in Bermuda, where Dalton gave a lecture proposing the island as the true setting of Shakespeare's *Tempest.* Meanwhile *Bacchante* was installed at Moresby's dockyards for a thorough scraping and a refit to set aright all the little troubles that show themselves on a maiden voyage.

Our course then lay south, via Brazil and the Argentine Republic to Tierra del Fuego. The plan was to enter the Pacific by the Straits of Magellan during the southern summer, when those waters are most tractable. Dalton had drawn up a great pedagogical tour that would take us to Chile and Peru, up the Andes to the Cyclopean ruins of Cuzco, then to the natural splendours of North America, principally the Yosemite Valley and Vancouver's Island, which we hoped to reach by May. From there we should proceed to China and Japan via the Sandwich Islands—in those days ruled by King Kalakaua, a friend of the Prince of Wales.

We began our run to Brazil in a great calm, only a few flecks of cloud above a sea of hyacinth blue. Although we made at best two or three knots under full sail, we were in no haste and boilers were unlit. Jellyfish floated around us, and a great mass the size of a house kept rolling itself out of the water, sinking, then rising again. Some thought it a colossal jellyfish, but Dalton pronounced it a monstrous squid risen from unimaginable depths.

Mother Carey's chickens wheeled in pairs, their breasts glancing yellow in the sunlight and their movements so graceful they seemed aware of us admiring their display. The seamen tempted smaller birds to alight on deck for morsels of food, whereupon the ship's cat, an old whiskerando named Gladstone, came prowling along the rail.

I painted these lazy scenes, and amused the Princes by dashing off charcoal caricatures with my right foot (a trick I mastered on youthful sketching trips with Ivry, being blessed with unusually long and supple toes). At night our wake was another Milky Way beneath the stars, and a white whale began to accompany us when we got up steam, turning and frolicking in our bow-wave as if bored with quiet seas. Such whales are rarely seen outside the polar oceans, and his presence struck me as a strange coincidence, for just recently I'd found in *Bacchante*'s library a curious romance called, with disingenuous simplicity, *The Whale*. It was written by an American who seemed to have spent a long time in the foul business of high-seas blubber-boiling, the last vocational resort of crooks, drunkards, lunatics, and renegade Quakers (the tribe to which we Hendersons belong). Yet the author was evidently a man of wide learning and rhetorical gifts.

The first time I read his tale of a madman's vendetta against Leviathan, it seemed, for all its Shakespearean and Biblical magniloquence, to be about a man trying to kill a whale. On a second reading the following year (for it was one of few volumes aboard *Bacchante* neither endorsed nor purged by the censorious Dalton, hence doubly precious) I concluded that whatever the confounded *Whale* was about it was certainly *not* about a man trying to kill a whale. What have we here? thought I, like Trinculo: a man or a fish?

Calm weather stayed with us to the equator. Here in mid-ocean we were to rendezvous with other Navy ships to form a Training Squadron, whose joint purpose was to prepare for war and preserve peace by a brandishing of cannon and a showing of the flag.

As we approached the fabled Line, Captain Scott took advantage of low seas to practise with his Whitehead torpedoes. We had only six of these costly weapons aboard (£500 apiece!) and the intention was merely to run the torpedo at a target without detonating. But something caused one to go off, killing a large number of fish, which were taken on for the galley.

The Chief Engineer then entertained the Princes by laying out charges with electrical fuses attached to chunks of salt pork. Whenever one of these was seized by a shark, the charge was detonated and the monster's head blown off. Such is the wonderful vitality of these fish that their headless bodies swam on and writhed for many minutes, until devoured by their fellows. At length Captain Scott ordered the Chief to desist, ostensibly to save supplies, but I believe Dalton had protested at seeing the Lord's creatures so wantonly slaughtered.

At last a dark smear lay across the rising sun—the smoke of the *Inconstant*, hull down, arriving at our rendezvous from the Cape Verde Islands. One by one the great ships showed themselves above the curving earth: the *Inconstant* (our flagship), the *Tourmaline*, the *Carysfort*, and the *Cleopatra*. By nightfall all members of the Squadron were assembled at their stations on the dozing sea.

"What know ye of Poseidon, son of Time, sunken Ruler of Atlantis? And of Amphitrite, Queen of the Oceans, she who girds the Earth?" asked Dalton of his charges, who made no response beyond a furrowing of smooth young brows. "Tomorrow we cross the Line." He wagged a finger. "And you will meet them face to face!" Beyond that he would say nothing of what the morning held in store for all on board who had never strayed below the Equator until that day.

Neptune (as the bluejackets preferred to call Poseidon) and Amphitrite arrived about ten o'clock along the port side, dripping and bedizened in seaweed and shells and bits of stinking tentacle and fishes' tails, risen from their watery palace far beneath the waves. The King of the Sea bore a marked resemblance to a thickset bluejacket by the name of Goodfellow. Beside him, with rouged cheeks, a bosom of scallop shells, and long tresses of hempen hair, sat his shy and fluttering Queen (a diminutive boatswain's yeoman).

George wore an amused, insouciant expression. Eddy's face lit up briefly at the feminine figure, then faded. His heavy lids fell, he pursed his mouth and began to tremble.

The two Princes were blindfolded and taken below with the rest of the initiates, more than two hundred all told, myself among them. King and Queen, tridents in hand, were enthroned on some crates over the engine-room hatchway, where Captain

Scott rendered homage, handing over a tribute of jam, clay pipes, pickles, tinned sardines, and cake.

A tank was fashioned from a sail in one of the gangways, and filled with seawater to the depth of a fathom. Above this a ladder led up to an extempore stage with the "shavers" upon it. These cut-throats ran from side to side, brandishing their "razors," a rusty assortment of old cutlasses and gutting knives. One by one we novices were brought up, still blindfold, and presented to Poseidon. You then felt rough hands upon you, a nauseating gust of smelling salts, a lather of soapsuds in the face and over the body—not neglecting ears and groin—and a tumbling backwards off the platform into the tank for many duckings by Neptune's fearsome retinue. A final squirt from the fire hose, and all were pronounced shorn, washed, and enrolled in the brotherhood of the Seven Seas.

The Princes were not spared at all by the rough sovereigns of the deep. Indeed, I heard afterwards from Dalton that their handling had been tougher than mine, which he thought all to the good, especially in Eddy's case.

These light-hearted rites were destined to be soon forgotten. On the very next day a man fell to his death from the fore-topsail yard.

As is customary, the Captain and whole ship's company assembled, bareheaded, the white ensign at half mast. At sunset the body of the fallen man was carried by his messmates for a last turn of the deck beneath a Union Jack, then sent to the bottom in his hammock freighted with a cannon ball.

On the following day another man fell overboard, from

the flagship. She hove to and lowered a boat, but he could not be found.

Thus began the ill fortune that seemed to shadow *Bacchante*, and to which Prince George alluded on my visit to London two years ago when he called her an unlucky ship. I remember how these men's deaths affected him at the time; I saw his slight figure bent over the gunroom table, inking a black border on his diary page. How Eddy responded, or if he did, I do not recall.

It was as if the bright pageant of the Line, believed by sailors to bring luck, was but a bitter parody, heralding storm-clouds of misfortune. Murmurings were soon heard among the men: Neptune had taken two of us; perhaps it was not he but Death who was ushering us into southern seas.

Seven

❧ ❧

TAHITI

Arue Women's Prison

As I LOOK OVER THIS NOW, on the point of sending it off to you, I remember how I felt while writing. It was two months ago—February—a month of constant rain. I was very low. Eighty days in here. Jail was ceasing to be cruel and unusual, starting to seem cruel and normal, a torment curving over the horizon.

Bob and the Canadian consul came to see me in the "bank," the visiting room, which has a counter down the middle with a wall of bars and mesh to the ceiling. Things were going well, they claimed. Their faces said otherwise. When the consul left, Bob took my hands through a small wicket where prisoners and visitors can touch, pass cigarettes. Amazing what a charge can crackle through one's fingers. Like being thirteen again.

Our time was nearly up but Toho, the warder—a mountainous Tahitian overflowing her blue uniform and orange plastic chair—smiled as if to say, go ahead, all the world loves lovers, and

158

left us alone in the room. She'd never done this before, and I should have been grateful. But on that day, in that mood, unsure of things, especially myself, all I thought was: They know me now. *L'écrivaine*. Not a runner or a doer. They've stopped worrying Bob's going to slip me a baguette with a file inside. And I knew I didn't deserve Bob.

"Aren't you tired of coming here?"

"I'll never get tired of being with you, Liv. Wherever you are." He kissed the palm of my hand. "You're salty." He nodded at the jailer's empty chair. "Look at that!"

"They think I'm resigned. A zoo creature. They can leave the cage open and it won't leave. Spirit broken." I burst into tears. "Sorry. This is one of those days when I'd feel better if I'd actually done something. Something really nasty."

"I prefer you innocent."

"I'm not innocent." I withdrew my hand. "And it's high time you knew."

"Christ, Liv!"

"No, not that! But I'm not the nice girl you think I am."

This was the first time I told him about you. The essentials. My test of Bob's faith, of his idea of me.

"At least now you know for sure I'll never want another kid. I couldn't risk it all going wrong again—blighting others' lives."

"You shouldn't be so altruistic, Liv. Don't get hung up on what you imagine might happen to others." He was thinking the best of me, as he always does.

"It's not altruism. It's for me. I can't risk another load of guilt. I've carried this around for more than twenty years. If I add another ounce I'll sink." I took his hand and squeezed it. "I'm a shit. I should've told you all this ages ago. Long before you threw away your life and came out here."

"Nothing's been thrown away." He stroked my fingers one by one, perhaps regretfully. "I'm working on Loti's *Mariage*, remember? Not wrecking mine. You mustn't take things on yourself so much."

I didn't seem to have diminished in his eyes, or shocked him, put him off. For he answered my secret with a secret of his own: why he'd left America in 1970.

"You've heard of the Kent State shooting, right?"

"The song was everywhere when I came to Canada. 'Four Dead in Ohio.' But you already told me you left because of Vietnam."

"It was more personal than that."

Bob said he'd been a "bit of a radical," roaming from campus to campus in an old Chevrolet with a young girlfriend who wove tapestries from seashells and doghair.

"I was having the time of my life. And all for a good cause. Then the National Guard shot those kids."

"You were there?"

"Thousands of miles away. In Berkeley. I was desperate to get there for the protest. I guess I thought—" (a dry laugh, more a squeak) "—my presence would stop Nixon flattening Cambodia. But Barbara was sick. Food poisoning, she said. I dithered. Then she seemed over the worst, so I left. Driving day and night, an hour's sleep here and there on the back seat." His voice fell. "The car had no radio. I was in Denver before I knew what had happened in Ohio. I rang Barb. No answer. Eventually I raised a friend. She was in hospital. It was blood poisoning, not food. Sepsis. She must have cut herself. She was always doing that. Poor Barb had hands like a fisherman."

They hadn't any money or medical insurance. He found her in a San Francisco charity ward. He sold his car and got her moved. But Barbara died within days. Bob left the States forever, appalled at his nation and himself.

"It was hardly your fault," I said. His hands were shivering in mine.

"Oh, sure. It was the war. It was Nixon. It was America. You probably think America's a modern country. America likes to think it's the *only* modern country. It isn't. It's primitive. A land of social Darwinists who don't believe Darwin. A decent hospital won't touch you if you can't flash a credit card!

"Circumstances pile up," he went on, "and you can unpile them any way you like after. But the difference between bad luck and tragedy lies in knowing what truly matters. *When* it matters. The thing—the thing I'd give anything to change—is I didn't know that. I didn't *think*."

I followed his gaze to a gecko high on the wall, wagging its head slowly from side to side as if it had heard and sympathized. Or disapproved. There was nothing else to say. He'd gone over and over his loss, as I had mine, for twenty years.

Toho returned, sinking cautiously onto her flimsy chair, ending the confessional. Bob got up to go. We tried kissing through the wire—not something we usually did. Too many others had done it, the mesh greasy with lipstick and lushly scented *monoi*.

•   •   •

It wasn't long after this that my outlook began to improve. Alain Tremblay, the Canadian consul, began coming more often, genuine cheer in his voice. He'd managed, at last, to get his superiors in Canada to make some diplomatic noise—no easy matter, given the tender state of relations between Ottawa and Paris ever since de Gaulle's "*Québec libre*" outburst.

Alain has become a real friend, but I remember my disappointment the first time we met. I'd expected someone older, more worldly, a heavyweight—not this slight, boyish man in white suit and black polo shirt that made him look like a tropical priest. He wore a rather floral cologne and a tiny pair of wire-rimmed glasses, perched on a nose even bigger than mine. He was younger than me, and Tahiti was his first foreign posting. I couldn't take him seriously.

His English was slangy and fluent, a Montreal accent I remembered from the years at Studio D. In my despair I thought he might be a Francophile with separatist sympathies, merely going through the motions, someone who'd never rock the boat. He didn't say much that first time. Just listened (that took patience!), explained he'd have to make his own enquiries.

I needn't have worried; Alain is no Gaullist. Now he's embroiled in this sticky political mess, the resolution of which may soon get us both out of Tahiti: me home to Vancouver, and him to a more senior but less agreeable posting such as Lima or Kiev.

My problem is the people I was with. Not that they're killers. Quite the contrary. They were interested in exposing death of a different order: the slow and possibly abundant death from the nuclear mess at Moruroa Atoll, where the French government tests its bombs. I'll come to this later; but in short the authorities know perfectly well we have nothing to do with that dead girl. This isn't just my view—Consul Tremblay said so too.

"We know you're not guilty. The French know you're not guilty. This isn't about the law. Soon as I can raise enough pressure, or we get near court, they'll let you go. Though you'll have to go quietly. Nothing to the press. It's a matter of face. We bring in the press only as a last resort. In my job we catch more flies with honey than vinegar—you can say this in English?"

We were smoking our way through the Gauloises he'd brought. I'd begun to trust Alain by then, but wasn't sure I trusted his optimism. I didn't like the sound of "last resort."

"This is just theatre," he was coughing into his sleeve. "To make people like your friends think twice about poking around. And put the *Rainbow Warrior* sinking in the shade. That was a big cock-up. . . . They killed a guy. Even if they didn't mean to. And they got caught. Very embarrassing."

"I know. I've heard all about it."

"They play hardball down here. Before this they played hardball with Pouvanaa."

"With what?"

"Tahiti's Nelson Mandela. Pouvanaa a Oopa. He died about ten years ago."

"They killed him?"

"Just locked him up and threw away the key. The guy was past eighty when he died. . . . Sorry! Don't worry—you're no Pouvanaa! But they play rough here. Always have. Though they may have to lighten up if the Cold War goes away, like people are saying. Not so easy to justify this crap." He chuckled scornfully and lowered his voice. "It's a joke. All this nuclear shit going down for twenty-five years and they've got about as much fire-power as one U.S. submarine."

Alain opened a fresh pack, tapped one out for himself and passed the rest under the wire. He cocked an eyebrow. "This is all off the record, Liv. Anything I say that's worth hearing, I haven't said. Diplomats are dead men. We don't tell tales. The nearest we get to the truth is to give it a massage."

I flew back to Canada from Hitchin in September—the September before last—back to my desirably situated apartment with its panoramas of water vapour and crippling mortgage. Things I'd shipped from Tilehouse Street began to arrive: Jon's photos, his books, Henderson's papers, Mother's china. The spear took months by sea in a container.

My flat was built to save money and make the world safe for vacuum cleaners—no skirting, no picture rail, no trim around doors and windows. Economies justified by the International Style. A previous owner in bourgeois despair had added a cosmetic fireplace with fake coals and a red bulb. Above this hideous fixture I hung Frank Henderson's spear.

It is fourteen feet three inches long (4.3 metres, if that's how you think) and carved from a dense dark wood that Mother used to call ebony. She was right about the weight. How could even the burliest warrior have wielded such a thing? I had to haul it up the outside of the building with a rope and bring it in over the balcony—unlawful, no doubt, but the delivery man helped me and we got the job done without breaking glass or impaling pedestrians.

Far from lending mystique, the spear lay reproachfully on my wall, accentuating the starkness, underlining Mother's death, the dispersal of a family past; and how much I missed Tilehouse Street, its cracks and ghosts, the smell of soot, the sprung floors that foretold who was coming down a passage, into a room.

It was mid-January. The whale film had aired the night before. Bob came up with flowers and a bottle of the Widow. By then we were seeing each other discreetly about once a week.

A great success, he insisted. So did friends and colleagues who rang. But hearing their voices only depressed me. I felt guilty for neglecting them. Friendship shrinks to a string of airy promises when I'm busy. Above all, I missed my "real" friends, women I'd got to know in my twenties and left behind in Montreal. The older one gets the harder it becomes to make those friends.

My West Coast friends I've met through work: a composer who does soundtracks, a sculptor who pays her way building stage sets. And Jane, a script editor who lives nearby. It was Jane who helped me find the flat. We have lunch, jog around Stanley Park sometimes, but I haven't told anyone in Vancouver about you, or Bob.

All I could think was: What now? What next? And the answer seemed to be that I was finished, that there was no way forward except to give up my pretensions, get a waitressing job.

"Fantastic, Liv. Well done! I didn't think about whales much. Except Moby Dick. Now I care."

"Don't patronize me, Robert. Tell the truth. Was it awful? What were the ads?"

"You mean you missed it?"

"I never watch them air. The last stage I see's the rehearsal print. Can't bear it otherwise. The rehearsal print's as good as a film ever gets. It's the last cut. All the other cutting—months and months of it—you've done on a grotty old work print covered in finger-smears and scratches. Looks like shit, but that's what you work with. Till the rehearsal. For the first time it's cut from your original negative by nice ladies in silk gloves. It's shown in a beautiful auditorium with perfect sound. It's breathtaking. And everyone comes, and they are breathtaken. It's the moment of truth and beauty. So why watch it again?"

He started to speak. I put an olive in his mouth and a whisky in his hand. "Drink this and listen. When it comes out of that box in the corner there, with its muddy little screen and tinny speakers, my film's ruined. And every ten minutes someone butts in and tries to sell me Tampax."

"Give yourself a break, Liv. It looked wonderful. They weren't selling Tampax. It was four-wheel-drives and winter cruises."

"You see! You remember the fucking commercials. Cruises in a film on whales! Have you any idea how many marine mammals are carved up every year by ships' propellers? How many turtles choke to death on all the plastic bags they dump over the side? Anyway, it doesn't matter what they're selling. Everyone I know in this business feels the same. You find the best locations, the best cameraman, great music—and when it's squeezed into that horrid little frame and interrupted by inane propaganda it looks just like everything else."

"Oh," he said, taken aback. "I thought tuning in to your latest would be like walking into Duthie's and seeing your own book in the window. I never get tired of that."

His eyes were roaming, searching for a change of subject. "*That's* extraordinary. Am I so unobservant? Or wasn't it here last time?"

"Just arrived. An ancestor—well, a cousin really—brought it back from Africa in the 1890s. We've always called it the assegai."

He walked the length of the spear, taking his time.

"Awful big for an assegai. Assegais are short stabbing things with steel blades. Like the Zulus have. Take a look next time Chief Buthelezi's pals are on the news."

"Well, that's what my mother used to call it. *The assegai.* As if it mattered somehow. She was funny about it. Always said it would be mine one day. Don't know why—she'd never let me touch it."

"I've seen things like this at the museum in Honolulu. I'd say it came from the Pacific. But I don't know this stuff. We should get someone over here from anthropology. They must have an Africanist. Or there's always Dermot Hough in astronomy. . . ."

"Astronomy?"

"He collects African and Melanesian carvings. His sideline's ethno-astronomy. Ancient star maps, constellations. We have lunch at the faculty club once in a while. Trouble with Dermot is he'll talk your ear off. His students call him the Gas Giant."

Bob took his drink and went to the window, ice chiming in his glass. The setting sun had oozed through a bank of mist, a ragged fir against the redness like stitching on a wound.

"How long have you been living up here, Liv? Looking at this ocean. Isn't it time to go there? You should take a trip. You need one. Really."

"Last time I took the boat to Nanaimo a kid threw up on my shoes."

"I mean a real trip. Hawaii, Fiji. Melville's mysterious divine Pacific. The tide-beating heart of Earth! We'll go together. You come up with a film project. I'll find some writers to visit."

I was thinking: If he's alive, he's sixty-eight. If I go out there I must go and go until I reach Korea. Until I find him. Or find nothing. Or bones in a jungle. A skull and some brass buttons in a killing field.

Bob left. Night came down on the sea, the ships lighting up one by one in the roadstead, pricking the dusk on the bay. It felt good to be alone. The whale film was dead to me, and Melville with it.

I switched on the TV, hopped channels, switched off. The Hitchin books and papers were stacked in a corner, untouched except to check they'd all arrived. I picked up Jon's school atlas, the one I'd saved from Mole. On the flyleaf:

Jonathan Wyvern, Fifth Form,
Harepark School, Walden St. Lawrence,
Near Hitchin, Hertfordshire,

England, Great Britain, Europe,
The World, Solar System,
Milky Way, The Universe.

My father at eleven or twelve, locating himself at the centre
of creation, as all kids do; now lost to the world. And there, near
the back, was Korea, which I'd looked at so many times in other
atlases, and which still seemed unknowable as Madagascar or
Mongolia. I had a good cry, then got another drink. I went on
leafing through idly, hoping for something—a doodle, a scribble,
an inky fingerprint. But Jon must have been a respecter of books,
even as a boy. Or maybe he just didn't like geography. Only
Northeast Asia was smudgy, where Mother's finger had often
brushed the mountains of Korea.

The Pacific lay across the centre pages, an ocean hemi-
sphere, the cracked spine like a geological fault. A bookmark, a
blue paper or card snagged in the binding, broke loose and flut-
tered to the floor.

An airmail envelope. Jon's handwriting. Addressed to
Mother at Tilehouse Street.

The flap was partly stuck; I tore it open savagely. Inside
were two sheets, covered in small script on both sides, as if this
was all the paper he had.

Dear Vivien,

I'm alive (obviously) and safe. Aboard a copra
schooner, the *Bremerhaven*, Captain Westermann.
Typical Jerry, obliging enough but vague about his

war. You'll have had a telegram, I assume. "Missing in action." I can imagine what you're going through. So I'm posting this off at first port of call, before anything else. I'll wire as soon I can.

Your last letter's still in my pocket. It's been in the drink—hard to read now—but I know every word. Should've answered in Korea, but couldn't think what to say. Then I got overtaken by events. Still haven't the foggiest notion how to respond to what you've told me, though I'd guessed something of the sort. The trick is to think clearly about the future, and I can't seem to manage that yet. A lot will depend on how things go when we make land tomorrow.

I'll get on with the easy bit—my ditching. Nothing heroic, just ran out of juice like a young fool. Usually they sent us to the Yalu, but that morning we were scrambled south, behind our own lines. Surprise attack. Bandits on the radar. My wingman found them—cheeky sod went off and jumped a MiG.

It was early, the sun still rising. We chased them out over the China Sea, above a layer of cirrus like the skin of a goldfish. I don't miss Korea one bit, but I miss those skies. Then a MiG jumped me. First real fight in weeks. I put some daylight in his tail but nothing more.

They'd given me a Sabre—quicker kite than my Meteor but shorter range. I remembered this too late.

Sheer bloody incompetence. Hadn't slept soundly for a fortnight, but that's no excuse in war.

I carried on south, looking for Okinawa or one of our carriers, holding the best airspeed till she flamed out. She was lightheaded without fuel but steady, gliding down gracefully, the cirrus turning to floss and gone at thirty thousand. Then just open sea, the risen sun, and the Sabre falling, eerily silent, a seven-ton paper dart.

I must say, Vivien, that it was dreadfully tempting to ride down all the way. There are things you don't know—I won't go into them now—and that hissing stillness was hypnotic. I felt paralysed, or perhaps I blacked for a while. Didn't snap out till I was under five thousand. The sea saved me, the sight of it—like hammered steel coming up to smack me in the face. And I saw a steamer, a rusty old bucket, her plates blazing in the sun.

Bailed out about two thousand. First time ever—quite a shock—like being slapped with a tennis racket from a passing car. They picked me up in an hour or so. Chinese, though Red or Kuomintang I never found out. We were evens there (I'd dumped my tags). Not a word of English but great mah-jong players. Fishermen, I gathered, outward bound for the Line Islands. I wanted them to put me on a British possession, but they stuck to the high seas. (They were up to something, smuggling most likely.)

Didn't see land for weeks. So I had them hand me
over to this little schooner off the Lines. I gave the
Chinese half my parachute to make silk thingies for
their wives. Westermann says he'll take the rest for a
passage to Tahiti (if I go that far on his tub).

You'll get a better letter from me soon. There's a
lot I have to get straight in my mind. And I have to
find him, if I can. Please understand this. I mean him
no harm. It's just impossible to come so close and
pass on by. Sometimes it seems to me that my fetching up here, of all places, must be providential. Barmy
I suppose—there's so little land out here it's probably
nothing extraordinary.

No matter what, Vivien, it'll be some time before
I come home. I hadn't meant to say this yet but I'd
better get it off my chest—I'm not sure whether I *can*
come home. I need your patience. A lot of patience.
Truth is, I'm none too well. The job's rather caught
up with me. So best not to tell the girls you've heard
anything. We'll cross this one next time I write.

Kiss them for me,

Jon

PS. Westermann says Korea's over—says a truce has
held. By God, I hope he's right!

I don't know how many times I read it, swept along in a
flash-flood of emotion, revelation, joy, panic. Mother's certainty of
Jon's return made sense for the first time. She'd *known* he hadn't

died in Korea. The odds he might still be alive increased enormously, despite his talk of illness. And what of that? Once I calmed down it struck me as an excuse. The letter sounded wary, distant, even chilly. Something was wrong between them. Who the hell was this "he"? Why didn't Jon sign off with love, as he did in his earlier letters, all four? Where was the following letter—the one he promised? And why, if he never came home, didn't Mother go looking for him? (This is something I still don't know. I can't answer every question for you.) Or had Jon come back to England after all? Had there been some showdown in Hitchin, too painful for Mother to reveal?

Another pain took me by surprise, though I should have seen it coming. Suddenly I felt abandoned, not bereaved. I'm sure you know this all too well, no matter how lucky you've been with your adoptive parents. Perhaps you think I deserve a taste of it. (I agree.) It occurred to me then that any fact of Jon's survival must also be a fact of his abandonment of Lottie and me, whatever the circumstances. And of Mother of course; but she seemed implicated in both the cause and the concealment.

The letter seemed to have been written at two slightly different times, his hand spidery in his words to Mother, steadier in his telling of the crash, as if he'd copied that part from something already written, perhaps a despatch he meant to send. He'd put no date. The stamp—faded and stained, the design some tropical flower, half missing even before I tore it—seemed to be from a French territory. I could just make out . . . *ments Français d l'O* . . . And part of the postmark: . . . *aiohae.* I got a magnifying glass. The name was no clearer. But the date stood out: *19-IX-53*. He'd reached land somewhere between the Line Islands and Tahiti—perhaps Tahiti itself—two months after his crash.

I combed every place-name in the index, looking for the sequence . . . *aiohae*. Nothing. I slept fitfully that night, a sleeping pill on top of booze, but was up at six and on the doorstep of the Vancouver Library when it opened. The map room soon supplied a perfect match: Taiohae, a town on an island called Nuku Hiva, in the Marquesas group, northeast of Tahiti.

I broke the rules, ringing Bob at the English department, babbling onto his message tape. He met me for lunch at a Greek restaurant, clearly worried about my stability. The shock of my discovery had disoriented me. I couldn't think. I'd even begun to fear that the letter might turn to ashes, prove to be some sort of fake. Bob heard me out, eating steadily while my moussaka congealed. Then he examined the stamp and postmark carefully.

"You're right," he said. "It's Nuku Hiva. And the date checks out fine. The Établissements Français de l'Océanie changed their name to Polynésie Française soon after, in the mid-fifties."

He promised to write to an author he knew who lived on Tahiti, a Lars Lindqvist. "Lars owes me. He came to the Vancouver Writers' Festival a few years back on my recommendation. Why don't you draw up a list of questions for him? And he'll be the first person to see if you decide to go there. The guy's been around." The name meant nothing to me just then, but this was one of Bob's great understatements; Lindqvist had

sailed with Heyerdahl on the *Kon-Tiki* from Peru to Polynesia
in 1947.

I rang Lottie. A sleepy male voice said she was "on tour." He'd
tell her I'd called. Meanwhile I haunted the library, reading anything that might help me understand. The Marquesas were
remote, far off airline routes and shipping lanes: a thousand
miles from Tahiti, two thousand from Hawaii, three thousand
from Peru. They were rugged and sparsely inhabited. There had-
n't been an airstrip on any of them until well into the sixties.
Taiohae, capital of Nuku Hiva and the whole group, had only
eight hundred inhabitants at last count, and far fewer in 1953.
Mail from there would have taken months. Did Jon just post his
letter and sail on to Tahiti with the trading schooner? Or could
he still *be* there, incognito, a sallow old white man with a local
wife and family?

If he was there, he'd be known. Everyone's business is an
open book in a place that size. The size of a school. Even if he left
years ago, people would remember him. Then I thought of those
Japanese soldiers who wander out of the bush from time to time
on Pacific islands, still fighting a war that ended in Nagasaki.
Could Jon have hidden in the mountains? But if he'd meant to
hide, why write at all?

And how should I read this letter, anyway? How rational
was he? I recalled Mole's speculation on Jon's state of mind, that
he might have had upsetting news. What on Earth had Mother
told him? Had it cost him his sleep—and nearly his life? Was the
illness mentioned physical or mental? From what I thought I

knew of Jon, he wasn't the type to be in awe of "providence." The stuff about looking for someone—someone they both seemed to know—and "meaning no harm" became more and more worrying as I brooded on it.

Then I remembered that the Henderson papers I'd found had been hidden, or at least put away very thoroughly, presumably by Jon. Given Mother's oddness about the spear, it seemed just possible there might be some Henderson relation out in Nuku Hiva or Tahiti. A black sheep, perhaps. Or even someone connected to Mother's being "disowned."

While in the Pacific shelves I looked at spears in Munro's *Polynesian Woodwork* and Clunie's darkly brilliant *Fijian Weapons and Warfare*. There was a macabre ingenuity and range of design: multiple prongs, detachable points, poisoned barbs, sting-ray spines, and one type "formed of a wood which bursts when moist, so that it can scarcely be extracted from a wound." Nothing illustrated was exactly like Henderson's spear, but there were things similar enough that Bob had to be right: it was from the South Seas, probably the Society Islands—Tahiti and its neighbours. Just possibly it had come from further afield, from the Marquesas.

Lottie rang back at last *(Will you accept charges?)* and we ran up a huge transatlantic bill. By then I was lost in a labyrinth of betrayal and intrigue so overwrought I can scarcely retrace it for you now. Jon, I was sure, had had a nervous breakdown shortly before his crash. He'd ditched his plane on purpose, a failed suicide. Then he'd shipped Mother the spear from Nuku Hiva, a bizarre gift to stand in stead of his return. The "assegai" was Marquesan, and she'd insisted it was African to throw us off, to make us believe she knew nothing of her mad, dishonoured husband, who even now might be shuffling round an asylum in Tahiti, or France, or England.

For the first time in my life it occurred to me that my mother, by hiding all this from me, making me fatherless, was partly to blame for you. Then it came to me that I—my birth—might be to blame for what went wrong. Was I my father's daughter?

Lottie listened aghast, unnaturally silent. She didn't share my urgency and outrage. She had clearer memories of our parents' life together, had known Jon almost twice as long as I. Lottie couldn't imagine him a suicide, let alone a deserter, even from a morally repugnant war. And she swore that everything she'd said over the years about my looks was only a joke. She thought I was cracking up.

"You've just finished a film, Liv, haven't you? In a month's time you'll be on to the next one, and all this will be back in proportion. We both need time to digest." I heard her hand muffle the receiver as she called out to someone; then: "I really wish I'd burnt that sodding spear. But no matter what happened to Jon, it can't have anything to do with him. I'm positive. You may not be old enough, Liv, but I am. I can remember seeing it on that wall all my life—long before he went missing. That spear was Henderson's. Or one of the Hendersons'. Has to be."

I sat in the window, gazing at the bay and the long whaleback of Vancouver Island. A paleness was gathering on the sea, the water turning soft and white, the whiteness thickening like light on film. All at the speed of a clock's hands.

❦ ❦

For weeks on end through the early months of 1989 my view was stolen by fog. I saw little of the bay or islands, knew nothing of the ships except their didgeridoo exhaust and doleful warnings answered by the glasses in my cupboard.

Bob came over whenever he could get an afternoon or a rare evening. I'd cook for him, or he'd cook in my kitchen. We'd switch on the cosmetic fire below the spear, get gently drunk in one another's arms. He was a good listener. I wanted to be away at once, but there was no point in going to the Marquesas for a two-week trip. I had to plan for half a year, or more. My search for Jon would begin on Nuku Hiva, but it might take me anywhere. French Polynesia was far-flung and expensive. I needed real money. And I'd have to rent out the flat.

One day he brought a small gift in a paper bag, presenting it in both hands with a little Asian bow. "Maybe this'll help you think. Melville's first book. Few people know it nowadays, but during his lifetime it outsold everything else he did. It's a true story, more or less. It's about Nuku Hiva. And running away."

Typee: A Peep at Polynesian Life. A lovely old edition that must have set him back a bit. Several Widows. The endpaper was an early map of the Marquesas Islands, sketchy, almost fanciful. I studied their simple shorelines and archaic names. *Santa Christina, or Taouata; Washington Island, or Houa-houna; Marchand Island, or Nukuheva.* And on Nuku Hiva was Typee, the "cannibal valley" where Melville was held captive after jumping off a whaleship.

•   •   •

Things fell slowly into place. Lottie warmed to the idea of a South Sea "expedition," as she called it, as long as I didn't expect her to come. She still thought I was mad, but knew I'd never rest until I'd done it. We agreed to sell Jon's old bike, she insisting I take all the proceeds. "You do the search for both of us, Liv. If there's any cash left over we'll argue about it when you get back."

Bob helped me work up a film proposal on *Typee*—to get seed money for research while I was there. The centenary of Melville's death would be in '91. Two and a half years away; tight but possible. It was a good idea on its own merits, but mainly I think he wanted me to have something on hand besides my quest for Jon, something to help me through the many false leads and dead ends I was likely to find. Not to mention total failure.

Apart from this proposal, I took on nothing except short-term work that paid well—keeping the decks clear so I could leave when ready. I'd forgotten what "whoring" was like: shooting ski gear at Whistler, ordering "heroes" for frozen food commercials (heroes are those suspiciously perfect grapes, tomatoes, sticks of celery, etc., that appear in loving close-up).

I lived on pasta, saved every penny, had dreams of Melville and major studio backing. (My proposal has yet to raise riches, but it brought in a few grand from Telefilm Canada and Blue Angel, a Los Angeles soft-core outfit with conscience money to burn.) Mostly, of course, I dreamed of Jon and Mother, of old schooners and green islands, of a warplane sailing down from the sky.

Eight

❦ ❧

ENGLAND

Riverhill. October, 1899

SOON AFTER OUR EQUATORIAL RITES, we met a tall Yankee clipper running north beneath a stack of fancy sail. She signalled that yellow fever had broken out in Brazil, which did nothing to allay the grim foreboding that pervaded our ship like a noxious gas.

We avoided that country altogether, sailing on south towards the Argentine through still waters that soothed our unease. The sea grew warm and brightly phosphorescent. By night each ship had a glowing bolster at her head, and when a boat was lowered for another man overboard—saved, thank Heaven—the water ran like quicksilver from the oars. From time to time the *Inconstant* signalled us with her electric searchlight. Even when she was hull down, her powerful dots and dashes could be read from their reflection on low cloud. Most nights were crystalline, Jupiter's moons clear in the telescope and Sirius very bright, higher in the sky than I had ever seen.

The ship brushed through shoals of paper nautili, their tiny pink sails spread to the wind, and a battalion of great turtles like the shields of some mediaeval host.

Shortly before Christmas the sea turned a sickly orange. Dalton lowered a cup and bid us taste: no salt at all, only mud. Though hundreds of miles from land, we were sailing on the mighty outflow of the River Plate.

"Drink here the soil you will be walking on by spring, boys," he said to the Princes with his usual flourish. "Or should we call it autumn down here? I'll wager this red earth has washed all the way from the Andes, where Inca monuments await us!"

George and Eddy were bent over the gunroom table with their South American texts, Squier's *Peru* and Prescott's *History*. Day after day they read of the Inca Empire, of its benign character and violent overthrow, of Cuzco, the City of the Sun, and the ancient buildings still to be seen there.

The subject was plainly of greater interest to the tutor than to either of his charges. In Dalton's eye, the Incas were sandal-wearing Utopians of the first water, instructive models for the future sovereign of the British Empire. "When the *conquistadores* set foot in that strange land of Cyclopean temples sheathed in gold—finding to their amazement no beggars, no hunger, neither slavery nor money—they feared they had strayed beyond the realm of normal men into the very kingdom of the Antichrist!"

As things turned out, the boys' sole glimpse of South America was of the present, not the past. Upon reaching Montevideo, they were taken to see the great Fray Bentos factory, where a hundred cattle were killed and tinned per hour.

One of the local gauchos gave Eddy some furs he had tanned, including a jaguar and three seals. The seals, in particular, began to stink on board and attract more than their share of vermin. Over the side they went before we reached the Falklands. The jaguar would have followed, but I asked Eddy if I might have him, and rescued the great beast from many smaller ones by anointing him with carbolic.

The nocturnal jaguar is for me the most beautiful of cats, much like a leopard in the coat, but the pattern bolder, freer, more hypnotic, meandering in pools and oxbows, the stuff of moon-shadow and starlight on jungle lakes.

On January 8th, 1881, Eddy celebrated his seventeenth birthday, his second of the voyage. A large plum cake was eaten in the gunroom, slices being reserved for Dalton and myself. Then the weather turned contrary, and *Bacchante* showed her weakness as a sailer. For days on end any progress made on one watch was lost on the next. Wishing to keep plenty of coal for the Magellan Strait, where he expected to face the roaring forties, Captain Scott lit no boilers. At last the wind swung northwest, bringing with it scents of Patagonia—slaked earth, alkali, burnt grass—strange things to sniff five hundred miles from land, as we ran full sail to the Falklands.

Dalton now had the boys reading *Adventures in the Beagle,* which inspired them even less than their Peruvian studies. I myself had long wanted to see Tierra del Fuego, its strange bird life and sea mammals, and its sad remnant of humanity, whom Darwin pronounced the lowest type in the world. That natural-ist's revolutionary ideas have now carried all before them, though my uncle Frank Morris kept up a rearguard action till he died. He would not accept the mechanical Earth of Lyell and Darwin.

"So you're Morris's nephew?" Dalton said when I let this slip one day. "Good heavens! I'd no idea. I met your uncle once at Lambeth. Admirable man, profoundly devout—a great humanitarian and great naturalist, in his day. But why attack science? The Church should never have allowed itself to be drawn into that. Where was the need? Darwin has shown us the *how*. But not the *why*. God is in the why. Who can say, Henderson, that each hour of Genesis was not an aeon? Who can say that the mutation of species is anything less than the divine hand at the loom of creation? The Lord's six days are long enough for Lyell's geology."

Dalton overflowed with Darwinism each night at the wardroom table, where the spectacle of a churchman who was such a partisan for science struck many of the officers as irresistibly absurd.

"I confess I do not think much of Darwin's theory, Chaplain," opined Lieutenant Smyth, bane of the hapless tutor. "How can man be descended from ape? Surely it's the other way round. My own men, given half a chance, descend rapidly to a simian state. Were it not for my example, most would degenerate further, into swine!" A titter circulated with the port.

"I would rather acknowledge an ape as my forebear than be a clergyman careless with the truth," said Dalton nimbly, though the allusion went over the assembled heads. Smyth turned on me:

"What do you say, Henderson—you of the prehensile toes? Have we all got monkey uncles? Or are you our lone example of the Missing Link?" Inspired by a glimpse of Gladstone making off with a bit of fish, I recalled an after-dinner theme of Uncle Frank's:

"I believe the Creator's highest accomplishment to be the cat, sir. We are a hasty work, yet to be finished. But the Lord did a splendid job when He designed the cat. Us He left half done, doomed to sit round tables and wonder what He has in store."

"I am ever at a loss to understand," Dr. Turnbull struck in, "why Americans are such great evolutionists. The course of evolution from Jefferson to Hayes is evidence enough against it."

Smyth waited until the mirth occasioned by this remark subsided, then pressed his ambush on the parson:

"Let me ask you this, Chaplain. How does Darwin account for the hairiness of apes and the nakedness of Man? This we must know."

"I don't believe he does account for it," Dalton answered huffily. "Darwin makes no claim to omniscience. He has merely offered an explanation for the descent of the myriad forms of life we find on earth, including fossils. No one has advanced a better."

"Then I'll advance one now. Here's a theory of me own to explain the hairlessness of Man, which you, sir, may present to the Royal Society if you wish." Smyth snipped the end from a cigar and grinned foxily. "You see it's quite simple, Mr. Dalton. Our ancestors, through countless ages, from the cave to the castle, got a taste for naked women."

❧ ❧

Unbeknownst to the Squadron, our plans were about to change abruptly. All this time, an urgent telegram had been shadowing us from Montevideo, aboard the *Swallow*. Within minutes of her catching us at the Falklands, the Admiral hoisted the Blue Peter, fired a gun, and signalled us not west to the Pacific, but east to Cape Town forthwith. Tierra del Fuego was not to be.

This was the first time Dalton spoke his mind to me about his duties. The man was beside himself with disappointment. His ears wagged, a tic appeared beneath his right eye, and his hair (what was left of it) crawled about his scalp like a tarantula.

"I hope the Admiral realizes, Henderson, what a carefully designed programme of study for the Heir Presumptive and his brother—the better part of an entire year's curriculum, no less— has been wiped away, broken up, utterly ruined by a single confounded telegram. Goodbye, Tierra del Fuego! Goodbye, Chile and Peru! The Andes, Cuzco, Lake Titicaca—gone! All those instructive places I've been preparing the Princes to greet with informed eyes, and which they may never see again. Gone at the tick of an undersea cable! It's too vexing. No Yosemite. No Vancouver's Island—to say nought of the Sandwich Islands. All we can look forward to now is a month among icebergs, followed by goodness knows how long among Boers and Hottentots! What the deuce am I to teach the young blighters now?" He checked himself, florid with rage, panting like a horse after a canter.

"Come aft for a drink in my cabin when you get off duty, Henderson. I should like to talk this over with you calmly."

Dalton was far from calm when he opened his door to me some hours later. There was a bottle of plum brandy on his cabin table, broached at Christmas and consumed parsimoniously until this day. He waved me into a chair and handed over the last of it in a tumbler.

"Sorry about the glass. But any port in a storm, what? Or any brandy, one should say. Haha." He lifted the empty bottle to one eye and peered inside, as if into a kaleidoscope, then put it down and cleared his throat.

"I should have liked to see a wild Patagonian, Henderson. Bougainville noted that the men there urinate like women, squatting. Since the great Rousseau was himself obliged by a congenital disorder to do the same, he believed this to be the way of Natural Man." Dalton allowed himself a chuckle, then remembered why he'd asked to see me.

"What hope can there be, Lieutenant, for the improvement of the Princes—and I refer to the elder in particular—when one's best efforts count for so little?" He gave me no time to answer, for which I was glad. "If the boy was . . . adaptable, I'd worry less. This would be a nuisance, nothing more. But, if I may speak in the strictest confidence, the boy is unable to fix his attention to any subject for more than a few minutes. In short he's failing, not in one or two subjects, but in all. This thing's empty, confound it. Steward!" A schoolmasterly bellow thundered down to the pantry.

"Thing is, Henderson, I want to ask you—again, I say, in confidence—how it's going on the nautical side. Any progress there? I'd value your candid answer." The steward knocked. Dalton ordered another bottle. Once this was brought and we were alone, I said that Prince George had taken to shipboard life like a duck to water. He particularly excelled at gunnery (one of my own interests) and had, in short, made an impressive start in the life of a naval officer.

"Don't beat about the bush, there's a good fellow. It's Prince Eddy we must talk about. You know that as well as I do. What would you say if I told you that I find him sadly deficient in any habits of promptitude and method, of manliness and self-reliance? That is how he is with me. Would such a description also fit his conduct in his naval duties?"

"I wouldn't go quite that far, sir." I said, mindful of our difference in rank, still bemused at this indiscreet, bibulous Dalton—a Dalton I'd not seen.

He let out a sigh of exasperation and refilled our glasses. "How far *would* you go then?"

"It's not really for me to say, is it, sir? May I suggest you ask Captain Scott, or some of the more senior officers?"

"No use asking Scott! Know what I overheard him say the other night? 'Trouble with Dalton is he's too damned clever. And clever people get silly ideas.'" The tutor checked himself, returning to his point. "So I'm asking *you*, Henderson, because it *is* for you to say. You know these boys better than anyone on board, save myself. You're nearer in age. They're less on guard with you. From what I can see, they have begun to view you as a friend. Their relations with the senior officers are purely formal and conventional. And not one of those gentlemen would give me a straight answer anyway."

I saw then the man's isolation. Until then he'd simply been, in my eyes, one of the "brass hats." But of course he wasn't. No place is kept warm for a private tutor on a man-of-war. He was extraneous to the workings of the ship, and an annoyance. His intellectual interests and opinions found few echoes around the captain's table. Who would have risked discussing anything freely—especially on the topic of the Princes—with an odd fish like Dalton who had the ear of the Queen? This insight, and the tutor's brandy, loosened my tongue.

"My impression, since you ask, is that Prince Edward will never be cut out for the life of the sea. But surely that is not expected of him, is it, sir—as eventual heir to the throne?"

"Quite so, to a point. It matters little in the long run. Except as training. We do not teach Greek that we may speak it. We do so for the discipline it brings to the mind and the tongue. Eddy is here to learn. This is his only schooling. He must learn to be with people of all stations and walks of life. Above all he must learn to lead, to inspire. Do you see any sign that he is starting to do any of this?"

I replied that I thought the young man deeply unhappy, that he struck me as a person ill at ease—with others and with himself. That it was to these causes that the . . . dormancy of his mental and physical powers could be traced. "It's as if he has locked himself away, sir. From everything and everyone, except perhaps his brother. We need to find the key, but I confess I haven't the first idea what it might be."

"Exactly! You've put your finger on it. *Dormancy* is the word. The ability is there. Has to be. Think of the stock he comes from! It's a matter of releasing, stimulating. . . . 'Leading out,' as the Latin *educare* tells us. I believe the key to be physical. It is to physical causes that we must look for an explanation of the dormancy of his mental powers. It's with physical remedies that we'll awaken them." I feared Dalton was about to broach the subject of self-abuse, and perhaps he was but shied away from it. "There's the pity, Henderson. I'd hoped that the South American tour—when we got inland, away from the ship—might be the very thing. High altitudes are always bracing. High altitudes and exercise. All this damp air, cramped quarters, and tossing about at sea level can't be good for anyone. I'm counting on your help. We've got to get him out and about as much as possible. Walking, shooting, climbing. You and I will speak of this again when we make land."

Rumours flew about the trouble in South Africa: it was to do with the Zulus, the Basutos, or perhaps the Dutch. The official word, relayed from the *Inconstant*, was merely that we were to make a "demonstration" at the Cape of Good Hope. I was kept busy with small arms, exercising the men in firing at an old rum barrel towed astern, while Dr. Turnbull initiated them into the penetralia of bandages and tourniquets.

Most days were sunny, the wind strong enough to bowl even *Bacchante* along at a good clip. But the air was cold, a chill intimation of polar regions to starboard.

It was a strange thing to look out over the heaving waters and wonder what might lie below those liquid hills at the rim of the world. Just water and ice, the lonely haunt of birds and sprites? Or a southern continent, a strange land of a one-day year, six months of sun, six months of night? What creatures, human or inhuman, might dwell in such extremes?

I confided these thoughts to Dalton at the rail late one evening when the aurora australis had erected a great conical tent above us, its apex overhead, and a wall of turquoise gossamer streaming down to the horizon all around, as if the Lord's finger had poked a hole in the night and allowed His glory to shower upon the world.

No man, said the Chaplain, had gone further than Ross, who'd reached seventy-eight degrees South and seen twin volcanoes, Erebus and Terror, rising from a marble wall, a great barrier of ice higher than the cliffs of Dover.

"An object unlike anything in Nature seen before, Henderson! Running to the horizon for hundreds of miles on either hand! Those volcanoes, and what lies beyond, are as mysterious to us as the Atlantean pillars to the Greeks. Some believe the earth to be dimpled at the poles, because the force of gravity is there unopposed by any centrifugal throw. At the polar regions, both north and south, there may be an anomaly, a vortex, in which the laws of Nature as we know them don't apply. This weird light may be evidence of that. Who knows?"

He fell silent for a while, gazing at the spectacle surrounding us, then resumed more dreamily. I couldn't see his face. My eyes were filled by the heavenly display, now twitching and rippling like the fur of a cat when it detects a fly. His voice had a note of intensity and wonder.

"Some think that the Antarctic dimple may contain a basin of much milder climate, a landlocked sea, ringed by mountains and heated by the midnight sun, retaining its warmth throughout the polar night. It is not inconceivable that such a land could be inhabited. Down there beneath this cone of light, the world's last isolated race might have built its own peculiar civilization. Imagine! One last Eldorado, unknown to the rest of mankind, strange as the golden cities of Peru! Keats was of the view that science fills the world with explanation and drains it of mystery. But who's to say there aren't one or two surprises left? Who knows what's down there, Henderson? Who can say?"

I suppose I should have seen then what a wild romantic Dalton was, for all his learning. Denied his visit to the land of the Incas, he was inventing another at the South Pole.

⟨⟩ ⟨⟩

We raised the Cape in mid-February, having made four thousand miles in three weeks and a half. In all that distance we saw no other sail, not even a whaler. As might have been predicted, the South African emergency, a revolt of the Transvaal Boers, had died down by the time we arrived. We encountered nothing worse than a general surliness and the flying of a few Dutch flags.

Dalton declared one evening that the Boers were not innately hostile to us, but had been rendered so by high-handed British policies. Needless to say, this was not a popular view in the wardroom. (Today, as war clouds again gather over the same region, his remarks seem wise and sadly prophetic.) He added that our diversion halfway round the world had been of no use to anyone but Cape Town innkeepers and beef contractors. As for the Princes, instead of ancient temples in the Andes they had toured an ostrich farm, where 32,000 flightless birds were hard at work growing ladies' hats and boas.

"Is not an ostrich farm perhaps more useful to them, Mr. Dalton," Lord Scott replied, "in these modern times, than the obscure remains of South American savages?"

"If one thinks a trip to Billingsgate of greater worth than a tour of Rome, then I'd have to agree with you," said Dalton tartly.

"Surely we've not missed any Colosseums, have we, Reverend?"

"Italy I have seen, Captain, but not Peru. So I can't say. There's my point precisely: many have been to Rome, few have walked the lofty streets of Cuzco. I can only report on the authority of others. We have missed the ruins of vast edifices which struck such superstitious awe into the Spaniards that they believed human hands could not have raised them unless aided by the Devil! Scientific observers tell us that the world has nothing to rival the skill and accuracy displayed in the Inca masonry of Cuzco. I dare say it might have been of greater benefit for their royal highnesses to encounter such marvels, and verify such claims for themselves, than to become conversant with the husbandry of *Struthio camelus*."

⋖⋟∘ ∘⋖⋟

The onward journey from South Africa to Western Australia was the longest *Bacchante* ever made: six thousand miles in six weeks. It was also the most perilous. The southern autumn was now upon those latitudes; again we sensed the icy breath of unknown seas and lands.

"Don't you feel, sir, that we're too near the edge of the world, sir?" Prince George, nearly sixteen, said to me one morning on the quarterdeck.

"How do you mean, P.G.?"

"If we go any further we might slip off the globe into space."

"Your tutor thinks there's another world down there, a land of the midnight sun."

"Let's down helm and discover it then!"

"That's the spirit! Where's your brother?"

"Catching albatrosses, sir."

And so he was, on the poop with the Chief Engineer, a long line astern and some barbed bacon for the great hook-billed birds that scythed along the combers and circled the ship for hours without a flap; such felicitous flyers that many seamen swear the albatross sleeps on the wind.

It saddened me to see them killed for nothing more than idle sport and the long hollow wing-bones from which young bluejackets make pipestems. All the albatross-catchers were youths, mocking the superstition of their elders. The latter shook their heads, saying the bird was a bringer of kind winds, and no good ever came of killing her.

"Look, sir!" Eddy called, measuring the span of the biggest he'd snared. "A beauty, what? Nine feet from tip to tip!" Torn between joy to see him so animated, and sorrow at its cause, I replied:

"But no sweet bird did follow,
Nor any day for food or play
Came to the mariners' hollo!

"And I had done a hellish thing,
And it would work 'em woe:
For all averred, I had killed the bird
That made the breeze to blow."

"I *say*, sir!" said Eddy with a frown. "I say, why care a fig for the wind when we've got steam?" The Chief Engineer nodded ingratiatingly.

"It never pays to tempt the Fates at sea, Midshipman. Steam engines have been known to break down. Is that not so, Chief?"

"Not these! Never. Your Rennies are built like the Rock of Gibraltar."

Well, the engines did not break. But the fair wind turned foul within hours of the murder of the bird that made the breeze to blow.

It came up stronger and colder, a steady blast off the unknown continent of ice. For a day *Bacchante* ran carefree before it with her canvas tight, 220 miles, her best day's run under sail. Then the wind rose to Force 10, and more in the squalls. The ship rolled heavily, thick seas sweeping her deck like a tidal bore. A wave filled the port cutter and washed it away. Another took the starboard cutter and hurled it against the mizzen rigging. A mainsail split, and every foot of canvas had to be struck, except a close-reefed jib for steering way.

By dusk we had lost sight of the Squadron.

I remember that night as magnificent and terrible. A full moon raced high above, throwing a wan intermittent light on frothing waters, through clouds like the roiling smoke of some industrial fire. I had never seen waves of such amplitude: fifty or sixty feet from crest to trough. Dwarfed by these mountains, *Bacchante* seemed a mere leaf, now sunk in a rapid with only her masts to be seen, now raised on a peak and leaping like a trout from the seas.

The noise was deafening, a venomous hiss above the moan of rigging and the Gatling clap of failing canvas. The last jib tore free and flew into the night. Then came the moment of truth for our untried ship. Every man on board held his breath, waiting for *Bacchante* to reveal her natural tendency.

A dozen hands were on the wheel but their efforts made no difference. Slowly and helplessly she broached-to, offering her side to the seas. The Princes, sheltering in their cabin under the poop, said later that they felt a strange grinding beneath the screw, as if we had struck a rock or shoal, though that was impossible in these deeps.

Had she stayed as she was, the waves would have stove the deck to matchwood. Luckily she chose, very slowly, to come up and lie-to, as if she knew this was her only hope. The only hope for every soul on board—and for England's royal line.

Another day and night she knocked about, head near the wind, until steam could be got up and the screw lowered. But even under power she'd neither answer helm nor fall off. Her rudder had broken, twisted sideways by a colossal sea, or floating wreckage, or perhaps by one of the giant whales known to exist in those waters.

❖ ❖

Temporary steering-gear was jury-rigged, and *Bacchante* limped on to King George's Sound. Because she needed extensive repair work in a Melbourne drydock, we spent more than three months in Australia. Dalton applied himself to finding manly excursions for his royal pupils. These included quail shooting, a kangaroo hunt (with subsequent consumption of kangaroo-tail soup), and a descent into a gold mine, the boys dressed in miner's rig.

After a dinner at Melbourne Town Hall, the mayor produced the home-made armour of Ned Kelly, an audacious horse thief and bushranger hanged that year. It was rudely made from ploughshares, pocked by police bullets, and weighed a hundred pounds. Kelly must have been a tough bandit indeed to have worn that portable oven amid the heat and flies of the Australian bush.

The Princes tried it on, staggering about under its weight like drunken knights. George, who can't have weighed more than the armour, had a particularly hard time, though as usual he outdid his elder brother, who called piteously from within for the helmet to be taken off him after only a few seconds.

The obligatory factory tour was Alcock's Billiard Works. Dalton, the boys, and I played doubles, after which the Princes were presented with their cues. Eddy stammered a speech of thanks, saying that these would be taken to Sandringham and always used there. But he passed his to me a few days later, having no interest in the game.

Ever since I'd asked for the malodorous jaguar, my cabin had become P.E.'s first resort for disposal of unwanted gifts. Noticing my growing collection of royal cast-offs, Dalton remarked that my quarters were littered with bits and bobs "like a jackdaw's nest." This tickled Prince George, perhaps for the apt allusion to my beak. Hence my nickname. During the long months ashore in Australia the easy informality of that land seeped into our relations; naval discipline was much relaxed between us. When not on duty or official business, I became Jackdaw to them, and they Eddy and George to me.

❧ ❧

In July we boarded *Inconstant* for an excursion to Hobart, Tasmania, a delightful sunny town beneath dark mountains with a powdering of snow. There was a row of noisy "pubs" along the waterfront, which grew much noisier once we docked. In one of these, a few years back, the last pure-blood Tasmanian man, a whaler named William Lanney, died of flux at thirty-four (an intelligence that haunted me later during my own bouts with dysentery). Several dockland characters with whom I shared an ale remembered him well. To them "King Billy" was a jovial, full-bearded fellow; in short, a seaman much like any other. But certain scientists supposed his race to be the last of the Cavemen remaining from the Age of Ice. There was an unseemly scuffle among these gentlemen to secure the Tasmanian's skull and bones.

Here, away from the ship and in a sparsely peopled land about as far from Britain as one can get without leaving Earth, Eddy began to relax and open up. People may have thought him simple and backward, but as one got to know him, one realized that though he was no genius and was certainly young for his age—always preferring young company—it was shyness that crippled him. That and the related fear of appearing stupid.

When he could forget himself, as it were, one saw qualities of spontaneity and good humour, a complete lack of any

197

royal "side." At such times it was easy to forget he was the Heir Presumptive. I recall a private dinner in Hobart given one night by the owner of a large sheep station and his son, whom Eddy had known in England. The Prince was perfectly at ease with this young man, and vice versa. We junior members of the company were in an ante-room, gaily helping ourselves to drinks. The Prince presumed to retail some second-hand advice (from Dalton) about the rearing of lambs. His friend replied in a jovial manner, "You stick to the soda siphon, dear chap, and don't try to teach your granny to suck eggs," remembering all too late who Eddy's grandmother was! I, too, felt so at ease that I scarcely noted what had been said until the poor fellow released a torrent of apology. But Eddy stopped him with a loud guffaw, greatly amused.

A few days later the same young man, on Dalton's suggestion, got up a party of us to hunt Tasmanian tiger on his father's estate. Assuming we were after a real tiger, or at least some sort of big cat, I was a little surprised at the amateur manner we strolled about on the high pastures, where a number of horribly mutilated sheep carcasses bore witness to the tigers' work.

It was strange country, hilly with bare ribs of rock and great eucalyptus dotted about like oaks in an English deer park. The hills had been shorn of their woods by settlers, and these spreading trees were the lonely survivors, filling the air with the scent of a bronchial remedy. The local "deer" were kangaroos, thicker-coated than those seen on the Australian mainland. The sight of them bouncing across this pastoral landscape in thirty-foot leaps was at once comical and unsettling.

Whenever I strayed outside Australia's cities I was struck by the force of what Darwin terms a "second creation." Every tree, animal, bird, and flower was ineffably strange. Even the light was unique, and the smells, the hue of the desert, the shape of the hills. One felt magically transported to another world or time.

"I fancy I should pinch myself." I remarked to Dalton, "All this. . . ."

He understood me perfectly. "Cardinal Newman used to say, when he visited the Eternal City, that in order to grasp the *genius loci* it helped him to mutter aloud as he walked the streets, *This is Rome, this is Rome!* Perhaps you and I should be uttering, *This is Australia, this is Australia!*"

"Tiger!" The yell went up. I glimpsed something like a huge pariah dog sloping off into the bush. There came more shouts. Eddy, who was some distance from me, raised his gun. Several weapons were discharged. "First blood to the Prince!" exclaimed a beater, a rough-looking fellow with a spade beard and the hands of a gorilla. "Well done, yer 'ighness, sir!"

The creature was lying on its side, as if resting, but it was nearly dead—shot through a lung. A pink foam of breath and blood issued from a nostril onto the grass. I doubted the shot was Eddy's, but he dropped to the ground and pressed his cheek against the dying body, his eyes closed in reverie, as if embracing a fallen comrade or a stricken wife.

It seemed an impossible or mythological beast, a cross between tiger and wolf, with some admixture of hyena, powerfully built, with a long jaw hinged so wide it resembled the maw of a python about to swallow a pig. Across the back were a dozen

199

bold stripes, continuing around a thick ringed tail as long as the body itself.

What I remember most clearly are its eyes: great black nocturnal eyes, bulging and deeply sad, already congealed with death like the eyes of a mouse one finds in a trap in the morning.

"I say, what a queer tiger!" Eddy got up and prodded the corpse with his gun, rousing Dalton from a scientific meditation.

"This is no cat, Eddy. And no wolf. The Tasmanian tiger is unique. Only the Latin is specific. *Thylacinus cynocephalus.*"

"Some call it the zebra-wolf . . . for the stripes, like," the beater added helpfully. "And I've 'eard 'em call it the nightmare-wolf, seein' as how it kills at night. Savage bastards these are. But gettin' thinner every year, I'm pleased to say. Thanks to sportsmen like yerself, sirs, and the gover'mint bounty. Take the 'ead off a sheep in one bite, they will, and leave the rest for the devils."

"Extraordinary!" Dalton was crouched beside the corpse, examining it minutely. "Extraordinary! Remind you of anything, P.E.? Something else that dwells in Australia?"

"What's that wild dog, sir? Drongo? Is this a drongo, sir?"

A bray of mirth escaped from the beater. "Them dogs is called dingos, yer 'ighness. There ain't none in Tassie, anyhow. A drongo . . . now that's somethin' else."

"What this gentleman tells you is correct, Eddy. The dingo is a true mammal, introduced from the Asian landmass by the Aborigines in relatively recent times. It never reached Tasmania, which may explain the presence here of this living fossil. This creature you have so skilfully shot is a purely autochthonous great carnivore, utterly unrelated to any other on the planet. Indeed,

the true tiger is closer kin to you and me, Eddy, than to this mar-
supial. Does that surprise you?"

The Prince, who seldom answered his tutor's rhetorical
questions, merely looked lost, as if he'd like to be somewhere else
or had, in his mind, already gone there.

Now the skin had been nimbly removed by one of the guides.
Eddy's prize was a female. Deep inside her silky pouch were three
tiny pups, naked and pink, the size of a human baby's finger, still fastened on their mother's severed teats. One by one, the beater
crushed them in his hand.

Nine

TAHITI

Arue Prison

AT TWO IN THE MORNING FAAA AIRPORT seemed a small, hot Marseilles. The red-eye flight from Los Angeles was packed and overheated. I was tired and sweaty, the thick T-shirt under my denim shift a mistake. I lay on the foreshore of sleep with dank memories of Lumley, as I've told you.

It seemed that card-carrying Anglo-Saxons were not really welcome in Tahiti. The officials—all white men—clearly would rather have been elsewhere. Admitting me to their country (whose country, actually?) was an exasperating inconvenience keeping them from imported wines and local mistresses. Young Tahitian vahines walked along the passport queue planting intensely scented gardenias behind visitors' ears. The girls were bored, and my first thought was that the bloom might contain a bugging device to detect insulting remarks directed at *la patrie*. But to be fair, it was two o'clock in the morning.

The officer said something in a lovely rolling language I'd never heard before. Perhaps the warm way I was dressed made him take me for a local, or was it my colour? The Vancouver summer had been fine, I'd ripened in the sun. Where did I fit in? With the jaundiced French, the *café-au-lait* Tahitians, or the *Demis*, the people in between? Maybe he thought I was a Demi.

Bloodshot eyes travelled up from my photo to my face and back several times, not hurrying over my chest on the way. He was short, his face pinched and suspicious, in a kepi complete with flap over his neck. A Legionnaire from a *Tintin* cartoon. He spoke again, this time in rapid French. I asked if there was some-one who spoke English.

"*Vous êtes Canadienne, non?*" He arched an eyebrow, imply-ing that all Canadians spoke French, or if they didn't, they should.

I was taken to a small room where laborious inspections were in progress. Large beetles were flying at the lights. Perhaps I was singled out because of my backpack and camping supplies. A customs man—also French, but without kepi—unrolled my tent, mosquito net, and sleeping pad; he took out my freeze-dried tandoori chicken and spaghetti. All this I'd brought for Nuku Hiva. A tent, I'd been warned, would be essential. There were few places to stay, it rained a lot, and the island had deadly centipedes as big as bacon rashers (Melville nearly lost his leg to one). Bob had bought me the camping gear himself months ago, at a store on Robson advertising its sale with *Now Is the Winter of Our Discount Tents*, a slogan no English prof could resist.

I missed him already. Term was starting soon. Bob wouldn't be able to join me for three or four months. The plan was that I'd get my travelling done, and he'd come early in December on "research." His wife would want him back for Christmas.

The man sliced open one of my factory-sealed dinners and spread the powdery contents on a tray, a Gauloise-yellow finger stirring wizened peas and orange flecks of carrot. He asked if I smoked marijuana, and suggested I might have to take off my clothes. I pretended I hadn't understood.

"Is this really necessary?" I said in my most English English, pointing furiously at my ruined food. "Haven't you got dogs? If you're looking for drugs why don't you use dogs? In Canada we use dogs."

"Dogs! Pah! We are more smartair than Canadian dogs."

He stuffed everything roughly into my pack.

"Aroha!" He let me go.

A taxi driver, larcenous but genial, took me to an overgrown hotel at the end of the Papeete waterfront—a relic of the thirties, thatched bungalows rotting amid hibiscus and bougainvillea. It seemed a refuge from the endless traffic, the pulsing disco of the sailors' bars. I liked the thought that my father might have seen this place, even stayed here. And the only alternative was a concrete box with a clattering air-conditioner at twice the price.

It's no good dropping out of the sky to a strange town in the middle of the night. I was disoriented, and dazed from the long flight. *What now?* I sipped Scotch and combed through the phone book till I fell asleep. No Wyverns in all French Polynesia.

Next morning I rang the only Henderson, who turned out to be a Mormon missionary from the States. Mormons are often well informed about genealogy, so I let him invite me for a lemonade. But he knew of no other Hendersons in Tahiti, past or present. What he wanted were my Henderson's details, so Frank could be posthumously baptized a Latter-day Saint. I did not oblige.

On the following day I met Lars Lindqvist, Bob's writer friend, for lunch out of town at the Taharaa Hotel. He'd picked the place not for its luxury, he said, but to show me Tahiti at its best.

"I suppose, Miss Wyvern, that you are already disappointed. Everyone is. The real place seldom lives up to outsiders' expectations. Especially men's."

"This comes close. But yes—I was getting off on the wrong foot." The Tahiti I'd seen so far was a wearing place, a small noisy city and an endless suburb, a two-strand necklace of bungalows along the coastal road. I rode buses through places that sounded like Gauguin titles—Te Rua Mao, Punaauia, Taata, Arue—but saw little open country. Occasionally I caught a glimpse of wild slopes, a pelt of vegetation climbing thousands of feet to a smoke-ring of cloud on Orohena's cone. Up there might be the old Tahiti, twilit glens and waterfalls, giant trees and rotting idols smothered in moss and orchids.

The dining terrace was on a bluff overlooking Matavai Bay, where Wallis, Cook and Bligh had anchored. My eyes must also have roamed inland, up over coconuts and mango trees to Orohena and its clouds. Perhaps I glimpsed the dark stone fortress where I'm sitting now. But I don't remember. Not eight months ago, and it seems eight years.

Nobody had called me Miss in a long time. I liked Lindqvist's elderly voice, its burled tone of sympathy and Scandinavian reserve. I also liked his written voice, from books of his that Bob had lent me—works of history, anthropology, and devastating polemics against nuclear testing in the waters he'd got to know from the deck of a raft, just two years after Hiroshima. Past seventy now, he had the beard, face and skull of a porcelain Confucius, his skin translucent, islanded with tiny moles; and sea eyes, cobalt or grey depending on the light. He was wearing a white T-shirt, khaki shorts, and lime-green flip-flops.

"Tahiti is a land of the past, Miss Wyvern. And it always has been." We clicked glasses. "Everyone will say to you, 'Ah, if only you could have seen this place thirty years ago!' Before the bombs. Before Papeete became a *boom* town." (He chuckled at his pun, which sounded rehearsed.) "And this is true. But when I first came here—back in '47—everyone said to me then, 'Ah, you should have seen this place thirty years ago!'"

I mentioned something I'd read while looking into spears: as early as the 1790s, Captain George Vancouver had complained about the Tahitians neglecting their genuine crafts to make rubbishy souvenirs for sailors. "Yes!" Lindqvist laughed and nodded at a wooden tiki guarding the cash register. "Tahiti invented airport art."

I'd sent him everything I knew about my father. I still hoped he might suddenly recall meeting Jon or hearing of him, though he'd told me in a letter that he didn't.

"I've been in Stockholm a lot lately. My wife's still there. Her sister's unwell. I haven't been able to do much for you, I'm afraid. I suggest you start at the Port Authority. Every ship that comes is entered in a register. There should be a record of the *Bremerhaven*." He dabbed his chin with an immaculate white napkin. "No. Records so old will be in the archives at the museum. Speak to Alphonse Manu. Tell him I sent you."

As I left I gave him the calling cards Bob had suggested, a bottle of aquavit and a film I made years ago about the Dew Line, a string of missile warning stations built across the Canadian Arctic by the Americans. I wasn't allowed in those radar bases, but I'd managed to film their spoor—middens of rusting drums and frozen garbage strewn over the ice. A biologist had found that the livers of polar bears were toxic waste sites, riddled with PCBs.

"These things are everywhere," said Lindqvist glumly. "In Peru they say that each night God cleans up the mess men make by day. But this is no longer true. I think we make too much. Even for God."

⋘ ⋙

Alphonse Manu came out of a back room at the Tahiti Museum, blinking in the sunlight splashed across the patio. He addressed me in Tahitian, then apologized in English for the mistake. I was getting used to this and rather liking it.

We found her quickly: the *Bremerhaven*, Apia, *goélette*, H. Westermann. She had arrived in Papeete on October 17, 1953, from Fakarava in the Tuamotu atolls. Evidently she'd called at the Marquesas before that, but the records gave only her last port of call and her next. On October 26th she'd left Tahiti for

Aitutaki in the Cook Islands. My heart shrank at the enormity of the Pacific and my task. Might Jon have stayed aboard until the Cooks, a British territory? And where might the schooner have gone next: Tonga, Fiji, New Zealand?

"What about police and immigration records? My father might have been detained here. I don't think he had any proof of identity or nationality."

"I wish we had these informations!" Alphonse Manu spread his hands in a Gallic gesture of regret and sympathy. "But these are not like shipping. Not open to the public. Papers that old, if they exist, will be in Paris. Have you tried the British consulate?"

I had; the consul was away on urgent business. (Later, after my arrest, I had a languid visit from Her Majesty's representative, an Etonian with schoolboy French. He spends most of his time in a mountain valley where, *on dit*, he grows orchids and beds underage girls in a hut stocked with fine editions of Shelley and Donne.)

Manu then took me through the museum galleries, waiting patiently whenever I stopped to make notes. There were no other visitors. Chickens were pecking at windfalls under a large mango tree shading a courtyard where old canoes were displayed, their planks sewn together like pieces of shoe. In boats like these, without charts or compass, the Polynesians had reached every habitable spot on half a world—the most farflung culture of antiquity. How had they known there was any land at all beyond the horizon? What made them gamble on the mere chance there might be?

I said, "It's as if they found the islands by prayer."

Manu's explanations were more mundane: "They knew the stars, the ways of winds and birds. They say a master navigator could identify currents by dipping his scrotum in the sea."

We entered the exhibition hall by the exit and worked down through time. Soon I was in the nineteenth century, among paintings of the Tahitian dynasty set up by the London Mission and its guns. More deadly were the white man's plagues. So many died of consumption in the royal household that the kings became known as *Pomare*, "Cough in the Night." Here was the last of them, Pomare V, the one who built my jail: a dandy with a pencil moustache, dressed like a Mexican general, the black pearls of his eyes boring maniacally into the lens.

Beyond him was his mother, Pomare Vahine, "Night Cough Woman," Tahiti's only queen, who reigned longer than all the men together. She'd sat for an oil painting at my age, plump but still supple and Polynesian in a pale silk dress, a red hibiscus and a tiara of gardenias on her long sleek hair. In later photos she was grimly Victorian and all in black, a sad old woman widowed by the past.

Nearby was her crown—a pantomime affair of gilt and velvet, with TAHITI spelt in big letters over the royal brow, as if both queen and subjects had to be reminded where they were.

I was glad to leave the irony of Methodists playing pope in the South Seas, and descend to first contact in the 1760s. The Tahitians had formed a theory about the *popaa* race: the gods had blessed the whites with iron but cursed them to be all one sex, roaming the sea for women until the teeth fell out of their heads. Girls swam out to the great stinking ships and gave *aroha* for a nail. Sailors pulled so many nails that the ships began falling apart.

I must have let out a whoop, for Manu was rubbing his eyes in astonishment. There, in a glass case crammed with heathen things of wood and stone, were half a dozen spears like Henderson's.

Well, not exactly alike—these were smaller, less impressive—but close enough in style to confirm that his came from the Society Islands, as he says in his last notebook. (I'll let Frank tell you about that in due course.)

Manu pronounced for me the assegai's true name: *omore*.

Like the Italian for love.

"You must not *fly* to Nuku Hiva," Lars Lindqvist said when I rang to thank him. "You must go by boat! And smaller the boat the better. You don't get seasick, do you, Miss Wyvern? Good. Come for a sunset drink next Tuesday. There will be people here who can help. And don't do too much unpacking, I think soon they will sail."

He gave me directions to his house, a kilometre number on the road around the island. It was now Thursday; I had five days on my hands—days I would otherwise have to spend badgering the air service to Nuku Hiva. They had only two flights a week, heavily booked, and couldn't find my reservation. There were also island steamers, which had replaced the schooners of my father's day. But Lindqvist's offer was much more appealing.

Months of tension and anticipation were starting to seep away. I felt free, excited, apprehensive, and at the same time very tired. I took a ferry to the neighbouring island of Moorea, a quieter place, "like Tahiti thirty years ago," someone told me. From a distance, Tahiti was magnificent, an emerald volcano on the water, conical and soft as a breast.

⋘⋙ ⋘⋙

I arrived at Lindqvist's late, after a rush-hour ride in a crush of portly Polynesians, trussed chickens, carrier bags, wicker hats and baskets. The bus went on its way in a whirlwind of smoke and noise, leaving me on the kerb. French commuters shot by in Renaults and Citroëns, gripping their steering-wheels with metropolitan ennui. The air was a sultry mix of fruit, seaweed, exhaust, coconut oil. My dress was sticking to my skin, underwear showing through. I felt hot, smelly, and indecent. Somehow Tahitian girls could ride two-up on a scooter and look gorgeous, not even ruffling the flowers in their hair.

A pair of high wooden gates set in a mossy breeze-block wall. I pressed a button corroded by salt air. The result was an explosion of large hounds, who hurled themselves at the gate and bayed on their hind legs, sending flecks of drool over the top. Then a few gruff Nordic words. The dogs settled, the gate shrieked on its hinges.

"Come! Come! Sorry about my watchdogs. But we need them, you know. Even out here." The old man's papery hand, mapped with blue, patted the Dalmatians' heads and reached for mine. He kissed my cheeks in the French way. "We are sitting in the library. Come!" He was wearing a faded red T-shirt and blue bathing trunks. I stopped worrying about my dress.

He walked briskly for his age, past the main house and across a lawn bordered with crotons. The land sloped down to a beach where piles of coconut husk were smouldering to drive away mosquitoes. The dogs lay down under a breadfruit, duty done, chins on paws. Lars looked at them indulgently. "It is true what is said about Dalmatians. Either they have spots or they have brains. These have spots."

His library was a small elegant building like a cricket pavilion. Light strained through wooden louvres onto bookshelves and wicker furniture. Books were interleaved like sleeping lovers across the mahogany floor. There was a musk of paper and glue slowly dissolving in the humid air.

A couple rose to greet me, perhaps late twenties: a man in frayed cut-offs, a slim woman with dark bobbed hair, bare feet, and a short black dress—the sort that makes you look more naked and alluring than if you have nothing on at all. I thought: She must have bought that here and I want one. She looked French, and had a French name—Natalie—but her "Glad to know ya, Liv" was pure Australian. Simon, her boyfriend, was also from New South Wales, an unkempt redhead "into molluscs."

"These two are leaving soon for Nuku Hiva," Lars added breathily. "Where Melville deserted! And where I deeply wish you will find what you are looking for. Taiohae Bay! By sea! What more can you ask, Miss Wyvern?"

"Liv, please." Evidently Lindqvist hadn't told them about Jon. I was grateful. It seemed too intimate a thing to reveal then.

I mentioned my interest in Melville and Henderson, adding only that my father had been to Nuku Hiva in the fifties, by schooner, and I'd always wanted to do the same.

"Before this goes any further, I'd better admit I know next to nothing about sailing. How long will it take you to get there? I've really no idea."

"Neither have we," said Natalie, glancing at Simon.

"All depends on winds," he said. "Could be anywhere from ten days to thirty. Hope you're not in a rush."

Lars produced a tray of beer. "Now we watch the sunset. This isn't the North. Or the South." (Smiling at the Australians.) "In these latitudes, if you blink you miss it." He was right. The low sun slipped from a bank of cloud, looking for a moment like a crescent moon on its back. Then it swelled to a magenta disc and melted onto the sea. We sat quietly, sipping thin Tahitian lager, our eyes adapting to the sudden dusk. I could hardly see the others or make out the spines of books. At length, Lars lit an oil lamp that hung above the table, and the old titles on history and exploration in half a dozen languages reappeared around us like benign ancestors.

Natalie had recently qualified as a GP, Simon was finishing a thesis. Something to do with snails. He was also an experienced sailor, with a master's ticket. And there was a third member of their crew not present, an islander with relatives in Papeete.

"How's your French?" Lars asked me, his pale eyes flashing in the lamplight.

"Not so good, I'm afraid."

"Good! This is good. Make sure you speak it very badly on Tahiti. Some of the local boys are . . . patriots. They like French money, but that doesn't mean they like the French. Three soldiers went to hospital last week. They won't bother Anglo-Saxons or Scandinavians so long as they can tell the difference. The French have made their colonies disappear by metafiction. *Mais non!* We have no colonies, they are all indivisible parts of France. A deputy in Paris and *voilà*, democracy. But things could be worse. Tahiti is not yet Hawaii."

I remarked how anachronistic it felt to be in a colonial possession. One can argue that most of the world's a de facto colony these days, but this was the real thing—a quaint affair of white officials in crisp uniforms, of flags raised and lowered beside palm trees.

"Basically they buy the locals off," Natalie said. "Subsidized Camembert and Vichy water in every tin-roof shop. Costs Paris a fortune. But if they gave Polynesia back they'd have nowhere to let off their bombs, poor dears."

"The cargo cult of Camembert!" said Lars. "We say to the French, if your bombs are so safe as you claim, why don't you let them off in France? And they reply, *But this is France!*"

A gecko began chirruping above us. I noticed a faded black-and-white photo on the wall behind his chair. "Is that the *Kon-Tiki*?"

"In final moments. A sad day. A painful one, too. I still have the coral scars." He went over to a map on the wall, tapping a worn spot. "Raroia Atoll. One of the Tuamotus. Old sailors called them the Dangerous Isles. With reason! They're so flat you can't see them coming." He uncapped more beer and handed it round, his eyes returning to the photo, tracked and eaten by tiny insects behind the glass.

"Last of the Inca ships. Of course, ours was small. Just for six. Pizarro saw ones that carried crews of twenty, and thirty tons of freight."

"How did you know what Inca ships looked like? Did the Spaniards leave descriptions?"

"Ha! A filmer's question! No, they didn't. They didn't even describe the gold very well. Only its weight. But smaller craft of the same type were still in use last century. Lucky for us, von Humboldt made good drawings. We did what we could to copy him."

"So you had no idea it would work?"

"Quite so. It was a tough trip! A heavy sea would wash through the deck-house. Through our bunks. But she handled better than anyone thought. Even we, and we were the believers. If we hadn't hit that reef we might have gone all the way to New Zealand!"

"Our boat's a white man's boat," Simon cut in, Lars taking on the ruffled look of someone seldom interrupted. "Fifty-two-footer. Bar fridge. Propane galley. And a flush head, you'll be relieved to hear. She *is* old, one of the last of the South Seas schooners. Built in Fiji about forty years ago. Old-fashioned even then. A rich bloke bought her recently and refitted her as a yacht. Rig's pretty much original. Two masts, gaffs, three jibs. Wants four to sail her, especially what we're doing, beating against the trades. Till now we've been a hand short, though Vatu—you'll meet him when we sail—Vatu's worth two of us."

"Everyone else goes the other way." Natalie was picking a fly from her beer. "Your typical yachtie winters in California or Mexico, waits till the cyclones are over, then heads southwest. Marquesas,

215

Tahiti, Cooks, Fiji, Oz. But we silly buggers thought we'd buck the trend. The owner made it worth our while. Wants his pride and joy delivered to Nuku Hiva, so he can sail back the easy way."

"So you're like Jack Kerouac and his pals. Driving an old geezer's Cadillac flat out across America."

"S'pose we are, Liv. S'pose we are." Simon chuckled and raised his glass. "Only we're not as well behaved."

Rather diffidently, they added that their trip had a serious side. Simon hoped to gather specimens on the way. "Shellfish, squid. Anything dead or alive I can get. We'd like to know how much plutonium, tritium and other Parisian fragrances are being sprinkled about down here. The French aren't talking. You can buy fish in Papeete market that'll make a Geiger counter roar."

"You might want to sleep on this," Natalie added. "We don't expect any bother, but you never know. By the way, not a word to anyone, please. Whether you decide to come with us or not. The DGSE have very long ears."

"Who?"

"The frog CIA," said Simon. "But she'll be apples. They won't touch us in international waters."

Lars explained that the Tahitian islands were downwind from Moruroa Atoll, where the French did atmospheric tests into the 1970s, long after other nuclear powers had stopped. Fallout had even rained on descendants of the *Bounty* mutineers at Pitcairn Island, a thousand kilometres upwind. Underground tests were continuing, about one a month.

He said that atolls—unstable crusts of coral on the lips of undersea volcanoes—were about the worst geological formation one could pick for nuclear tests. Bikini Atoll, in the Marshalls, had been blown in two by an early American bomb. The French tests were smaller, but after more than a hundred blasts their testing sites were "like crushed meringue," leaking radiation and plutonium from countless cracks and pores. They were also sinking fast. Hurricanes had swept right over them, washing stockpiled waste into the sea. No one outside the French military knew how widespread the contamination was. Hence the need for samples.

"If the French hadn't lost Algeria," he added wistfully, "this would never have happened here. They could have used the desert. Not that I wish ill on the Algerians. But I am often thinking Tahiti might still be the quiet place I found in '47." The lamp was faltering, releasing a warm kerosene smell into the room.

I'd read some of this in Lindqvist's books, but to hear him speak of it in that half-darkness, to the tolling of swells on the reef, brought an immediacy to these concerns that made my own quest seem small and self-absorbed. My interest was one man's fate; theirs the fate of an ocean, perhaps a world.

I decided to sail with the Australians. Their schooner would bring me near to Jon, to his experience in 1953. The trip would help me prepare for whatever I might find. And if nothing else it was a way to honour his memory. The risk of trouble from the authorities seemed slight. I worried more about my seamanship.

"All I know is that a sheet's a rope, not a sail. Isn't it? I sailed a dinghy a few times as a girl. But someone warned me never to mention dinghy sailing to yachtsmen."

"No drama, Liv. We'd rather have a filmmaker than a yacht bum. Yachties are two a penny round here. It's much harder to find someone you can stand listening to for weeks on end in a stuffy cabin. Reckon we can stand you. Question is, can you stand us? If you think you can, you're in."

"Then I'm in! Thank you."

Papeete waterfront, two days later. I got there early and breakfasted on *pain au chocolat* with strong coffee at a stall by the cruise docks. Traffic was squealing along the corniche. Reggae throbbed from a bar. A barefoot man was swabbing the floor, washing small tides of black water, cigarette butts, and dead beetles into the gutter.

"Ça va, Liv?"

"Atrocious accent. Coffee?"

Traffic lights changed, releasing a pack of motorbikes. "Knock yours back," Simon shouted, "and we'll head down to the marina. Lars is meeting us there. The old gaffer can't resist a lovely boat. Or a lovely woman. Reckon you turned his head."

Even from a distance the broad navy-blue hull stood out. She looked authentic, a working boat, while those lined up each side of her were plastic toys with jangly aluminium masts. She was creaking gently on the tide.

"The *Tui Marama*." Lindqvist's measured voice. "Vatu here should translate for you." A large amiable man stepped into the circle of the ship's admirers. I'd half noticed him, taken him for a bystander. Now I saw one of the most perfectly formed human beings I've ever met. In a white man his physique would have been narcissistic, the result of long hours with exercise machines.

But it was clearly natural to him, as natural as the smile—warm but reserved, no beach-boy grin.

"Miss Olivia Wyvern. Mr. Tevita Nadarivatu." We shook hands. "I'm Liv. What do I call you?"

"Vatu. Everyone calls me Vatu. Since my army days. It means Stone." The nickname, he explained in a resonant voice I wanted on film, referred to his reluctance to get up early after drinking "grog." He'd been with Fiji's UN troops in Lebanon. I noticed his T-shirt, a sort of traffic sign—a red circle with a diagonal slash enclosing a mushroom cloud; below it was the question, *When Will I Be Blown Up?* attributed to *William Faulkner, 1950, accepting his Nobel Prize.*

"Now we've got a little Lebanon of our own," Vatu added sheepishly, making it clear he didn't approve of the coup in Fiji.

"You couldn't be in better hands," Lars said. "This man speaks English, French, Fijian of course, and Tahitian."

Vatu laughed off the compliment. "Everyone in this part of the world has languages. Otherwise it's awkward when you leave home."

"Which is?"

"Suva, same as the *Tui Marama*. In Fijian her name means something like Lady Chief, like Queen. In Tahiti *Marama* means moon. All this—" he waved at the open sea outside the reef, where Moorea rose green behind a waiting tanker "—is Moana Marama, the Moon Sea. Tahitian legend. The Societies are fallen moons."

He was anthracite dark, with a high furrowed forehead and a helmet of springy hair resembling well-trimmed topiary. I'd seen engravings of men like Vatu in old books, ferocious figures with punky warpaint, stretched earlobes, and towering bouffants dyed orange and red. But he was calm and soft-spoken, with such easy manners they seemed a state of grace.

"How did you learn Tahitian?"

"The best way. My wife's Tahitian."

"Is she coming to see you off?" I glanced around for her. Tourists were admiring the boat. And I believe—this may only be hindsight—that I have an echo of a hardbitten man in slacks and aviator sunglasses, a professional of some kind, taking photographs.

"Tara's in Paris, at the Sorbonne. I've been staying with her mum and dad. They'll be down soon. We'll sail after lunch. Less traffic on the water."

Lars handed me a letter. "This came for you. I forgot it the other night." *English Department, University of British Columbia, Vancouver V6T 1Z1.* I turned aside, reeling with homesickness.

"Farewell, all. Bon voyage!" The Confucian figure glided away on his lime-green flip-flops.

❧ ❧

Smell. Not a filmmaker's long suit. A boat is a thing of smells, carrying her years about in bilges, lockers, beneath her ribs, in the hidden footings of her masts. Diesel, new paint, varnish, these were superficial. A few seasons of leisure hadn't banished thirty years of working life. Below, in strata of time, lay exhalations of pineapple and banana, drifts of cocoa, spilt rum, crushed sardines, tarred rope, tobacco coils, lye and quicklime, bully beef and withered bêche-de-mer—all that had sweltered under the *Tui Marama*'s decks. And through everything the rancid tang of copra.

Copra, bringer of cargo—knives, guns, watches, radios and calico—a life rendered into soaps and oils, like the whale. The only thing a lonely atoll has to sell. Except itself: a place to practise blowing up the world.

I'm not sure when I began to notice things were wrong. For the first few days it was calm in the evenings, the auxiliary chugging, the old ship nodding and ambling beneath us like a mule. We'd gather on the forward hatch around Vatu's *tanoa*—his kava bowl—a beautiful, bellied thing hollowed from a giant tree, the Fijian sitting regally behind it like a muscled Buddha. This was his "grog," not alcoholic but a mild opiate. He taught me the etiquette: crossed legs and upright back, the respectful handclap before accepting the coconut-shell cup, the importance of draining it in one and clapping again quietly.

I got to like the earthy taste with its numbing hint of drug. Three or four rounds before supper, one formal, showing respect for the holy plant, then a stretching of legs and stories. The South Seas! There was nowhere on earth, during those first, good days, I'd rather have been.

Natalie and Simon seemed affectionate by the bowl, knees touching, fingers interlaced on the pandanus mat that Vatu always unrolled on the hatch, Simon interested in her lecture on the pharmacology of kava (given for my benefit), she boasting of her husband, his degrees in zoology and botany, his collections, his cartoon strip for a greenie magazine.

"Show us the latest, Si," she said. He was good: the line strong, the captions making the point. Frame One: A lovely blue-white Earth orbited by an alien spacecraft, a laughable Buck Rogers thing, two squid-like creatures reclining inside and sipping cocktails with little umbrellas. "What did I tell you?" one says to the other, "the perfect honeymoon spot." Frame Two: second alien frowning, its large eye goggling through a telescope. "I thought you said this place was unspoiled. It's overrun by toolmakers! See for yourself." Frame three: close-up on factory chimneys, a traffic jam, airliners circling a congested airport. Frame four: "Don't worry, darling. That'll all be gone by the time we land. Those infestations are self-limiting."

Simon showed his work sheepishly, like a small boy ashamed of a stamp collection he's outgrowing. I saw that Natalie was being strenuously nice to him.

At breakfast next morning he was moody, giving short answers, avoiding my eye. It was a Sunday, Vatu on watch, Natalie with a week-old *Sydney Morning Herald*, bought at great price in Papeete, spread out on the doghouse table.

Simon: "Go on. Read the paper, then."

Natalie: "Sorry, you want some? Sports or Books?"

Simon: "You know perfectly well what I want. I want to talk. I like talking at breakfast. Together five years and you don't even know that. Jesus!"

"Simon, that's not fair. You know we haven't had news from home since Suva. And you know there's nothing I like better on a Sunday morning than to curl up with a coffee and spread out the paper for a quiet half hour."

"A quiet two hours, more like. Liv, you tell her. How long have we been sitting here? How long's she had her nose in that?"

"Sorry. This one's for you two to sort. I'm taking coffee up to Vatu."

"Oh, yes. Vatu. Oh yes. Fine specimen, isn't he? You should see how your tongue hangs out. It's revolting."

"Simon! Say what you like to me. But don't you ever speak to Liv like that again."

"Or what?"

"Why do you always have to be so bloody pugnacious?"

"I'm not pugnacious. I just defend my turf against habitual trespassers."

"What sort of life is it, Simon, when you see your whole existence as bits of turf to be defended?"

I didn't know Simon and Natalie well enough to judge how serious their bickering was, but it alarmed me. Only Vatu stayed the same, radiating his polite goodwill. He must have noticed things weren't right, but was too well-bred to let it show. I kept to my duties and myself, avoiding the Australians because I wanted to, avoiding Vatu because I didn't. I don't hold the agony-aunt view that the "other woman" is always a villain or fool. That's not how I see it. As Bob's other woman I was keeping that marriage alive, supplying something it lacked, for him anyway. (And for her, too, if she couldn't stand sleeping with the guy, but I didn't ask.) That said, I was hardly a social worker. I was there for my own rewards. I'd rather share an interesting man than have a dull one all to myself. But one affair like that's enough. So I treated Vatu with a formality that seemed to suit his own code of behaviour. I stayed out of his cabin; he stayed out of mine.

That night there was a storm, our first, the dark sea blossoming white under a backlit overcast. The old ship leapt and skittered until dawn, as if shrunk to a bathtoy, tiny on the waves. I felt overwhelmed, inadequate. And plain scared. I'd never seen weather like that from a boat.

❧ ❧

We thought it a turtle or a dolphin. They're often caught in driftnets, Natalie said, where if they can't surface to breathe they drown in about half an hour. If breathing is possible, they die more slowly trying to thrash free, the nylon slicing into necks and flippers.

She'd just relieved me on lookout at the masthead. Vatu thought there might be uncharted reefs. "Charts can't be trusted, Liv," he'd said. "Coral is a stone that grows." We took turns aloft, fighting nausea and hypnosis, watching for a change from green to turquoise, for a tell-tale stitch of waves. Natalie sang out again. She'd seen colour.

"Nothing. Only human. Filthy bastards."

She meant flotsam, rubbish from a ship. She'd said more than she knew.

The woman was floating face down, her yellow hair fanned and pulsing in the swell like fronds of seaweed. Her shadow lanced away through green infinity, a shaft of darkness with the outline of a bird. She wore a red shirt and white shorts. Her feet were bare, the soles very pale as she slipped by. It seemed impossible that she could be here, so far from land. We'd seen no ships or islands, not even any gulls for days.

A breath of nightmare touched my scalp and set me shivering in all that heat. Vatu started the engine and reversed, spilling the wind. Natalie was pulling on a pair of fins. "I'm going in for her. Simon, get ready to lift her over the stern. Liv, go back aloft, would you, and look for a sail. The boat she came from might still be around. Keep a sharp eye out for wreckage."

I did as I was told, swarming up the ratlines (the rope ladders between the *Tui's* shrouds), scanning through binoculars. The sea was gentle again, acting innocent. I was at the centre of a still and empty world, a bare disc drawn from the compass-tip at which I stood. The body had materialized from nothing, a sleeping beauty on the ocean fields.

The only variations were the fall of sunlight, cloud shadows, an occasional flash when a heavy swell collapsed in a grin of foam. No sail, no funnel, no smoke. Nothing but isolated clouds overhead, and larger ones growing up from the horizon on slender stalks, spreading out in caps like toadstools. We might have been the last people on Earth. On water. I think I was in shock.

A shout summoned me on deck. I helped Simon and Vatu grasp the woman by her arms and heave her up the transom. In the water she'd looked merely unconscious; out of it she was clearly dead, her buoyant repose transformed into a sodden lifelessness. Eyes staring like a doll's, sky blue, till Natalie brushed down the lids.

We laid her out beside the companionway. She looked young. Sixteen, twenty-two? The dead don't show their age like the living. Natalie knelt astride the girl, kneading her, dislodging a gush of bloody water from the lungs. I noticed Natalie's hair, how the sun had burnt a pink line along her parting. The hair shook. She inhaled sharply, a moment of horror before regaining her professional detachment.

"My God, look here. She's been hit! On the head."

She rolled the body onto its front to show us the wound, then pulled up the shirt, exposing a purple welt over most of the back. The backs of the thighs were the same. Vatu turned away, respectful of woman, of the dead. Simon began to cough, his voice narrow. "Sunburn?"

"Sunburn doesn't crack ribs. If I open her up, I'm sure I'll find internal injuries. She fell from a height. The water hit her like concrete. Or something did."

We threw hasty questions. Where could she have fallen from so hard? A mast? A cruise ship? Vatu didn't think last night's storm had been bad enough to sink anything seaworthy. "More likely a propane leak in the galley. Gas sinks more boats than weather."

"I don't think she fell from a ship at all." Simon was glaring upwards, fury in his eyes. "I say she fell from the sky. The Argies do that. When they 'disappear' people, verb transitive. Heave-ho from a chopper out at sea. She was probably a guerrilla or something. A teacher who got uppity and joined a union."

"We're a long way from Argentina, Simon," Natalie said.

"Not as far as you think. Only a couple of hours by air from Easter Island. That belongs to the Argies."

"Chile. It belongs to Chile."

"Same difference."

"We're jumping to conclusions." Vatu's resonant voice, calming. "We know very little."

The body was fresh—only hours dead—but wouldn't stay fresh much longer. It couldn't last to the nearest village, let alone a port with a police station. The *Tui*'s fridge was smaller than a TV set, enough for milk, butter and a few beers. We couldn't keep her.

"I'd like privacy for an hour or so, below," Natalie said. "I'm going to take photos, then do a post-mortem. It won't be pretty. When I've got her sewn up we'll bury her at sea. We'll keep her clothes and try to get some fingerprints. Can we find some ink, Simon? Maybe squeeze it out of a biro or something?"

The three of us sat at the bow, as far as possible from Natalie's operating slab—the doghouse table. I went aft briefly, to help with the fingerprinting. She was coolly efficient with the corpse. I wasn't; this girl was the first I'd ever seen. (Except for Mother, "at rest" in an undertaker's chapel, her make-up done all wrong.)

There'd been a flurry of words and speculations. Now no one spoke. Vatu and I studied the water for wreckage, a wallet, anything. For a time the *Tui* was adrift, head to the faint wind, sheets slack, sails jowly. A sorry bit of seamanship, had there been other eyes to see it. A ship is lovely only when she's taut. A flapping sail is a sign of tragedy, like a horse on its side.

Simon went to the wheel, let the ship fall off and gather way for steadiness while Natalie worked.

It was four o'clock when she emerged, arms bloody to the elbows, face drawn. She was wearing a yellow plastic apron that said *Captain Cook.*

"You better take a dip, sheila. Then you'll need a drink." Simon's old voice was back, amiable, confident, the voice he'd had in Tahiti. "Luff—and tots of grog all round. Real grog, Navy style. Then we'll do the honours. Anyone got a prayerbook?"

No one had, not even Vatu.

"What a mob of heathens! Still, she might be a heathen herself. Might have been. . . ." He went below and came back with a salt-rimed Bible, an Australian ensign, some glasses and a bottle of rum. "To those in peril on the sea. Bottoms up." Simon jerked his thumb at Vatu. "You and me, mate. We'll fetch her. Ladies stay on deck."

While they were below, Natalie bathed in the sea, then came forward, wringing her hair inside a towel. "You're good with words, Liv. Would you, you know . . . read something?" She put the old book in my hands. There was a purple ribbon marking Psalm 104:

O Lord my God . . .

Who layeth the beams of his chambers in the waters:
Who maketh the clouds his chariot:
Who walketh upon the wings of the wind. . . .

Who laid the foundations of the earth, that it should not be removed for ever.

Thou coveredst it with the deep as with a garment. . . .

There go the ships: there is that Leviathan, whom thou hast made to play therein. These wait all upon thee. . . .

Let the wicked be no more.
Praise ye the Lord.

The small corpse shrank quickly, weighted by a spare anchor, a paleness in the green, smaller and smaller, until it was only a writhing opalescence, a white otter diving to the bottom of the world.

Ten

⟨⟩ ⟨⟩

ENGLAND

Riverhill. October, 1899

I DID NOT WITNESS IT MYSELF, but doubt anyway that I could have adduced a rational explanation for what was seen as we sailed back to Melbourne from Tasmania. I am not mystically inclined, nor was I then. Table-rapping, ball-gazing, spirit-calling, planchette— all that seems to me sheer trickery and nonsense, unworthy of civilized beings. The Holy Ghost's as far as I go. Yet a very queer thing happened out there on the Bass Strait, and no-one, not even Reverend Dalton or the Admiral, was able to account for it.

There was little wind that night, the ships all but becalmed, and the waters of the strait, which have a well-earned name for treachery, were on their best behaviour, glittering like beaten pewter in the path of the moon. At about four a.m., a lookout shouted that "the Flying Dutchman" was across our bows.

It wasn't my watch. I was sound asleep in my bunk. Let Dalton,

230

who questioned the eye witnesses, describe what they reported: "A strange red light as of a phantom ship all aglow, in the midst of which light the masts, spars, and sails of a brig two hundred yards distant stood out in strong relief as she came up on the port bow."

The apparition was next sighted from the bridge by the officer of the watch. The quarterdeck midshipman also saw it, and was sent forward to investigate from the forecastle. But by the time he got there the thing had vanished, and nothing—no ship or light or wreckage, no fog or reflection of the moon—could offer a material source for either the glow itself or the silhouette within it. The sea was still, its surface clear and empty from our stem to the horizon.

Thirteen men all told, of varying rank and experience, saw the ghostly craft, and any suggestion that our ship might have fallen prey to collective delusion was quashed when the *Tourmaline* and *Cleopatra* flashed to report the same phenomenon, asking if we had seen it.

Unhappily, this was not the end of the strange affair. Later the same morning, the very man who had first sighted the Dutchman—a smart royal yardman, one of the best young hands aboard—fell from the foretopmast and died instantly upon striking the forecastle.

Nor did this exhaust misfortune. Within ten days the Admiral became gravely ill, obliging us to postpone our departure from Australia while he fought for his life.

❦ ❦

In August we celebrated two years on board together, and I my twenty-second birthday. Prince George gave me a sturdy pocket knife and Prince Edward a smart little cigarette case. Dalton had taken up cigarettes in Australia; Eddy and I had followed his example. George was too young, but his tutor slipped him the odd one as a reward for lessons learnt. The lid of the case bore an inscription which I recall to this day, though the gift itself became another's within weeks:

To "Jackdaw" Henderson on his birthday, from his shipmate "P.E."
Two years aboard Bacchante and twenty-two aboard this world.
August 6th, 1881.

If the style seemed Dalton's, I believe the thought was Eddy's, an example of the kindliness within him which merely needed time to emerge from its cocoon of ineffable sorrows.

Dalton was impatient to move on, as was the Admiral, winning at last his long battle with ill health. Near the end of the month the Squadron set course for Levuka, capital of the Fiji Islands. After showing the flag in this new child of the Empire, ceded only a few years past by its famous cannibal king, our orders were to proceed to Japan.

Soon we were in the tropics again, the thermometer at eighty, the wind aft, the seas lazy and aromatic. The Princes had brought aboard a young kangaroo who became very tame, begging for tidbits and coming like a dog when called. I believe it sprang ashore at Levuka, where I'm afraid one must conclude that the Fijians, promiscuous meat-eaters, could not deny themselves so singular a delicacy.

George was heartbroken, but Eddy seemed utterly indifferent to this loss, as he was to all the tokens of esteem lavished on him wherever *Bacchante* touched. Not two days after sailing he gave me his Tasmanian tiger skin, expertly tanned for him in Sydney. Nothing in life seemed to interest the Prince for more than half a day; once that brief flicker had died he was keen to rid himself of any reminder, as if he dreaded encumbrance. It was George who honoured official gifts and keepsakes, who played with the pet kangaroo.

Dalton had been sorely taxed to find improving activities for the Princes during our month at Sydney, a place offering plenty of draws in the opposite direction. He got them out of town as much as possible, up into the Blue Mountains by train, and west to the great tawny plains, greening here and there under the balm of artesian water. These downs, he declared in the crisp air of a New South Wales hilltop, gripping each Prince by the elbow like Moses showing off the Promised Land, were destined to soak up all the surfeit multitudes of Britain. One sight of the great Australian plains was enough to banish the darkest threats of Malthusianism.

"*Crescite et multiplicamini, et ingredimini super terram.* Translation, Eddy?"

At about this time I began to notice that the Princes had indeed begun to ponder human multiplication, though more the prerequisite act than the happy result. Prince George was then sixteen, Prince Edward seventeen and a half. The former's eyes were acquiring their father's well-known sparkle in female company, roving after the many pretty figures to be seen in Sydney, whether at the Governor's table or under the gaslights of the quay. Eddy was also delighted to be once again among feminine influences, but not, I believe, for the same reasons.

It could no longer be denied that Eddy's physical desires were awakening and, in his long separation from the opposite sex, seemed to be taking a predictable direction. Although I did not admit as much to those hyenas who grilled me in London, their gibes at navy life were true enough. Men at sea learn to go without women, to form friendships that may become amours. Once ashore, most sailors return to the natural appetite of male for female. A small minority do not, and Eddy seemed to be among these.

I cannot say exactly when he began to act on his desires, though I noticed a change in his manner around the time he affected a moustache. It was thin and precisely tended, like the work of a gardener for whom greenery exists only to to be cut into shapes unknown to Nature. This lean herbaceous border to Eddy's luxuriant mouth changed his expression from a vacant languor to that of the languid voluptuary; it was possible to divine a faintly sinister air, which Eddy until then really had not merited.

One afternoon I came below and spotted a young sailor furtively quitting the Princes' cabin. I rapped on the door, which was answered by Eddy as if he had been expecting someone else. His clothing was disordered, his face flushed.

"Oh, it's you, Jackdaw. Come in."

"Thank you, no. It's my watch. Did that man try to steal something? Did he offer some affront, Prince Edward?"

"Er no, Jackdaw. Rather the other way round. I gave him a shilling."

"What for, may I ask?"

"For a kiss," he said guilelessly. "Look, I should prefer to be alone. I'm not feeling quite myself. Carry on. There's a good fellow."

Taken aback by his disclosure, I was at pains to point out that since I was on duty, and we were on board a ship of the Royal Navy, "Jackdaw" and "good fellow" would not do. As for what he'd just revealed, I chose to ignore it. Kisses between men could be innocent—did not the great Nelson asked Hardy for a kiss? However, I doubted Hardy got a shilling in return.

While at sea between Australia and Fiji I attempted, in a round-about way, to broach the matter with Dalton over a whisky. But he was not prepared to explore this terrain with me. He har-rumphed and wheezed, tugged on a greying whisker, cast his gaze around my tiny cabin for another topic.

"You know there should be four, really," he said, eyeing my Three Wise Monkeys, a souvenir from Gibraltar. "In India there's always a fourth. A little fellow with a wide grin and his hands over his whatnots." He harrumphed again, suddenly aware he hadn't changed the subject after all.

"I say, I'd keep *that* if I were you, Henderson." He gestured towards Eddy's hunting trophy. "Get rid of the dratted jaguar—I can smell him all the way from my berth—but keep the marsupi-al tiger. In a few more years he'll be as rare a specimen as poor King Billy. They're dying out, you see. That's what Gould believes, and he's the man to know. It's a crying shame. If not a blasphemy! A unique, outlandish beast, condemned to extinction in our day."

At such moments I envied the Princes their teacher, having had none like him while a cadet myself, and I worried, as he did, that much of what he offered them was falling on stony ground. I kept the striped pelt with its long ringed tail; it hangs to this day (and to Ivry's disapproval) in our hall. Dalton was right about the jaguar. Carbolic could not save him. With heavy heart I flung him into the deep off New Caledonia, where he was smartly swallowed by a shark.

Our proximity to that island, a recent French acquisition, exercised Dalton in the wardroom. New Caledonia had been found, named, and claimed for Britain by Cook, he maintained, but nothing had been done to follow up. So France had hoisted her flag there without challenge a few years back, and was now busy stocking the place with felons, anarchists, and communists. The same, he said, would soon be done in the Loyalties, the Marquesas, and other possessions.

"It is France's plan to turn the Pacific into an outdoor jail for the offscourings of Paris, with all that that implies for the native islanders and our own colonies."

"Really, Dalton? How shocking!" said Smyth sarcastically. "Mightn't the French say that we *Anglais* have already done the very thing you deplore. With Australia?" He leant back in his chair and began to light an after-dinner cigar, his eyebrow cocked.

"The situations are not comparable in the least," the tutor replied hotly. "We are building a great new Britain. They are intent on nothing more than prison camps and naval stations."

Smyth harrumphed. "That sounds a touch Jesuitical to me,

Dalton. Johnny Crapaud's no different from us. What are we here
for? Same as he is. Gold and glory."

"Never underestimate the Jesuits. Or those they've schooled,
Lieutenant Smyth. That's a mistake too often made. Accuse a
Jesuit of killing ten men and a dog, and he'll produce the dog alive
and make you a liar. It is the French who are Jesuitical, for all their
half-baked atheism."

To a condescending murmur from the nautical men, Dalton
flourished an atlas to illustrate "the Gallic chess position" being
artfully deployed across the Pacific whilst our squadron was
"yachting about like millionaires." He ran a finger diagonally
across the page. "There is not now a single island group of importance between New Zealand and Panama which hasn't fallen to
France. By the time the Panama Canal is built, they'll be sitting
on every harbour and coaling station between our colonies and
America." The normal atmosphere that filled the wardroom
when Dalton mounted a hobbyhorse, one of irritable boredom,
changed visibly to interest. Smyth's cigar went out in his hand;
one could see his mind turning over strategic implications, even
as Dalton continued:

"The pity of it is, we could have had these islands for the
asking. Time and again the natives begged us for protection.
Gladstone's government rebuffed them. The French, though, have
lost no time. In the past year alone they've taken over Tahiti and
Moorea—islands where the missions and trade have been in
English hands from the start, where English was, until lately, the
language spoken by every educated native, and where the British
consul's word was next to law! Islands whose chiefs and sovereigns

have repeatedly asked for the right to hoist the Union Jack. Their pleas fell on penny-wise ears in London. Now we see the cost!"

No doubt it was a surprise for them to hear Dalton, the radical, voicing support for Disraeli, Empire, and the Tory party. I believe the explanation is that the tutor took his cue from the Queen. As is well known, Her Majesty and Disraeli used to get along like a house on fire; the same could not be said of Mr. Gladstone. Dalton's socialist leanings were subordinate to his imperialism. Like Disraeli, he saw a moral imperative for empire. The British were the instrument of Providence. If, at times, we were despotic, this was in the long run for the best, a firm paternal hand, a benign despotism like that of the ancient Incas he so admired.

But Dalton did not regard the French in the same light at all. Their actions were purely selfish, and their similar claim—their *mission civilisatrice*—was in his view a tawdry sham concocted to obscure the base motives of cynical Jesuits, godless masons, and grasping *petits bourgeois*.

Dalton's rosy view of Britain's mission could hardly have found a happier practical expression than in the Fijis. These islands had voluntarily joined the Empire after a period of misrule by various cabals of white settlers and black chiefs, culminating in the short-lived monarchy of Thakombau, Fiji's once and only king.

Nothing prepared me for the beauty of the islands, my first true glimpse of the South Seas. The coast of Viti Levu, the largest island, was steep and thickly wooded above dense mangroves. From the gleaming sea the land rose darkly to a great height, mountain piled upon mountain, gashed by ravines and dappled with rags of shadow from attendant clouds. A dark storm loured over the southeast, resting, so it seemed, on the towering throat of an extinct volcano festooned in vegetation. Here and there the island's jungle fleece was shorn away in bright green patches—the fields of the natives—and through the glass I spied a village quavering in the heat, its houses a neat ring of haystacks round a lawn.

A new capital for the colony has since been built at Suva, but our destination was Levuka, the old trading town on Ovalau, which we reached at dusk. We anchored outside the reef until dawn, then got up steam and proceeded slowly between coral heads on which the swell had seethed all night. An offshore breeze carried the fragrance of the land: spices, fruit, molasses, leafmould, cooking fires. The sun rose astern from a puddle of mist, spreading a brassy light over the bay and gilding the town's backdrop, a rough pyramid of verdant mountains with shoulders of black rock. The gimcrack buildings, weatherboard with roofs of zinc or thatch, sprawled along a ledge between water and hillside; others dotted the steep slopes behind.

In its heyday, during the cotton boom ignited by the American Civil War, Levuka became a notorious lair of gunrunners, blackbirders, beachcombers, and bush lawyers. Every second building was a tavern, and ships seeking the harbour had only to make their way up the stream of rum bottles drifting out. Land changed hands for gas-pipe muskets, whilst slavers prowled the Pacific, seizing islanders for the plantations, or, in the case of pretty girls verging on womanhood, for duties less likely to involve the cotton plant.

The harbour was dotted that day not with bottles but with shipping: three or four schooners, an old side-wheeler, gigs, dinghies, and strange sleek catamarans—my first sight of native ocean-going craft. Some had single hulls with an outrigger, others were twin-canoes linked by a deck on which stood a small cabin. Our word "canoe" fails to do them justice, for the largest held a hundred men or more. Their sails were great lateens, the yards lashed to the prow, their free ends aloft, with the spread between them giving a horned look to the craft. They came to greet us in formation, as if for war, steered by long trailing oars, ochre sails hung with white streamers snapping in the wind, and the words of a song carrying over the water—a marvellous sight, like a scene from Homer.

In the boats were tall, well-built fellows ranging in hue from deep bronze to black, their great heads of hair giving each a bushy halo in the sun. They wore boar's-tooth necklaces and not much else besides a kilt of tapa, their chests and limbs glistening with coconut oil. As their fleet neared ours, they ceased their song and gave a sudden chant in unison, a deep-throated *Woh! Woh! Woh!* that boomed like the surf.

Several high chiefs boarded the *Inconstant* and welcomed the Admiral by bestowing on him a whale's tooth, a great honour, Dalton said, equivalent to the keys of a city.

"Fiji men," he instructed the Princes, "set an importance on etiquette and ritual matched only by the Japanese, whom you will meet a little later on our voyage. Consider this a rehearsal. As in Japan, an elevated sense of honour, manners, and refinement coexisted, until recently, with a capacity for warfare of the utmost savagery. Prisoners were clubbed at the war temples, baked, and eaten in orgiastic feasts. Such behaviour was widespread only twenty years ago. In a single generation Fiji has passed from cannibalism to Christ, from the age of stone to steam. As Launcelot observes to Jessica, this making of Christians will raise the price of hogs!"

Here Dalton's noble vision of empire had been realized, a happy dream to set before Prince Eddy, future king and emperor— a dream that would soon veer into nightmare.

I do not know how long Dalton's schemes were forming in his mind. His harangues about the French imply a gestation of several months, and long before that I think he was casting around for some master-stroke that might awaken Eddy to his kingly destiny. The tutor was acutely sensible that he soon would cease to be the young heir's guiding light. When *Bacchante*'s voyage came to an end, in a year at most, Eddy would go to Oxford or Cambridge, to a sybaritic world that might undo everything Dalton had striven to achieve. His desperation stemmed from the paucity of these achievements in the two years we'd been at sea, and the knowledge that so little time remained.

However long Dalton's plan may have been germinating, events conspired to ripen it swiftly at Levuka. There was a lot of coming and going—messages too important to be entrusted to subordinates and clerks—for I saw him hurrying along the waterfront between the dock and Government House, rain or shine (and it rained a great deal). But I do not think Dalton would ever have had the drive to put his plan into action, and to make others help or at least acquiesce, without the example and inspiration of the old man Thakombau, Fiji's erstwhile King.

I do not mean that Thakombau was party to the plan in any way, merely that he had a galvanizing effect. Looking back on it now, nearly twenty years later, the whole business seems quite mad. But then, on those faraway islands, in the presence of an old black king who had turned the sacrificial stone of his war temple into the baptismal font of his church, we seemed to have strayed into a cantle of the globe where the days of gods and heroes were still warm; where anything might be essayed, anything won.

Had we come a few years later, with Thakombau dead, and the map of the South Seas inked with the hues of the Great Powers, nothing could have happened. But to sit cross-legged on a mat beside a man who became chief at a feast where eighteen men were eaten—ah, that was a thing not often done! The old king was a lion, now wise and docile but once the fiercest in the forest, and the sight of him ignited in Dalton, man of books, a wild and all-consuming fire to be for once in his cold life a man of deeds.

Had Thakombau dressed as a beggar, you would still have known him for a king. He stood well over six foot, with a chest like a weightlifter's, an august brow, and a broad face with hooded eyes that seemed incapable of surprise. He must have been close to seventy years old in 1881; no one knew the year of his birth exactly. His father had been the most powerful chief in the islands, renowned as the "Hot Stone"—because his terrible oven was seldom cool.

The day we met Thakombau, a Sunday, began with the throb of large sharkskin drums carrying over the water. Some ratings joked about the locals getting hungry, but we were told these retired war-drums now did nothing more alarming than summon worshippers to church. After divine service on board, Mr. John Thurston, the country's leading European and former Chief Minister to Thakombau, came in a gig to greet us and convey the Princes, their tutor, and officers not on duty to the King's hall.

Unlike the Fijians, few of whom stood under six foot, Thurston was a midget, a wiry Scotch-terrier of a man with truculent eyes that bulged like a terrier's, and a jutting chin thicketed with beard. He said very little on this occasion. Not until later did I understand the power he wielded behind the thrones of Fiji, black and white.

The King's house was a large structure on a stone platform about two yards high. The roof was as prettily thatched as any in Suffolk but with a flaring Oriental line and heavy eaves. The walls were tightly woven of rattan in diamond patterns, and the entrance was flanked by posts topped with conch shells. We entered by a low door and were ushered crouching through the gloom to spots where we sat on the floor, it being an outrage for anyone to raise his head higher than a chief's.

The Governor, Sir William Des Voeux, came in with his wife, children, and native attendants—Fijians of rank, wearing white kilts trimmed with scarlet, a boar's tusk pendant on each sable chest, and their great frizzes of hair in red, ochre, natural black, or combinations of all three. Not until my eyes adjusted to the gloaming did I see Thakombau clearly, at the far end among his chiefs, like the king of an ebony chess set.

No garments concealed his upper body, which was that of a man half his age. He wore only a great band of tapa around his middle like a cummerbund, and below that a native kilt. His head and feet were bare. I heard that when the whites had crowned him King, lowering a cheap diadem with paste gems onto his bushy hair, the scene had been irresistibly absurd. A titter ran through the crowd and only Thakombau's great dignity of bearing prevented uproar. That same night he threw his crown in the sea.

When all were assembled, the old man gave a speech of welcome, rendered into English by Mr. Thurston. He spoke of how he had never dreamed, when he ceded Fiji to the Queen seven years ago, that his old eyes would ever live to behold her blood and sinew; for though the lands of Fiji seemed great to him, he had seen the globe that represents the world and understood how many great lands Her Majesty ruled from the rising to the setting sun, and that by comparison with all those lands, Fiji appeared no bigger than the dung of a fly.

"We were too small to stand alone on the sea any longer," Thakombau continued, looking steadfastly at Eddy through his rheumy eyes. "These islands are our riches. Tumult and strife are poverty. Many of the whites who came here were bad men, mere stalkers on the beach. If matters had remained as they were, Fiji would have become like a piece of driftwood, to be picked up by the first passer-by. I understood in my heart that if I and my chiefs did not cede Fiji to your grandmother, the white stalkers on the beach, the cormorants, would open their maws and swallow us.

"When I gave Fiji to the Queen I added a small gift. I sent her my old and favourite war club, which in war was called the 'Bloodbather' and in peace the 'Queen's Bedspread,' for with it by my hand the Lady of Bau slept soundly. With that emblem of the former law of Fiji, I sent my love to Her Majesty, that she might watch over us as I had watched over my lady.

"Your Queen is now our Queen. Our two races are bound together. Law makes us as one, and the stronger nation lends strength to the weaker. For this we thank you, and we ask that you convey our gratitude to Queen Victoria, and our hopes that she, and you who after her will one day be Kings of Fiji, shall ever remember and care for us and our beloved islands."

Clearly it was Eddy's duty to respond. I glanced anxiously at Dalton, who glanced just as anxiously at me. Eddy had seldom spoken in public during the voyage, and those few occasions had not been successes. He was tongue-tied and awkward, prone to stammer, blush and fidget.

The Prince stood up, drawing a gasp from the natives. But the old man, without saying or doing anything, managed to radiate serenity, conveying to all present that he was aware that while Fijians sit to do honour, British rise, and that the taboo against raising one's head above a chief's could not apply to Eddy, for he represented the highest Chief in this world.

The natives immediately relaxed, and Eddy . . . well, I've no idea if Eddy understood that he had made a *faux pas* already, but he managed to conduct himself all right. The air of goodwill in the room seemed to enter his being and endow him with confidence. His reply was short and, if not distinguished, adequate and well received. No doubt Thurston added lustre when rendering it into the native tongue.

While this was going on my eyes strayed over the chiefs around Thakombau. Some evidently were the product of mission schools, with tamed hair and starched shirts. A few were women draped in calico. Others were wild, white-eyed old men from the mountainous interior, clad in little save animal teeth and oil, the lobes of their ears stretched like napkin rings and stuffed with rolls of banknotes and tobacco.

Thakombau's house, according to Thurston, was a smaller version of his palace on Bau, said to be the finest native edifice in the South Seas. What raised the rustic building to distinction was its strong, curious workmanship. The pillars, thick as *Bacchante*'s masts, were of polished hardwood. The top of each was adorned with a band of carving and a sperm whale's tooth hanging like a bugle from a cord. The walls were lined in tapa cloth stamped with rectangles, diamonds, hatchings, etc., in brown and black.

The ceiling was perhaps the best feature of all, comparable in effect to hammerbeam work in an English church. Its tiebeams and king posts, stringers and struts were fastened together by sinnet lashings, very tight and neat, with chequering and houndstooth in black and white against the chestnut-red of the rope.

When Eddy had finished, a smile creased Thakombau's face, and he was heard to say, as if to himself, *Vinaka, vinaka*, 'It is good, thank you." He gave a brief command to one of his heralds who, using a stick, fished the finest of the whale teeth from its pillar, and held it out to Thakombau, who touched it. Thurston explained afterwards that these specimens of ivory constitute a form of currency among Fijians, yet were something greater, for their value was more spiritual than financial. Even the most Christian of natives regarded them as repositories of *mana*, or metaphysical power.

Thurston whispered to Eddy, who sat down cross-legged where he was. A hush descended. I became aware of sounds outside: chickens, birds, cicadas, the muffled thud of the reef. Lulled by these, by the heat, the hay smell and softness of the mats, which were laid over a thick cushion of grass, I began to doze.

Smyth nudged me awake. The King's herald, risen to a kneeling pose, was holding up the whale tooth and its cord while he recited a formula. When the man finished, Thurston accepted the gift with a similar speech, and held it before Eddy, who touched it as Thakombau had done.

It was a splendid moment, the once and future Kings of Fiji, face to face; the passing of a spark of *mana*, the divinity that hedges kings, from the old man to the young.

Dalton's face was alight with triumph—and relief.

❦ ❦

When weather permitted, the squadron played cricket against Levuka Town. Prince George was a strong batsman. Eddy was more often seen strolling northward along the beach road, ostensibly to take the air, but really to vanish for hours on end into what remained of the roaring district, a few muddy lanes of taverns and bordellos.

One sunny afternoon Mr. Thurston took us to see his botanical gardens on the hillside, reached by a long flight of steps affording fine views of harbour and sea. While walking he told us a little of his life—seaman, botanist, trader, planter, and now, as he put it, "panjandrum." He'd arrived on the islands many years before, soaked and coral-gored, to the sound of a brig breaking up on the reef. I remember his piercing eyes framed by brows like the fibre of a coconut. He spoke energetically and floridly, using odd allusions and expressions, the style of a man who must assert himself with words, though he did so wittily, not pompously.

Chief architect of the system of indirect rule, which included a strict ban on land sales to whites and alcohol sales to natives, he'd earned the respect of Fijians and the hatred of many of his fellow settlers. On this slope above Levuka he had established a collection of local plants, foods and medicines as well as flowers and ornamentals, above all the stately fan-palm. Export of these to collectors round the world brought a steady income with which he acquired staples such as maize and cassava, distributing seed to villages throughout the archipelago.

Dalton and he talked learnedly for an hour, scattering the Latin pedigrees of plants like so much pollen as they walked along the terraces. Reaching the upper limit of his Kew, Thurston took us into the woods along a path beside a torrent, from bright sun to a leafy gloom that reminded Prince George of Trinidad and the cautionary tale of the "indiarubber man." Indeed, this Eden too had its vegetal serpent, harmless to man but a patient murderer of trees.

"We call this gentleman the 'Scotch Lawyer,'" Thurston said to the Princes, his hand on a trunk resembling a column of tangled snakes, "because he's like a crooked attorney who fastens onto an estate and wrings it dry." He explained that the aspiring creeper, properly known as the strangler fig, begins as a seemingly innocent shoot beside a tall, vigorous tree. Slowly it climbs its neighbour, lacing and enmeshing the trunk, choking off the flow of sap. The host dies and rots within its assailant's embrace, leaving the Scotch Lawyer, now sturdy enough to stand alone, flourishing over the remains.

"Coming as I do from a line of Scots," I remarked, "I think 'Lawyer' nickname enough for this odious plant."

Thurston laughed, unloading the heavy bags of care below his bloodshot eyes. "Indeed! Shall we call it the 'English Planter,' then? Or perhaps the Rampant Anglo-Saxon? Can't leave out the Americans, can we? Your South Seas Englishman's a lazy devil. Your American's part alligator and all the rest steam engine. We had a little civil war in Levuka on their account—they set up a branch of the Ku Klux Klan here. Called Thakombau an old nigger and me a nigger-lover. Had they prevailed, Fiji would have come to resemble this odious tree all too closely, as is happening apace in the Kingdom of Hawaii. Have you seen Honolulu?"

"No, worse luck," said George. "We were going to. Father and King Kalakaua are friends. But we had to go to Cape Town."

"Well, if you do go, you'll hardly see a native face on the street. The whole place is Scotch Lawyers—subspecies missionary, subspecies planter, subspecies republican and democrat."

We walked down from the gardens to town, looking out over the harbour and our great black ships. Like many small men, Thurston didn't walk, he stalked—hands thrust into the pockets of his linen jacket. The mental and verbal energy contained under pressure, as it were, in his diminutive frame continued to bubble out and follow us like lava down the mountainside: "Justice for the Fijians is of greater consequence than cotton growing. Or even empire building." He shot a fraught look at Eddy and George. "I hope Mother England will remember that. God help us if she doesn't. The Fijian is the finest friend you can ever make—and the fiercest, most tenacious foe. You don't want another New Zealand on your hands. Ten million pounds wasted in campaigns, hundreds of settlers slaughtered, half the Maori race destroyed, and no hope of lasting peace except by destroying the rest. Or, at the eleventh hour, admitting them to government. Which is what should have been done from the start."

Beyond the lace of spars and rigging, the sea ran smooth to the ruled line of the sky, a sheet of cyan blue with islands near and far, and the distant loom of others below the curve of the Earth.

❖ ❖

On Levuka's waterfront near the cricket ground stood the Royal Hotel, which had the best dining-room we'd seen since Sydney.

The building had an airy verandah where officers resorted in the evening for a quiet cigar. Being young and underpaid, I did not go often myself. However, one evening, having dined less grandly elsewhere, I was strolling by quite late when Dalton's mighty voice boomed from the lantern glow into the night, stilling the crickets and frogs who observed a respectful pause before cautiously resuming their usual clamour.

"Henderson! Speak of the devil! Join us."

He and Thurston were sitting at a corner table, and looked as though they'd been there some time. The other patrons had gone home. Dalton's spectacles were smudged and his cravat disordered. Thurston's eyes, always a trifle bloodshot, looked redder and glossier than usual, the whites jaundiced, though it could have been the lamplight. He seemed old and sickly, much older than the vigorous tutor, though the two were about the same age.

Dalton was in one of his confiding moods. I accepted a glass while he finished a train of thought: "Well, you've done it, Thurston! A capital job of work. Fiji's an exception to the past and a model for the future. There's no reason in the world why the experiment shouldn't be repeated . . . and soon!" The tutor winked at his companion, then addressed me.

"What did you think of Prince Eddy the other day, Henderson—progress, eh?" I agreed.

"I believe the time has come. . . ." Dalton was topping up my glass. "Drink up, dear fellow. We're streets ahead of you. . . . The time has come for him to strike out on his own. Until now he's taken his cues from Georgie, and that's not right. It's not natural for a young man, nearly eighteen, to look to his little brother for initiative. I want to see him build on this recent triumph. By himself. Opportunity has knocked! Can't say more now. You'll be getting orders. May one assume you'd have no objection to a little time away from the Squadron? Just myself, Prince Eddy, and a chap you'll meet later—captain of a charter boat. Friend of Mr. Thurston's here. Have I said too much?"

"I wouldn't say so." Thurston replied, giving me a fore-and-aft look and reporting his impression as if I wasn't there. "This young fellow looks steady enough to me. Though he'd better steel himself to meet an island character." He turned to me. "Bit of a rough diamond, this captain you'll be sailing with, but there's no one alive knows the waters or the natives better. I was telling your shipmate how he fetched up here back in the sixties—sailed an open dinghy seven hundred miles from Apia, one hand on the tiller and the other on a missionary's wife." Thurston chuckled, a grinding of unsound lungs. "Cigar? Manila not Havana, I'm afraid."

The lamp went out, leaving an air of scorched oil about us. For ten or twenty minutes we smoked in silence, the tips of our cheroots illuminating each face in turn, answering fireflies in the palms. My eyes widened to the night. I could just make out the Brazil-nut shape of Wakaya across the bay, a black void bitten from the stars. Faint strains of Eastern music were drifting intermittently across the water, perhaps from the quarantine station for Indian coolies brought in to satisfy the planters' appetite for labour.

"Well, young man—what's your answer?"

"Oh, I'm sorry. . . . Of course I'll do anything you suggest, so long as it's square with my superiors and the Governor. Wouldn't mind a few more days away from the tub." I waved my cigar towards the dark hull of *Bacchante*.

"Des Voeux usually takes my advice." Thurston said quietly, in a tone that implied, *the Governor does as I say*. I discovered later that this remark, which struck me then as arrogant, was nothing but the truth. Des Voeux was new to Fiji, a match neither in knowledge nor in personality for Thurston.

"When do we leave?"

"Well, that's it, Henderson," said the tutor. "We're not leaving from here. We sail with the Squadron, then transfer to a smaller vessel at sea."

"An open dinghy?"

"Hardly," Thurston said. "You'll like her. Belonged to a South American *supremo*. No expense spared. Like a French cathouse below decks and the fastest thing afloat. Steam and all, triple expansion. But whatever you do, don't ask Captain Whosit any questions. Especially about how he came by this vessel of his. I never do. Though one hears things, of course. I'm damned glad he's on my side. So will you be if there's any sort of scrape."

"Don't let him alarm you," Dalton struck in nervously, more to stanch Thurston's flow than to reassure me. "Everyone who needs to approve this . . . this excursion—and I mean *everyone* —has given his, and *her*, approval. But nothing more must be said of it for now. And that applies to what's already been said." He shook the last of the bottle into our glasses. "We're having brandy and cigars, enjoying the night air, and complimenting Mr. Thurston on his botanical accomplishments. Nothing more."

Strange how much of Fiji comes back to me now as night scenes. Why doesn't the mind's eye light up with blazing sun and blinding sea, the emerald forest, the curtains of rain, the coral gardens? But there it is: Fiji for me is a land of soft nights, cigars glowing against the darkness, and great fires with dancing tribesmen.

The festivities seemed to happen on their own without hint of the choreography behind the show, though Thurston must have been stage manager. It was a farewell never to be forgotten.

In late afternoon we gathered on the green below Government House, where the Princes were resting in the cool of a summerhouse built for them by the local chiefs' own hands. The sun sank behind the volcanoes, its rufous light sliding up the masts and rigging of the fleet. The aged King came down with his entourage, wearing brown tapa stamped with discs of black. Mats were spread along the top of the slope, facing the sea. Here the Governor sat in the native way, Thakombau at his right hand, the Admiral to his left, the Princes in front. Around them gathered all the ships' officers, all the high-born Fijians; whilst on the lower side, across an open space, young men and women sat neatly arrayed like companies of infantry.

In the middle of the open green was a great wooden bowl, the size and shape of a church font, supported on eight squat legs, the whole carved in one piece from a prodigious tree. A burly giant was mixing and straining a muddy-looking liquid into the bowl through a muslin. His actions, formal but strenuous, were those of a potter kneading clay. He wore a boar's-tusk necklace and a skirt of leaves, with other leaves and vines draped over his body (not unlike the figure painted on the Wild Man Inn near Bramford). At length, he lifted the pulp on high and squeezed it mightily, forcing a cascade through clenched fingers to show that the liquor had reached full strength.

Thakombau then dedicated the ceremonial drink as a farewell toast, wishing us a safe and pleasant voyage to England.

Dalton was grinning from ear to ear, smiling on Eddy and George—but especially Eddy—like a proud father. It wasn't hard to

divine his thoughts: these unearthly islands with their race of courtly cannibals were the answer to his prayers. Here the Heir
Presumptive was maturing like a tardy flower brought into sunlight.
The necrotic countenance had quickened, the hooded eyes flashed,
the mouth essayed reactions, opinions, even jokes. Each day in these
enchanted latitudes seemed worth a year of normal life.

The mixer walked slowly from his huge bowl to each drinker
in turn, bearing a coconut-shell in outstretched hands. The
Governor and Thakombau were served first, draining their cups in
one draft. Eddy and George did the same. The crowd clapped as
one, calling out *matha* and *vinaka*—"It is empty, it is good."

Having already sampled the drink in a grog-shop on the
waterfront, I knew what to expect: a cool, earthy taste followed by
a numbing of the mouth and a sensation of relaxed well-being.
(On some islands missionaries have unwisely stamped kava out,
only to find it replaced by the scourge of rum.)

By the time the great bowl was dry, the light too had
drained away, leaving a purple residue across the western sky
above the blackness of the mountains. A man began to make fire
in the old way, drilling a stick into tinder until a feather of smoke
arose—a scene, remarked Dalton, from the Stone Age. This
hard-won fire was used to light others; soon the greensward flickered with leaping flames. The purpose of the young men and
women seated in companies now became evident. They were
dancers, or perhaps actors is the word, for they performed epics
of war, mythology and love.

The scenes were wild and dramatic, impossible to convey.
Men danced and ran in the fiercest and most abandoned figures,

yet kept formation perfectly like shoals of fish, all turning as one, all landing on the same foot at the same beat, sending a shudder through the earth into one's spine. They wore fringes of grass and water-weed, kilts of leaves, bracelets and bandoliers of vines and ferns. Their faces were fantastically hued—some scarlet, some yellow, others blue; some were half one colour, half another, split vertically or horizontally; yet others were done in spots and stripes. One heard the dry flutter of leaves as they passed, smelled smoke and coconut oil, and were it not for the sable hue of their skins might imagine oneself transported back to the rites of Dionysus.

The women sang and beat time with hollow tubes of bamboo. Their own dances were subtle, graceful compositions, many done while seated, movement being achieved only with arms, hands and fans, which wheeled like flocking birds and heaved like sea-anemone.

A gibbous moon rose as if by command from the dark crest of Wakaya, pouring quicksilver over the waves beyond the warships. Food was brought briskly and efficiently, as always in Fiji, and eaten with little conversation. All heads were bent over heaps of fish, pork and yam served on glossy leaves. Frogs and crickets played their busy rhythms. The imperious *woof-woof* of a barking pigeon could be heard on a hillside, and the shriek of the laughing jackass, or kookaburra, rang in the woods.

Dinner done, the crowd fell still and the old King advanced into the firelight with Thurston to say his goodbye. He looked tired, perhaps saddened by the parting, yet proud—proud that the political course he had embraced at the end of a long and changeful life had turned out as he'd hoped. Thakombau's herald came forth with a whale's tooth in his hand.

"When you arrived," the King said, "I welcomed the elder Prince with a *tabua*. We now say our goodbye by giving this tabua, younger brother of the first, to the younger Prince of England. These teeth from an ocean giant are the gift of Fiji, not of myself alone. They are yours so that your time among us here begins and ends in *mana*, and that they may guard you in your homeward journey across the seas."

George received the tabua with a graceful reply. He thanked Fiji for its hospitality and loyalty, for the many gifts that symbolized the great gift of the islands themselves, a gift that Britain would treasure and honour for evermore.

The night ended with a war dance that eclipsed all others in energy and ferocity. It was a splendid, even frightening scene, the mock battle carried to the edge of woods and sea, war clubs whistling past our heads so close that those in front could feel their breeze.

Clouds had begun to run before the moon, driven by a freshening southeast trade, and the fires had died to glowing heaps. The dancers were wings of battle rushing in the night. Suddenly, a brilliant ray seared out from the harbour, revealing one wing in silhouette, restoring the other to full colour, blinding us all to fire and moon. The lush vegetation around us came alive, every leaf and branch picked out. The sailors cheered and the Fijians, who never before had seen electric light, burst into yells of amazement. The dancers, however, neither skipped a beat nor showed surprise, except to greet the awesome beam with a great flourish of weapons, and to continue by its weird glare until their battle was done.

I heard the Admiral boast to Thakombau, saying we British had succeeded in outdoing the moon, and it was only a matter of time before we should discover "how to make a light like the sun."

The King answered that though he was very old, he hoped he might live on for many years yet to see the great wonders Progress held in store.

Eleven

⊰ ⊱

TAHITI

Arue Prison

THE WIND HAD DIED. Smooth water lay around the *Tui* like oil. A mandala of ripples, an empty flag.

Not until later, near sundown, did Natalie speak about her labours at the doghouse table. She and Simon were standing together by the rail, reconciled. He seemed meek, his moods humbled by the girl.

Natalie, rum bottle by the neck, was vacantly taking swigs as she gazed aft across the ocean, less at the sunset, I think, than at the waters we'd left behind, the place the body had appeared and disappeared. "That girl had had booze. And sex. I can't stop thinking there might have been foul play. I know that sounds melodramatic. But bad things happen to young women travelling. I don't know what we should do."

Simon had abandoned his theory about "Argies." "She probably just fell overboard," he offered warily. "During a party on some

259

rich fart's gin palace. Hit her head on something. Or a sea slammed her against the hull. I'm with Vatu—we don't know a thing."

"We don't know *much*," Natalie said sharply. "But I found out quite a bit down there."

"Sorry, Nat. Didn't mean to piss on what you did. You were amazing." She smiled, as if to encourage his humility.

"We may know *too* much." Now Vatu sounded suspicious. "We have to think very carefully. Do we get on the radio with this? I don't think so. Not here."

"Why not?" I said.

The others exchanged glances.

"Better reef now. We're in for another blow." Vatu's eye was on a charcoal stain in the southwest, blotting across the sunset. Cat's-paws ran to meet us, fanning out. A warm rain emptied itself. Then the *Tui Marama* heeled suddenly, as if someone had struck the mast. Vatu at the helm. The Australians hauling in sail. I looked on helplessly, then went below.

The storm drove us east all night. I lay in my bunk, braced against the corkscrew pitch and roll, sleepless with visions of a yacht (hers or ours?) crushed like an eggshell, snagged on coral, or sunk in an ocean trench, a place of inconceivable pressures and endless dark with great luminous squid and blind translucent eels like whips of living ice. The dead girl wasn't merely a shock; our lives seemed as precarious as hers, our boat stalked by every flaw and hazard.

By the following noon the wind dropped to a steady breeze and the chop went down, the water heaving with the memory of last night's seas. It was my turn on lookout, but Vatu relieved me. I didn't argue. The strength had left my body; it had been all I could do to keep myself in bed last night. Natalie touched my arm *(You okay?)* and handed me a mug of coffee.

Simon was absorbed in fishing, netting things and bottling them in jars. His neck and arms were badly blistered; he was too involved to take care with the sun, no matter how often Natalie urged him to cover up. Later, when I felt better, she gave me the wheel, my first time at the helm. I hung on like a child allowed to steer a car—the ship huge to me now—hoping the wind wouldn't rise or shift, but pleased to be trusted.

We stood together quietly, she thoughtful, as though wanting to talk but unsure how to begin. Then we heard a distant engine. It grew louder, the throb of a helicopter, racing low across the sea towards us. The machine—a large military chopper with twin rotors—hovered off our bow above a maelstrom of foam. The *Tui* stalled, her sails in a frenzy. Natalie seized the spokes. Simon gathered his gear and ran below. Their actions, the way the chopper behaved, the appalling noise after days of wind and water, all made it seem like an attack, though I'd little reason to think this was anything but a rescue mission looking for survivors of the wreck the girl had come from.

"No worries," Simon shouted, re-emerging. "No way the bastards can land!" He and Vatu sprang about, lowering canvas. The chopper circled several times, a side door open, one man taking photos with a long lens, another shouting at us over a PA. The words blew down as nothing but jagged shards of warning, or anger, embedded in the deafening pulse of the blades.

The helicopter left. Our sails went up again. The ocean peace returned. But the remoteness I'd felt ever since leaving land was shattered. This seemed only an opening act, a prelude. I remembered a hike in the mountains a few years ago, when I'd startled a grizzly. The bear—far bigger and more powerful than I'd imagined—peered at me with its weak eyes, reared up, and sniffed. I saw its claws, long as my fingers. *Do nothing, play dead, don't run, a grizzly is fast as a racehorse.* It had merely scratched at a tree and gone on its way. But the wilderness that had seemed so welcoming and calming was suddenly a place through which I moved in fear—like a cave woman, when other creatures owned the Earth and we were weak and few and hunted.

"You wouldn't have a gasper, would you?" Natalie said soon after we got under way.

"Thought you didn't."

"I don't. Only other people's. Give us one. I know you've got some. It was wafting under your cabin door. Smelt beaut. What are they?" I withdrew two Sobranies from my bag, leaving nine for the rest of the voyage.

"Look, Liv. I've been meaning to say something. Should've levelled with you by now. Simon's . . . headstrong. As you may have noticed." She gave a nervous laugh. "It's the best and worst of him." She inhaled deeply, tilting her head back, closing her eyes against the sun. Then she admitted that we'd come further east than planned. Simon had manoeuvred us towards the Forbidden Zone, a great disc of ocean round the testing atolls.

"Fact is, we're not much nearer Nuku Hiva now than when we left Tahiti. If you were a sailor you'd have realized. Si can be a crafty sod. Often gets a storm to blow him where he wants to go. And not only at sea." She chuckled again, mirthlessly. "I told him it's not fair to you. I thought he'd accepted that. Believe me." She blew a plume into the sail. "I should've known better. You've seen how he's been lately."

"We're still in international waters, aren't we?"

"More or less. Shipping is 'advised' to stay out of the Zone. Just a 'precaution.' Naturally! What they're really worried about is that we'll find something, or do something. That chopper was here to put the wind up us." She added that Simon had nobbled the radio. We were completely cut off, a good thing under the circumstances.

"If they board us and find we've been keeping quiet about a suspicious death, we're stuffed. And not just us. The frogs could use it to discredit the whole movement. I can see the headlines: 'Greens Held in Tourist Death.'"

Simon's recklessness, his arrogance, infuriated me. This voyage was turning out to be a waste of my time. Worse, we could get held up, even deported. I might never reach Nuku Hiva. "Do you have to call them frogs? It's as bad as nigger where I come from. I used to live in Montreal."

"Sorry. No offence. Don't mean the people. Just the government." She then told me something I half remembered from the news a few years ago: the sinking of the *Rainbow Warrior* by French agents in Auckland harbour, the killing of a man on board.

I listened. She was right. Governments who regard themselves as world players are capable of anything. "What are his doubts?" I said. Simon, I'd decided, was more than an activist; he was a zealot. And zealotry feeds on doubt. It seemed to me that Simon's doubts had to do with himself: whether he was worthy of, and equal to, his cause. This was the worm that gnawed him.

A worm I knew myself. Was I good enough? Would I ever make a film that lasted? Had I whatever it would take to find the truth about my father?

That evening we gathered round Vatu's kava bowl, the first time in a week. Evidently Natalie had given Simon a talking-to, and spoken privately to Vatu. After a formal round, the Fijian took the initiative.

"The girl changes everything. We have to report her death. If we hang about in the Forbidden Zone, we must report it here. On a military base. Perfect excuse for them to hold us as long as they like, pending inquiries." He clapped lightly, handed me a cup of grog.

"All right," said Natalie. "We'll change course after dark. To throw them off. We'll report at Nuku Hiva. We can always come back here later. And it's better for Liv." She smiled at me. "You're on my conscience."

The others agreed, even Simon.

"What about the *Tui Marama*'s owner?" I said. "Does he know what you're up to? Or is this really Lars's boat?"

"There is a benefactor. Anonymous. A wealthy sympathizer. Not Lars. I doubt Lars has pockets this deep. Officially the boat belongs to Fletcher Christian Tours. Of Panama."

"Whoever he is," said Vatu after a pause to make sure everyone had finished speaking, "he has a sense of humour."

❧ ❧

So we ran from the sea grave and the greater death at Moruroa, threading under power and sail through the Dangerous Isles. All the Tuamotus are low, a hundred paint-drops flung on a canvas the size of Europe, none higher than a mirage and as hard to find. But solid enough to grind a ship to pieces. Some were tiny cartoon islands tufted with a single palm, others great rings of land with huge lagoons inside, forty or fifty miles in diameter, draping over the horizon like Dalí watches.

We landed on one of these to swim and stretch our legs, to get away from the ship, the lingering presence of the girl. I borrowed Natalie's snorkelling gear and gloried in the lukewarm water, watching fish, surprised by how the fish watched me— intelligence in their eyes, a knowingness I'd not expected. I swam over gardens of light to where the coral wall dropped away into indigo depths and oceanic chill, saw sharks in the offing, and rays like sheets of newsprint on a wind.

But still I felt her touch, her frozen-sausage fingers inked and pressed against a card. She was in my dreams, her empty belly stitched up like a sail. And in the dreams her face was yours. I'd wake with this lunging fear she might *be* you; that you had come looking for me somehow and fate had thrown your body in my path. A fear I've known for twenty years. I hear the news, or glimpse a headline, or see MISSING posters in shop windows, and always I read the details, the age, the description, to make sure.

I took a stroll along the inner beach, a scimitar of sand. I could walk forever on this atoll and the land would never change. It was a place with no hills or streams, no stony trace of time, no escape from the scratching of the palms and the surf *hush-hushing* on the outer shore.

Within an hour I felt imprisoned—I know this sounds quite mad as I write to you behind high walls—imprisoned in a vast panopticon watched by the eye of the sun.

A feeling of confinement stayed with me on the boat. I saw what Johnson meant, how a ship is a jail with the chance of being drowned. I couldn't wait to get off it.

Leaving the Tuamotus astern, we crossed some of the deepest water in the world, the long striding swells rolling the old schooner this way and that. I remember the *Tui Marama*'s sounds: the trickle on her hull, the humming shrouds, the deep nameless notes her body made as she nudged across water-hills that raised her and hid her, and curled on her deck.

It rained often and the winds were fickle. To raise the Marquesas took nearly a fortnight. When not on watch I kept below, alone inside wooden walls with their ingrained air of tar and old cargoes, behind a small brass-rimmed eye through which on one tack I'd see the clouds and on the other vitreous depths. Once I saw a turtle's beaky face, wagging from side to side like a toothless old sadhu as he gazed into my shell.

I thought of the turtle army Henderson describes. He'd seen hundreds; I saw one. The seas had teemed around *Bacchante*, but we sailed waters eerily lifeless and denuded. For Simon this was proof of nature's dying, of the oceans' rape by human appetite, of the poisons flushing in from every coast, and the measureless lesions of the weapon tests.

"A blue whale," he said one evening, "can hear another's sonic boom across a thousand miles of ocean. Imagine what a nuclear blast must do to ears like that. Maybe that's why their numbers aren't recovering. We've deafened them all and they can't find each other."

It seemed almost beyond belief that between Frank's voyage and Jon's the Pacific had passed from cannibal kings to nuclear powers. One lifespan: Mole's avalanche of human time. And it came to me in a rush of historical vertigo that if Henderson had lived into his eighties, he'd have seen the atom bombing of Japan.

Most evenings I turned in early to read Henderson, or Stevenson's travels—he wandered the South Seas a few years after Frank. I'd spend hours listening to my Walkman. Or I'd take out Bob's letter for the smile it gave me, the glow of him warm in his tweed over there in Vancouver watching the waves roll in, waves that might have passed beneath my bottom—and just to hear the old guy's voice.

Liv, my darling:

You left a mug in my briefcase with crimson lipstick on the rim. Every morning I give it a kiss. The marks you left on me have faded (just as well), but *Olivia* is engraved on my heart.

You've been gone . . . what? A week? Already I'm desolate. Your voice—I miss your voice almost as much as the rest of you. No one to call after class.

And who will help me drink the Widow? You should see the students I have this term. Not a kindred soul among them. When I mention Rimbaud they think I mean Sylvester Stallone.

If you've gotten this you'll have met Lars by now. Anything he has to say is worth listening to. But don't let his air of *éminence grise* overawe you. He and I got stinking drunk on Granville Island when he was here for the Writers' Festival. He fell off one of those little bathtub water-taxis, and we had to fish him out of False Creek by the seat of his pants. Imagine that—a guy who sailed the *Kon-Tiki*!

Are you off to Nuku Hiva? I want a long letter from there no matter what you find. Or don't find. I know things look promising, but brace yourself for the worst. What you're doing is an act of exploration that will demand as much bravery from you as any physical danger I can think of. Call me collect at work if things get rough—if you can get to a phone. Promise.

Send a card from somewhere warm and sticky. I'll join you *anywhere* when term's over. Name the place, and I'll invent a grand Pacific writer there, whom I need to interview before he croaks.

Dance the obscene Lory-Lory in the moonlight and think of me.

Already there are whiskers on my palm. XXXX B.

With this Bob had enclosed notes for a lecture he was working on. Or so he said. I think this was really a gift to me, his ideas for my film. He even hinted I might steal his title. "Titles aren't copyright, my love."

Literature 307, Pacific Authors. "Melville's Ghosts."
Prof. Robert————

"In life the great whale's body may have been a real terror to his foes; in death his ghost becomes a powerless panic to a world. Are you a believer in ghosts, my friend?"
Moby Dick

Widely regarded as the greatest novel written by an American, *Moby Dick* is the only Melville work well known to modern readers. But during his lifetime, his first book, *Typee: A Peep at Polynesian Life*, outsold everything else he wrote.

Closely based on the true story of his running away to sea, and desertion at Nuku Hiva, *Typee* brought Melville fame and scandal at the age of twenty-six. He was "the man who lived among cannibals," who witnessed scenes of "savage" love, and took part in them with the winsome Fayaway and her adolescent friends.

Omoo (1847) continued the yarn with the author's mutiny and imprisonment at Tahiti. Readers wanted

more of the same. But not long after his thirtieth
birthday Melville began *Moby Dick*, publishing it in
1851. Far from being hailed as the masterpiece we recognize today, *The Whale* (as it was known in Britain)
marked the start of a long dive in its author's reputation. After its commercial failure, and the failure of all
later books, the once dashing adventurer became a
customs clerk to support his wife and children.
Melville's career ended much as it began, in obscurity
and genteel poverty. Twenty years after his death, the
Encyclopaedia Britannica had only this to say:

> His works of fiction and travel are of irregular exe-
> cution. *Typee* and his other records of adventure
> were followed by tales so turgid, eccentric, opin-
> ionative, and loosely written as to seem the work
> of another author.

Such was the judgement of the 19th century.
And there things lay until Melville's rediscovery in
the 1920s by modernists such as D.H. Lawrence and
Virginia Woolf, who recognized him as a visionary
ahead of his time—a literary Gauguin.

Melville's Lies.
Were his early books travelogues, as American read-
ers generally took them? Or ingenious fictions, as
British critics suspected? This course will argue they

are both, and that in their dual nature is the key to understanding all of Melville's writing. His "ghosts" are not only those of the Polynesians he glimpsed in their last free days but also the shades of makebelieve with which he coloured his experience.

Melville's Loves.
Contemporary readers were shocked and titillated by Fayaway, the naked Marquesan girl. Modern critics have been more intrigued by homoerotic undertones, to say nothing of "Buggerry Island"—a venue purged from later editions by the author's widow.

Melville's Hates.
Melville deemed the white man "the most blood-thirsty, atrocious and diabolical race in the world." Yet he was no simple follower of the Noble Savage. He was disturbed by the evil he found in paradise, and within himself. At the moment of escape from the Typee Valley, he used violence against the Marquesans who, despite his fears, had never raised a hand against him. "Even at the moment I felt horror at the act I was about to commit"—a horror heard fifty years later from the mouth of Conrad's Kurtz.

Melville's Expulsion from the Garden.
In the Typee Valley Herman Melville found a flawed Eden, a better place than the civilized world. Yet he

could not remake himself enough to stay there. Neither could he leave his Eden without violating it. This dilemma, the dilemma of the Fall, would echo through his whole life's work. Beyond *Typee* lay a pilgrimage of despair, not to atheism but down to the sunless deep of the old Ophitic heresy: that the world being what it is, God must be evil or mad.

In short, Herman Melville's encounter with Natural Man (and Woman) in the cannibal valley equipped him to explore man's place in nature so profoundly and splendidly in *Moby Dick*.

It was hard to think about my film now Nuku Hiva lay within reach, a ripening presence over the horizon. I was close, close to where Jon had been (however briefly), to the one certain proof of his existence after Korea. I was consumed with dread that the authorities might reappear. I was both hunted and hunter, filled with turmoil by the mounting gravity of waters my father had sailed more than thirty years ago. Where was he now? Could he have left any trace or clue? Would I be able to recognize it if he had?

I reread the *Typee* Bob gave me in Vancouver. Melville's Nuku Hiva might beguile me, might take my mind off Jon enough to let me sleep.

❖ ❖

Early in October I woke to a shout at dawn, summoned on deck for a first sight of the Marquesas. The sky had cleared and the ocean glittered in Canaletto wavelets to the rising sun. The spires of

Ua Pou could just be seen from the masthead with binoculars, great shafts of stone poking like a mule's ears through a frayed sombrero of cloud. We toasted landfall in malt whisky, the ship bowling along under her spinnaker while the island rose and grew into a dizzying Gaudí ruin of pinnacles, shadows, and rank greenery.

The Tuamotus had been a deceptive place of swirling horizontals, the rise or fall of a few yards defining land from sea. Now I saw mountaintops that might have marched here from the Andes. The Marquesas had none of Tahiti's softness, no coastal lagoon behind a barrier reef. They shared no shallows, nothing that might be called a sea. Each island was vertical and solitary, standing in oceanic depths.

Our last night at sea was clear and lovely. Venus followed the sun, a sinking flare in the twilight. Later the moon rose, near to full. We motored slowly by its light, aiming to reach Taiohae Bay before dawn, before anyone could know we were there. Taiohae, where Jon's letter had been posted in 1953, was also the place we'd have to report the death. Anything might happen then.

At last I told them why I'd come. I couldn't stop talking. This might be the moment of truth, a moment of contact and discovery I hardly dared imagine. Or it might prove to be the end of hope, when everything would crumble like the contents of an opened tomb. I stayed on deck all night, unable to turn in without a glimpse of Nuku Hiva, as if afraid we'd miss the island altogether and sail on round the world.

The smell of land preceded any sight of it—damp earth, blossom, the wet bonfire scent of a village.

In the small hours there it was, a long pallor like the bone in a ship's teeth. The moonlit glow of surf on a rocky coast.

Taiohae's great anchorage was once a crater. Aeons ago its outer wall gave way and the ocean rolled in, forming a horseshoe bay two miles across. Most of the wall still stands, rising from a lune of beach to a dark sugarloaf three thousand feet high, mossy with ferns and threaded with tiny waterfalls shattering in the wind. From this central cusp the crater rim embraces the bay in two steep headlands, closing like crab claws on the entrance. In a finish that is almost too much, needles of rock rise sheer from the water just beyond each pincer.

"Lost in admiration at its beauty," Melville wrote, "I experienced a pang of regret that a scene so enchanting should be hidden from the world."

My own feeling was the opposite: thank heaven this place was inaccessible. If not, it would've become another Rio or Acapulco. And there'd be no chance an Englishman could have hidden here thirty-six years.

We approached the police station beneath an avenue of flamboyants, their flames lying all around on the white dust. A pig was basking in a wallow fed by a leaky tap on the gendarmerie wall. "Vatu, old mate!" said Simon. "Do the honours with the imperialists once more, would you? I might say the wrong thing."

The four of us trooped into the stone building, passports and ship's papers in hand. A secretary and two gendarmes: a small French sergeant, a large Marquesan constable. They looked bored stiff and delighted to see us, taking us for American yachties seeking admission to French Polynesia.

The sergeant had the look of a man who prefers talking to listening, a square face with a small jaw, its smallness emphasized by a droopy moustache and a tall brow that gave a top-heavy impression, as if it might topple forwards like a loose façade. With growing shock he listened to Vatu's solemn relation of events, interjecting *Alors! Non! Mon Dieu!* The other said nothing. He was rotund and shy, concentrating on a pencil in front of him, setting it on end like an obelisk, catching it as it fell.

When Natalie began describing her post-mortem, the secretary, a matronly Polynesian in a Mother Hubbard printed with red hibiscus blooms, excused herself and went outside. Natalie handed over the roll of film she'd shot during her investigation (I was thankful the nearest photo lab was a thousand miles away), a bag with the girl's clothes, and a padded envelope containing the forensic evidence she'd gathered—samples of blood, hair, saliva, stomach contents, and vaginal swabs sealed in plastic bags. "These should be kept refrigerated all the time." I saw a card I recognized—on one side an aerial view of Moorea; on the other were fingerprints.

As each relic was set out on the desk in the rustic police station, beneath an old photo of de Gaulle and a fading tricolour stirred by a fan, the dead girl came before my eyes. She was much too near life (the life of a tourist, a nurse, a volunteer?) to have left her body like these empty clothes. That was one thing. The rest of it, the theories, our fears, the evils we'd imagined, now seemed nothing but a shipboard madness evaporating on dry land. The dreaded French authorities were only a pair of village bobbies, and this sad business would soon have an explanation.

We asked Sergeant Benoit (the talkative one) if he knew of any missing vessel, wreck, or loss overboard. Natalie also asked if there'd been any reports of foul play. He was astonished by this question. In his experience murder was extremely rare. There hadn't been a murder on his beat for six years, and that had been like all the others here, a *crime passionnel* sparked off by alcohol. This was a very quiet part of the world with delightful people. Only 7,358 (he was absurdly precise) in the whole archipelago, and only a fourth of these on Nuku Hiva. His duties seldom went beyond enforcing fishing regulations and breaking up a brawl.

"As for deaths of foreigners at sea, they too are rare. Except for losses overboard, of course, but those are seldom found. People who are ill do not go yachting. The last one was before my time, and it was straightforward. Heart attack. An elderly gentleman with a young wife. . . ." A smile threatened to bolt from the tottering façade and was reined in.

"Please understand. I must report everything you have told me to Papeete, and await instructions. I expect they will require us to take formal statements, so I must ask you not to leave Taiohae for now. You have been most helpful. All this is . . . is most professional in the care you have taken. I commend you all. Especially you, Madame Doctor." Benoit aimed a courtly bow at Natalie.

The pencil man looked at his watch. The sergeant frowned at an electric wall clock, stalled at ten to five. A procession of tiny ants was ascending single file from the floor into the casing. "It is now nearly midday. Please be so good as to come back this afternoon. Not too soon after lunch. There's no point in inconveniencing yourselves before we have some word. I can recommend the cuisine and the ambience at Chez Merivi. Madame is a charming American lady. Madame Lily. *Au revoir.*"

The policemen shook our hands.

Lily McIver spoke cheerful English, fluent French, and a smattering of Marquesan, all with the same Tennessee accent. She was slim, girlish, perhaps mid-forties, and still attractive to young men. Vatu and Simon preened unconsciously when she sat at our table for a chat. She wore a bright yellow sun dress, white sandals, and had taken time with her face.

Chez Merivi, or Melville's Place, clung to a hillside with a broad view of the bay, the flame trees scarlet and green over the houses, blue wisps rising from backyard kitchens as the village cooked its lunch. There was a Mr. McIver in a photo by the bar. Lily said they'd come to Nuku Hiva by boat many years ago, and built the restaurant and cabins with their own hands. She'd never left. He went back to Tennessee each winter, homesick for the cold, returning in spring to Nuku Hiva, a countermigrating bird.

I asked her if she could think of anyone, any old island character, who might fit the description of my father. Nobody came to mind. While we ate she went to some trouble phoning and putting the word around. There was no "Britisher" of the right age on any of the islands except a priest on Hiva Oa, a Father Damian who'd arrived in the 1970s and was probably Irish.

"I don't go back that far myself, you understand, but if a guy'd wanted to get lost here in the fifties I guess he could have. Ask the gendarmes. They're usually back by four. Good luck!"

"Liv, you're not eating," Vatu said. "If you don't eat up we won't be able to see you when you turn sideways. *Kana vaka levu!*" He was tucking in heartily as he always did, elegant portions of swordfish soon devoured, followed by a large order of chips. Natalie was eating absent-mindedly, worrying again about the police. Not these here, but the real ones back in Papeete, and the unseen power behind French Polynesia, the military command on Hao near Moruroa.

I wanted only for this lunch to end. I had no appetite, couldn't swallow. My stomach was hard and swollen. I couldn't take my eyes off the view. *He* had been here. The *Bremerhaven* must have anchored where the *Tui Marama* lay, tiny and far below. He had walked under that avenue of flame trees to post his letter. In truth, the only reason to think Jon had lingered on this island was his mysterious reference to a man he wanted to see. That, and the absence of any further letter or wire—though they might have been destroyed by Mother. Yet no amount of reasoning could dislodge the thought that he *had* stayed on Nuku Hiva. That he could be here still, beneath a tin roof, a Marquesan wife cooking his lunch. Or somewhere beyond these mountains. Or living like a bear in the wild uninhabited interior, where Melville had roamed for days, utterly lost.

Twelve

❖ ❖

ENGLAND

Riverhill. November, 1899

I FOUND MYSELF ON A SHIP without running lights, without name on transom or bow, flying a flag seven years extinct: a blue ground charged with a white shield, dove and olive branch, a device of crown and cross, and the words: *Rerevaka na Kalou ka Doka na Tui,* Fear God, Honour the King. The flag of Thakombau's old kingdom, as if I'd shipped aboard a craft sailing out of the past.

Nothing of this did I see till daybreak, having left *Bacchante* in the middle of an overcast night on a still ocean, half a watch from Levuka. No questions, Thurston had said. There was no one to ask anyway, only a strange seaman at the helm, a Polynesian in a calico kilt of purple sunflowers, with a wild mane and blue eyeglasses, grasping the spokes in tattooed hands and staring at the dawn. So we were headed due east, where no land bigger than a cricket field would be met for fifteen hundred miles. No questions!

The sun leapt smartly from the curving sea and I tumbled towards it; the Copernican order seemed as blindingly true as the sun himself. *Of course* that great furnace burns motionless in space; *of course* our wet green world merely spins like a ballerina in the court of the fiery king.

My word, she was fast, this ship without name. She had three masts, schooner-rigged, and the sleek hull of a grand yacht. Her sails were furled. A powerful engine urged her towards the sunrise, swallowing the ocean at the bow and spewing it astern. Two furrows marked our progress: a white trace from her screw, and a black boa in the air like the breath of an express.

Ornate she was, as Thurston had said, all brightwork and varnish, a hull of emerald green with gilt frippery along the rail, her stanchions elegant as table legs. The cabin to which I'd been ushered in the night by a silent Chinese could hardly have presented a greater contrast to my Spartan quarters on *Bacchante*: crimson plush, lace flounces about the port-hole, a large gilt mirror over my bunk.

The companion slammed. Dalton's bulky form emerged from below, strode forth and joined me at the bowsprit.

"Like a hot knife through lard, eh, Henderson?"

"Twenty knots, I reckon. Such lines! And I don't even know her name. . . ."

"Neither do I. Didn't like to press the point with our skipper. When I alluded to this mystery he said he was painting the hull. Do you see any sign of paint, any scraping, any brushes? Blessed if I do." He thumped the rail. "Never thought I'd sail aboard the yacht of a South American tyrant!" Dalton lowered his voice. "It seems that in return for helping the head of state keep his own head by a brisk flit over the horizon, our captain contrived to keep the ship of state. His name's Skinner. Carny Skinner."

"Are we in the hands of a circus man?"

"Carny, one gathers, is short for *Encarnación*. These Spanish Christian names! Imagine christening someone 'Incarnation.' Nothing's sacred. At least his mother didn't call him Jesus. They do that too, you know. Many a Latin brigand wears the Holy Name." Dalton hacked roughly. Cigarettes had been cheap and abundant at Levuka, perhaps smuggled there beneath these very decks. "Captain Encarnación Skinner. Son of a Newfoundlander and a . . . a *woman* of Peru. She lives in Levuka, marvellous old girl. A dozen words of English, not one of them repeatable. Skinner's father—dead now—jumped ship in Lima forty years ago. Made a fortune in the guano boom. Lost it. Made another when cotton and Thakombau were king."

"We must be burning a king's ransom in coal."

"Skinner can afford it. Keen to serve H.M. Government, in exchange for our forgetfulness. He provides this passage; certain irregularities are allowed to lapse from official memory. Thurston says there's enough on Carny to string him up more than once, but if we were to do that we'd have to dangle half the whites in Levuka, himself not excepted, just to be fair. Odd things happened under Thakombau."

I asked if Skinner was in slaving.

"Couldn't say. Thurston gets garrulous enough over brandy, but the more he *talks* the less he *says*. My guess is the Far East trade: pearls, trepang, sandalwood. Anything where speed and shallow draught are trumps. No doubt he brings back Oriental 'medicine.'" Dalton coughed significantly. "One gathers there's many a sweet dream to be had in the South Seas thanks to Captain Skinner. Come below and meet him. Best he doesn't know who we are just yet, in case anything goes awry. Must be time for breakfast, though I'm dashed if I know how a chap's to keep his watch adjusted when we're tearing up longitude like this. Rouse Eddy on the way, would you?"

The Prince emerged from his quarters beaming, the "French cathouse" *décor* predictably to his taste. "I say, Jackdaw, this *is* a pleasant change!" In the saloon the Chinese steward had set out appetizing plates of melon, pineapple, boiled breadfruit, sea biscuit and jam. The narrow room was lavishly appointed with crimson cushions and cut-glass sconce lamps swinging in gimbals. The walls were panelled in mahogany, hung with watercolours of South American scenes: women in mantillas at a well, a poncho-clad horseman crossing a mountain pass, an Indian porter grotesquely laden with a piano beside a wall of gigantic stones, presumably an Inca temple.

"I say, Captain . . . ," Dalton began diffidently, after scrutinizing the pictures. "Allow me to present the rest of your guests. You'll forgive me if I can't exactly introduce them. I think it better for all concerned if we remain *incognito* for now."

"Well, I'm Carny Skinner, and I don't care who's asking. You gentlemen can be the Three Musketeers. Your business is your business, but I'll tell ye the same as I tells all the lads aboard— ye're on a good and lucky ship. Stick with me, gents, and we'll all be fartin' through silk."

He chatted on in a roughly amiable way, as if he often carried anonymous passengers, which I'm sure he did. He wore the irregular outfit of the South Seas trader, white cotton pyjamas given a dash of colour by a red kerchief and two large, very brown bare feet. His accent was a mix of Spanish and Celtic. He rendered "three" as "tree," dropped some aitches and rasped others like a Castilian. Eddy he referred to as "the boy," pronounced as "bye."

Physically, Skinner was perhaps the most ill-favoured human specimen I'd ever set eyes on, combining the stunted frame of a mudlark with the sallow skin of an Andean muleteer. Nearly beardless, he did not trouble to pluck out the sparse black whiskers that thrust from his chin like horsehairs breaking out of an old armchair. The hair of his head was raven, straight and sleek. But his swarthiness was belied by his eyes—a pale yellow, like those of a dog one instantly mistrusts.

"Fine vessel you have, Captain," said I. "Makes one realize what a sluggard is a man-of-war."

"Nimble enough, isn't she? Lunenburg built, not seven year ago. Everyting the very best. I moors 'er up a river now and then. That way she keeps her bottom clean like a sweet young lady should."

Eddy smirked; his tutor blushed. "Will you say grace, Captain?" Dalton asked frostily. "Or shall I?"

Skinner rapped a biscuit on the table to demonstrate its quality, evicting no tenants. "Please yerselves, sirs. We'll chase it with a tot of Hon Sen's calibogus. Best grace-cup ye'll find in the South Seas."

Tumblers of this liquid, which smelled and looked like furniture polish, appeared before our inclined heads while Dalton was still intoning *benedictus benedicat*. It seemed to be a mixture of rum, coconut toddy, molasses, bottled beer, and hot pepper. Skinner drained his in one draught. "I'm needed on deck. Excuse me, gents. *Buen provecho.*" He clicked his horny heels in a mock salute and left with a slice of breadfruit in his hand.

The cleric frowned at a South American icon above the captain's empty chair, a rustic Madonna with a pink face in a little bright blue retable. "What is it Kingsley writes?" he mused: "Take your saints and Virgins; give me the political economist, the engineer. The railroad and the telegraph are signs enough that we're in harmony with the universe."

Only Dalton, Prince Eddy, and I had transferred from the Squadron. It felt odd, this sudden intimacy, we three under false colours on a nameless ship and tipsy at breakfast-time, as if we were deserters or conspirators. Eddy stopped eating and looked up through the ports (there were five or six on each side, high on the saloon walls where the coaming broke above deck) at the Captain's passing feet. "I wonder what Georgie's doing this very minute. I wish he were here. He'd enjoy this."

Dalton cleared his throat. "George is visiting Rotuma today, I believe, P.E. From now on in your voyage—I refer also to the voyage of *life*, Eddy—there will be more and more occasions when you take up duties different from your brother's. Weightier duties. You two boys must follow different paths as soon as you set foot in England. It's as well to begin now."

❧ ❧

For days the wind stayed low, a bosomy swell heaving in from the northeast. Our rogue ship (so I called her) scaled the watery hills like a powerful locomotive, sluicing eagerly down each trough. I stayed on deck sketching or reading in the lattice shade of bare spars, fanned by the breeze our headway made through the salt air.

Prince Eddy came up and strolled around from time to time, quite lost for things to do without his brother. Dalton tried to busy him with *Polynesian Researches,* the exhaustive work of Reverend Ellis, missionary to the Tahitians.

"I say! You're not flying a valid flag," the Prince exclaimed to the Captain, pleased with himself for noticing. Skinner recoiled in mock alarm: "Am I not, bye? Swat me pink! Better not use the red duster, had we? Not where we're goin'. Like a red rag to a bull with Johnny Crapaud."

"Who's Johnny Crapaud?"

"What some call a Frenchman, shipmate. He's a merry-begot. I'll tell ye that for nothing. So mean he won't give ye the steam off his pee. And a hard man to please in the way of flags, since the only one he wants to see aflyin' is his own. Come aft with me, Admiral, and we'll pick out a tidy one." The captain rummaged theatrically through the signals locker, yanking out mildewed ensigns, holding them up quizzically before the Prince as a lady's maid might offer her mistress a choice of gowns.

"Republic of Liberia—Kingdom of Hawaii—República del Ecuador—Jolly Roger—Plague on Board—República de Bolivia.

Bolivia! *Carajo!* Nobody can rightly say whether that godfor-saken country has any coast or not. Run it up, Mister Oputu."

"If you don't care what you fly," Eddy persisted, "why not go under French colours and have done with it?" Skinner regarded him for a moment, tickled by his naivety. "Cuz . . . come here so I tells ye . . . cuz there's a difference between scratching your arse, bye, and rippin' it to bits with a wire brush!"

I doubt Eddy had ever been spoken to like this in his life. Nonplussed, he withdrew into his customary silence until Dalton appeared. "What sort of man," he asked his tutor, "is a Frenchman?"

"Your Frenchman, P.E., is a great idealist, his highest ideal being himself. He is a lover of art, and an artful lover. His motto is excess in all things. His two obsessions are his language and his liver. He makes a science of cookery and a dog's breakfast of sci-ence. Like the Chinese, he will eat anything at all, as long as it's sufficiently scarce or expensive. He adores Liberty and asks Tyranny to enthrone her. He expects to be born a god, to live as a poet, and die of a surfeit of ortolans to the sound of soft music."

"What's an ortolan, sir?"

"*Emberiza hortulana*, a rare bunting, grotesquely fattened, killed by an overdose of Armagnac, and consumed whole without sparing the innards of bird or man. You take my point?"

The Polynesian mate meanwhile struck the obsolete colours of Fiji and ran up the dubious credentials of Bolivia. Mr. Oputu was almost as singular a personage as his master. Noting that he had a fair degree of "beach" English, I tried several times to engage him in conversation when he was alone at the wheel after dark, his bronze face with its web of tattoos lighted like a fearsome idol in the binnacle glow.

"Good skipper to work for, the Captain?"

"Good skipper."

"I'm told he knows these waters awfully well."

"He know water!"

"Which would be the nearest island on this course?"

"Many island."

The conversation always foundered. How to cut through these terse replies? "A little bird told me," I ventured at last, "that Captain Skinner once sailed an open boat from Samoa to Fiji with one hand on the tiller and the other on a missionary's wife." At this the mate's savage mask cracked into a watermelon grin.

"Two hand, sah! No hand on tiller—two on lady. Cap'n Skina make missonaree husband steer whole damn way. Devil he!"

But Oputu's lockjaw returned at the next leading question; he would not be drawn out.

My curiosity was eventually satisfied, in part, by Dalton. On the third evening, *Bacchante* now a thousand miles astern, he beckoned me into his cabin with a wink and a flourish of the cherry brandy.

"Forgive me for having kept you in the dark so long, Henderson. As you'll have guessed, our destination lies outside the Fiji group."

"I should think so! We must be halfway to Tahiti." I asked if that celebrated island was our goal.

"Well, yes and no." He lowered his voice and began to explain that the main island—Tahiti itself—had just become a full-blown French colony, the Tahitian king having abdicated the previous year. There was now a resident governor, a garrison of several hundred marines, and a chain of blockhouses along the shore. "We can't set foot there. And neither can our skipper. One gathers he's earnestly desired by the French for filling certain local wants." Dalton regarded me intently, as if trying to make up his mind how much more he should tell.

"The Tahitian *group* is another matter, Henderson. Exactly how many of the Society Islands—which ones other than Tahiti and Moorea—were included in King Pomare's gift of sovereignty to Paris is still moot."

He made a little box of his thumbs and forefingers, on his left. "We have Fiji." The box moved to his right. "The French have Tahiti." The box came apart and he spread his palms in bafflement. "But where on the deep shall the line be drawn between us? Some of the intervening islands are unclaimed, others under the loosest of protectorates. I have no doubt, Henderson, that some have yet to feel the booted foot of a white man! Skinner has alluded to places known to him personally that are not on any chart. No doubt these are useful in his work."

Dalton refilled our glasses, took up his and strode to the open porthole, where he stood breathing heavily and gazing into the night.

"These islands lie sprinkled on vast tracts of ocean like stars in constellations. Which Power shall join the far-flung dots, and give them form?" Suddenly his fist shot out and thumped the bulkhead, eliciting a bass response from the well-found timbers. "Even the confounded Germans are sniffing round the Leewards. The *Bismarck* has been seen at Huahine and Raiatea. Politics, dear fellow. Politics! We are coming to a time and place where the clay of history is soft. Let us give it a British shape, and set Prince Eddy's stamp upon it!"

Of these politics there remained many gaps in my understanding, only some of which I have since been able to fill. I am satisfied that Dalton was essentially correct in his assessment of the positions of the Great Powers. The French had secured Tahiti and its sister island of Moorea, the Windward half of the Societies, but their dominion did not extend over the whole archipelago. The Leeward Islands—Bora Bora, Raiatea, Huahine and others—retained their ancient independence, even though they'd had close ties with the late Queen Pomare.

Indeed, under an Anglo-French protocol these islands were guaranteed free from intervention by any Power. This agreement was still in effect at the time of our visit, though the French and others had begun to challenge it even before the old Queen's death in 1877.

Things might have been very different if her son and heir had shown the vigour of his ancestors, or even his mother's stubborn attachment to tradition. But he was weak, extravagant, self-indulgent, probably syphilitic and, in his own words, "already French at heart."

In Fiji Thurston had spoken to Eddy and Dalton of this King, contrasting him unfavourably with Thakombau. "The young bugger's fat as Falstaff. Drinks Benedictine like soda-water. Wanted to abdicate from the day he was crowned, the only issue being the size of his pension. I hear he settled for sixty thousand francs."

Eddy did not draw the desired inference. "I know how the poor chap feels," he said. "All this. . . ." He waved his arm, as if to embrace Levuka, the tall ships, the great globe beyond and the many lands of which he would one day be the sovereign. "I'd chuck all of this up for five thousand guineas a year."

Dalton later said that he thought it a good sign Eddy was making jokes, however poor in taste. It was plain to me that Eddy was perfectly serious. This was neither the first nor the last time I heard him express the sentiment.

I raised with Dalton something which had troubled me ever since the night in Levuka when he and Thurston first sounded me out. Why me? I wanted to know. Why such a junior man on this adventure with imperial implications?

"Because, dear fellow, this business is *sub rosa*, and it is imperative that it should be, as Whitehall chaps say in their specious lingo, *deniable*. In other words, should our presence be discovered, we must be able to pass it off as an innocent mistake—a pleasure cruise blown off course. If senior officers were present such an explanation would scarcely be credible."

"But you yourself, sir, are not a junior officer."

"I'm not here as *Bacchante*'s Chaplain. My presence on this excursion is purely that of a tutor escorting a young gentleman on a venturesome world tour. You are my factotum. Blown off course, that's all we need to say. Circumstances may have obliged us to ship aboard a vessel with questionable colours, but that is not unusual in these parts. We're breaking no law in going where we go. There are islands quite nearby, Rarotonga for one, that lie clearly within our Empire's sphere of influence. It's hardly unusual for a contrary gale to blow a ship from Rarotonga to Tahiti."

"But she's a steamer."

Dalton coughed into his hand.

"Steamers break down."

Dalton specifically condemned the fantastic impulse in life (beyond, of course, the tenets of his faith, which may seem fantastic to those of other persuasions). "One third of each day we sleep, and when all our days are done we sleep and dream forever," said he from time to time in a favourite sermon. "This world is not for dreaming. There will be time enough for that in the hereafter. Do Heaven and Hell possess geographies as real as Westminster and Wapping? No. Our finite minds cannot grasp the infinite, nor our material natures conceive the immaterial. The afterlife is a country of the soul and spirit, a dreamworld as sunny—or as dark—as each living soul has earned. Heaven is the sweetest of all dreams, a dream that neither doubts itself, nor tires, nor ends. And Hell? Hell, too, is a dream: an everlasting nightmare furnished with terrors begot by our own evil, and from which there is no awaking. So it behoves us, while we walk upon God's good Earth, not to dream our days away but to apply our reason to the tasks He sets us. Daydreams are for children and opium smokers. Life is for thinking, for understanding. Let us therefore live it thoughtfully, in the risen Lord!"

Dalton's scheme for Eddy's awakening was, in his mind, founded upon sound pedagogical principles. Yet Dalton, as I've noted, was hardly the apostle of reason he imagined himself to be. And it must not be forgotten, when contemplating the tragedy that ensued, that quite apart from Eddy's listlessness, Dalton, however secretive on the matter, was deeply disturbed by the Prince's wayward physical desires.

As I write now, approaching a new century in an English winter, it seems absurd to suggest that an upright churchman and royal tutor might have winked at fornication. But Dalton was beside himself with worry, desperate to achieve a *coup de théâtre*. We were entering the orbit of a fabled island which must have seemed to him, freethinker and sexual reformist, a heaven-sent specific for straightening Cupid's arrows. No doubt he had read many tales, both factual and fanciful, of the beauty, voluptuousness, and free spirit of Tahitian women.

Bougainville named Tahiti "New Cythera," after Aphrodite's birthplace; and Cook witnessed bacchanalia to make Nero blush. Despite the coming of Europeans, these islands still lay far from the sea-lanes, thousands of miles from the sobering undertow of any copper cable. It seemed to us then, as to so many before, that they might be the last acres of Eden remaining on this Earth, lands of innocence and joy where God kept to the garden shadows, watching but not judging, allowing providential Nature to fill the wants of man; where maidens swam like fish in moonlight pools, and one had only to stretch his hand to pluck the tropic fruit, of which none was forbidden. *Ils ne connaissent d'autre Dieu que l'amour.*

Native legend held that Taaroa, the Creator, made the Society Islands from moons he plucked from the sky, leaving aloft only the moon we see today. On Tahiti itself, the days of Taaroa were all but done with the death of the old Queen who, like Thakombau, had been born a heathen. Her Eden fell with her into the endless night of the past, its approaches sealed not by an angel with a flaming sword but by iron steamships flying the *tri-colore*. Yet the Leewards, remotest of Taaroa's moons, still slumbered fitfully in the primordial dream, still free in the 1880s, if ultimately doomed.

I know now what goes on where the palm tree blows, how Eden dies of a melancholy for which opium, rum, and death are the only cures, how its white strand is bloodstained, how its soil grows loamy with the bodies of its people as they sicken from the very breath of the white man. Yet when these isles rise up for the first time before one's eyes—ah! it is impossible to believe they are anything less than living shoots of Paradise.

My first sight of them was Bora Bora's mountain, a square, dark thunderhead within a halo of white, so upthrusting that it seemed about to burst, as one day it may, for in the telescope the silhouette resolved into a volcanic tower, slumbering under ferns and vines.

The wind was freshening astern, giving those on deck the illusion of gliding by magic, for we steamed at the speed of the wind. The only sounds were the slapping of stays and thrash of pistons. I set up my easel and tried to capture the forest greens and turquoise reef as the island slid past, an enchantment, a weathered castle from a far-off age, its lower ramparts shimmering above a still lagoon. We saw no other shipping, not even a native sail. No smoke curled from Bora Bora's woods, and the next islands to rise—the twins Raiatea and Tahaa—were still too far off to show any sign of habitation, though their form was clear: a greater and a lesser land within an hourglass of reef.

Dalton was at the port rail with Eddy, transfixed by the scene. At length he came over to where I worked. "May one peep?" he asked, as he usually did, though his appraisal of my brushwork, a matter of nods and grunts, invariably began before I had time to consent.

"*Les Îles Sous-le-vent!* Doesn't it strike you as extraordinary, Henderson, that this corner of the Earth has any name at all? To the Brahmin sage the physical world is an illusion and we are all mere characters in a dream dreamt by God. Here, before this marvellous scene, I begin to see what he's driving at. And I see it in your painting there. Well done."

I remarked upon the resemblance of Bora Bora's volcano to a vast and ancient tower, the relic of a giant race of builders, unknown to Palaeontology, who might have dominated the world and left their mark upon it long before Darwin's Adam swung down from the trees. Such fancies did not seem too far-fetched on the Sea of Moons.

"Gautama the Buddha was once asked to define the length of an aeon. Do you know his answer?"

I shook my head.

"Once every thousand years a man climbs a mountain with a cloth in his hand. He gives the mountain one wipe and goes away. That mountain will be worn to nothing before an aeon passes! The Buddha should never be taken literally. Yet science now tells us that the days of Creation were long indeed. The world was in place aeons before our simian minds began to ponder their own existence. And I have no doubt it will be spinning still, sunrise after sunrise, for aeons more after our moment in the sun is gone; when nothing shall remain of us but fossils in stone and a few great works—pyramids, castles, canals, viaducts—fading like smiles from the planet's face."

These musings were ended by the bark of Captain Skinner ordering us below. He did not like the weather, saying a westerly at this season in these waters was sure to be trouble. Almost as he spoke, the wind outpaced the ship, tipping her chin into the swells. My poor watercolour was ripped from its pins and blown to sea, where it drew a sour inspection from a frigate bird.

Skinner ran up a steadying jib and let the ship have her head, on past Raiatea, past Huahine, on across the open sea towards Tahiti. He did not explain his actions. My conjecture is that he was making a reconnaissance to satisfy himself no warships were at the Leewards or bound there from the Windwards. Around five, when the wind had abated after a swift run of several hours, the lookout sang that he could see Tahiti's loom. I took my telescope and went aloft, finding myself swung about the foretop like a monkey on a stick. But once settled in my perch, I caught sight of a great heap of cumulus on the horizon, turning gold in the last of the sun. I must have stayed aloft an hour, watching flying fish leap from the shadow of our bow, as the shining albacore closed on them, and slip back into the water like thrown coins. The gold reddened and the image began to melt into the rosy dusk. Then came a brief glimpse of land under the cloud, a cone that could only be Orohena, the great mountain of Tahiti—seven thousand feet high and visible from seventy miles.

Neither I nor the lookout descried any sail or smoke. In that lonely Sea of Moons we might have been back in the days before any brimstone blew across a quarterdeck; before steam-engines clambered into hulls and began puffing back and forth across the world.

Skinner held course until the light failed, then ordered bare spars and turned half circle, back to the Leewards and the embers where the sun had drowned.

We steamed half that night, cutting through oncoming seas, confident no man-of-war could catch us, even had our trace been sighted.

I was awakened in the small hours by a clang of the engine telegraph and a change in rhythm as the revolutions slowed. The ship flumped on the swell for a while, then steadied quickly. The menacing seethe and dunt of a reef grew loud in my porthole. I threw a native cloth around my waist and went on deck. The binnacle was unlit, but the trollish form silhouetted at the helm was unmistakably Skinner himself. The wind had dropped, or rather we were sheltered from it, for strips of buttonhook cloud were driving across the moon.

I made out a black mass of cliffs or hills dead ahead and the phosphorescent grin of the reef astern, nothing more. Skinner seemed to steer by smell, by the perfume of orange blossom, gardenia, and wet earth wafting from the darkness. It was madness, I thought, to be under way like this, however slowly. A strange flute was trilling to port, whilst a conch moaned to starboard, as if we were being lured onshore by wreckers.

Dark walls drew in, the sky shrank to a wedge, the scent of land grew strong, the screw throbbing no quicker than a heartbeat. We were inching up a narrow bay or estuary. With a sudden hiss and flurry the engine reversed. The heartbeat stopped.

The anchors made a shallow dive.

Thirteen

❧ ❧

TAHITI

Women's Prison

Taiohae, Nuku Hiva. October 23, 1989.

Dear Bob:

Living here on the beach where Melville and my
father ran away, the crossover land of stray whites
and errant locals, the place where our centuries have
made their deepest erasure of island time. You see,
I've done my homework. I'm also literally on the
beach, sitting at a picnic table beneath a barringtonia,
which drops red and white brushes every night on
the strand.

I'm staying at Hotel Hikokua, the best my
budget will allow, a tiny guest house just above the
tideline where jetsam gathers. I include myself: I am
certainly jetsam. The Marquesans let you know.

These are the Surly Isles, though one can hardly blame them.

Mine host, a taciturn Nuku Hivan, cuts a figure like Schwarzenegger playing the Illustrated Man. A promising extra for my film. His tattoos are mysterious. No hearts and anchors and winged swords. They look like hieroglyphs or heraldry, and are a work-in-progress. The left foot is done from toenails to mid-calf but the right one isn't, so he seems to be wearing one blue tartan sock. Round his neck is a choker of whirls and chevrons. Each shoulder and elbow has a large dark oval, as if he once wore a motorcycle jacket of which only the pads remain, while the right fore-arm is intricately inscribed to the wrist, stopping short of his diver's Rolex (a fake). I asked what this armful might mean: *C'est une histoire longue, M'selle.* What kind of story? *Longue.*

His daily attire: hot pink bathing trunks, yellow flip-flops, a seashell necklace. All morning he reads bodybuilder mags, sips Hinano beer, and is augustly drunk by lunch, when friends drop in to watch TV and help him eat the profits. His wife—a pretty waif with a baby on her hip, a mauve pareu round her waist, and nothing above it save a black lace bra— eventually drives them away by swearing a blue streak in Marquesan.

Yesterday afternoon the tattooist came to continue the Work, and my siesta was punctuated not by the tap-tap-tap of mallet on shark's tooth that Melville describes, but a familiar mechanical buzzing. The twentieth-century gear is an old Philishave with a needle soldered to the heads. The artist was carrying dog-eared photocopies of Krusenstern, Steinen, and Willowdean Handy; hence the designs, entirely authentic, recorded before the last original canvases rotted with their owners. Long story indeed.

My neighbours. Room 3: a tall Tahitian, a nurse I think, her black hair in a single plait to her bum.

Room 4, next to mine: a vintage Kiwi hippie "finding himself." Possibly a divorced computer salesman. Spends long hours practising the ukulele. This morning I uttered a threat to fill it with concrete.

Room 5, across the passage: an Englishman, about my age, toffish voice and an expensive surfboard he "never travels without." Bummed with the Marquesas because there's nowhere to go surfing "unless one fancies being splattered on the rocks." His girlfriend, a wilting rose named Lavinia, is tired of travel and very bored with the surfboard. She talks about the kitchen she wants to put in their Hampstead house. She touched her knee to mine last night at dinner and kept it there. Enough of man, apparently.

But I don't want to talk kitchens. Come here and rescue me, you old wanker.

Missing you like hell. Come and treat me to Chez Merivi, Melville's Place, the best and most

romantic on the island. Gorgeous view and you'd like
the owner, an exiled American *comme toi*. I've a lot to
tell you, especially about those contacts of yours.
We've been "helping the police." I'll save that for
next time, when things have shaken out. Nothing yet
on my dad, but the police are also helping me.

XXXXXX Liv

Well, I was missing him, and I don't mind letting you peek at my
letters (parts of them). I owe you so much—twenty-two years—
yet I don't know how much of this you really want or need. In low
moments I think you may be getting in touch just for the medical records, to make sure there's nothing nasty up the family tree.
And that's fine. If those are all you want, you shall have them
with my blessing. This long letter to you is, above all, about the
blood in our veins. Whether you and I will ever have more than
blood in common remains to be seen.

We returned to the gendarmerie at four that first day in Taiohae,
and went back there every day for a week, but no word came from
Papeete. Strange how that brash port now loomed in our minds
as a metropolis, as it did for the Marquesans. The police took
sworn statements and asked us tactfully not to leave town without letting them know.

Sergeant Benoit wasn't sure, at first, how to take my own
search. I think the story of Jon seemed almost as incredible to
him as the unprecedented matter of the girl. The *Alors* and *Mon*

Dieus came thickly. But he listened and tried to help. No immigration records survived from those days. His were routinely sent to Papeete after five years and kept, he thought, for five more before being discarded or sent on microfiche to Paris. The police records of the Marquesas—he indicated some metal cabinets—went back twenty years. Anything older would also have been sent to a warehouse in Papeete, where . . . he shrugged and allowed himself a smile, "Let us just say, Mademoiselle, that the little grey mice and the little white ants have relieved many a felon of his anxieties."

I left him my father's details, asking if someone might be able to go through the records. Or perhaps, if they were too busy, I could look myself? The latter was out of the question, especially as I and my friends were under investigation. But he introduced me to Heikua, his secretary, asking her to spend any slack hours on my request.

Nothing was going to happen quickly. And the benign languor of the island must have begun to soak into me, for I saw how unreasonable, how *métropolitain*, it would be to expect that anything should.

I was bitterly homesick, missing Lottie and Mother, missing Jon—my old idea of him seemed so distant now, and my imaginings of what I might find were washing away in the tides of daily life. And I was thinking of a Yankee in a rainy city at the top right-hand corner of this ocean, of the day he looked at the postmark on a letter I'd hoped might tell me everything, and which was starting to seem a dead end.

If there were clues, they were forgotten or so deeply buried I hadn't the archaeological skill to unearth them. No one remembered the 1950s, or wanted to. The Marquesans seemed to live in a continual present. Most were young, younger than I, their numbers bouncing back from catastrophic decline. I'd seen the figures: perhaps 80,000 on these islands when contact with the outside world began; by 1860 fewer than 10,000; by 1920 only 2,000. In 1936 a mere 1,300 Marquesans were counted, and experts foretold their imminent extinction. Syphilis, smallpox, tuberculosis, alcohol, opium, murder, suicide.

The Nuku Hiva I saw was twenty miles across, with this one small town and two or three tiny hamlets. But old Nuku Hiva had been a teeming, edgy place, ethnically and geographically as convoluted as a brain, each valley a nation, each ridge a frontier. That was how the old civilization died, in disease and rum to be sure, but also in a last conflagration of ancient feuds, modern firearms, and despair.

Small wonder the survivors were so withdrawn, so divorced from their past, so given to silence and drink.

"I'm *fiu* with Taiohae!" Natalie and I were having coffee below my hotel, sitting by the middle of the horseshoe beach, opposite the ocean passage, hard below the dark cusp of Muake, at the focal point of the land. "If you're bored, fed up, exasperated with husband, job, place or weather, the word is *fiu*. Are we under house arrest or what?"

There'd been no word from the *Tui*'s owner, the anonymous angel of Fletcher Christian Tours. Attempts to ring Lars had raised only a recorded voice apologizing for difficulties with the line. Natalie felt watched and trapped in all this beauty, on centre stage in an amphitheatre filled with ghosts. When she left I jotted in my notebook: *I have come for ghosts.*

I was seeing him on the road, the way one does at the beginning and end of an affair; your heart quickens, you peer inquiringly—*it can't be!* And no, it isn't. I had a picture of Jon in my handbag, Lottie on his knee. I'd been stumping up and down streets, knocking on doors like a Jehovah's Witness, showing it to everyone, especially the old. But what would he look like now, half a lifetime later?

My father could be anywhere in the world, or dead thirty years, but if I moved on without searching the Marquesas inside out, I'd spend the rest of my life haunted by the thought that while I sat at a café table, he might have shuffled past: the white-haired fisherman disappearing into a shop, the muttering street-sweeper with his head bent, the old fellow in a crash-helmet starting his scooter.

And if he'd found a woman there might be people like me, my half-brothers and sisters, his Nordic features mingled with their colour. These younger ghosts were everywhere. Many islanders had European looks, a legacy of whalers, beachcombers, slavers, marines, or even of Spaniards from the sixteenth century, when Mendaña fetched up here and butchered hundreds while looking for a New Jerusalem. Several mistook me for a local until I opened my mouth, and of course I was wondering about this. If I had a touch of the tarbrush (as Lottie liked to say), was it only mine? Was that my mother's secret? Or had it surfaced from deeper in the family gene pool, from Henderson's time? Jon himself might not be here, but there could well be descendants of the man he'd come looking for, distant cousins of ours walking the street.

I wanted to go everywhere at once, every village and valley, all six inhabited islands. The task may seem overwhelming to you, as it did to me while I was stuck in Taiohae. But the tiny population was a tragedy in my favour. Only a few dozen people on each island could have been adults in 1953. I'd stay until I'd spoken to them all.

At the mairie—an old fort that Americans, British, and French had all held at one time or another—I bought a topographical map showing every house and feature on Nuku Hiva, except for white spaces in the mountains where cloud had blanked the aerial survey. The mayor, who had a Xerox machine, helped me make up a poster with Jon's photo to put in shops and offices: *CON-NAISSEZ-VOUS CET HOMME?*

Simon announced he was flying to Papeete to talk to Lars and the Australian consul. All seats on the whimsical air service were still booked solid, and the airstrip was several hours away across the mountains. But he was going to camp there for a stand-by seat "and be such a bastard they'll bounce someone just to get rid of me." This seemed a workable plan. The gendarmes raised no objection, and he left in Taiohae's only taxi, a battered jeep.

Meanwhile I covered church, state, and free enterprise with my posters and enquiries. The schoolteacher, a young Demi from

Tahiti named Monique, listened well but knew nothing. The priest, a Father Yves, had been on Nuku Hiva only a year; his heart was still in France. He poured out coffee and memories of Avignon. He showed me his church and took me to the cemetery, where I spent hours pulling weeds from weathered stones and lacy cast-iron crosses, in a welter of emotion, hardly knowing whether I wanted to find Jon or not to find him there.

Was there anywhere else the dead might be buried; in house platforms, for example, as I'd read?

"No! Not in the nineteen-fifties." Father Yves laughed awkwardly, as if the persistence of heathen customs might be a professional embarrassment. "I doubt anyone has been buried in a *paepae* this century. Of course, two villages also have churchyards. Hatiheu. Taipivai." *Taipi-vai*, the Taipi Valley: Melville's Typee. Since landing on Nuku Hiva I'd hardly thought about him, his book, my film.

"The only other place I can suggest," the priest added, "is an old Protestant cemetery, beyond the fort. No one's been buried there in years. Marquesans are Catholics. But occasionally, when a Tahitian or a foreigner dies here. . . ."

I left fuming. I should have gone there first. Surely a French priest would know that an Englishman was likely to be a Protestant? Either Father Yves was a bit dim-witted (Nuku Hiva was hardly the plummest parish in the French empire) or he'd stalled from some ridiculous sectarian rivalry.

The small burial ground lay up a track beyond the government wharf at the far end of the village. I had to ask directions several times to find it. When I got there I saw I'd judged the priest harshly; the place might easily have slipped his mind. Cliffs rose sharply behind, their wild vegetation tiptoeing back among the graves. Elderly frangipani, leafless but in bloom, tottered like branching coral over the headstones. I found a stick and began slashing at the undergrowth.

My discovery took less than an hour, but raised many more questions than it answered. I peeled a poultice of moss and roots from a simple concrete slab edged with pebbles. I swept away loose earth, and read:

J. HENDERSON
† 1953
Age inconnu
Inhumé 25·8·1959
R.I.P

It began to rain but I hardly noticed. I knelt down on the brush I'd felled, ran my finger over the crude letters, confirming they'd been scratched into the cement when it was soft. Could this be the man Jon was looking for—some descendant of Frank's? Or was it Jon himself, under a false name? But why the precise date of burial and vague time of death? No one else had a pair of dates like these.

Of course it was just possible that this Henderson had no connection to Jon whatsoever, like the Mormon in Tahiti. The name is common enough. But surely not in a place the size of Nuku Hiva. There can't have been eight hundred people on the whole island in 1953. If this was coincidence, it was cruel enough to make one believe the Greeks were right about the gods: that they're a bunch of overgrown wastrels roistering away in the clouds, and every now and again one of them gets bored—gets tired of brawling and screwing with the rest—and decides to toss down a lump of shit or gold in the path of us mortals, just to see what we'll do.

Sergeant Benoit gripped my elbow warmly and handed me into a chair. We'd fallen into a pattern of communication: I understood his French if he spoke slowly, he understood my English if I did the same. He came round from his desk and sat opposite me, his fingers in a cat's cradle.

"My secretary has checked the earliest papers." He looked over at Heikua, who nodded glumly. "She has found nothing yet. No Englishman of the right age. Not even an American or Australian. . . ."

I burst in with my discovery, explaining that Henderson was a family name. He thought for a moment, then snatched up a bunch of keys. "Come!" We jounced back to the graveyard in his Land Rover. Soon we were standing by the slab, in light rain and the moist fetor of slashed weeds.

"As you describe," he muttered. "It is curious, two dates. This person—and let us keep in mind that we don't know if this is a man or a woman—this individual must have been moved or reburied. Or found six years after death. This is possible." He got down and scraped at the letters. "The grave is very plain, even for a Protestant. No headstone. No Christian name. Only an initial. Facts, nothing more. This looks to me like an official inscription."

"Except R.I.P."

"R.I.P. is something one might put when one knows nothing. On the grave of a sailor or a soldier, for example. It is possible this belongs to a body washed up from the sea, from a wreck."

"Who might know? There must be people around who'd remember. It was only thirty years ago."

"I'm afraid thirty years is a long time on Nuku Hiva, Mademoiselle. If this grave were in the Catholic cemetery there might be some connection with a local family. But here, and the age unknown. . . . It must have been an outsider. If I were you I'd ask anyone over fifty. But you've already been doing so." He turned and gazed down through the trees to the sheen of the bay. "There may be records in Papeete of a shipwreck at that time."

He fell silent, thinking, eager to help, oblivious of the rain soaking into his starched shirt. Suddenly he stamped his foot, a winning, childish gesture. "*Comme je suis vachement stupide!* Tari Kautai is the one for you! Many years ago he was constable here. Long before my time."

This man, very old now, lived in Taipivai but wasn't on the island at the moment. He'd been flown to Tahiti some weeks ago for an operation, but was expected back soon. "A hip replacement. They say he has a new woman! Some wood on the old tree must still be green." The sergeant allowed himself a smirk. "Though you wouldn't think so. Tari is half blind and deaf as a stone. But his brain is not bad. Well conserved in alcohol, like that of Einstein. Or is it Comte? Is it Comte whose preserved brain is no bigger than a chimpanzee's?"

"Where will he go when he comes back? Will he come to Taiohae?"

"He'll go straight home. We'll send our helicopter to the airstrip. He'll be home in twenty minutes. Old Tari's too frail to go by road. The Taipivai road's washed out anyway. You should visit him at his house. If this rain ever stops."

I begged him to let me go immediately. I wanted to be on the spot when the old man returned. Benoit was cagy, saying I might still be needed as a witness. I was terrified of being summoned to Papeete before having a chance to talk to this ex-constable. I wanted to be hard to find.

"How would you get there? I regret I can't let you go by boat. My orders. And more important for me, how would you get back?"

"I'll walk. I'm a keen hiker. How bad is the road?"

He pointed at the sugarloaf above the bay, thrusting darkly into cloud. "There's a landslide about three kilometres beyond Muake."

"Let me try. I've got a good map. If I reach Taipivai, and you need me in a hurry, you can always fetch me by boat or helicopter."

"If you knew our helicopter, Mademoiselle, you would not say such a thing! Only the very ill are not afraid of it." He laughed. Then he went silent, looking at the grave, and his eyes said he'd decided to let me go.

"You may go. But please, no boats." He wagged a finger. "Not even little ones." Then he shook his head, as if clearing water from his ears. His expression was strained, his voice low.

"You yourself were only a passenger with the others, is that not true?"

I said it was. He hissed in exasperation.

"This is what I have been telling Papeete!"

At sundown I went to Lily McIver's for dinner, to find the others and say goodbye. I got there before them and sat by the window. A stout man was unpacking woodcarvings he made to sell to yachtsmen, setting out a row of incised bowls and weirdly foetal tikis—gods and ancestors with pursed lips and bulging eyes. Like the tattooist, he copied ancient examples. Two or three generations ago, Marquesan society had shrunk to where there were not enough hands to pass the culture on. This happens in families, too, I thought. The road from the past is washed out, and all one can do is rescue a few artifacts and echoes and bits of paper.

I showed him Jon's photograph. He shook his head.

The sun had fallen behind the western rim but its light, coppery in the thick air, still lit a shoulder of Muake and the ridge above the little graveyard. The bay filled gently with dusk.

The others came in. Natalie sat down and puckered at the wine list. "Only one Aussie and it's a shit. Dunno about the Chilean. Won't touch French on principle. Doubt it's fit to drink by the time it gets here anyway. Even though we're in France right now!" she cawed sardonically.

Lily appeared, bright as ever.

"When are y'all going Melville hunting?"

"Just me. These two aren't crazy enough. I'm going up that ridge tomorrow, rain or shine."

"Last year I had some professor from . . . I don't rightly recall. Maybe Noo Yawk? He said the boys went *that* way." She pointed to a hollow far below the ridge. "There's a big ruin down in there, a place where they used to dance in the old days. What Melville called a hula-hula ground, on account of his time in Hawaii." A French oath issued from the kitchen. Lily glided away gracefully, a dancer herself, rolling a clear blue eye.

"I can't agree with that professor," I said *sotto voce*. "They stuck to the ridge all the way. You can read *Typee* like a guide-book. . . ."

"Listen, Liv." said Natalie, glancing at Vatu. "We have to say our final goodbyes tonight. Simon got out on a plane this morning. He's being questioned in Papeete. Sent a telex. They still have those here. We've got to go back to Tahiti."

"Flying?"

"Sailing. They may want to look over the boat."

I wondered what the authorities would make of Simon's samples. But I kept this to myself; I didn't want to take care of them.

"Can you sail her, just the pair of you?"

"We'll manage. It's true about Vatu—he's worth two." Natalie patted the Fijian's burly forearm. "The trades'll be with us. We'll motor if it gets rough."

They didn't seem too put out by this change of plan. Indeed, they were relieved to be off. They even planned to do some more "snooping," as they put it—something they'd have done on our way here if we hadn't had the death to report. They'd heard rumours the French were preparing a new test site on Eiao, an uninhabited rock island only sixty miles from Nuku Hiva.

I'd seen it on the charts but given it no thought, till now.

"Could someone live there?"

"You mean your father?"

"I'd leave Eiao till the very end," Vatu said. "Too barren. Good for goats and bombs, and not much else. Long time ago, four Navy blokes deserted there. Three died of thirst." He topped up my glass and grinned. "The last one survived by using the others' skulls as water bottles."

It seemed very foolish of Natalie and Vatu to do more spying. But their plans weren't my business. I told them about the Henderson grave, the old constable in Taipivai. Hours later, after brandy with Lily and a conversation that seemed haunted by the dead—by Melville, Henderson, the girl, and perhaps by Jon—we walked along the beach to their dinghy, beneath a field of stars.

"Maybe we'll see you when you're back on Tahiti," Natalie said. "Ring Lars. He'll know where we are." She hugged me, a little desperately.

This was the last I saw of them until I spotted Natalie here in the prison yard.

⟨⟩ ⟨⟩

The *Tui Marama* was gone from her mooring by sunrise. There were no other boats. I walked down to the beach for a swim. In its stillness and emptiness the bay might have belonged to a time before man, to any of the twenty thousand centuries since Nuku Hiva rose and cooled.

"When I was a boy," my hotelier said unexpectedly at breakfast, after watching me study my map, "people used to walk that way to Taipivai across Hapaa. Before there were cars."

The menace of his silence, his bulk, and his tattoos vanished with these words. I asked him what he meant by Hapaa, which wasn't on the map. Soon we were chatting easily. His name was Pierre. Marquesans weren't surly, just shy and reserved—as I should have known, being English.

Taipivai and Hapaa: Melville's Typee and Happar. The first hundred pages of *Typee* resound with the question of these names. The Happar were said to be peaceful folk, already half tamed by missionaries, who might shelter Melville and his friend until their ship sailed off. But at all costs the runaways had to steer clear of the heathen Typee, "inveterate gormandizers of human flesh."

Pierre's large finger settled on a green blank running east from the crater rim. Across the contours was a dotted line, marked *Sentier*. "That's Hapaa. No one goes up there now except to hunt pig."

He thought this path joined the Taipivai road, probably beyond the landslide. From there it was only a few kilometres down to the village of Taipivai, where Tari Kautai lived.

I left most of my luggage with Pierre, taking only camping things and a change of clothes. His wife (a fuchsia bra that day) packed me a lunch. I made my way to the edge of town, found the path, and began climbing the crater rim.

Melville had been on board the *Acushnet* a year and half when she anchored at Taiohae in 1842. He'd seen no land in six months. Provisions were low. "The bark that once clung to the wood we use for fuel has been gnawed off and devoured by the captain's pig; and ... the pig himself has in turn been devoured." He decided to risk his luck "among the savages of the island."

From the *Acushnet*'s deck it had looked easy: a dash down a village lane and up the nearest spur, a scramble along the crab-claw ridge until they reached the high mountains. Opportunity came when the starboard watch were given a few hours' shore leave. A storm drove the Marquesans into their houses and the sailors into a boat shed. When their shipmates grew drowsy and began to doze among the war canoes, the two runaways sprinted through breadfruit groves and gardens, unseen in the misty downpour.

Even though I had a path to follow, the first stage of Melville's route was tough going—steep, overgrown, the humidity enervating. My pack seemed heavier than it should be; I blamed the bottle of whisky it held for Tari Kautai, bought on Sergeant Benoit's advice. It took more than an hour to gain the ridge and a phaeton's view of the Taiohae amphitheatre, its heights fogged, a tarnish on the bay. Due south, across a windy sea, I could just make out the spires of Ua Pou.

The trail wound through a grove of Tahitian chestnut into an empty wooded valley, the sun winking through heavy leaves.

Here and there the land sloped away, giving views of folded greenery ringed by mountains. There was no sight of the sea, no sound whatever of man. Only parakeets and bees, and wild cockerels flashing gaudily in the woods. I was enthralled. It was wonderful to be alone. If Jon had wanted to hide from the world he could hardly have picked a more delightful spot. But the thought faded as soon as it took full shape in my mind. No one could live here without supplies—matches, for a start. Sooner or later the most elusive hermit would become known to travellers and hunters.

There was a snort, the crunch of a large animal bullying through undergrowth, leaving a piggy scent on the air. This Eden had its dangers. Then I began to worry more about the hunters than the prey. What might they do to a foreign woman alone? I walked on nervously, considered turning back before dark, but the trail showed no recent footprints; I had Hapaa to myself.

Nearly all the trees—mango, guava, pandanus, banana, breadfruit—were food trees, descendants of old Marquesan orchards. This jungle was the work of woman and man, the overgrown garden of a ruined estate. And soon I saw ruins in the shadows, walls of *paepae*, the high rafts of stone on which wooden houses once stood. A neolithic civilization had thrived on these islands, glimpsed by Melville in its last good days. Now it was lost as Stonehenge, in only a hundred years.

The last two Hapaa, a man and a woman, had crossed the ridge to Taiohae a century ago, leaving their tribal home behind, a memory still fresh when Stevenson came, himself tubercular and doomed. Now nothing remained of them, and even their name was no longer written on maps. These were islands of oblivion, where people tattooed themselves with glyphs they couldn't read.

E hari te fau,	The palm tree will grow,
E toro te faaro,	The coral will spread,
E mo te taata.	But man will die.

By mid-afternoon the path had branched several times, bearing no relation to the confident line on paper. The way I chose became clogged with recent growth; soon I was breaking trail with a stick. I wasn't exactly lost—map and compass told me I'd hit the road beyond Muake eventually—but I was running on dead reckoning.

The sky whitened to a lifeless haze. The air became oppressive. I stopped to drink at every stream that looked undisturbed by pigs, beginning to see the wisdom in Vichy water. The more I drank, the more I sweated.

Then rain came, thick cool rain, welcome until I stopped for the night and began to feel downright chilled. I had trouble finding a level spot to pitch the tent. Eventually I flattened some bush on an ancient paepae, and slept under nylon where a Marquesan family had lived under thatch.

I woke often from frightening dreams to more tangible fears of drunken hunters and wild boars. Once, I had to force myself outside to pee. Squatting in the bushes (always the worst part of camping) I remembered the giant centipede: *a bite characterized by immediate severe pain, followed by tissue necrosis.* It took a long time to fall asleep after that. There were things in the night beyond the nylon membrane—snapping branches, footfalls, breaths, grunts, stifled cries. It wasn't hard to understand the old Polynesian dread of *tupapau*, the restless ghosts who lurk in lonely places. No doubt there were plenty of them in Hapaa. And as I floated between sleep and wakefulness, I was visited by a ghost of my own—scenes of my father lost and starving, stumbling about up here like Melville, sick in body or mind. He was buried in this very paepae, and I was lying on his bones.

The rain ended by dawn. I wriggled from my cocoon into a world of mist. Somehow I got a fire going and made tea. After that I pressed on miserably, each step bringing down a shower of drips. At last, around midday, I saw open light through the trees: a track, presumably the road to Taipivai. But Muake seemed too close.

I sat under a mango tree and ate some nuts and chocolate. Revived, I left my pack there and took a look around. I could hear the roar of a waterfall; if I could see it, it might fix my position. The central plateau of Nuku Hiva is a raised dish of swamps and streams overflowing in three great waterfalls, two of which drop into the forked canyon of Typee.

This high wilderness had been a no man's land in ancient times, avoided by the Marquesan tribes except when they swarmed up here to make war in clearings strewn with bones and broken weapons. Again it struck me how Balkanized these islands had become, as if the history of whole continents had had to be repeated here in miniature. The people might know themselves to be descended from a single fleet, yet still they divided and fought—as if human enmity must always fill the space allowed it, whether an island or a world.

The roaring strengthened until I was certainly above a large waterfall. But all I could see was a swollen river, narrow, deep, and fast, vanishing over the lip of a chasm brimming with spray. I went closer, lured by an illusion of safety spun by the mist. The edge was dangerous, an overhang of slippery grass, loose stones, and clay. Suddenly the mist rose in an updraft, revealing a long canyon gouged a thousand feet deep into the land. This great waterfall had to be Vaiahu. Not far from here, Melville had pushed aside a bough and looked "straight down into the bosom of a valley" like "a glimpse of the gardens of Paradise."

He had seen thatched houses, bleached and glistening, but now there was no sign of human beings at all. Jungle covered everything except the steepest cliffs. Small clouds were sailing like balloons between the sheer green walls.

I wondered if Jon had seen this. I felt certain he had. He sought out such places—for their own sake and for photographs. I felt him with me, looking through my eyes. And I thought of you. If you were like me, you'd want to see this too.

There was no way down. It took Melville and Toby several days and nights of great hardship to cross the Vaiahu River higher up, reach the second branch of the Y-shaped Typee Valley, and literally drop into the canyon, launching themselves from a precipice onto the crown of a palm tree as if it were a safety net.

By then Melville was feverish and lame, his leg bitten by some "congenial inhabitant of the chasm," probably a centipede.

"The continual roaring of the cataract—the dismal moaning of the gale through the trees—the pattering of the rain, and the profound darkness, affected my spirits to a degree which nothing had ever before produced. Wet, half famished, . . . nearly wild with the pain I endured, I abandoned myself to frightful anticipations of evil."

I went back to where I'd had lunch and started along the road towards Taipivai. After an hour I came to the slide, a cone of red earth and chunks of basalt. It wasn't hard to scramble across. I'd not gone much further when I heard a vehicle. A Marquesan family went past in a red pick-up, inspected the barrier, and turned round, giving me a welcome lift to Typee.

They were free with smiles, but taciturn as the rest. I thought: Getting people to speak to me (let alone to camera) will be difficult. No one here seems even faintly curious about outsiders. I suppose they've had enough of us.

Fourteen

❦ ❦

ENGLAND

Riverhill. January, 1900

HOW STRANGE TO WRITE THE DATE of a new century, tho'
mathematicos tell us we're stuck in the old one for another year
yet. What will it bring, one wonders? Or should I be sanguine
and ask, What wonders will it bring? Twelfth Night last night,
and we gathered—the whole tribe and sundry neighbours—for
our yearly reading of the play in Mother's drawing-room. Ivry
was a radiant Olivia, and Admiral George a salty Antonio.
Gertrude read both Viola and Maria, equally well. Henry had great
fun as Aguecheek. But I believe I can honestly say, without fear or
favour, that I stole the show with my Sir Toby Belch. Ivry says
that's nothing to be proud of, since I didn't have to act! Well, she'll
soon have a break from my coarse male presence about the house:
back to Kumasi in a month. And she has hinted, though I hardly
dare hope—and the news brings almost as great apprehension as
joy—that when I return, a little stranger may have joined us.

So much in the future! But back, now, to that anonymous landfall in the South Pacific, and the conclusion of my voyage in troubled waters of the past.

❦ ❦

I had to admire Skinner's midnight seamanship when I went on deck next morning. Cirrus raced across a turbulent heaven, but we lay snug as any ship in a bottle. He'd brought his vessel several miles up a narrow reach gashed into the steep island as if by a titanic axe, and had anchored in water scarcely deeper than her draft in the one spot where no passing vessel beyond the reef could see us, because of an intervening *motu*, or islet, tufted with coconuts.

The cleft (a "tickle" he called it) resembled a firth or fiord, though cold northern words can't convey the luxuriant verdure draping the cliffs: here a tracery of ferns on pillowed basalt, there an overhanging rainforest, the great trees nearly touching across waters Skinner had navigated in the dark. Phaetons wheeled far above between the cliffs, snowy plumage flashing and their long tailfeathers trailing like kite ribbons, white and pink. Silver torrents threaded down from a peak lost in cloud, vanishing into dark ravines and leaping from ledges in bridal veils.

I was roused from contemplation of this scene, which I longed to paint at the first opportunity, by a shout from a double canoe emerging from the river at the head of the gorge. It held three big men attired in red-and-white kilts, who came alongside, shouting *Karani! Karani!* until Carny emerged and bade them aboard. From the hearty greeting and warm embraces the diminutive skipper received from these bronze giants, it was clear

322

that Skinner was a frequent visitor to this smugglers' cove. All went below for "calibogus."

After half an hour or so Prince Eddy, Dalton, and I were called. Skinner introduced us to the islanders, one of whom had a smattering of English. "These gentleman," he said to them, "have business of their own to discuss with you. So I'll take me leave. *Con permiso.*" His manner with us had become more respectful since Dalton had at last told him who we were. There could be no keeping the secret now that Eddy would have to play a ceremonial role, for if Skinner didn't treat the Prince with due deference it would have disparaged him before the natives.

The name of the island was never divulged to me by Dalton, though I know very well it was Raiatea. I would recognize instantly, should ever I see them again, its turquoise reefs, dark woods, and lofty mountains. While Tahiti itself had been lost to the French beyond any hope of recovery since Pomare V's abdication, affairs in the Leewards hung in the balance, and this island of our landfall was the key, in Dalton's view, to the outcome for the whole Leeward group.

The French had suborned the chief of neighbouring Tahaa, setting him up with a flagpole and two hundred marines as "King" of both. His dominion, however, extended no further than a cannon shot from the only haven deep enough for a man-of-war. The rest of Raiatea and others in the group were united in their opposition to French designs by a *guerrilla* leader operating from the mountains, a man named Teraupoo.

My latest intelligence is that these islands remained in a state of warfare throughout the 1880s and '90s, the native faction opposed to France yielding to the *tricolore* only a year ago as I write, its leader packed off to New Caledonia in chains.

Dalton explained to the skipper's guests that we were British, that one of us was a grandson of Queen Victoria, and that we had weighty matters to discuss with their chief. When the three men grasped that Eddy was a Prince, they fell prone before him and launched into a long harangue. The gist of this, conveyed by Skinner, was that they were commoners who had come aboard under orders to obtain certain supplies; they had never expected to meet an *Arii Peretani*, a High Chief of Britain. They were not worthy to welcome him, and begged our leave to alert their own chiefs, in order that a suitable reception might be prepared.

So we waited several hours, and I got in my painting after all. Skinner minded his own business, which included the swift unloading of heavy kegs and boxes. He warped his vessel round neatly until she faced the sea. During our whole time on that island, he kept fires lit and steam up—a wise and prescient precaution.

Not long after midday there emerged from the shade of a coconut grove near the river a crowd of several dozen Polynesians attired in a mix of foreign and local fashions—top hats, pandanus wreaths, phaeton-plume headdresses, bustles and ponchos of tapa cloth, cotton pyjamas, silk waistcoats. The mature women wore decorous cloak-like dresses of Wesleyan *couture*, but their black hair was gay with orange blossom, gardenias, and hibiscus blooms. The nubile girls had on nothing but the pareu, a bright rectangle of muslin or calico wrapped tightly round their slender forms and knotted like a bathtowel just above the bosom.

What caught all eyes, as we rowed ashore, was a tableau of Britannia sitting regally under a breadfruit tree, so startling and incongruous a sight it seemed an hallucination induced by Skinner's grog. The goddess was posed more or less as she appears on the back of every penny: a lovely statuesque young girl draped like Athena, a long spear in one hand and her other resting on a shield emblazoned with the Union Jack.

Dalton and myself stayed in the gig, but the *Arii Peretani* was hoisted out bodily by a man standing in the water. This giant, who wore a Norfolk jacket and deerstalker but no trousers, and who proved to be seven feet tall when he strode ashore, bore Eddy on his shoulders as a man might carry a three-year-old along the beach at Weston-Super-Mare.

"Not so much an honour, Henderson, as an insurance policy," Dalton commented, citing Reverend Ellis. "In the old days, if a high chief's feet touched ground it immediately became his property. So they kept visiting dignitaries aloft. Hard work. Many of them weighed three hundred pounds."

Once Eddy was safely deposited on a stool, his white suit a trifle wet about the ankles, Britannia approached to lay her shield and spear gracefully before him. Smiling and uttering *maeva*, "welcome," the dusky avatar of our national goddess placed a garland of petals around his neck, as is done among the Hindoos. We too were given the same honour as we stepped ashore. This, said Dalton, was not merely a welcome but a precaution against the island's ghosts and spirits, unusually plentiful hereabouts because the mountain above us was a sort of elephants' graveyard for migrating souls from all over the Societies.

"But they're Christians!" Eddy exclaimed.

"So are we," replied his tutor. "But how many in England do not believe in ghosts?" The evangelization of this place, he added, had been done in an irregular way by a pair of Cockney Dissenters, a blacksmith and a ham actor.

"They set themselves up as little kings, as that type of missionary often does." He sniffed disdainfully. "Fellows were out of their depth. Here they were, in the very Mecca of heathenism, with a temple to Taaroa on one side and to Oro, God of War, on the other. It was all too much for our East End divines. The actor went native, or off his head, or both—I forget—and the blacksmith became more interested in building schooners than toiling in the Lord's vineyard. He kept sailing away, years at a time, seeking softer ground in which to plant the Wesleyan seed. The islanders made do without him, cobbling together heretical beliefs from the new faith and the old."

Dalton's voice fell confidentially. "I have no doubt that half the people gathered here today could, if pressed, recall the last great sacrifice to Oro, when a hundred enemy were slain. Including a Frenchman or two. Anyone over thirty might have seen it."

I ventured a predictable joke about French cooking.

"Actually, you're wrong there, Henderson. The Tahitians were not cannibals. Strictly speaking. But a high chief might exercise the privilege of swallowing a victim's eye. They say Cook had to do it when he was here, to show what a great man he was. Down the hatch like a Brightlingsea oyster!"

The day's ceremony consisted mainly of feasting, though a few abstained altogether on the grounds of some taboo. The

Fijian dines heartily and quickly, keen to resume the important business of kava drinking. These Tahitians made a great show of food—course after course of fish, yams, breadfruit, tubers, baked pork, corned beef, bananas, and paw-paw—until all of us were full as ticks. One saw how the person of a chief might easily attain three hundredweight.

We were asked to be patient while their leader readied himself to greet us, which would happen on the morrow. At dusk we returned to the ship, had brandy and cigars, and went to our bunks. Britannia insisted that Eddy keep her regalia, and when these were brought aboard we saw that the shield was a large green turtle shell over which an old Union flag had been stretched. The spear seemed to date from earlier times, when the islanders had no iron. It was wholly of a hard, dark wood, very finely worked and polished, with a shaggy braid of human hair set into a groove at its base.

With dawn came a moaning of conchshells, the sound wavering, for wind was scudding down the firth in broomstrokes. A whaleboat came alongside while we breakfasted. Sensing that a certain buoyancy might be required of Eddy, Dalton made no objection to a round of calibogus.

We proceeded under oars to the mouth of the bay. Skinner came with us, having again enjoined Oputu to keep up steam even if we were gone several days. As the gorge widened, the forest on the cliffs began heaving and tossing, shedding many a leaf and frond into our boat. Skinner seemed worried by the weather but otherwise at home. I admired the views of island and reef as we passed between the two, the land rising in bold sweeps from the inside waters, choppy now but nothing like the open sea, where rollers ran murderously upon the reef and spent themselves in gouts of spume with a report of heavy guns.

Cook wrote that these shores, when first he saw them, were so thickly ringed by habitations that he could hardly tell where one village ended and the next began. Now a house was a rare sight. Dalton remarked that civilization was threatening to exterminate the native race. A thousand had died on Tahiti in the last 'flu epidemic, while not a single European perished. Jeremiahs had arisen, preaching that the white man sent these plagues intentionally, and it was only a matter of time before the last survivors would be rounded up and shot like pigs.

In mid-morning we drew into a bay, beaching below a village of burnt and ruined houses, testimony to a recent French bombardment. We were asked to follow on foot along the beach and up an overgrown path through young woods reclaiming former cultivations. As we climbed, this bush gave way to primaeval fern trees, gloomy banyans, and gnarled Tahitian chestnuts whose buttress roots snaked along the ground like spilled intestines. These moody trees had stood here long before the white man. A chill ran down my back and I had the notion of trespassing on Druidical groves.

We emerged at length into what had once been a large paved clearing, now half covered with scrub. Here and there were ancient buildings—walls of basalt blocks, platforms with seats made of slabs, and a standing stone of phallic shape and heroic size, being taller than myself. Here, on their ancestors' thrones, sat three men of aristocratic bearing arrayed in feathers and tapa. They rose to greet us. All were *arii*, or chiefs, and one a deacon of the church. Their military commander was not among them, for which they apologized, saying Teraupoo would join us at dusk, if not before.

The gathering was small: these three, we four whites, and a dozen other natives of both sexes. Eddy was enthroned on a stone seat, but the rest of us, not being *arii* of any sort, were obliged to sit on the ground. Skinner presented our hosts with a massy kava root from Fiji, which struck them as a gift beyond price, for the sacred plant had died out on their island. Expecting another gargantuan feast, we had eaten little at breakfast, but no food was in evidence. Instead, a girl approached Eddy, a tall beauty who might have stepped from the romantic pages of *Rarahu*. Her slim body was wound in pale muslin printed with large crimson flowers. Behind each ear was a hibiscus of matching hue, and her dark hair, which flowed abundantly to her waist, was studded with the small white stars of *tiare tahiti*, the wild gardenia whose heady fragrance beggars all description. So different was her attire and manner that it took me a moment to recognize this nymph as the very same who'd played Britannia.

Dalton glanced at her longingly, perhaps in expectation of her effect on the Prince. But instead of singing a pretty song of welcome, or planting a wreath on Eddy's head, or a kiss upon his cheek, the girl knelt opposite him, put her face within a few inches of his, and opened her mouth with her fingers as if displaying her ivory to a dentist. One of the chiefs whispered something in the Prince's ear. An astonished Eddy then performed a minute oral inspection, pronouncing the damsel's mouth to be flawless and spotlessly clean. She then approached each one of us and did the same.

Though the procedure struck me as a shocking intimacy, the girl's youth and beauty outshone any awkwardness when her eyes met mine. She had the large liquid eyes of Polynesia, dark and clear as forest pools, radiating a calm dignity as if to say that this was an honour for both of us, a happy meeting, the most natural thing in the world. Her nose was typical for her race, soft and wide like a baby's, and I caught a trace of mischief in her glance as she inspected my much sharper organ. I heard her inhale, and at the same time I breathed the gardenia scent of her hair, the coconut oil and cinnamon on her golden skin.

The girl withdrew to the platform and began to chew some of the roots we had brought, decorously spitting the proceeds into a wooden bowl. This was the local method for making kava, and very effective it proved to be. We drank round after round, breaking off only for some fruit, and by mid-afternoon were in a state not far removed from that of opium smokers. Indeed, I remember little of those hours but a drowsy reverie among old stones and trees, the wind keening in the upper branches. The sun slid down; shadows lengthened and filled the clearing, restoring to perfection the jagged walls and mossy pavements, until I seemed back in the heyday of this ancient temple, a languid worshipper of Oro.

We revived ourselves with pipes, cigars, and large cigarettes rolled in leaves, the Tahitians being much addicted to their home-grown tobacco. At about five o'clock some women brought food for us, a fine repast of fish, clams, and cold roast pig. Our hosts would not eat, saying it was "taboo" for them. This taboo did not extend to Skinner's keg of calibogus, which went down very well with everyone.

The light in the clearing was poor but not too faint to see that Eddy was hitting it off with a member of the opposite sex. She was handsome rather than pretty, a little fleshy but full-framed, taller than Britannia, beautifully turned out in a silk pareu and floral wreath, her long black lashes and red cheeks enhanced, respectively, with kohl and rouge.

Dalton, now in conversation with the deacon, who spoke English, looked on approvingly, as did the lovely kava girl, seated between me and Skinner on the grass, laughing and rolling her eyes. She had enough English to tell me her name: Tiurai, Tahitian for July, the month in which she had been born sixteen summers past. I told her mine, but the bunched consonants were beyond her lips' command. Skinner rendered me as Faraniki Henesoni, taking pains to explain the distinction between Faraniki (Frank) and Farani (France), an important one under the circumstances. With my "beach" Polynesian I asked her who Eddy's *vahine* (woman) might be. This produced a cascade of laughter from her pretty mouth and the information that the individual was not a *vahine* but a *mahu*. Thinking she might mean that Eddy's friend was married or betrothed, I pressed for details. Skinner came to my aid with a number of opaque definitions.

"How good are ye, sir, with a fousty secret?"

"Good enough, I hope."

"Then let me tell ye that a mahu is a Polynesian poodlefaker."
He paused, searching my face for comprehension. "A kanaka John-
Jane, sir. A *maricón* what's janneyed-up. A midnight surprise. What
them belowdecks calls . . . savin' your grace. . . ."

"Out with it, Captain, I'm still no wiser."

"The lads, sir, they calls 'em fuckaladies, sir. For, er . . . hob-
vious reasons."

"You mean a prostitute?"

"Well, some is and some hisn't. But I don't tink ye're getting me."

At this moment I was appalled to see Reverend Dalton in the
offing.

"Actually, Henderson," he said, lowering himself didactical-
ly to the grass, "the word is not the English profanity you might
suppose. The term is Polynesian: *faka leiti*. It means 'in the manner of a woman.' The custom is indeed curious. If a family has
only sons and wants a daughter, they may raise a boy as a girl. He
assumes a girl's name, wears flowers and feminine attire, becomes
proficient in cooking, mat-making—all the distaff arts. He is
treated in every way as a normal woman. He may even marry."

"Marry aye, Reverend," said Skinner. "But I've never known
one drop a kid."

"But I fail to see the point," I broke in. "The Chinese or
Hindoo wants a son so badly he'll leave a baby girl to die. Why
should the South Sea islander, in his state of Nature, want counterfeit daughters?"

"Perhaps it has to do with the voluptuous character of the
Polynesian and, more practically, with Malthusian pressure. An

island can support only so many mouths. When it's full up, as many of these seem to have been when first discovered, there's no premium on fertility. A barren wife is no disgrace. On the contrary, a counterfeit woman, proficient in . . . er . . . female arts. . . ." He coughed into a hand and lowered his voice. "Captain Cook and others observed such practices."

Dalton had taken our discussion as purely ethnological. That Eddy's companion was not what "she" seemed had escaped him. And so, mercifully, did Eddy's reaction, when the understanding that eluded Dalton dawned upon the Prince. This I saw: it was the look of a tarantula that has just spied prey. But can a tarantula be said to have a look at all? Of course not. No, it was merely a predatory stillness; but one knew where it would lead.

I regarded the mahu with fresh eyes. Indeed, I could hardly take my eyes off the amphibious creature. He was lovely—not a word I normally employ for my own sex, but even without the silk, the make-up, the hibiscus bloom behind his ear, he would still have been lovely. This godling vouchsafed to those of normal appetites a glimpse of the magnetic force of the abnormal. And (leaving aside the question of what may be normal and abnormal in such a place) he vouchsafed to other men—to me, at least—an intimation of what women see in us, of *how* they see us.

"One feels it in the air, among these pagan stones, don't you agree, Henderson?" the tutor naively observed. "A certain indefinable voluptuousness, what? Ellis reports that Oro was an Eros as well as a Mars. Carnal love was a god amongst these children of Nature. Such capital women! So free! Though they may be sinners in our eyes, let us remember they are not sinners in their own hearts. Unlike ourselves."

A messenger came from the woods with ponies, announcing that Teraupoo had sent these to convey us to his fastness in the hills.

We ascended a dank ravine. Streamers of mist formed at chest height and wove between the trees. We rode in silence; doubtless the French and their puppet King had many spies on the island. As the path rose into the highlands it grew muddy where wild animals had passed. Our mounts began to stumble on clay and roots. We were obliged to continue on foot, Eddy soon slipping in a puddle. I saw the tall figure of the mahu beside him, whispering reassurance, steering him with a gentle touch on the elbow, the shoulder, in the small of his back.

The slim hand of Tiurai slipped into mine like a child's.

The sun left without any farewell glow. Soon it was dark. I began to doubt the wisdom of this march. Were we perhaps being lured into ambush, as Skinner was muttering under his breath? He admitted he'd never met their leader face to face. He did not know these people or these hills. The weather was gathering itself for some mighty outburst, and he was miles from where he should be—with his ship. He did not share our interest in the secrets of the land. Sailors go round and round the world, but they never get far into it.

Our mysterious destination came to us as a hot blast and a strange glow filtering between the trunks of giant trees. Ahead was a clearing of light—light cast upward on the boughs. In the ground was a shimmering pool of white and red, figures moving darkly at its perimeter, stirring the source of light and heat with long poles, like devils torturing the damned.

"*Aue!*" Tiurai exclaimed in delight, squeezing my hand.

The pit was about ten paces long and half as wide. A great fire, which had raged there for a day or more, was in the last stages of combustion, having transferred its energy to several tons of glowing volcanic stones. The demons were levelling and turning these to make an even bed of coals. At close quarters the scene resembled some industrial process, and I couldn't fix my eyes for long against the incandescence. Any leaf or twig that fell burst into flames.

"The learned Ellis must have been mistaken," I remarked to Dalton. "What can this be but an oven for roasting 'long pigs'—in this case four white ones?"

"I have the deacon's assurance that we are about to witness something remarkable—even inexplicable—but will live to tell the tale."

The deacon joined us, saying that though his people had lacked precise knowledge of *Te Atua*, the Lord God, until white men brought His Book across the sea, yet they had known in their innocence some elements of His Truth which the white man had not been given, or had forgotten. Chief of these was the miracle of the fiery furnace—the very same by which Shadrach, Meshach, and Abednego had struck the fear of the Lord into the King of Babylon.

Dalton assured the deacon that we worshipped the same God he did in every way, and trusted that it would therefore be unnecessary to cast us into the furnace as a test of our faith.

"Well, I don't say as I agree with that," Skinner struck in. "Me dear old Ma baptized me a Roman in the church of Santa Rosa de Lima! I worships a different Lord from the likes of Swaddlers and heathens."

The deacon smiled ironically. "The white people," said he, "brought us this Book but they do not believe in its miracles!" No foreigner, to his knowledge, had ever walked the fire. We were to watch, nothing more. Indeed, he begged us not to follow the example of the firewalkers, no matter how strongly we might feel "called" to do so, because we had not observed certain indispensable taboos. To tread the oven in an unclean state was sure to end in death or terrible injury.

Religion of all kinds was evidently the family business, for the deacon's own brother was the *tahua*, or holy man, who knew the rites for walking the furnace, namely certain prayers in an ancient tongue which, the deacon assured us, was identical with that spoken by the Israelites in Babylon. This tahua would soon emerge from a little kiosk of leaves on the far side of the pit, quavering in the oily light of candlenut torches.

In the dancing air there appeared a ghostly figure dressed in the ancient style of the Tahitian islands, white tapa about his waist. He wore a headdress of long leaves, whose tips jutted out like the crowning spikes of an aloe and bobbed as he walked, and in his hand was a leafy wand. His face and limbs were nearly invisible against the darkness, so he seemed a hollow man, a thing of nightmare.

The spectre halted by the far edge of the pit and began a long chant to some spirit or deity, which (*pace* the deacon) I was sure had scant relation to the God of Israel. Some fifty people were around the pit: men, women, children, and we four unclean *popaa*. The oration done, nothing could be heard but the cracking and spitting of the furnace, and the wind soughing in the trees. All present seemed to hold their breath as, with upright carriage and wizened face fixed on heaven, the tahua stepped down onto the white-hot stones and calmly walked the oven's length towards us.

I could see the hem of his pareu, which hung to his knees, agitated by the rising heat but not scorched, and there was no sizzle or smell of burning flesh from his bare feet. Neither was there any flinch in his movements or expression, no sign whatever of pain. He seemed entranced, far removed from daily consciousness. When he reached the end of the pit where we four sat transfixed, he stopped, turned, lifted his wand majestically, and walked slowly back to where he had begun.

He raised his wand again. Now others got to their feet and began to file behind him. One by one they stepped down into the furnace as if entering a paddling pool, except that all kept their eyes upturned to the night sky. It seemed the tahua had the power to confer his mastery on them. Some forty people were soon moving through the incandescence, all under the same enchantment. Each time the priest reached an end of the pit he called out, and in this way the walkers followed him back and forth six times.

I was astounded to see the deacon there, and the other chiefs who had received us, but my amazement knew no bounds when I descried the slender form of Tiurai rippling in the midst of the heat.

The last to enter the pit, and to leave it, was the seven-foot Triton who had borne Eddy on his shoulders from the sea. Here, among several others well beyond six foot, his stature did not seem so exceptional, yet his tall form moving in the haze and glow was an unforgettable sight, and as I watched him pass calmly back for the last time, back to safety and the normal world where fire and flesh are foes, I heard Dalton softly quoting to himself in wonder: *Lo, I see four men loose, walking in the midst of the fire, and they have no hurt; and the form of the fourth is like the Son of God.*

The holy man withdrew to his hut, the walkers fell back to the rim of the light, a hush fell on the outlandish scene.

"Jaysus!" Skinner exploded. "Lord liftin' Jaysus!" There followed a litany of "Can ye believe your eyes?" and "Never in all me years," and less repeatable expressions of incredulity. He'd heard talk of this "pishogue" all over the South Seas. He'd always thought there had to be some circus trick behind it. But now. . . . His hand trembled as he passed the jug of calibogus, and so did mine as I took it.

Years afterwards I had occcasion to speak with a medical officer who witnessed a firewalk in Fiji. He was utterly at a loss to account for the phenomenon. The only observation he could add was that he saw one man lapse from trance and look down, whereupon the poor fellow was dreadfully burnt, his feet taking months to heal.

•   •   •

Young men threw bundles of leaves on the stones, sending up billows of steamy smoke. Out of this cloud a tall, regal figure appeared before Eddy and Dalton. It was the seven-footer who was last to tread the oven. He could hardly have contrived a more dramatic entrance.

"I am Teraupoo, Your 'ighness," said he incongruously, for like all who had English on the island, he spoke with the Cockney savour of the missionaries. He was about thirty, having a broad, dark face with a small goatee, and long hair braided in a knot at the nape of his neck. His eyes were bloodshot from the smoke. He was lean and fit, his musculature showing to advantage through the greenery he wore like a sprite. He apologized for remaining *incognito* at the bay. On the coast the French had many eyes and ears. Indeed we had passed the ruins of his home, the work of a gunboat and a squad of marines.

Eddy was lost for words. Dalton made an obsequious reply, addressing his interlocutor as "King."

"I ain't a king, sir, and never 'ope to become one. We have a so-called king on this island, but he's a blackguard and a traitor. The king we had before him was a bad man too. We knew nothing of kings before the white man. The first Pomare was made king by the thieves of the *Bounty*, with their muskets. The second by the men of God, with theirs. The third died young. The fourth lost her kingdom and fled here to the Leewards, the only place she could sleep without fear. Then she went back to Tahiti and became the knife and fork of the French. Now the last of these upstart kings has given away the kingdom that was never his to give, like a man who sells a house which belongs to his relations."

He added there would be occasion enough for politics tomorrow. The taboo had lifted; it was time to feast and dance.

The people brought out instruments: drums, mouth organs, jew's harps, nose-flutes, rustic banjos. The forest rang with music and laughter, and with the girls' sweet voices singing *himene*, those promiscuous South Sea songs that may begin with a line of Blake or Cowper in stately Tahitian, and end with "Barnacle Bill" or "Fanny Be Good" bequeathed by a beachcomber.

We dined gorgeously that night, and after much dancing of the *upa-upa*, were led a short way through the woods by torchlight to a settlement of a dozen huts, the headquarters of our elusive host. We slept native fashion, on palm mats, Dalton and Eddy in one hut, Skinner and myself in another. I fell asleep to the sound of distant flutes, rising wind, and loud crashes as branches snapped and fell in the woods. I believe Skinner lay awake all night, worried by the gale and perhaps by things of which he had a better grasp than we.

The others were risen and gone when I awoke. A bloody sky filled the door, and the air was already heavy, gathering itself for the day's blow. I arose and went outside, still groggy from kava and calibogus. It occurred to me I might get away quietly and do some sketching. Dalton had made it clear that I was to keep to the background here. The show must be Eddy's. My day was free.

I had just settled in a picturesque spot with a view across a succession of green ridges and mist-filled valleys—a vista worthy of the brush of Sesshu—when Tiurai appeared, none the worse for her ordeal by fire. Stretching out her hand she drew me up, having touched a finger to my lips. I gathered my sketching kit and followed down a path descending a ravine. Without her guidance I doubt I should have seen a path at all after the first hundred yards.

Thunderclaps were sounding on the mountain. After a long scramble, we came to a pool amid smooth rocks beneath a silver thread of water, the whole surrounded by lianas and giant ferns. She tried to ask me about myself and the others, especially our Arii, but we had too little language in common for me to oblige. For this I was grateful; I was falling under the spell of this strange girl, and might have told her anything she'd asked. Instead, I bade her pose on a boulder above the pool, and there, with a charcoal between the obedient toes of my right foot, dashed off a likeness that struck a pleasing echo of her beauty.

My party trick delighted her. She accepted the sketch eagerly, comparing it with her reflection in the water. The pearly teeth I'd inspected the day before parted in a winning smile. She looked up, as if inviting a kiss. But when I bent to do so, she shook her head and instead placed her soft nose against mine, breathing deeply.

Without any shyness, she unwound her garment and slipped into the pool. I did the same. *And they were both naked . . . and were not ashamed.*

For a long time we frolicked there, whilst clouds flung volleys of rain across the hills, and our silver thread became a mighty hawser. Sheet lightning flickered in the overcast, bringing an unwelcome thought of Captain Scott and his electrical experiments. *Bacchante!* That world of iron and men seemed a distant purgatory; its contemplation lasted only seconds, until Tiurai pinned me under her brown limbs, tenting my face in her abundant mane. We played like otters in the waterfall, which pummelled us and shot us down the race. And when this game became too hazardous—Tiurai miming that stones and logs might soon tumble on our heads—we clambered from the pool and lay on a smooth boulder in the steaming rain.

I was a tyro lover. Years before, still children, Ivry and I had tiptoed to the brink of love, with sighing and hugging and a little pressing of one another's bulges (explorations that would not be resumed until we married, so many years later). I'd lain with a woman for the first time at seventeen, when I patronized a brothel with fellow midshipmen in Cadiz. The escapade was more educational than I'd bargained for; my initiation into the mysteries of Venus being followed some days later by worrisome discharges, which required painful ramroddings of my homunculus with a tincture of poisonous metals. The experience had kept me chaste till now.

Tiurai was an expert; she delighted in teaching, and I in being taught. There was a freedom and innocence to her worldliness that one never finds among the civilized. For those few golden hours in the downpour, the romance of the South Seas seemed nothing less than truth.

Oh happy place! I cried aloud to the sky, my mouth filling with rain. And I showed Tiurai the one advantage my civilization possessed over hers in things of love: I taught her how to kiss.

Upon returning from the waterfall, I found Eddy sheltering in his quarters with his new-found friend. The Prince seemed greatly relieved to be away from matters of state, adjourned for an afternoon siesta. "Ah, Jackdaw! Have you two met? The vahine doesn't speak much English I'm afraid."

I acted the prig. Perhaps I wanted my love for Tiurai to stay unique and pure, far from the taint of P.E.'s murky lusts. I told Eddy that though I had little authority over him here, I should nevertheless be much obliged if he would give me five minutes in private, right away.

"Do you realize what sort of creature your 'vahine' is?" I demanded. "Have you no concern for your reputation? What if Dalton finds out? Worst of all—what if the French do? What if they're spying on you as we speak?"

"'Course I realize, dear fellow. Wasn't born yesterday. So what?" Eddy was the worse for drink. "As for reputations, I saw you slipping off with a vahine yourself. A real one. Tut-tut! Whatever will Nelly say?" (Nelly was a nickname Prince George had coined for Dalton, from Neale, his middle name.)

"Never mind Dalton. Think of your grandmother, P.E. To say nothing of your father."

"My father!" Eddy shot back. "How dare you speak for my father!" He tried on a fierce look, but his expression soon wilted to one of peevishness. "Do you know what my father was doing last I heard, Henderson?"

"Of course not."

"Well, I'll tell you. He was in Paris. His apartments at the Chabanais. A very expensive bordello near the Bibliothèque Nationale, in case you don't know. And do you want to know what he was doing in the Chabanais?" I began to splutter, but there was no stopping him. "My father was consulting with a rather clever furniture maker about a special chair he's having made to his own design. A chair with stirrups, handles, and ball-bearings which will allow a man of his bulk to enjoy three women at once in comfort. When he wasn't doing that he was bathing in a marble tub filled with trollops and champagne." Eddy paused. "You see, Jackdaw—he has *his* affairs and I have mine."

I was dumbfounded. Here was an Eddy I didn't know: cynical, worldly, contemptuous, *royal*. His tone accomplished exactly what he intended: Who was I, a lowly sub-lieutenant, to pry into the personal affairs of a future King of England?

I was not privy to the political talks held throughout the day between Dalton, the island patriot, and Eddy (when he could be torn away from his bed). I saw only what passed at dinner that evening, before our visit was cut short by acts of God and men. Teraupoo was a man of few words and little ceremony by Polynesian norms. Eddy's role was that of a talking dummy on a ventriloquist's knee, and the fluency of Dalton's ventriloquism was dealt a blow by Eddy's intoxication and the islander's knowledge of English. As for the divinity that hedges kings—that was a damp squib. These Tahitians certainly esteemed birth and chieftainship, but their sour experience of royalty meant that Eddy carried little of the symbolic weight he'd had in Fiji.

How much Dalton had prepared the Prince for this episode in his education, I cannot reliably say. My impression is that he'd been told relatively little, since its purpose was to awaken his initiative. The idea was for him to discover things for himself, as if he were the prime mover in momentous affairs. On this far-flung island Eddy might shine, as he had begun to shine with Thakombau.

It is my belief that even had things gone well, the tutor was not in a position to offer the islanders much beyond some boxes of guns and a promise to press their suit in London. In Fiji he had stood on Thurston's shoulders. Here he was on his own, and among islanders whose knowledge of Englishmen was of beach-combers, schooner captains, Cockney evangels.

Subsequent events have borne out the sincerity of Teraupoo himself. He was what he claimed to be, and paid a heavy price for it when the French eventually caught him, years after our visit. Our misfortune cannot be blamed on him; the treachery (if it was treachery) did not lie there. But can it be blamed on some hostile agency sent to destroy us? Or was the seed of our destruction carried with us from the start, in Dalton's dreams and Eddy's weaknesses? I still do not know. I can only set down what I saw and heard that fateful night in the hills.

The cyclone Skinner had dreaded for days broke upon us. By midafternoon the ground about the huts was waterlogged, even though their situation wasn't low-lying. Rain simply fell faster than it could run away through the undergrowth. Men were busy outside, throwing ropes over buildings to hold the roofs down, lashing these to great stakes driven into the earth. Teraupoo did not reside in Thakombau's barbaric splendour, surrounded by carved wood and whale ivory. His headquarters were adequate but simple, offering no prize for the French. Doubtless he had several camps like this, hidden in the mountains.

I remember that it became difficult to listen at dinner over the peculiar din of the gale. In our northern clime a wind of this order whistles and moans; but here the sound produced was a deafening hiss like that of steam escaping from a boiler, rising and falling but never relenting, as the rain tore sideways through the jungle with such velocity that any boughs not snapped were blasted bare of leaves.

Confined inside the leader's shivering house, with conversation all but impossible, we drank far into the night. Skinner's keg of calibogus (borrowed by Eddy for his dalliance with the mahu) at last ran dry but our host substituted a local arrack, distilled in gunbarrels from palm toddy. The women, including the mahu, were not present. My thoughts dwelt on Tiurai. I worried for her safety, consoling myself that she would know what to do in such weather. But my thoughts of her went far beyond worry. There was nowhere on Earth I wanted to be but in her arms. I hoped the talks would be slow, drawn out for a week at least, and dreamt of going to the waterfall with her every day. I wondered where she lived, whether there was a way for us to spend these precious nights together. In short, I was in love.

Some time after midnight the hissing abated a little, and the moment was judged propitious for each to retire to his own quarters. Eddy was the first to leave, reeling but bipedal, and that was the last we saw of him for some hours. I suppose Dalton understood by then the true nature of his ward's companion. If so, he must have rued the day he thought a Polynesian *affaire* would be the very thing to straighten Eddy's heart.

I found myself shaken awake by an agitated Dalton, who had just realized that the form on the mat beside him was not a sleeping Prince but a bundle of clothing with a coconut for a head. Dalton ordered Skinner and myself to dress at once and search through the stormy woods. His greatest fear was that the Prince might have fainted or tripped and be drowning awash on the ground. So the three of us fanned out as best we could through the wet and darkness. It was an impossible task. No lantern or torch could be lit; the night was pitch black, though now and again great sheets of lightning threw the settlement into stark relief against a weird tracery of shadow. Several times I tripped over guy ropes rigged to buildings.

I had an idea where Eddy was—warm and dry with his beloved, as I should like to be. So I made my way in the direction where I believed both Tiurai and the mahu might be living, rather hoping to stumble upon my darling girl.

I found a hut—or it found me, its rattan wall slapping me in the face. I groped round to the door, which swung open to my knock. Inside a candle guttered in a jar. It is difficult to reconstruct my thoughts, for they came on a tide of panic. The scene, however, is clear, a horrible tableau like an instant of battle lit up by a starshell, as lightning filled the doorway: the man-woman, his wrists tied behind him, his painted face pale and strangely restful, drained of its coquetry, a dark creek of blood ebbing from his naked body, congealing on the floor like molten iron.

I bent over him, and it took some moments to discover the ghastly, hidden wound and the nature of his death, a death unspeakably cruel and vile. A cutlass—it seemed the kind used for cutting sugarcane—had been plunged into his fundament. The blade must have severed his internal organs. Only its wooden handle could be seen. He was thoroughly dead but still warm.

Who had done this? Who would be capable of such a thing? Had an assassin stolen into camp under cover of the storm? Where was Eddy? Had the two of them been ambushed? Eddy too, I feared, was somewhere dying, having crawled off like a maimed cat. He might be out there under the thrashing palms—so loud they were!—his life-force, which always seemed in short supply, draining into the flood. I blundered out, searching by lightning, by a succession of magnesium photographs that made no sense. Was that a shadow or a corpse? Was that Eddy bent in pain, or an enemy, or a fallen branch? Who was out there in the dark and the rain? Where was Tiurai?

It was Dalton found him, not half-dead as I'd imagined, but sitting in a wicker chair in their own hut, a cigarette smouldering between his fingers. I shall never forget Eddy's face: the face of a man watching a lantern show—rapt and faraway, the eyes glassy in the candlelight. Words made no impression on him. Dalton took away the cigarette and shook him by the shoulders; his head lolled like that of a rag doll. Above the hiss outside came a regular smack of heavy drips. I thought it was blood, but it was only a leak falling from the ridgepole onto the mat. What I'd seen minutes ago in that other hut might have been an hallucination. Yet its reality was plain enough from the blood on Eddy's shirt—a long nightshirt, its front stiffening with blood, his calves bare and scratched and pale.

"My God, he's wounded!" I shouted.

"It's not his blood," Dalton replied. He thought Eddy had merely been the victim of a prank, that he'd been daubed with pig's blood. The tutor hadn't seen the mahu.

I pulled Dalton aside and described what I'd found. It took a long time to make him understand that a grisly murder had occurred. The unspoken question that remained was whether Eddy had had a lucky escape from the same fate or—heaven forfend— had somehow been the perpetrator. I have never believed the Prince capable of violence, but it was clear from Dalton's reaction that the tutor was not so sure. He rambled incoherently about Eddy's drinking and fragile state of mind, of wildness, of "unnatural provocations." Then he abruptly checked himself, as if he'd only just remembered who I was, and took a more cautious tack.

"Don't you see, Henderson?" he hissed. "It's a traitor's death. The death of Montezuma! They've done this to incriminate the boy."

"Who?"

"The French!" He railed against the mahu, saying his very presence here was proof of treachery. He was a French spy, disguised as a prostitute. Or a Tahitian agent, engaged by a Pomarist faction. Or a republican, a hireling of Dissenters intent on blackening the monarchy and Church of England. And as for the mahu's killer, well, there was the master-stroke; the creature had been intended from the start for double duty, to work his wiles, then perish as a sacrifice.

I said we'd better fetch someone.

"Who would you fetch?" asked Dalton, suddenly weary. He seemed utterly exhausted. He went over to Eddy with the candle, passing his hand back and forth to throw light and shadow into the Prince's eyes. There was no response.

"Oh dear boy! My poor, poor darling boy!" Dalton was quite overcome. He fainted away, his breathing coming very hard and his face glowing like a coal. I loosened his clothing, threw water on him. When he came round he didn't know who I was or where he was. He raved for a long time—snatches of conversations, scenes from the Princes' boyhood and his own. *Shoot me! Eddy, shoot me!* Then suddenly his eyes looked into mine, and he said, "Good Lord! The strangest dream! I was running through the woods at Sandringham with antlers on my head—I do that for fun with Eddy and Georgie, you know. I gave them bows and arrows for Christmas. They shoot at me as I dodge through the woods. Only Eddy was all grown up, and he'd really shot me and I was lying here in my own blood. . . ." Then a look of terror seized him. "Who are you? Why is there blood on your clothes? Answer me, man! Don't kill him!" At that, mercifully, he passed out again.

It must have been three or four in the morning when Skinner burst in, followed by my beloved Tiurai. Dalton's reason seemed to be returning, and Eddy was conscious enough to resume smoking his cigarettes—like a tramp, down to the butt, as if each breath of tobacco might be his last.

The Captain was frightened but still thinking clearly. He'd found that hut and seen what I had seen. He thought killers might still be lurking about, ready to pick us off one by one. (This hadn't occurred to me.) Our only hope was to make for the ship at once. The girl, he said, knew a way. She would guide us down the mountain. Tiurai looked at me imploringly. *Come! Come!* she seemed to say. I took charge, making Dalton and Eddy gather some essentials, herding them out into the storm.

Somehow we got down to the coast, by a shorter, steeper route than our ascent, blundering and sliding through the darkness, over boulders and fallen trees, through mud and waist-deep floodwater, following the course of a stream, perhaps the very one in which Tiurai and I had frolicked only that morning. Those quiet hours in her arms already seemed a year ago.

First light was breaking when we reached the cove, to find the ship riding at her anchors, smoke fleeing from her funnel. Oputu had stuck to orders; steam was up. While the gig put out to get us, Tiurai and I shared one last embrace, a rending moment that has haunted me for years. I tore off a shirt-tail and scribbled my address in charcoal. One day, perhaps, the wars would cease; high commissioners and consuls and battleships would tame this corner of the ocean, and a mail steamer would call here twice a year, and she would have the deacon read my letters, and he would set down her far-off words to me.

I folded the cloth inside the only pretty thing I could bestow on her—the cigarette case given me by Eddy. This I put in Tiurai's hand, closing her fingers over it. I drew her against me and said my farewells with a kiss.

Skinner got us out at dawn. No other captain and no other ship could have done it, even though the cyclone was abating, visible now as a great galactic arm sweeping off to the southeast. Had the winds come the other way—from their prevailing direction—we should have been bottled up in that cove for days. But we shot out smartly under full steam and a pocket handkerchief of jib. Once in deep water, Skinner set out sheet anchors and kept in the island's lee until evening. Then, with the gale fallen to Force Eight, he steamed for Bora Bora and the western Pacific. A week later we made a nocturnal rendezvous with *Bacchante* in the ocean wastes of Micronesia.

Dalton and I never spoke of these events again. Nothing of our excursion was entered in *Bacchante*'s log (the eighteen days of our absence being covered by a slow run to Yokohama). Later, the whole sorry mess was diligently buried under Dalton's monumental history of the voyage, as if beneath twin tombstones of great weight. And so it might have remained, had not those Whitehall hyenas somehow got a whiff of it. Someone must have talked, though who, when, and where is still impossible to say. Perhaps it was Carny Skinner, but I hardly think so; a rogue he may have been, but he was a man whose life depended upon secrecy. His life was brief enough in any case. I heard he involved himself in the Pacific War between Peru and Chile, selling guns to both sides; one of his clients paid the bill with a firing squad. My view is that French agents are the most likely source, and that they passed information to republican sympathizers in London.

For some time, on our way Home, I wondered whether Dalton had questioned Eddy about what happened in that hut, though I doubt that he did. The Prince's mental and emotional states were delicate. He avoided me as much as possible. The ground he'd made in Fiji was lost and never recouped. At best, his level of development returned to the unsatisfactory state that had prompted the tutor's desperate move in the first place.

The rest of the voyage—Japan, Singapore, Egypt—passed quickly, a mere nine months for half the world. Whatever some bluejackets might have wondered about our comings and goings on the high seas, such thoughts were soon forgotten in the thrill of going home, and overshadowed near the cruise's end by trouble at Alexandria during the Arabi revolt.

I am certain Dalton himself locked these things away in his mind forever. He stood to lose most from their disclosure—everything, his whole life's work. Indeed, I'd wager he lost all recollection of them, except perhaps in nightmares.

Nothing might have surfaced from the South Sea débâcle had Prince Eddy's name not been linked, however unfairly, with other scandals less easily suppressed, and had he not died so suddenly (and to some suspiciously) in 1892. I also fear, given the misfortunes in my own life which I mentioned at the outset, that the person or persons responsible may still be active.

Not long after *Bacchante* reached England in the summer of 1882, I fell very ill and remained so for many years. I was invalided out of the Navy in '84, and my health allowed me to undertake few duties until I was sent to the Gold Coast a decade later. The medicos couldn't agree on what was wrong, though they did agree I was lucky to survive. I leave it for my reader to judge whether a human hand lay behind this or any subsequent illness. To this day, I do not know; I merely have suspicions. And, as I've already said, these may be nothing more than delusions. I pray that they are. Nevertheless, I cannot rule out the possibility that, should I die prematurely, the manner of my death may finally illuminate the truth. For this reason I have set down this account and now seal it for the rest of my life.

I shall end by underlining that not a word of these things has ever escaped my confidence, nor shall it until these papers are opened. I will however confess to one harmless lapse in the erasure of all trace of that excursion to the Leeward Islands.

Some days after we'd left that archipelago far behind, and the east winds normal to the region had returned to speed us westward, Dalton must have remembered the spear and shield presented to Prince Edward. They'd been stowed in the hold by Skinner's steward, Hon Sen. One night I was on deck for a late stroll when I saw the Chinaman about to heave these items over the side. Green turtle shells and old flags are common enough, but I recalled at that moment how intrigued I'd been by the antique workmanship of the great Tahitian spear. No sooner had this thought come to mind than I remembered the one whose pretty hands had clasped it on the sunny morning when the *tableau* of Britannia was enacted for Prince Eddy.

I laid an arresting hand on the steward's shoulder, and placed an arresting half-guinea in his palm, explaining that the other half would greet the spear's discreet transfer to my ship. A similar tip to a bluejacket saw the spear well stowed in a dark recess of *Bacchante*'s magazine.

So it is that I have kept, through all these years, one strange memento of my island love. And I wonder sometimes whether she still has the silver keepsake that I left with her.

If you, dear Ivry, are my reader, I pray you will forgive my youthful indiscretions as well as my adult silences. I believe I have not misjudged you by thinking that, should I depart this Earth in your lifetime, you would rather have my candour than a sinister mystery. You have often paid me the compliment of saying I am aptly named, so I leave you this frank and private memoir,

Your ever loving and devoted Frank.

Fifteen

 ◁▷ ◁▷

TAHITI

Women's Prison

IT RAINED ON AND OFF FOR DAYS IN TAIPIVAI, rain like a child's tears: sudden, copious, without apparent cause, as if the pent emotions of the atmosphere simply got the better of it. The showers ended in the same spirit, sun beaming through the last drops, a smile after sorrow.

I found a good place to stay—the only place—an airy cabin with bright coral curtains. Unlike Happar, Typee still lives, home to a few dozen families near the river's mouth. Madame Kekela, my landlady, was descended from the ancient tribe. But my lodgings might have been in the Dordogne: jam and baguette with coffee on her verandah in the morning, fresh flowers on my table in the afternoon. She was a stocky woman in her late forties. Her husband was away, working on a freighter. Their children had grown and left for Tahiti. She'd travelled a bit herself—San Francisco and New Zealand—which gave her the idea to cater for wanderers and Melville buffs who made their way to Taipivai.

The river bordered her property, behind a waterlogged orchard of breadfruit and bananas. Further upstream it was a stony torrent, but here it ran deep between mud banks. A contemplative heron often stood beside a whirlpool, and great land crabs scuttled about looking for dry burrows, scratching at my door on rainy nights.

Madame Kekela was a heavy smoker, and the *nono* flies were making me one too. We'd sit on her verandah for a while in the evenings, puffing away. Jon's picture rang no bells, but she listened to my story and offered to put the word around. She agreed that Tari Kautai was the man to see. He'd been chief of Taipivai when she was little, during the Second World War. Later he went into the police, though she wasn't sure when. "He is the oldest in the valley. No one can say precisely how old—not even himself. That's old, no?"

"Will he talk to me?"

"Take him a bottle." Her motherly face smiled in the light of a match. "Then he'll talk. And take some flowers from my garden. He has a young woman with him. She moved in not long ago. A cousin, he says, from Hiva Oa. She's got a little girl. The story is her husband left her. But we never heard about this cousin before. People are talking." She laughed. "Can you imagine? He's old as a turtle!"

⋖⋗ ⋖⋗

Taipivai village occupied only the lowest part of the valley, straggling along one side of the river for about a mile, up and down

from a small wooden church. A tiny shop sold soap, batteries, cigarettes, and dubious tinned meats named Klik and Spork. I
bought a carton of Gitanes and pinned one of my posters by the
door.

The houses were mostly clapboard bungalows smothered in
clouds of bougainvillea, some built on ancient platforms. I
stopped at every one and showed Jon's picture. People were sympathetic and not in the least surprised—Polynesians, I found,
took matters of family and descent very seriously. Some even
became talkative, speaking of situations like mine among themselves: men who'd never returned from fishing trips, from jobs
across the sea; women who'd run away to Papeete and never been
heard from again. But so few were old. At least half the villagers
were children. I met only five who'd been adults in 1953.

Two of these were an old couple who lived up the valley by
a neglected coconut grove belonging to the church. The wife
began to speak then stopped herself. When I pressed her, she said
very hesitantly that she thought she recalled a white man being
found dead in Taipivai, in the 1950s; the husband said it was the
1970s, and not a white man, merely an unidentified skeleton—
someone who'd drowned or fallen from the cliffs.

I felt disheartened. Their story was unsettling but too vague;
nobody else recalled anything like it. And Tari Kautai was taking
a long time. A new hip in a man his age was no joke, no matter
how amusing it might be to Sergeant Benoit. What if there were
complications? He might never be well enough to come home.
And why should his memory be better than anyone else's? I
decided to give him a few more days. After that I'd have to take

my chances on Nuku Hiva's roads, making my way over the mountains to Hatiheu, the last village of any size. If I learned nothing there, I'd have to roam the rest of the island, going to every farm and fishing camp.

Each day I went out, taking a lunch, and each evening Madame Kekela read my face and shook her head. When I'd spoken to every living soul in Taipivai, I began exploring the upper valley, finding my way through guava thickets and banyans to an imposing platform called Paepae Merivi, said to be where Melville had stayed, half guest, half captive of the Typees. Like all the finer ruins, it was made of boulders skilfully fitted without mortar, with a flight of steps at the front; the back had a raised footing of cut stone for the wooden house, the rest being an open terrace where Fayaway's family had buried their dead and spent their sunny days. Melville's or not, it would look good on film, its mystery deepened by the thick woods all around and the snarling river below.

High on a slope I saw the "taboo grove" he'd feared, scene of "horrible idols, heathenish rites and human sacrifices." It was eerie even now, with its deified ancestors overthrown by missionaries and time. The stone tiki figures were roughly life-size, some headless, others without feet or on their backs. Perhaps they had once been fearsome; now they were merely outlandish and forlorn. More poignant than their physical decay was the thought that these ancestors had lost their descendants. No one alive remembered who these beings were; and in losing their past, the offspring, like you and me, had lost their way.

They made me think of you, of who and where you might be now. I pictured you here, the two of us searching for your grandfather on these mountains in the sea.

As I got to know the valley, I saw that Typee had been a garden city from one end to the other, a succession of terraced orchards, houses, temples, and dancing platforms, running below the mountain walls for several miles. It must have been home to thousands.

The Vaiahu fork, which I'd seen from above, and which Melville had described as a park-like mix of buildings and fruit trees, is completely cut off and overgrown today, not even a game trail leading in towards the falls at its head. But the main branch has a track as far as a small hydroelectric plant that lights the village. One morning I walked up there, beyond all the ruins, determined to reach the twin cascade of Teuakueenui, the Two Great Eels, down which Melville and Toby had tumbled like shot monkeys.

It looked easy on the map, but wasn't. Above the hydro shed the valley was very narrow, and looked as wild as in 1842. I had to spider over boulders beneath trees crowding the torrent's edge, or wade to my thighs in fast water. I saw no machete cuts, no sign that anyone had come this way in years.

After an hour I reached the end, a great broken bowl of dark basalt, water-carved from mountains boiling with mist. Here the Two Great Eels thundered into a broad, revolving pool.

I took off my clothes and stood in the spray. I swam into deep water and let it take me round and round beneath the shifting arc of a rainbow. I thought of Henderson and Tiurai, their waterfall romance, and how, ultimately, they seemed to have led both Jon and me to this island they had never seen.

The voice of the falls drowned every other sound, though from time to time I thought I heard a human voice, calling or singing. I glanced around, but it was only a trick of my ears, or perhaps the chiming of stones washed down from the heights.

⋘ ⋙

Next morning I woke to the throb of a helicopter, shockingly loud, echoing between the canyon walls. I'd slept late, and my first thought was that the chopper had come for me, caught me unawares, and I hadn't time to lose myself in the woods. My legs were stiff, and the din was fading by the time I got to the window. The craft looked small and old, a bulbous dragonfly body with a thin tail, like a Bell I used to hire for aerial shots.

Madame Kekela broke into a wide smile at breakfast—Tari Kautai was home! I waited two more days while she gathered the news. It was good. His operation had gone well; they'd kept him in Papeete for such a long time because of his age, nothing more.

He lived on a windy headland down the Typee bay, overlooking the beach where Melville fled Nuku Hiva. Here the river meets the sea, a brown surge into clear jade.

I turned up late in the afternoon, to catch him fresh from his siesta. A baby was crying inside. A short plump woman of about thirty came out at my knock, and I gave her a spray of oleanders and hibiscus. She seemed a country person, shy and plainly dressed in a dark green shift. Without a word she led me through a banana grove against the house.

The old Typee was slumped in an armchair on his back porch, the ocean flopping and seething on the shingle below. Chickens and puppies dozed by his feet. He had been braiding rope. Nearby were sacks of coconut fibre and new coils hanging from the eaves. He wore one earring and a pair of khaki shorts. His flesh was lean, pale yellow, and vaguely translucent like a mummy's. A zipper of neat stitches ran up his thigh. He had a good head of iron-grey hair, a coarse goatee, and thick eyebrows ending in long whiskers like the feelers of a prawn. He might have been anywhere from seventy to ninety years old. If he's eighty, I thought, he'd have been about my age when Jon posted that letter.

"He won't speak to you outside," the woman said. "He can't hear over the surf." She eased him up and helped him into the dark interior. The window louvres were closed, admitting only slats of light. When my eyes adjusted I saw that it was one large room, with sleeping quarters behind a cotton screen. There was a pleasant smell of strong tobacco, dried fruit, sinnet, spices. I gave him my name.

"Speak up, please!" He settled himself into a chair and motioned for me to sit opposite, across a small table made from a cable drum. I repeated who I was and briefly why I'd come, adding that Madame Kekela and Sergeant Benoit had suggested I visit him. If this was an inconvenient time, perhaps I could come back another day?

"Not at all, Mademoiselle." His hands ran inquiringly over the bottle I presented, recognizing its shape, the best Taiohae could provide. "Johnny Walker!" He chuckled amiably, showing empty gums and wide eyes like milky quartz. The young woman went outside.

"I don't see well any more. They told me I should let them do my cataracts. I told them I'd think about it. But I won't. I'd have to wear glasses!" He touched my arm.

He was surprisingly vigorous, contorting his face histrionically like a character in a silent movie, the shrimp whiskers adding greatly to the effect. He made me think of Fidel Castro at his most engaging, in seductive interviews with pretty foreign journalists. His French was good, the product of a Catholic boarding school.

"A knife at my eyes! I won't have it," he repeated, gripping my arm more urgently. "I said I've seen enough." He released me and paused; then, "Will you allow me, Mademoiselle, to touch your face?"

His fingers, bony and calloused from years of rope-making, walked lightly over my skin as if reading Braille. The woman came back with three glasses and some water on a tray. "My young cousin," he said. "Martine. Her name is Martine. She's looking after me." We shook hands.

"If you feel strong enough," I began. "I'd like to ask about a long time ago. Nineteen fifty-three. Do you remember a stranger, an Englishman, turning up on Nuku Hiva back then?"

"I'm plenty strong enough! They fuss so much. Wouldn't let me home for weeks. I've never liked Papeete. Do you?"

"Not much," I said. Martine patted his shoulder, reminding him what I'd asked.

"Strangers? Many strangers came to Nuku Hiva in those days. The government sent them here after the war. Gave them land. We had a man with no lungs. Mustard gas! And there were ...," he groped for words he hadn't used in years, "pacifists. Conscientious objectors. The authorities wanted them off Tahiti. Some of them never went home. They fell in love with Nuku Hiva girls." He smiled towards Martine. He seemed to be talking about the forties. Or even the twenties. I steered him back to 1953. What was he doing then? Was he a policeman in Taiohae, or still chief of Taipivai?

"I was chief three times. Can't remember the years. Why do you want to know?"

"The man I'm looking for was my father."

The bottle stood unopened beside three empty tumblers and a pitcher of water. I wondered if he was waiting for me.

"Shall I?"

"Bien sûr!"

"Santé!" Raised glasses in the semi-darkness. Kautai swallowed greedily, set down his glass, and sent a bony hand to the floor for a tobacco pouch. He began rolling a huge cigarette in a six-inch square of newspaper. "Why did your father come to Nuku Hiva?"

"To hide, maybe." I explained about the Korean War, the downing of Jon's plane. "I think he was unwell. I don't know how. Perhaps he was confused." I didn't know the French for shell-shock or post-traumatic syndrome. "It's also possible he was looking for someone. Someone called Henderson. A Demi. This person might have come from the Leewards. From Raiatea."

"Ah! Les Îles Sous-le-vent." The lovely name fell dreamily from Kautai's tortoise lips. He knew them well; he'd worked on a gunboat before the war. He put down his cigarette and beckoned.

"Let me feel your face again."

"I don't look much like my father," I said. "He was fair, blue eyes, average height. I'm dark and tall."

"Yes, I know." From the darkness under the roof came a gecko's call, like the kissing sound one makes at a baby or a cat. His hands took a longer, deeper reading than before. "The bones!" He laughed. "You might almost be Maohi!"

My looks again. Several had called me that—the Tahitian form of Maori, meaning any Polynesian.

"Except my nose."

"Oui! Except your nose!"

The Typee sat back pensively, nearly invisible in the darkening house. From behind the curtain came whimpering and suckling. Martine and her baby. His baby? I've still no idea, but I wouldn't rule it out. The light between the boards faded quickly, as the sun slipped behind the Hapaa mountain.

"I can tell you a story," he said abruptly. "For a long time I have believed that one day I would have to tell this story. For many years I hoped to tell it. Lately I've been thinking it is better to forget. It may not be your story. It may be the wrong story altogether. But if it is yours, it will be very sad for you. Do you want to hear it? You should think carefully."

"It's always better to know."

"So one thinks when one is young! When one is old there's too much time for going over things. The sorrows of a lifetime run through the mind. Again and again before your eyes, when all you want is sleep. I wish I knew less! But the older I get the more clearly things come back." He gave a brittle laugh, then resumed smoking and taking sips of whisky like a lizard.

What tormented the old fellow? I lit up, kept quiet, as if mulling over what he'd said. But I agreed with Frank: *Explanations, however distressing, are more consoling than mysteries.*

"I should like to hear everything you can tell me, Monsieur."

"Very well. You've decided. I remember those years. It was the time of the big bomb scare. The *Lucky Dragon*. I was constable in Taiohae."

"You mean the H-bomb tests?"

He nodded. "The American bombs. Boom!" His glowing cigarette traced a mushroom cloud in the twilight. "They were a long way from Nuku Hiva, but wind and water go anywhere, no? Each was bigger than the one before. There was a ship, a fishing vessel—Chinese, Japanese, I'm not sure. But I remember her name. The *Lucky Dragon*. One doesn't forget a name like that, not after what happened. Her crew saw blossom floating down from the sky. Pink petals, settling on them like when you sleep under a *hutu* tree. And they felt lucky. Heaven was smiling! You know how the Chinese are." He coughed again, his face stony. "Soon all those men are dying. And people on some islands too. It was the . . . ," he fished for the word, "*retombées*. The fallout. People here were frightened. 'Kaoha, Tari,' they'd say, 'if this is what the Americans are doing, what will the Russians do?'"

He was warming to the story, doing voice parts, moving his gaunt hands like shadow-puppets.

"How about the French? At Mururoa."

"That was later. Those bombs are safe."

Martine came in with some slices of fried yam. The old man softened them in whisky and sucked them down, quiet a long time, recollection seeping like water into a dredged well.

"There *was* an Englishman here. A man who spoke English. He might have been American, Australian, who knows? He had the bearing of a military man. He arrived without papers on a schooner. He came to the gendarmerie and told us he'd been shipwrecked. We had no telephone. No airstrip. Schooners came and went with the wind. Sometimes two or three would arrive together, sometimes we'd go months with none. We didn't worry about people who turned up as he did. Many had no papers in those days. We'd put them aboard the next boat and they'd be dealt with in Papeete." Another silence. The gecko called again above my head, agitated, or perhaps two of them were fighting.

"We had an old motorcycle at the gendarmerie, left over from the war. British make. A BSA. I loved that thing! A *moto* is a fine thing when you're young. I rode it everywhere, like a horse. Police business, naturally! It had no springs like they do now. I'd stand up on the footpegs and let it bounce, the saddle coming up to slap my bottom!"

His mind seemed to be wandering. And so was mine—back to my father's Royal Enfield. Once or twice each summer, when we were girls, Lottie and I would brave the greenhouse spiders to rediscover the machine under its old rug. I'd stare at the great finned engine—its art deco castings had a monumental look—

awed by the bike's fossil power, by its remoteness from my memories of Jon. Lottie claimed she could remember riding pillion, clinging to his back, but I think she made that up. In 1953 she was only four years old.

We became aware that the machine was changing, aging in a way that he, frozen in memory and photographs, could not. The tyres softened and sank; oxide dulled the castings; rust lifted the maroon enamel. It became impossible to see how our father's bike could ever have been new. I began to think of it romantically as his last passion, a hostage to time, rotting in his stead like the picture of Dorian Gray.

Suddenly Kautai gargled, yanking me back from Tilehouse Street. He spat a tarry bulb of phlegm into a jam jar he used as an ashtray.

"I remember the Englishman helped us get it working. He wanted to make friends. Always a good idea with the cops, no? That's how he kept himself in Taiohae. Mending things. Boat engines, pumps, kerosene fridges. He hadn't a sou to his name."

"What name did he give?"

"Silly! I have the name of the bike but not the man." Kautai thought the Englishman was on Nuku Hiva for about two months, between one schooner and the next. He was often seen with the doctor, a man from Raiatea who'd been in Europe, in the war.

"We thought it was because they were both military men that they became friends. Later we found out there was a connection."

"What was *his* name—the doctor? Was it Henderson?"

"Faraniki. Faraniki Teraupoo." The milky eyes turned up as
he remembered. "Jim! That was the Englishman. Monsieur Jim.
As for his surname, I think you'll find it over there." He raised his
chin in the direction of the bedroom. "You can check presently.
Martine will show you. Let me go on while the mind is clear." The
house was nearly dark, only a slatted pallor from the cracks, and
the paleness of the old man's eyes. Now and then a match would
flare, for Kautai's cigarette or mine, and the rustic walls hung with
rope and clothing would imprint themselves, a retinal flash.

Faraniki Teraupoo! I was certain now. Tiurai must have
been a sister or daughter of the guerrilla chief; Frank had left her
with more than a cigarette case. And Jim! My father had used his
parrot's name.

"This Monsieur Jim became well known along the beach.
Tang, the Chinaman with the store, gave him an empty hut to
live in. The Englishman loved walking. Every day he'd go up the
ridge behind the fort, sometimes for hours. He said he was interested in Merivi, the American writer. This writer must be very
famous, no? Every stranger who comes here wants to follow that
man's route through the hills! Most of them give up. Some get
lost. Three or four have died. They fall in the rain, they are bitten
by the centipede, they have a heart attack. . . . But Merivi wasn't
the only reason Jim did so much walking. He was watching out
for the next schooner."

"To get away?"

"On the contrary. He wanted to make sure he was off in the
hills when she anchored. So we couldn't deport him to Tahiti!
That's when he vanished. While a schooner was in port."

Martine came in from the porch with a hurricane lamp, bathing the house in saffron light. The old Typee took a swallow of his Scotch and looked at me beseechingly.

"Monsieur Jim walked out of the village when the schooner came and he was never seen alive again. I am sorry, Mademoiselle. This is why I asked you to reflect. . . ." He strained to hear how I was taking it.

"Can you be sure he died?" An old hope returned: Jon stowing away to another island; or hiding in the hills, living like a hermit, perhaps for years. It was soon dashed.

"We expected him to turn up in a day or two, once the ship had sailed. When he didn't we were puzzled. Unfortunately, as time went by, suspicion fell on Faraniki, the doctor from Raiatea. There was talk in the village that the two men had been fighting shortly before Jim disappeared. Teraupoo could get unruly when he drank. He was a big man. Heavy and tall. He used to make liqueur with his medical equipment, his glass tubes. Good stuff—better than the schooners sold. I drank plenty myself. Against the law, of course!" He shrugged. "But as Tang used to say when we'd catch him selling opium, 'Heaven is high and the emperor is far away.' Poor Faraniki! His face was always sad. But he looked happy when he drank."

Teraupoo had been taken prisoner by the Germans after the fall of France. He'd been forced to work in a concentration camp, or several camps. Kautai thought only his medical skills had saved him.

"Who knows what a man has inside him after such an experience? He never looked well. But how he worked! Always helping people, neglecting himself. Everyone loved him."

I asked why the doctor had come to Nuku Hiva instead of his home island. Kautai said he'd been posted here by the government. In those days, still reeling from the war, Paris was thinking of letting its ocean colonies go. Islanders were being given white men's jobs.

"If *I* alone had heard that story about a fight, I wouldn't have acted on it, Mademoiselle. Teraupoo and I were friends. No one wanted the police bothering him. But the sergeant was French—they usually are—a man named. . . ." He stopped and thought. "Rivard. Sergeant Rivard. All spit and polish. For him the disappearance of a European was a very serious matter. When the Englishman failed to return, Rivard and I searched his hut. Because of what we found there we had to question Faraniki. I still regret what we put that poor man through. It was very hard on him. I can still see it in his eyes—the fear of being locked up again! He was never charged, but never exonerated either. Not until it was too late. He died before we learnt the truth."

Kautai paused, and after a minute or so I noticed a regular sound, like a boat engine on the wind. But it was the old man. He'd fallen asleep. The temptation to wake him—to bump his chair, drop my glass, strike a noisy match, was almost irresistible. After a battle with myself I got up quietly to leave, but I was hardly on my feet before he gave a snort. Then came a rustling sound, like a mouse in a kitchen drawer. He was tearing off a square of newsprint and rolling another smoke.

"It was plain that Monsieur Jim had left in a hurry. In his hut was a long letter. We found another letter with it, on the table. One he was writing. Not finished. The sergeant's English

wasn't too good, and I have only three words: *Anuzzer beer please!*"
The old Typee chuckled, then coughed respectfully, recalling the
gravity of his tale.

"Rivard took the papers to the schoolteacher. A nun. A woman
of education, naturally. She had difficulty with the first letter,
which was in a bad state. But she translated the other. There was
still much we didn't understand. To read strangers' letters. . . ."

He began speaking in Marquesan to Martine, who went to
the bedroom, retrieving an old tin box.

"Now, Mademoiselle, you can read the rest for yourself. I
haven't looked at these things in twenty years. Not since my eyes
started going. Often I've wondered whether someone like you
would come to me before I die. I thank God that you have!" He
toasted the Almighty. Martine fossicked in the box, following his
instructions. She handed him a brown envelope. He took out the
contents carefully, caressing each item in the same way he'd
touched my face.

"It wasn't my job to keep these things, but if I hadn't. . . ."
Another shrug. "Anything that goes to Tahiti vanishes. They
demand everything, but they pay no attention to what happens
on faraway islands. Nobody cares about us here. I think we sent
them the schoolteacher's translation. These should be the originals." He added that Sergeant Rivard left Nuku Hiva in the early
sixties, shortly after the mystery of the Englishman was "solved."
The letters sat in a drawer at the police post, along with one other
piece of evidence: a silver cigarette case.

"For a while after Rivard left I was on my own at the gendarmerie. I confess, Mademoiselle, that I had my eye—I had

sharp eyes then!—on that pretty *étui à cigarettes*. I ask myself, Why surrender this to Papeete when everyone concerned is dead? So I take it into my own custody, and for the sake of my conscience, I keep the letters with it. 'Tari Kautai,' I tell myself very sternly, 'if a rightful owner ever turns up, you must give them back.' They are yours now."

Martine trimmed the wick on the lamp, but I could hardly read a word. One of the letters was disintegrating, little more than papier mâché, salty and damp to the touch. This had to be my mother's letter, the one that went "in the drink" when Jon crashed. I poured out the last of the whisky and gulped mine down. My eyes were wet and stinging. I couldn't read here. I wanted nothing more than to be away, alone.

"There!" said Kautai, unwrapping a flat silver box from a square of cloth, his ropemaker's hands still nimble. He held it out. "Inside the lid. The Englishman's name, no? We sent Papeete that name. Never heard anything more."

Sea air had turned the outside gunbarrel black, but the tarnish inside was a light tan. When my hand steadied I could make out the engraving:

To "Jackdaw" Henderson on his birthday, from his shipmate "P.E."
Two years aboard Bacchante and twenty-two aboard this world.
August 6th, 1881.

Eddy, Henderson, Tiurai. It was as if the case's owners had entered and sat down. A hundred years collapsed into a rectangle of blackened metal in a dim house. Perspiration stung my face.

When I felt calm enough to make myself understood, I thanked the old man warmly, enfolding a hand like a bird's foot in both of mine. These letters, I said, and all he'd remembered, were gifts beyond price. But I couldn't accept the pretty silver case.

I had no desire for it. All I wanted was to go and read.

"Keep it, my dear. What use are pretty things when one no longer has eyes to see them?"

"Martine should keep it. I insist." Then I asked how my father's disappearance had been "solved." The old man began wheezing alarmingly, quite angry with himself. "Forgive me. This is the most important!

"It was by chance. A few years after Monsieur Jim's disappearance, the authorities decided to bring us electric light. A team of surveyors and engineers came to inspect the Taipivai waterfalls for a generating plant. Do you know Teuakueenui, the Two Big Eels?" I told him I did. "That's where they built it in the end. But they also examined the other one. The one called Vaiahu." His chin pointed across Hapaa towards Muake, to where I'd seen the Vaiahu River make its leap into the Typee gorge.

"I was their guide. There were no roads like today. Only old paths and animal trails. The Big Eels weren't so hard, but Vaiahu took us days, cutting in with knives. Nobody had been up that fork of the valley in my lifetime. Not in fifty years. No one goes there even now! The rain and the flies were terrible." He swallowed noisily. "At last we reached the bottom of the falls. We made camp there. Every day I cleared bush for the survey. One morning I am cutting and I find a human skull. This doesn't surprise me. The old people used to make. . . ." He lowered his voice, a mix of awe and shame, the shadow of the mission school. "Offerings. They made offerings there. That's what Vaiahu means in our language. *Vai* is water or river, *ahu* is an altar. Soon we found more bones from the same body. All together, not like a sacrifice. Scraps of clothing. A belt buckle. And this silver case. Clearly these were the remains of an unfortunate who had fallen from the cliffs in recent times. I had never seen the cigarette case before but I thought I recognized the buckle. So did others in Taiohae. It was the body of the Englishman, Monsieur Jim. He must have gone walking up there while the schooner was in port." A papery arm reached out and touched my knee. "Mademoiselle, I am so sorry to bring you this news. But at least you can be certain that your . . . your father was not killed by Teraupoo. The doctor would never have climbed up there. He wasn't well enough."

I'd noted his hesitation. *Your father.* He remembered something in the letters.

"What was done with the remains?"

"They were respectfully removed, Mademoiselle. By myself. We buried him in the old Protestant cemetery. We assumed an Englishman would be a Protestant. By then poor Faraniki was dead two years himself. He's there too, not far away. Tahitians are also Protestants."

"Did Faraniki leave any children, any kin?"

Kautai started at this.

"Not here. Not here on Nuku Hiva. . . ." He halted, on the point of telling me what I was going to read. "He never spoke of any. Perhaps there are kin on Raiatea or Tahiti, but I don't believe so, none that are close. You must understand, Mademoiselle, that if he were alive today he'd be nearly my own age. We who were born back then are very few. Women gave birth, but the babies died. Or they grew to fourteen, fifteen, and coughed blood. Ours was the smallest generation. The whites said we would be the last. We thought this too. So many ghosts, so few alive. When I was a boy in Taipivai only twelve people were living here. And three of them were French! I was the last one of my family. I believe it was the same with Teraupoo."

The old Typee went silent, as if falling asleep again, but it was just his way of letting me know he'd finished and I could leave.

I slipped the letters gently into my bag and got up. I gave Martine the cigarette case. How else could I repay them? Perhaps I still feared that the case might prove to be tainted by jealousy and anger. What was it doing on Jon that day, when it must have belonged to Faraniki?

Taiohae, November 11, 1953.

Dearest Vivien:
Armistice Day and I'm still on Nuku Hiva. Did you get my last letter? I sent it the moment I got here. A lot's happened since then. Afraid I still don't know what I'm doing from one day to the next. But first, yes—I forgive you.

You're right about the Marshalls. I didn't have to
go. We were all volunteers. Though it wasn't only
allies. Some Yanks got fried as well. Everyone
believed the range was safe. I have a confession of my
own, Vivien, something I should have admitted years
ago. I stayed up a bit longer than my orders, to get a
few snaps. At the time it seemed nothing. Later of
course, when they warned us about genetic damage, I
rued it bitterly. I asked myself countless times
whether the price of those pictures might be Livvy
turning out a freak. On this score it's a relief to know
she isn't mine.

That cloud was magnificent, macabre, mesmeriz-
ing—I can't find words. At the time I kept thinking
of what Oppenheimer said: that physicists have
known sin. And his pithy bit of Sanskrit: *I am become
Death, the destroyer of worlds.* (Everyone wondered
how long he'd practised that.)

If you didn't want risk in life, Vivien, you
shouldn't have married a pilot. But understand I
didn't go to Enewetak lightly. Overflying those
clouds was necessary. Someone had to get readings.
We believed these weapons would make war as
obsolete as witchcraft. Our weapons have outgrown
us. Of course, *we* may not have outgrown our
weapons. There lies the danger, but it's a chance
we had to take.

Mole used to say there weren't a First and

Second War, just one long war that lasted thirty-one years, with half-time in the middle. He was right. Without the A-bomb it might have gone on and on, with Russia after Japan. The bomb was the lesser evil—the alternative's a shambles like the Somme or Stalingrad every twenty years. Or so I believed then. After Korea I'm not so sure. We seem to have the worst of both worlds. We've got the bomb, and we've still got the meat-grinders. We did things in Korea that no one should ever do. I can't speak about this.

As for who Livvy's father is, I didn't *want* the details. That's the hardest thing about your letter. I know you meant well, but now I can't think of you or her without seeing you in his arms.

So if I didn't want to know about Frank Henderson's grandson, what am I doing on Nuku Hiva, helping him drink his moonshine? Fair question. Not sure I can answer, but I'll try.

What I wanted—the opportunity coming along so unexpectedly it seemed providential, though most schooners put in here on their way to Tahiti—was to see what sort of man he was. In my finer moments I hoped I'd like him, as you suggest, that I'd find him worthy of being my daughter's father.

Thing is, Vivien, when I ditched that Sabre I knew I hadn't long to live. About the time your letter came I got bad news from the M.O. Myeloid leukemia. Par for the course apparently—thyroid, gonads, then everything goes pear-shaped. He gave me three to four months. I'm beating the odds a bit, but I won't walk away from this. You must understand there isn't time for me to get home from here—certainly not in a state you'd want to see. Or the girls. I don't want Lottie and Livvy to watch their father die. So I think it best to stick to what you were told by the War Office. Missing in action. Let's tell them their old Dad went down in a good cause, helping to make a better world for little girls.

Nobody here knows who I am. (Except Teraupoo now, and he's given his word.) They think I'm a shipwrecked yachtsman. It's rather fun—the odd thing about playing someone else is that you *become* someone else. I'm sure you know all about this from your acting days, but it's a revelation to me. It's how I made friends with Livvy's father. Couldn't miss him in this place—a big brown chap with a stoop and the Henderson nose. He's everything you say he is, but he hadn't a clue who I was. Not till last week.

I can see why he lives here. Tahiti sounds too busy, too many reminders of the war and who's in charge. This is the most breathtaking spot on Earth. Wild, insanely mountainous, nothing like the Marshalls. (I'd give a lot to have my Leica.) The people are silent and brooding till you get to know them. You've seen them in every Gauguin painting. The girls make one ache.

The men look like they'd eat you at the drop of a hat.
But really it's like any English village—some people
are tight as peas in a pod, others haven't spoken to
their next-door neighbour in years.

The storekeeper's lent me a hut of his by the
beach. In return I keep his fridges going (always
playing up). He's Chinese—sometimes he lets me
have a whiff of poppy, which makes me feel right as
rain. I'm still pretty good, still getting out for walks.

A week ago Teraupoo and I got squiffed on the
hooch he makes with his medical kit. Began exchang-
ing confidences. He's none too well himself, though
he'll outrun me by miles. I got a bit carried away—
got the notion that since I wouldn't make it back to
Hitchin, he should go in my place. Husband for you
and a father for both girls. So I told him who I was.
Didn't think he'd turn a hair. Women used to have
several husbands at once on these islands.

Evidently that's not how they do things nowadays.
Never seen a man so frightened. Thought I was playing
cat and mouse with him. He's like all those poor devils
who went through the camps, always watching from
the corner of his eye. Suddenly this mild-mannered
chap, none too fit but heavy enough, is on me like a
sumo wrestler. Luckily Tang hears the rumpus. He
and a couple of his customers pull us apart.

Two days later we're pals again. Faraniki under-
stands now that my suggestion's serious. (I told him

everything—he's even examined me and I'm afraid his opinion is the same as the M.O.'s.) From what he's said about his own family, I gather he's a sort of last of the Mohicans. So for him to learn he has a three-year-old is immensely good news. He became ecstatic, hugging me, weeping and moaning.

When he calmed down he told me about Frank and Tiurai. Same as he told you. Then he brought out Frank's old cigarette case. A lovely thing, inscribed to "Jackdaw" Henderson. He absolutely insisted I take it— that I be the one to give it to Livvy, or I should send it if I wasn't going back. I said he should keep it and give it her himself, when time's ripe. Good calling card. He balked at that. Perhaps he . . .

There Jon stopped, in the middle of a page. I turned the sheet over in disbelief. I stood up and sat down, read the whole letter again and again, as if I could somehow extend its length by repetition. I got nowhere with Mother's. Every time I tried to peel it open, the damp wad threatened to disintegrate. It needed drying, tweezers, a steady hand.

When I couldn't read any longer, I wrote up what Tari Kautai had told me. Then I lay awake until just before dawn, speculations tunnelling in my mind like worms. Perhaps Faraniki *what?* Felt guilty? Didn't want to see my mother? Didn't think he could face Europe again, not even Hitchin? Or was it that he knew more about the state of his own health than he was letting on, had decided to stay in Taiohae for the rest of a short life, like Jon?

Most of all I thought about Jon's fall from Vaiahu. It can't have been his first trip behind Muake, not if he was walking so much. He would have known that ground. Perhaps familiarity made him careless, made him peer from a slippery cornice after a storm, as I did. Perhaps he was frailer than he admits. Or it really might have been a centipede. Or was it the same demon that made him forget his fuel gauge, a reckless invitation for death to take him whole instead of piecemeal? All this I still don't know, and never will.

But why not finish the line? Schooners don't move that fast. Why not end the paragraph and write *I love you*?

Rain woke me mid-morning, loud as hail on the metal roof. Through the window came a smell of earth and wet ashes. I didn't feel like a tourist or a filmmaker anymore. I had a claim on this corner of the world, and it on me: a blood-and-soil thing. If you work it out, I'm three-eighths Polynesian, which makes you three-sixteenths. (Unless Lumley also had some warm blood in his veins, but I doubt that very much.)

I sat on Madame Kekela's verandah, rereading the fragile blue pages by daylight, thinking over the trace of that wheel trundling down upon our lives through a century. Because Frank Henderson took a lover in 1881, my mother takes a lover in 1949. Because of this, I exist. Obvious yet indigestible. But does Jon also crash because of this? Am I prone to seduction in 1966 because of his disappearance in 1953? Is that why I abandoned you?

• • •

About noon the sun came out, and we heard the helicopter. I worried I'd overtaxed old Kautai, sent him back to hospital. But it landed in a small field beside Madame Kekela's, scattering her goats. It had come for me.

For some time I stayed put, obstinately smoking. Eventually the pilot came and helped me pack. Then I heard voices. It was Martine, breathless from running, speaking quickly in Marquesan.

"She has something for you," said Madame Kekela. Martine pressed Henderson's cigarette case into my hand and kissed me on both cheeks.

"She thanks you but she can't keep it. It has many ghosts. The ghosts are yours."

Sixteen

⋙ ⋘

THERE'S ONE MORE DOCUMENT in the Henderson papers from my father's darkroom. (I can't break the habit of a lifetime: Jon is still my father, though I haven't a drop of his blood. I tell you this even if it cooks my goose with you. The woman who raised you is your mother. I gave birth like a turtle who drops her eggs in the sand and swims away. No illusions there.)

If Frank wrote more about *Bacchante*'s voyage or his later life, nothing else remains. This letter was tucked into his last notebook.

Whitehall. May 24th, 1918

Mr. G. D. Samuels,
Samuels and Fraser, Solicitors,
27 Harrington Street,
London S.W.

My Dear Gerald,

Our schooldays are long ago now, and our paths
have crossed too seldom since. I very much regret
that misfortune should be the occasion of my writing
to you after being so long out of touch. Only yesterday I learnt that you too are a victim of the air raids.
With the greatest relief I heard you weren't in the
building at the time, but I am deeply distressed a
young employee lost his life. I don't know his name,
but if you judge the sentiment appropriate, please
pass on my condolences to his family, from a fellow
sufferer in this foul roulette.

I trust that all your family and the rest of the staff
are safe, and that this will be forwarded promptly.
Where will you be living and working until your prem-
ises can be rebuilt?

Our own loss—not three months ago—is so
painful that I've been unable to let many people
know. I shall come to it later in this letter. Forgive
me for waiting until now. Allow me first to address
something that will strike you as utterly trivial by
comparison. I refer to the sealed papers I left with
you many years ago, which I now fear may be blasted
over half of Chelsea, if they weren't destroyed in the
hit. (If they were, well and good, so long as the
destruction is *total*.)

I realize there must be a great many things

demanding your attention at this dreadful time, but I'm afraid it is urgent that these old writings of mine not fall into the wrong hands (onlookers, looters, members of the press, police, etc.), indeed, into any hands but yours or mine, even in a fragmentary state. Since, if memory serves, I never divulged their contents when I left them with you, I should do so briefly now in order that they may be recognized if they turn up in the rubble.

About twenty years ago, when I was still a young man (though at the time I felt old and spent, and my health was far from robust) I fell prey to certain fears about what struck me as a sinister pattern of events. I was unwise enough—this was in the years 1899 and 1900, whilst home on sick leave from the Gold Coast—to set down a rambling narrative in several notebooks which, as you may recall, were to remain sealed until my death. In my feverish condition, I believed certain persons might want me out of the way; indeed, I thought attempts on my life had already been made, either by poison or through agents colluding with anti-British forces against whom I fought a disastrous engagement in West Africa. I prefer not to go into the ultimate source of this obsession, except to say that it sprang from much earlier events to which I was privy as a young naval officer, during a period of high imperial tension between us and the French in the South Seas.

I need hardly make the trite observation that those Victorian manoeuvrings belong to another world—remote as the War of Jenkins' Ear from the suicidal catastrophe in which Mankind has now embroiled itself. In those days France was our eternal foe; now she is our friend, and the fount of evil isn't Paris but Berlin. In those days we counted losses in thousands; now they are reckoned in millions. In those days men of arms fought one another in more or less chivalrous engagements; now cowards hurl down death from on high, neither knowing nor caring upon whom it lands. These attackers who drone across our skies on moonlit nights may not be cowardly in themselves, but this new form of warfare, waged against women, children and the old, is inherently dishonourable. We did right to try to ban it before it could take wing. (I had a small part in that initiative at The Hague about ten years ago.) Would that we'd succeeded!

I have served this country all my life, and serve it still, in a capacity of which I can say nothing except that it touches on security. If my youthful imaginings had any substance to them, I doubt I'd be entrusted with my present duties. Yet it could be very serious—not merely for myself but for public morale—if my old papers fell into the wrong hands. A prominent figure was involved, and the enemy might find my indiscretions grist for propaganda.

To have said even this much is indiscreet. When
you've read this note, please be so good as to destroy
it at once (or secure it with my notebooks to the same
end). Long before the War, I meant to retrieve these
old papers from you and make a bonfire of them. I
kept putting it off. After the Entente Cordiale and
the shift in our alliances the whole business seemed
so outdated. Other things were always more pressing,
and I was abroad much of the time.

I suppose there may also have been a reluctance
to confront my younger self. What man wants to
revisit himself as he was during dark hours of insta-
bility and weakness? Yet what man can be sure he
would resist such an opportunity were it presented?
Perhaps I feared that the resolve needed to throw
those books into the flames unopened might elude
me. Curiosity is the downfall of men as well as cats. In
short, my old nonsense was safer with you than with
me, and I am anxious about it now only because of the
bombing. Who could have foreseen this war of
Zeppelins and Gothas, the first invasion in nine centuries carried to the very bedrooms of our nation? It
seems (to one who trod teak decks and learnt his gunnery with muzzle-loading cannon) a hellish vision
from the pen of Mr. Wells.

Were I to be charitable towards my callow self,
I would say that the mania to which I fell prey
stemmed from an inability to accept that much of the

suffering in life has no logic, no trajectory of cause
and effect; that it is mere random misfortune, the
common lot of mankind, stemming from our imper-
fect, grasping, violent natures. How thoroughly we
have all learnt that lesson now!

In the far-off days before this unending and perhaps unendable war, we believed that reason governed
human events, more or less; that the domain of reason
was enlarged by the march of science; and that when
things went wrong, a rational explanation was there to
be discovered. Now we have only to open a newspaper,
or talk to our many bereaved friends and relations, to
know that Man is not a rational being but an unfin-
ished and rather nasty piece of work: clever enough
to get himself in trouble, but not clever enough to get
himself out. In short, we know ourselves to be
doomed by our own hand and cursed by whatever
gods there may be, peering down on us from their
corrupt heaven like schoolboys pouring acid onto
an ants' nest.

I've tossed my religion on the dust heap. How
can one keep faith with a Prince of Peace who has
brought us to this? But I hope the Lord has not for-
saken you. The world is a lonely place without
Him—a frightening place once one begins to think
that Man, not God, is in charge.

Most of my life has been spent serving the
Empire. When the World War ends, if ever it does,

how will we look our colonies in the face? What can we say to those we told, in the sunny afternoon of our arrogance, that we knew best? How can they possibly look up to us now, when our civilization tears at itself with a barbarity that makes the savageries of Africa appear like a village brawl? How shall our churchmen persuade the heathen we bring the True God, when ten million have died in whirlwinds of steel, each side having called upon His name?

We had a daughter, Ivry and I—our only child, for we married late. When my dear wife revealed she was a mother-to-be, I worried, above all, that I might lose her to childbirth. Now we have both outlived our offspring.

We christened her Olivia, because Ivry took Olivia's part in a family reading of *Twelfth Night* at the time she gave me her news. I can't remember whether you ever met our daughter; if you did she must have been quite small. She grew into a lovely, vivacious, intelligent girl, with her mother's poise, sagacity, good humour and good looks, tempered by a moody introspection inherited from me. In short, she enjoyed life but also took it seriously—especially in what she saw as her duty towards fellow creatures.

Last year she left school, determined to do something for the war effort. There was no stopping her. I had to admire the Henderson blood coming out in

one so young, and the wrong sex, but I admired
much more the fact that she did not endorse the
slaughter. She was not among those silly girls who
sent white feathers to sensible young men. She did
not exult over enemy dead. She saw that this war can
have no winners, that we are all immeasurably ruined
by it, no matter where ultimate victory may fall.

So Olivia would not work in munitions or other
furtherance of the carnage. Had she been medically
inclined she might have taken up nursing, at Home
or the Front. (I thank heaven she never saw the
trenches.) But her one shyness of character, since a
young child, was a dislike of things medical. I doubt
she could have endured the lot of a nurse, watching
men die slowly of terrible mutilations, seeing even
the lucky ones traverse great seas of pain.

Olivia was particularly outraged by the onrush
of death from the air. This started the summer
before last, when she turned sixteen and grew up
very quickly, faint lines appearing on her brow.
That June a school was hit in Poplar, killing twenty
children. A hundred rail passengers died at
Liverpool Street in the same raid. She had been at
that station only a few days before, and naturally
she asked herself, *Why them, not me?* It was the victims' innocence that especially appalled her. I
remember the fury of her tears when a bomb fell
into the Serpentine, killing all the fish. Children,

housewives, pets, even fish: why should they suffer
for the madness of men?

So Olivia found an original way in which to
make a contribution. She had me teach her how to
drive a motor, and when still seventeen became an
auxiliary driver of a fire engine. There is a great
shortage of drivers everywhere, of course, but especially in London around each full moon, when
German bombing squadrons take advantage of the
light. Obstacles were thrown in her way by petty
officialdom, but she overcame them all. (I prodded
the pen-pushers a little, but Olivia never knew of
that.) I'm very proud of how she served, but nothing
can console us for her loss. Now I'd give anything in
the world to have locked my daughter away for the
duration and have her still alive.

Olivia's work began last January, when the
Germans started sending over their new Giant
machines with three-hundred-kilogram bombs. She
went up to stay at my sister's in Warrington
Crescent, five minutes from a fire station. She was
called to Long Acre, where many died in a direct hit
on an air-raid shelter, and I'm told she did her duties
well. She wasn't needed again until the next full
moon, when houses were razed near Chelsea
Hospital.

A cruel irony, Gerald, is that our daughter did
not die in the thick of her brave war work, though

she died because of it. She was sleeping at her aunt's
when a surprise raid began on March 7th, the only
time, so far, that London has been attacked without a
moon. That night the aurora borealis was so bright
and constant that the enemy found their way by its
spectral light. Most of the houses in Warrington
Crescent were wrecked. My sister Gertrude escaped
without a scratch, but a bomb fragment pierced
Olivia in the stomach. She developed peritonitis, and
died three days later. Ivry and I were at her bedside,
though she did not know us at the end.

   Forgive this ramble, Gerald. I'd meant to write a
few lines, no more. But your own misfortune has
loosed a flood of sorrow and outrage which I have
contained, though scarcely been able to express,
until now. I can't speak of this to Ivry, nor she to
me. She is unconsolable. But I feel I can speak to
you. You and I—tho' we have seen so little of each
other as grown men—had much in common in our
younger years. Now we are both stricken by this
new kind of war in which evil falls from heaven
upon innocents.

   Again, my deepest sympathy to you and yours,
   Frank

⋨⋩ ⋨⋩

Olivia! Well, there's proof, if any were still needed, that my mother
meant to tell me I'm Henderson's great-grandchild. I see now, as

I type his letter out for you, that it must have been Mother, not Jon, who hid Frank's papers in the basement. They were her gift to me, a gift that brings her closer than she's been in years.

She locked them in that darkroom and lost the key, knowing I'd be the one to find them. (She knew her daughters, knew it wouldn't be Lottie who'd tackle the cellar.) I believe she also meant to tell me everything she told Jon in that last letter, but put it off too long.

As for what Frank tells his solicitor and schoolfriend, I think he may protest a bit too much about his old suspicions being unfounded. Not long ago, Bob wrote for me, on University stationery, to the Royal Archives at Windsor Castle, asking what materials they might have from that period of Prince Edward's life. The Queen's Librarian sent the following reply: "I regret to inform you that the Royal Archives have no holdings pertaining to Prince Albert Victor Edward, Duke of Clarence and Avondale. His file has not survived."

Whatever Prince Eddy did or did not do, in the Pacific or elsewhere, he was erased from official history.

How Frank's own journals survived his wish to destroy them isn't clear. I presume Ivry was given the papers when he died, as originally intended. Towards the end of her life she left Riverhill, with its tropical conservatory and blighted orchard, and moved back to Tilehouse Street. She outlived all the Hendersons by a few years, and after her death the house passed to Frank's cousin, my Wyvern grandfather.

Poor Frank and Ivry: "without issue." So much was hidden by that dry expression in their wills. It wasn't Prince Eddy, or Samory, or dysentery, or even the loss of his eye that cursed Frank Henderson. It was Olivia's death that broke him, that turned him from a wry adventurer to an old man fretting about fruit trees.

Seventeen

⟨⟐⟩ ⟨⟐⟩

TAHITI

Arue Prison

THE POLICE HELICOPTER ALIGHTED in the gendarmerie yard. Sergeant Benoit, with genuine regret on his tall face, said that my friends had reached Tahiti and were "assisting police in their inquiries" (an expression shared by French and English). This was of course the moment at which I lost control of my life.

The silent Marquesan constable was there, setting up pencil obelisks, knocking them down. I thought: Years ago old Kautai must have sat at that same desk.

"The *Aranui* will be in port this evening," Benoit went on. "She sails for Papeete tomorrow at noon. I have orders to put you on board. She's a fine ship. We'll get you a good cabin. But I must ask you to surrender your passport now. The captain will hold it. I am sorry." His words washed over me until his hand reached out and hovered for the passport. I had to ask him to repeat what he'd just said.

I had the rest of the day to myself, and an urgent task. I thanked him for all his help, and told how things had gone in Taipivai. Looking back now on those last hours of freedom, I wish I'd thanked more warmly. I'm sure he put off fetching me until he knew I'd seen old Tari Kautai. He'll be higher in heaven for that.

Faraniki was in the overgrown Protestant cemetery not far from Jon, as Kautai had said. I must have passed him on my previous visit, but he lay in the grasp of a young fig and I hadn't been looking for Polynesian names. His grave was more elaborate, edged with hewn blocks of reddish stone from a Marquesan building. The headstone was tall and irregular; its weathered outline seemed an echo of Muake's basalt cusp.

F. H. Teraupoo
1911–1958
Officier Médical
avec l'affection et gratitude
du peuple de Nuku Hiva

My two fathers. Your grandfathers. I wept there for some time, and found myself doing so again beside Jon's rough concrete slab. He deserved better. And to have his real name; though his false identity proclaimed a trust between these men. Faraniki had kept Jon's secrets to the end.

Taiohae was big and brash that last Marquesan evening. Bright shops, a thumping bar, the lights of the *Aranui* and two or three yachts trickling red and green across the bay.

Pierre welcomed me back with a handshake, gloomily wagging his head at my poster. The surfboarders and the Kiwi were gone, but the Work was progressing, a bloody graft of fresh tattoo taking root on his calf.

The terrace was full of sailors from the ship, belting down beer and watching TV. I'd forgotten that winking presence in the corner: French cartoons and puppet shows all day, news at six, then Mexican soap operas dubbed into Tahitian. I did not want television to exist on Nuku Hiva.

⤝⤞ ⤝⤞

As soon as the *Aranui* docked at Papeete, two humourless types in dark blue rollnecks, sunglasses, and beige slacks marched up the gangplank and ordered me to go with them for questioning. We slid down Boulevard Pomare in a Citroën with smoked windows, through a buzz of mopeds and scooters, past anti-speeding posters showing a wheelchair: *Si Ce Modèle de Voiture Ne Séduit Pas. . . .*

They kept me at the main police station behind the Palais de Justice. It took them three days to charge me (Napoleon didn't burden his Code with habeas corpus), adding that in a "crime of blood" bail was out of the question. I did not fall for the ruse that my former shipmates had confessed, and that if I wanted leniency I should do the same and give evidence against them. I wondered, though, how long the others had been held and what pressures had been brought to bear. And what about Lars? Was he there on the outside, poised to help—or in the slammer too?

So I landed in the last Pomare's old stone jail. Natalie was already here, but we were kept apart. That was the worst thing, the impossibility of talking it out with anyone. I expected deliverance at any minute. Apologies, admissions of a mistake.

I sulked on my cot, too angry and depressed to read, gormlessly watching the little caged TV with the sound off half the time. One evening there was something unusual. A riot or massacre, a mob against a wall. A street party. Men spraying champagne, women dancing in the spume. People attacking daubed masonry with picks and chisels. It was a year-end roundup: the Berlin Wall had fallen weeks ago, and I hadn't heard.

The Cold War seemed to be breaking up at last, like an ice age, this hope in all the faces on the screen. But what I felt was fury—at the waste of it all, at the beggaring cost to man and nature, at two generations ridden by a fear unrivalled since mediaeval hellfire. This peace had cost the world too much.

A week went by. Then I was taken to the visiting room, the place I now know as "the bank," where I met the Canadian consul, Alain Tremblay. He'd already been briefed by his Australian counterpart. Simon had been picked up the day he got off the plane from Nuku Hiva. He and Natalie were jointly charged with murder and conspiracy to commit espionage. Vatu and I were accessories.

Much of this you already know, but I should add that the police have a surprise: a photograph taken on the morning the *Tui Marama* sailed from Papeete, conveniently snapped by a passing "journalist"—probably a DGSE man taking routine shots because of our association with Lars. Somehow there is a woman in the picture whom none of us remembers seeing there. A young blonde, similar enough to the one we fished from the sea. Either this photo is a forgery, or some passer-by was caught at an angle that makes her appear to be one of our group. They're too clever to give her an identity; our alleged victim is "a person unknown"—just as she still is to us. The police also claim they have witnesses who are prepared to swear that five people, not four, embarked on the *Tui* that day. Even so, their case is absurdly flimsy. What could have been our motive for killing her, and then documenting our crime so conscientiously?

"It'll be laughed out of court the minute it gets there," Tremblay said, once he'd satisfied himself on the details. "But I'm afraid you still have to be prepared for a bit of a stay. This is what happens to foreigners in trouble here. Usually it's drugs, and no one feels too sorry for them. The *détention préventive* can be so long it amounts to punishment anyway." He added that the spying charge against the Australians just might stick, because of samples and papers found on the boat.

I blew up at him. Didn't he realize how much he'd just demoralized me? *How* long was "a bit of a stay"?

"Sorry. I wanted to be straight with you. You don't look to me like the type for bullshit. I don't know how long. . . ." He shrugged. "Three or four months is par for a drug charge coming to trial. But this is politics—to scare people away from their nuclear sandbox. Lars Lindqvist's the one they're really after. He's been a thorn in their side for years. But he's world famous and he doesn't scare easy. So they hassle who goes near him. You guys gave them a chance on a plate."

An inevitability was building, dropping into place around me brick by brick. I wrote to Bob, not asking him to come here (I could hardly hold him to our holiday plans) but to see if he would find a realtor and put my flat on the market. I'd need the cash for lawyers.

The dear man turned up so quickly that his reply to my letter arrived after he did. For the first of many times we held hands through the barred wicket. He was wan and jet-lagged, a creature pulled from a Vancouver winter, grey and creased like a beached whale, his voice hollow and falsely hearty.

"Good timing, Liv! You couldn't have picked a better moment to get arrested. I'd already bought my tickets. Here's your mail."

He pushed through a bundle of letters (inspected when he came in). There were already some early Christmas cards. I thought: What about Christmas? Will he have to go back so soon? I couldn't ask.

"How are you, love? How are you really?" He'd never called me love before. It seemed too British for Bob.

"Oh, I'm having a great time. I'm locked away with hookers having the DTs, and cockroaches big enough to ride on, and ghastly stinks coming up the drain in my washbasin. Can you be gassed this way? Maybe that's the idea. No need to sharpen the guillotine."

•   •   •

I don't know what Bob told his wife—I never want to know the lies—but somehow he got out of Christmas. Then his work on Pierre Loti's *Mariage* became so significant that he really *had* to stay in Tahiti (this one he did tell me because it was partly true). He bought himself a laptop, and another one for me, saying there was nothing like writing to make the time fly by.

Later, when he'd talked about Kent State and Barbara, I saw he wouldn't leave until I got out; Bob wouldn't walk away from a woman in crisis ever again. He's as haunted by his guilts as I am.

In the mail he'd brought from home was your letter. I couldn't have had a more wonderful or unexpected gift. I'd been thinking only of myself. Then your letter comes and opens up a door. I don't know where it will lead, or if it leads anywhere at all, but its sheer existence is enough for now. Every word I've written has seemed a step towards that door. And even if you never read this, and never see me, you've still done something wonderful, something I don't deserve and may never be able to repay.

I made several attempts to unfold Mother's letter. Bob also examined the compacted mass, concluding the only hope was to take it to a professional conservator. He doubted that anyone with the right skills existed locally, which would mean leaving it unopened until I got back to Canada. Lars, however, knew someone who did such work for the Tahiti Museum. The letter left my hands for about six weeks, while I tormented myself with hopes and fears for its survival and what it might, or might not, hold.

When it came back I could hardly recognize it. Five sheets were sealed inside archival plastic sleeves. Their muddy colour had washed to a pale straw mottled with traces of blue-black ink that had run a long time ago. All had savage creases meeting at a hole worn in the middle, from being folded and carried so long in Jon's pocket. The edges looked like an eroded coastline, the margins mostly gone, and deep coves eaten into the text.

The conservator had done a good job (paid for by Lars, I gather, in remorse for getting me involved with his Australian friends), but the results were disappointing. Even in the best parts, the paper was badly decomposed. I could read nothing. But in the course of her work, with special lighting and solvents, the conservator had glimpsed a few readings. She enclosed a transcript—merely disjointed words, phrases, and broken pieces linked by strings of dots.

I could probably make anything I want from these fragments, like the poetry people assemble from magnetic words stuck on their fridge doors. That said, I do think one question can be settled: the matter of how and where my mother met Faraniki Teraupoo. I now believe he came to Tilehouse Street. There's the phrase "put the kettle on," mention of a "veterans' sanat[orium]," and, most telling of all, something about "Henderson's spear." It seems that Teraupoo's poor health when he was freed from the camps detained him in Europe long after the Second World War, that his family had kept or remembered Frank's address, and that he came looking for his English kin before going back to the South Seas. I think my mother snapped her lover's picture and kept it in her desk with Henderson's glass eye. That tall man in a demob suit is my Polynesian father, paled by overexposure, stooped by his war.

It must have been August 1949 (my birthday is in May). Presumably Jon was away somewhere, though he'd left the Pacific by then. Perhaps Mother already knew that her husband was contaminated, and saw this as her only way to have another child. But now I'm just making up excuses for my own existence!

This is all I can tell you. My other questions are still unanswered. I've no inkling who might have "disowned" my mother, though of course I wonder if she did have family who rejected her, perhaps because of me. I don't know why she didn't go to Nuku Hiva—or ask someone to—after she got Jon's first reply to her confession, the one in the atlas. I can only assume she thought he'd be on his way home soon, and worried she might get there to find him gone—in those days it would have taken months from England. Or did Faraniki write, thinking Jon had left the island as a stowaway?

I've also thought about the cigarette case. I believe Jon accepted it because he meant to send it to Hitchin, either by post or, after further persuasion, with Teraupoo. He didn't mean to jump that day at Vaiahu. He fell. He'd intended to come back and finish writing. He was going to tell my mother that he loved her.

Alain came this morning, bringing some floppy discs and news I hardly dare believe—as of this week, a deal is "in the pipeline." Vatu and I could be out any day. Tomorrow this goes to Papeete for printing up, and then a big fat jiffy bag will make its way to you.

• • •

While I've been locked in here, Bob and Alain helped arrange one other thing. I gave some thought to bringing Jon's remains to England, putting him beside my mother. But it seemed too invasive and presumptuous. I wouldn't want anyone digging me up, not unless they had a very good reason for thinking I was unhappy where I was. So I feel it's best to leave him where he's been for all these years. On Nuku Hiva he found forgiveness in himself, and with that I believe he found his peace.

Next time the *Aranui* sails for Taiohae there'll be a stone on board, a slab of reddish basalt. Sergeant Benoit has offered to take care of things that end.

Jonathan Barkley Wyvern
1920–1953
Group Captain, RAF
Husband of Vivien
Father of Charlotte and Olivia
In Loving Memory

Come with me one day. We'll visit your grandfathers together. And I still have a film to make.

Now over to you. I want to know everything.

Will you tell me?

ACKNOWLEDGMENTS

My thanks to the following for generosity with their time and many helpful suggestions: Shirley Wright, Amanda McConnell, Mike Poole, Rose Corser, Robert Suggs, Robert Koenig, Inga Clendinnen, Greg Dening, Bengt Danielsson, Rod Vickers, Nicholas Dennys, Beryl Sims, John Leaberry, Andrea Duncan Tanner, Paul Quarrington, Cassandra Pybus, Peter Shinnie, Peter Hulme, Peter Gorrell, Rob Kay, Sandra Berg, Michael Wallace, Richard Landon, Jim Galozo, Doris Cowan, Bella Pomer, Henry Dunow, and Antony Harwood.

Special thanks to Janice Boddy, Claire and Farley Mowat, Louise Doughty, Anthony Weller; also to Louise Dennys and Diane Martin at Knopf Canada, to Bill Scott-Kerr and Sarah Westcott at Transworld, and to Jack Macrae and Katy Hope at Henry Holt.

A NOTE ON SOURCES:

This book is a fiction inspired by certain events in the life of my cousin Francis Barkley Henderson, C.M.G., D.S.O., who was born in 1859. Chapter 2 and parts of Chapter 4 are based on his own account of his capture by the Sofas in 1897, published in Jerome K. Jerome's *The Idler* (London, 1898), and on his official report in the Public Record Office, Kew (reference CO 96/308). Details of the *Bacchante* voyage are drawn from *The Cruise of H.M.S. Bacchante, 1879–1882*, compiled by John N. Dalton, ostensibly from the journals of Prince Edward and Prince George (London: Macmillan, 1886). The ship's logs are also in the

Public Record Office (reference ADM-53-11621 ff). Henderson retired with the rank of commander in 1919, after serving in Naval Intelligence and MI5 during the First World War.

While I have allowed my imagination free run with this material, the historical context of *Henderson's Spear*, in both the nineteenth and twentieth centuries, is as accurate as I could make it. There was, for example, a guerrilla leader named Teraupoo on Raiatea in the 1880s and '90s; but only the existence of the spear itself (and *Bacchante*'s exceptionally slow passage from Fiji to Japan) suggested to me the events on that island in which my characters take part. I hope Frank, Ivry, and the others will forgive me for the liberties I have taken with their lives.

Books I found especially useful include: *Prince Eddy and the Homosexual Underworld* by Theo Aronson; *Poisoned Reign* by Bengt and Marie-Thérèse Danielsson, (originally published as *Moruroa, mon amour*); *Islands and Beaches* by Greg Dening; *The Hidden Worlds of Polynesia* by Robert Suggs; *Hugh Dalton* by Ben Pimlott; *Hope and Glory* by Peter Clarke; *Age of Extremes* by Eric Hobsbawn; *The Gold Coast Past and Present* by George Macdonald; *Melville in the South Seas* by Charles Anderson; *Herman Melville* by Hershel Parker; *I, The Very Bayonet* by Deryck Scarr; *Fijian Weapons & Warfare* by Fergus Clunie; *Dead Man's Chest* by Nicholas Rankin; *A Dream of Islands* by Gavan Daws; *Tahitians* by Robert Levy; *Mystic Isles of the South Seas* by Frederick O'Brien; *Forever the Land of Men* by Willowdean Handy; *Polynesia's Sacred Isle* by Edward Dodd; *Tahiti-Polynesia Handbook* by David Stanley; *Tahiti & French Polynesia* by Robert Kay. The quotation from *The New York Times* in Chapter 4 is dated November 17, 1889, and given more fully in Aronson's *Prince Eddy*.